INFINITY

ANTIPODES SERIES BOOK 3

ANTIPODES SERIES BOOK 3

INFINITY

T.S. SIMONS

4 Horsemen
Publications, Inc.

Infinity
Antipodes Book 3
Copyright © 2022 T.S. Simons. All rights reserved.

4 Horsemen Publications, Inc.
1497 Main St. Suite 169
Dunedin, FL 34698
4horsemenpublications.com
info@4horsemenpublications.com

Cover Design by Jen Kotick

Library of Congress Control Number: 2021951245

Audio ISBN: 978-1-64450-375-1
Hardcover ISBN: 978-1-64450-954-8
EBOOK ISBN: 978-1-64450-376-8
Print ISBN: 978-1-64450-377-5

For Maxine and Lynda (always remembered)

What value do YOU place on friendship?

HEARTBROKEN, CAM EMBARKS ON a voyage to seek answers. Will the journey answer his burning questions? Or will he learn more than he bargained for? His journey presents both challenges and opportunities as he builds new friendships along the way, as well as reuniting with old acquaintances. Just as Cam and Freyja's life comes full circle, their friends and community are threatened, forcing them to defend those they love.

In this third installment of the Antipodes series, friendships are tested when the survivors learn the horrifying truth about why they were chosen. Which relationships will survive?

Melbourne

Kerguelen Islands

August Island
Auckland Island
Bellcamp Island

Arnol

Carloway

LEWIS

Callanish

Garrynahine

Stornoway

Leurbost

Balallan

Tarbert

HARRIS

TABLE
OF CONTENTS

ACKNOWLEDGEMENTS

I ALWAYS GET TO THIS part of a book and go blank. You would think after writing several novels, and all the drafts that precede them, I would be able to write a list of people to thank. But no. One day, I will remember to keep that list as I go along. Sadly, it is not today.

To all the wonderful people who have bought or recommended my books, and even waited patiently for the next in the series–thank you. I can't tell you what it means to me that people actually enjoy my work. The feedback you provide is invaluable.

Maxine—thank you for a lifelong friendship and so much laughter. We may go months without seeing each other, but I know you always have my back. Love you.

Bob – Thanks for being one of the good ones. Hope you like this edition better.

Caitlin—thank you for telling me how much you love my books. When an intelligent, articulate, and resilient woman like you tells me she likes my books,

I know I have done something right. Wishing you all the best.

To my family, friends, and colleagues—thanks for putting up with me.

If you enjoyed this book, it would mean a great deal to me if you could spare a few minutes to leave a quick review on GoodReads, Amazon, BookBub, or any other platform.

GoodReads: www.goodreads.com/author/show/20861749.T_S_Simons

Amazon: www.amazon.com/T-S-Simons/e/B08MT6YYDL

Bookbub: www.bookbub.com/profile/t-s-simons

CHAPTER 1

MOORING THE SMALL FISHING boat in the harbor at Kirkwall, I paused, wondering what sort of reception I would receive. Had I made a mistake in coming here? The last time I visited the Orkney community was almost a year ago, and for vastly different reasons.

Knowing how to open the access hatches in the geodesic domes that protected us from infected rain, a raiding party had kidnapped eleven women to enslave, my wife Lae being among them. In pursuit, but a full day behind, our crew had stopped here briefly and been welcomed. A quick meal, a precis of our mission, three volunteers to join us, and we were on our way. I had been in no fit state to communicate on our return voyage when we returned the six abducted Orcadian women. Reeling from the violent death of my wife Laetitia at the hands of the raiders and battling a severe infection, I hadn't left the cabin of our vessel.

As I slowly entered the village, I could see people watching me from a distance, apprehensive. Knowing that the people here were likely as wary of strangers as the residents in my home community on the Hebridean island of Lewis were, I entered with my hands in front of me, indicating that I held no weapon. Cautiously approaching, I was about to call out a greeting when a tall shadowy figure spoke enquiringly toward me. "Cam?"

"It is," I responded and looked over to see the male speaker. The afternoon sun was behind him, the glare in my face making me squint.

"Will?" I guessed as I stepped farther forward and into the shade of the home's eaves.

A wide grin crossed his face as he extended his arm. "How are you, Cam? *So* good to see you! You recovered alright then?"

Grateful for the warm welcome, I smiled. "I'm well, thank you. My profuse thanks to you for the antibiotics and painkillers. They undoubtedly saved my life."

"Our pleasure, and it was a fair price too. We never got the chance to thank you personally for returning our friends. I... I heard your wife didn't make it."

"No. She didn't."

"I'm sorry, man. I can't imagine what that feels like."

Hell is what it feels like, I thought with fresh pain piercing my chest, making me want to double over from the stabbing sensation, but said nothing.

"Not that we aren't thrilled to see you, Campbell, but I assume you haven't come all this way for a random neighborly call. Is there something we can do for you?"

Even after all these years, I still appreciated the direct Scottish approach—there was no beating around the bush with social niceties. People just asked, and you responded.

Out with it, then. "I was hoping... if you don't mind, to speak... with them. The women... that were taken. If that is okay? I... I just need closure."

Will paused, and I waited as he responded haltingly.

"I'm not sure, Cam. It has taken them a long time to deal with what happened. I know it has been a year, but they are still struggling with nightmares and flashbacks. Most of them still cannot leave the village. But for you, I will ask, okay?"

Realizing that this was the best that I could expect, I nodded in agreement.

"You can stay with us. I'll let Liesl know."

A small group had gathered, interested in the newcomer. They were watching us apprehensively but visibly relaxed as they saw Will shake my hand enthusiastically, chatter springing up among them. Will turned to re-introduce me to the community here, and the look of fear broke on many faces as they recognized me. Several people approached to thank me, genuinely appreciative of my role in the rescue, small as my part had been.

A small woman stood slightly apart from the group that had gathered. She looked familiar but out of place here. Dark hair tied back in a ponytail, she was tiny, delicate, with features like a bird—classically beautiful with pale skin and sparkling blue eyes enhanced by her dark lashes and brows. I hadn't seen her last time I was here, but that was hardly surprising because I was focused on the rescue. Was she one of the rescued women? I had only seen them as they came out of the broch, filthy and scared, their hands still tied until Freyja cut their bonds in the daylight. Wracking my brain, I couldn't place her. *Why do I know her?*

Realization struck, and I recognized her as the tiny bird-like woman with the booming voice from my briefing session in Melbourne. Military budgie. *What the bloody hell is she doing on Orkney?* Then again, I realized in the next instant, the same thing could be asked of me. Once the crowd had dispersed after Will's introduction, she made her approach forcefully.

"I'm Illyria," she chirped pleasantly, thrusting her hand out. "Campbell, isn't it?"

"It is. But please, Cam." I wondered if she remembered me or if she had just heard about what happened. "We've met before," I started cautiously. "Well, not really. You were part of the team in Melbourne."

"Oh, I remember you. The deployment team discussed each candidate at length, so I feel like I know you. Wonderful to meet you."

"You talked about us?"

"Well, of course! Days were spent choosing candidates. Did you think we would let just anyone survive?"

"True enough. How did you end up here?" I blurted, realizing as the words left my mouth that it was quite rude.

She laughed again, a warm, charming laugh. Despite her booming voice that day, she was lovely and easy to speak to.

"They seconded me to the Department. You know, for the project."

"Military?" I guessed.

"Major Morgan, Intelligence Officer, Australian Army." She saluted in formal greeting. "What gave it away?"

"Honestly, your voice. I had never heard such a commanding voice from someone so tiny," I confessed.

"A learned skill." She twinkled at me with her brilliant blue eyes, the dark lashes gleaming in the sun. "And one I used many times with recruits. They offered me a place on Auckland Island with the scientific community, then I traveled through to Clava. Now tell me, how did *you* get here? Though it is not your first visit, I understand?"

Will, realizing that we were going to be awhile, took the backpack I had left on the ground, caught my eye, and gestured into a nearby house before disappearing through the door.

Up close, I realized she couldn't be more than a few years older than I was; she just appeared more worldly. Intelligent and with a razor-sharp wit, nothing got past her, reminding me very much of Freyja. But I hadn't spoken with another Australian in some time, outside of my immediate family and Freyja, and I enjoyed doing so now. We spoke of Melbourne, August, and Auckland; the portals and how awful they were; the differences between Australia and Scotland; words we found amusing; and strange customs.

"If you were in the Clava community, why did you come here?" I asked, somewhat cautiously, as we re-entered the village. As lovely as she was, we didn't know each other.

"Let's just say that I didn't entirely agree with some of their decisions. Besides, I had personal reasons to come here."

I must have looked confused as she laughed. "My parents were from Kirkwall. They migrated to Australia before I was born, but I had always wanted to visit here. After I graduated from university and went to Duntroon, well, my military career took up all of my time. Now, I live here."

"You weren't here when I last visited?" I quizzed. While I hadn't met everyone here, I was certain I would have remembered her. Military trained, she would have been an asset in our retrieval of the captive women from Mousa. Freyja would certainly have roped her in to assist.

"No, I first came about eighteen months ago, just to visit. Test the waters, you could say. Then I moved, permanently, about eight months ago."

"What does an intelligence officer do on an island community?" I asked, genuinely interested.

"Not much!" she laughed delightfully. "But here, I started a market of sorts, based on a barter system. Four days a week, I travel to different areas of the community, collecting excess produce for trade. I facilitate the trade, and I get to keep a small percentage of the goods. So, it keeps me fed and clothed, and everyone else gets to maximize their time doing what they do best."

"That sounds like a great idea," I said enthusiastically, and I meant it. "Lewis would love something like this." Now that the community was widespread, having someone travel between settlements to take your excess produce and trade it for other items was a fantastic idea.

"It sounds like a great idea when you have no skills!" She giggled merrily. "But they all seem happy enough."

Making plans to accompany her on her rounds during my stay and excusing myself, I entered the house after Will, a little tentatively. I didn't want to barge into their private space. But I could hear low voices and followed the sound, standing hesitantly in the doorway, not wanting to intrude. Will looked up, smiled, and introduced me to his wife, Liesl, and their two children, Thor and little Thea.

Thor, a rambunctious four-year-old, was racing around the kitchen like a tornado, much to Liesl's frustration, and barely gave me a second glance. Thea, a golden-haired two-year-old, blinked at me with fascination before handing me her knitted teddy. I thanked her profusely, and after introducing myself formally to the bear, solemnly returned it to her, watching the look of self-satisfaction cross her chubby cheeks. With her sharp green eyes and blonde curls, she looked just like I expected Katrin to look at the same age. Intelligent and testing people who came into her sphere to see if they measured up to her expectations.

Invited to clean up by Liesl, I did so with gusto. Days spent on a boat with no clean water for washing meant I was desperate for a shower, even if it was a barely lukewarm, dripping shower. If only I had known that I would never get to have a shower with water pressure again, I would have enjoyed it much more, recalling the hot forceful showers of my original home in Melbourne.

It had been six years since the waterborne virus had spread from Europe and killed every living thing through simple dehydration, but the result had been no person, plant, or animal had survived. The exception was the few thousand of us who had been lucky enough to be chosen to live in a domed community, a terrarium of sorts, where the water was safe. We lived in communities of shared resources, but with limited contact with the outside world. Since I had been ensconced in my new world, I had traveled more than most. But I had not yet seen life outside of these domed communities—the exception being Mousa, the tiny island off the coast of the Shetlands, where the raiders had taken the kidnapped women. That journey had previously brought me here.

When I left the bathroom, Will gestured me toward the table, and I soon found myself tucking into a delicious vegetable soup with fresh bread.

"This is *so* good! How I have missed fresh vegetables!" I gushed, making Liesl blush with pride. Eating with children was something I was surprised to find that I also missed after days alone and enjoyed helping Thea with her spoon, Liesl enjoying the break from parenting for a short time.

It was the sense of sublime relaxation that came with being back in a protected environment that I hadn't expected. No longer needing to worry about getting caught in the rain, eating something contaminated, or constantly suiting up to avoid having a random wave splash into my face, I relished that bone-deep sense of intrinsically *knowing* I was safe. If my attention lapsed for a second, it wouldn't be life-threatening.

Eighteen months ago, I had traveled back to Australia to find my sister, Sorcha, who lived in an inland, isolated community. The first leg had been through the antipodal point back to August, my original settlement. Then by boat to New Zealand and Australia.

On our way back to Scotland, Sorcha and I had stopped at our old holiday property, where our parents had isolated themselves after the pandemic had struck Melbourne, and it was impossible to get food, fuel, or safe water. It had been a time when people were raiding shops, attacking neighbors, and breaking into houses to survive. It was clear from the freshness of their remains that our parents had survived for some years after the virus struck. The handmade dome my father had built from tarpaulins had developed a minuscule tear that allowed water to pass through. But it made me wonder—*how many people still survived outside of the geodesic domes?*

After a blissful night spent in an actual bed, a hand-carved wooden car driven up my leg woke me. Liesl found Thor and me sitting on the guest room floor sometime later, racing cars along tracks made from shoes and my belt. Thea insisted I sit with Holly, her teddy, at breakfast, chattering away to me the entire time while Liesl made tattie scones.

Will spent the next two days showing me around the community, introducing me, and ensuring that everyone we spoke to knew my role in saving the abducted women. We had returned all the Orcadian women unharmed. Laetitia had been the sole female casualty, though the raiders had killed three men on Lewis who were simply in the wrong place at the wrong time.

Despite her pleasantness and appreciation of the time spent with her children, I sensed Liesl was apprehensive around me. Assuming that she was shy, I was polite but didn't push. Perhaps, like me, she enjoyed the solitude of her own home. I had shown up unannounced. It wasn't until after dinner on the third night, after their children had gone to bed, that she admitted, highly embarrassed, that she had initially feared me.

Will and I looked at her in amazement.

"Alize told me you went ballistic," she admitted, "when you heard your wife had died."

Flushing, I had no reply. Freyja had told me this, but honestly, I recalled nothing about that time. I remembered one woman telling me that Lae hadn't stopped screaming, so they had slit her throat. After that, my memory went blank.

Will looked at her, bewildered. "And you don't think I would lose *my* shit if I was told that they had murdered my wife?"

Liesl blushed at that. "Maybe. It was just... they made it sound like Cam was an animal, completely out of control."

"I was," I admitted quietly, realizing that honesty was best. "Out of my mind with grief. Nearly four years ago, my first wife went missing. I spent a year searching for her. I didn't think I ever would survive the loss, the bone-deep grief of losing someone I loved that much. I didn't think I could live without her, and honestly, I wanted to die. It took me a very long time to recover. But then I met Laetitia, the sweetest, kindest woman I had ever met. I fell in love again, and we married. Now we have a son, Louis. He had just turned one when those ... men .... took her ... on her birthday. She was five months pregnant with our second child. After Lae went missing, I spent days not sleeping or eating, just desperate to catch up to them, to find her. Then to learn that they had murdered her? That those animals had killed our baby too? I admit I lost control. I remember nothing after being told how she died. I woke up, fevered, on the yacht. The other women were all safe, but not her."

Will sniffed. "Mate, the way I hear it from Gerry, you were restrained. I am not sure there would have been a man left alive if that had been Liesl or my child."

Liesl reddened further as Will reached over the table to take his wife's hand.

"I'm sorry," she whispered, half choked. "I didn't know."

After making the initial introductions, Will returned to his work in charge of the fish farm. While invited to accompany him, it was something I could not bring myself to do. Fishing had never been my favorite pastime, unable to kill the thrashing fish on a hook or in a net.

Recognizing that the women needed time before being comfortable enough to speak to me, and simply being here, in their faces, might be confronting, most days I spent with Illyria. She took me traveling across the community, meeting the different families, learning bits and pieces about what they raised and grew and how they lived. I shared information from August and Lewis: things that grew well, companion planting tips from Diana. Illy's military training came through occasionally, and I saw the leader in her. It was never blatant. She was helpful and had a natural way with people, adapting her communication style to her audience. In the end, it was Illy that advocated on my behalf to convince the six women to speak with me, something they were reticent to do. After Liesl's confession, I knew why.

As I accompanied her on her rounds and learned the basics of her business, I recognized it was a fantastic concept. One farmer had a surplus of pumpkins, another of wool. Illyria took a minor cut of each item but passed the rest on to others. They gifted those with skills like doctors and engineers with their goods in exchange for their service to the community. Those who gave away their surplus got to choose from other produce. Everyone seemed happy with the arrangement.

"It is a terrific system," I told her. "But how do you keep everyone happy?"

"That is where my psychology training comes in." She grinned. "Recognizing how much people are prepared to donate. Reading them, if you like. Everyone is willing to trade but to differing levels. Some are exceedingly generous, prepared to give away all their excess, and not want anything in return. Others want something in return, every time—a fair trade, you could call it. A small number want to feel that they have gained from the trade, that it was in their favor. It is about ensuring that everyone feels like they are getting a good deal, not taking advantage of the generous ones, and ensuring that the tight-asses feel rewarded. Most of all, the trick is to keep absolutely everything confidential. Let no one know what trade you have done with another."

"Well, from what I saw, you are doing an amazing job," I admitted.

"It keeps me busy ... and fed."

Five days after I arrived, Illyria sat with the six women and myself in Illyria's small, neat cottage. She provided tea and cake. Small talk dominated the conversation as everyone arrived and settled in for the evening. Work was finished for the day. No interruptions from children or partners. What was it like here compared to Lewis? What was it like on August? What was the world outside like now? I felt quite nervous about raising the real reason we were here.

One of them started eventually, saying how sad they were about Laetitia. I recognized the voice, but not her face. It was the woman who had told me about Lae's fate, Alize.

The look of apprehension in her eyes illustrated she remembered me losing control, and I knew I was better off addressing that immediately.

"The truth is..." I started, forcing my voice to remain calm, "I remember you telling me they had murdered my wife. I heard you, but I remember nothing after that. I am told that I lost my mind, temporarily. I loved her so very much. The day they took her was her birthday. She was five months pregnant with our second child. I lost my first wife several years before and thought I would never recover. Then I met Laetitia. She was my world. We were madly in love, devoted to each other. Then in a single day, to lose both her and our child, leaving our little boy without a mother? Well … I need to make sense of what happened."

One of the other women spoke, barely audible.

"What I witnessed was the most profound manifestation of grief that I have ever seen. How I think I would react if that were my child. You must have really loved her."

"I did," I admitted. "I still do. That is why I am here. I need closure. I can't sleep. I dream about her. I can't move forward with my life, not until I know what happened."

The women looked around at each other and at Alize. Without speaking, they had appointed her to the spokesperson role.

She started slowly. "They took us unaware. We were all working near the coast, individually, some of us in pairs. We had seen no one from outside other than Illyria here, and we genuinely believed we were safe. Some of us waved to the ship, and they attacked us from behind. Others were simply outnumbered. There were eight of them on the ship; another two remained on their island. Over the course of a single morning, we all ended up on that filthy stinking ship, where we found five women we didn't know. We were tied and gagged so that we couldn't speak to them. But they were prisoners too, tied as we were. Some were bruised and filthy and had been there for some time. But it was the terror in their eyes that we could see, even in the poor light from across the room, which made us even more scared."

Pausing for a moment, Alize continued, swallowing hard, trying to retain control as the memories flooded back.

"The men were foul, stank terribly, and were quite abusive to us. We knew from the start why they had taken us, as they leered and slobbered. Made nasty, judgmental comments about our appearance, your friend Isla and Saba here in particular. They took every opportunity to grope us, test the merchandise as they referred to it. The saving grace was that they had agreed in advance that they would only have one each. Ten men to ten women. Jason, the leader, described it to us as, 'I don't want someone else's slops.'"

Several of the women cringed slightly with the memory, but Alize continued, more matter-of-factly, now that she had begun.

"We arrived on their island two nights later, which we know now was lucky. We were terrified, not knowing where we were, and couldn't see where they were taking us. They had already told us they planned to strip us naked and parade us along the beach upon arrival so that each man could choose. Fight over us, I guess. They didn't care if we soiled our clothes. But it was dark, and there was no light to see us properly, so they forced us into the broch overnight so they could see us better by daylight. We tried to escape. Contemplated suicide. But it was so dark in that stone tower that we couldn't see anything. We couldn't see each other or what was around us. The door was solid, and there was no light at all. After what they did to your wife, we knew they were serious. If we climbed the narrow stairwell in the dark and all we did was break our legs, then we had no chance of ever getting away. It was plain that there would be no medical treatment. There were no boats on Orkney... then. We knew we would never make it home."

A sob punctuated the sentence, and another woman put her arm around the crying one.

"We didn't sleep. We huddled together. Some of us cried, others not. The smell of fear and piss was overwhelming. Then morning came, and you were there. We heard the screaming and yelling, and we were absolutely terrified. We had no idea what was going on. Then we heard a gunshot. Your leader opened the door, and as soon as the light hit her and our eyes adjusted, we could see that she was a woman. Words cannot describe the sense of relief I felt to know that there was a woman. Just with her sheer presence, I knew she wouldn't let them hurt us. She didn't. After you... beat them... she dealt with it. Cool, calm, no qualms. She knew what those monsters were, and what they planned to do to us. She looked us in the eye and promised that she would never let them hurt us, or anyone else, ever again. She told us we would never really rest unless we knew it was over. So ... she ended it."

Freyja. She would have taken charge; I knew that without question. Even if she didn't feel confident, she was a master at projecting it.

"And Laetitia?" I asked softly, seeking an answer to what I really wanted to know.

"She was on the boat when they took us. The other women ... from Lewis, I mean ... were in the cabin, down below. The men had taken them the day before. When we were well out to sea, they dragged all eleven of us back up onto the deck. Lined us up so they could see us in the light. Poor thing, she was terrified. You could see it plainly from across the deck. They had hit her, hard. She had bruises across her face and a nasty black eye. She could barely open it. But she kept crying, crouching, and refusing to stand up. It pissed them off. They had already been talking about what to do with the spare, and... and..." Alize couldn't finish, choked with the emotion of reliving that awful day, twelve months ago.

"I know what they did," I whispered. "Isla, a friend ... our neighbor from Lewis. She told me. Laetitia screamed in his face, and he cut her throat."

Alize nodded in agreement. Just a tiny flick of her eyelids.

"It all happened so quickly. Jason, the leader, was yelling at her, hitting her around the head, trying to make her shut up, stand with the others, and be quiet. As he was smacking her, the gag moved. She screamed so loudly it made my ears hurt. She was just panicked. We could all see that. She didn't scream to antagonize him. She was just beside herself with terror. I didn't even see the knife in his belt until he had it on her. She was just suddenly... silent. She fell onto the deck. Her cloak fell back as she landed, and that was when we all saw *why* she was upset. Refusing to stand."

"She was five months pregnant. She was protecting our child," I finished, choking on the last word.

Tears welled up in all the women's eyes at that point.

"We didn't know that until then. They didn't either. She was so tiny, lying there."

Silence filled the room as we all pictured Lae's still form, bleeding on the deck.

"We are grateful to all of you," Alize finished, tears streaming down her face with the memory. "Without you, we wouldn't be here today, with our partners, our children. We owe you our lives. Future generations will exist because of you. One day I hope we can repay you."

"Thank you," I breathed. Recognizing that this was enough and standing to leave, several of the women came to hug me.

As genuinely as I could, I managed, "I am glad you are all home with your families."

Illyria stood quietly, and taking me by the arm, led me out into the cool night air.

"They needed that as much as you did," she whispered. "They have been holding on to that guilt for a year—survivor guilt. Healing can only start when you recognize what happened, and you can talk about it. Once you can distance yourself from the event, you can become objective. Only then can you process, let it go, and move forward."

"Thank you," I whispered, unsure of what else to say.

"I'll see you in the morning," she promised.

CHAPTER 2

INITIALLY, ILLYRIA REMINDED ME very much of Freyja in manner, forthright, direct, and highly intelligent. She could read people and adapt quickly. She knew how people were going to react before they did. But I soon learned that when she wasn't negotiating, she was kind and easy to talk to, much like Lae.

"Where to from here, Mr. Mackintosh?" she asked cheekily one day on our way back from a farm near Stenness. She was driving the golf cart containing her trade goods.

"Mousa, then Edinburgh," I replied. "I really would like to visit Clava too, although I can't say why."

"That isn't what I meant, but I can radio ahead to let them know you are coming to Clava." She stopped the cart and turned to face me. "What I meant was you are nearly thirty. You have your entire life ahead of you. What next?"

"Why would anyone want to be near me?" I asked, astonished, baffled by the question. "I have lost two wives in four years. They aren't great odds, you know. Can't see too many women wanting to sign up to *that*."

"One went through the portal. That wasn't your fault. Disgusting excuses for men kidnapped the second. Also, not your fault. You, Campbell, need to forgive yourself. You are only human. Both were random acts. None of this was your fault."

"You don't think..."

"Think what?"

"That perhaps I am just bad luck? Cursed?"

"Do you *really* believe that?"

"I..." I started, but she cut me off with a kiss.

"Forgive yourself!" Delivered in that forceful military tone, it was an order. "Then you can move on."

"You make it sound so easy. How do I do that?"

"You make a conscious effort. You recognize that none of it was your fault, and you let it go."

She paused and looked at me, assessing. "After you left the other night, I led the women on a guided meditation. To help them seek closure and heal. Maybe that could help?"

It had been many years since I had meditated. "I'm happy to try anything," I admitted.

"Come."

Illy beckoned me off the path, and we found a lush patch of grass under some trees. It was serene, calm, and safe.

"Lie down and get comfortable," she instructed in a slow, peaceful voice.

Following her instructions, I loosened my boots and lay under the tree, the shade darkening my face.

"Lightly close your eyes. Feel your face relax; feel all the tension melting away. Unclench your teeth and your jaw; feel them become soft and relaxed. Starting from the top of your head, feel the tension drain out of your body and into the earth. Feel it pull away from you as the earth takes all the pressure away. Feel the heaviness of your body, soft and relaxed. Empty all the thoughts from your mind. Acknowledge them, one by one, and let them go.

Focus on your breath. Breathe in slowly, then out slowly. Physically see your breath as you bring it in, inhaling, then see it outside your body as you let it go.

Visualize your challenges as a kite. See them. Manifest them as the kite. See the color, the size, and shape. Feel it as the kite vibrates in the breeze. You are holding onto the tail as it fights you to take off; it wants to be free. Picture the portal and Freyja falling in. She didn't want to go. See the men on Mousa. Large and strong. Picture them in your mind. Remember the details, the sounds, the colors, the smell. Really focus on them. It wasn't your fault, Cam. None of it. No matter what you did, or didn't do, you didn't kill Laetitia. You didn't force Freyja to go through the portal. None of this is your fault. Really *feel* that."

Behind my closed lids, I could see the kite soaring above me. Red, ragged, and fighting to be free.

"When you are ready, when you have fought with the kite enough, just let it go. Let it go. Forgive yourself."

The sun was beating down through the tree, the orange tinge glowing behind my closed eyes. I still held onto the large red kite. Buffeting in the breeze. All of my fears, terrible memories, bound up in that single object. Losing Freyja. Spending months searching for her. Being isolated and feared. Thinking she had betrayed me. Hugh's death. Learning that Heidi had deceived me, that Freyja hadn't left me for Angus. Hearing about Laetitia's death. With a final deep sigh that went all the way to my spine, pressed into the grass, I let go of the kite and watched it as it soared higher and higher. Onward and upward it flew, up into the brilliant blue sky, shrinking, until it was finally out of sight.

Feeling lighter than I had in years, I opened my eyes and saw Illy watching me.

When she leaned in again, this time, I was ready.

Kissing her was arousing me in a way I hadn't felt in a very long time, taking me by surprise. My stomach was jittery, my skin tingling. After Lae, I didn't think I would ever feel this way again, and it surprised me how I felt now. Guilt knotted my stomach. But surprisingly, I felt *alive*. As she touched my face, I felt like I had awakened from a long sleep. It was new and exciting.

"Illy," I murmured in her ear, "I can't start anything. It wouldn't be fair to you. I have a life on Lewis. My sister, my children. I have to go back."

"Well then. Let's just enjoy the time you have left," she said simply.

Life on Orkney was very similar to Lewis. There was a genuine sense of community. People appeared to care about each other, stopping to have a chat and help. People shared harvests and meals. Illy, despite not being an original resident here, was liked and respected. Traveling between homes took ages as everyone wanted to catch up on the news, learn how everyone was faring. It got me thinking again about why she had left Clava and Auckland before that. But that triggered another question.

"Illy, I have to ask, why didn't your colleagues on Clava offer Angus a place with the other scientists? Why send him to Lewis, I mean?"

"Angus MacLeod? Goodness, why would we want him? Have you met him? Opinionated, excruciating, oxygen-thieving fucktard. Until they mobilized us, I had to deal with him via teleconference. That was bad enough. He was in a similar role for the British government, selecting the best candidates to settle the offshore communities. But he was a civilian. We collaborated to ensure that we had sent complementary teams to our ground zero sites. We spoke most days. I used to dread it—demeaning, argumentative pedant, always trying to one-up me. God, I was happy when they posted him."

I smirked at the apt description.

"Why was he posted?"

"From what I understand, they sent him to Lewis, as the British knew he was a valuable asset and would likely aid the resettlement. There were meetings about allowing him to join the scientific community at Clava or even on Auckland. The issue was none of us could stand him. Then, I assume somehow he learned about the Clava community and visited."

That was news. Freyja had said nothing about visiting Clava.

"When?" I asked.

"Oh, recently, maybe eight or nine months ago. I was still there, but in my planning stages to leave. Maybe closer to nine months."

That made sense. Freyja was on Lewis by then, heavily pregnant with Katrin.

"Was he pissed? That he hadn't been told about Clava, I mean."

"Honestly, I have no idea. I had resigned from my post and was leaving anyway, so I was no longer included in briefings. I just saw him one day. We had never met in real life, but I recognized him easily enough. He was coming out of the headquarters. He spotted me, made a beeline for me, and started talking at me. Boasted that he was being tasked with a special mission to visit the other domed communities like they had promoted him above me or something. Honestly, I had always thought he was an arrogant twat, so I nodded sweetly, made my excuses, and left. After that, I avoided him until he left a few days later."

"Illy, what do you mean by you could radio ahead? You said that the other day."

"Oh, I forgot you wouldn't know. Most communities have a satellite radio capable of transmission."

"They do?"

"Let's just say that the discrepancies between the resourcing of the communities were one of the many reasons I decided I wasn't suited to life at Clava. But I can contact them if you like. I have the radio here."

Illy's tone was a little off. She wasn't telling me something, but I wasn't sure that we were close enough for me to ask.

"No, it's okay," I replied quickly. "It is only a thought, and weeks away, even if I make it. I have things I want to do first. What is it like on Auckland? At Clava?"

Illy sighed. "Very different from here. Come on. It is getting dark, and Will and Liesl will wonder where you are."

CHAPTER 3

AFTER NINE DAYS, IT was time to move on. After wishing Illyria goodbye, a surprising sense of sadness washed over me. She was an amazing woman, one I genuinely liked and respected. There was a good chance we could be happy together. I had made my peace with what had happened but knew that I needed to visit Mousa, just once, to put this chapter behind me. While I knew Lae never made it this far, that was where those brutes had intended to take her, enslave her. It is where my memory skipped, and I was missing a fragment. Orkney was lovely, but my children were on Lewis. My sister and Di. Louis was my mini Lae, and being here, away from him, was more painful than I would have thought. It was my longing to hold Katrin, to see her happy, cheeky face beaming up at me, that surprised me. She was as much my child as Louis, and I could never be away from her either.

The formidable solid gray stone broch was visible from quite a distance. I had taken care to arrive in the mid-morning to avoid flashbacks. Mooring near the broch, instead of the cove where we had anchored the

Selkie, I stood on the beach and listened. I'm not sure why or what I was listening *for* exactly. But there was nothing—just wind echoing through the small valley, whistling past the ominous broch. The broch stood on the grassy hillside and commanded attention with its imposing authority.

Staring up at the broch, I noticed they had affixed a flat metal roof, a solid steel door on the single doorway. They covered the slitted windows from the inside. Likely the raiders had used it for protection before its use as a prison, drawn to this place for its tiny speck of greenery, so out of place in the sea of death. The door was ajar, and I stepped inside, imagining those poor women, terrified out of their minds, trapped here in the dark, amid the filth and stench. Exactly one year ago today, on her birthday, Lae had left, never to return. Never to hold Louis, or me, in her arms again.

The broch was much higher and far more intact than the one at Carloway, and I fervently wished that Lae had been here to see it. The tall ancient cylindrical stone tower was Norse, I think she said. But thousands of years old. If it hadn't been for her love of the broch at Carloway, I would never have known about Mousa. Then the outcome would have been vastly different. It had been Lae who had saved the other women. How conflicted she would have been to see something she had only dreamed about but in the vilest of circumstances.

Standing in the doorway, my back to the broch, I could see several houses visible in the cleared area below. The shacks were crudely built, uneven structures that were barely more than sheds with a flat roof that overhung the stone walls of repurposed stone—each with a single door and window. Entering the nearest one, I discovered it was a basic fishing cabin. A single room with a filthy mattress on the floor, it had once been silver or pale blue. Now it was mottled shades of brown, stains of all sizes marring the stitched surface. It held a simple wooden table and chair opposite—no sign of life. Even though Lae never made it here, I knew I needed to come here to see where they lived and had planned to enslave her and our child. Somehow, over the past year, I had built up the notion they were ogres, sub-human. But in truth, they were just men. Brutal, repulsive men.

I spent several hours wandering through the settlement, not sure what I was looking for. Slowly I retraced my steps, walking along the path where we advanced on the camp in the early dawn light. Locating the tree where I slammed the first man, indentations still faintly visible in the bark, I paused and closed my eyes. This was the place I had been standing when I heard, the last place I remembered standing before waking on the *Selkie*, several days later. Gazing out to sea, I knew that there was no closure here. She was gone, and for Louis' sake, I needed to keep on living. Louis was my focus now. Closing my eyes, I visualized her seated on our couch, baby Louis in her arms. That charming smile as she gazed lovingly at our son. *Happy birthday, kitten.* I sent the wish out to wherever she was, taking care of our child. The child I would never meet.

Slowly I boarded, being careful not to splash water on myself, and sailed back to the northernmost point and down the eastern coast of mainland Scotland. The solitude was a balm to my wounded soul, watching the blues of the sky and sea drift past, day after day.

There was no sign of life. But wind, blessed wind. As the days passed, the pain lessened, and I looked forward to seeing Louis and Katrin. Just one more mission. A trip to Edinburgh, possibly Clava, then home.

CHAPTER 4

WALKING ALONG THE EDINBURGH High Street, I was astonished to see that the beautiful buildings that had stood for hundreds of years were still mostly intact. Rubbish was strewn everywhere, forcing me to step over it carefully and watch where I walked. Broken windows and smashed cars littered the cobbled streets, but the charismatic buildings remained intact. Solid stone in various shades of gray, sand, and fawn, with chimney pots poking out of black slate rooftops, most were several hundred years old and withstood the test of time. Imposing and silent, these buildings stood sentry, watching generations be born, grow up, and die. They had seen wars and celebrations alike. Now, they may be the only part of Edinburgh that remained.

I had walked the Royal Mile many times on visits here, across the North Bridge, and past Waverley station. Casting my eye upward, I could see Edinburgh Castle atop the volcanic rock. A place I had visited several times, it remained silently judging, surveying all that lay below. The city I loved, so alive with people, sound, and full of life was familiar, and yet now, it wasn't. Stillness and a foul stench filled the air, unlike any memory I held of this place.

Turning into Princes Street, it didn't take me long to locate the building that housed the National Records of Scotland. An imposing multi-floor sandstone building with solid black painted doors, small chips in the glossy paintwork showed evidence of someone trying to enter. Sighing, I realized that smashing a window was my only option. I was creating quite a habit of breaking into abandoned buildings. Eyeing the small multi-paned windows on the lower floor, I tried to locate one that would be easier to access.

The Records room was a spectacular circular space, well lit with natural light and large tables in the center. Computers and lamps, now dead, were still plugged in, awaiting their next user. Fortunately, the walls were covered, floor to ceiling with enormous leather volumes, embossed with gold lettering containing all the recorded births, deaths, marriages, census data, church data, and court findings since the mid-1800s.

Knowing her birthday, it wasn't hard to find what I sought.

Rose, Laetitia Katherine.

Born 16 September.

Mother: Jasmine Rose, aged 19 years.

Occupation: Student Nurse.

Father: information withheld.

Place of birth: Raigmore Hospital, Inverness-shire.

It was the place of birth that came as a surprise: Inverness. She hadn't always lived in Glasgow then. I smiled, thinking of that. Lae had believed that she had never been farther from Glasgow than Edinburgh until she moved to Lewis.

Her mother's name was on the certificate: Jasmine Rose, aged 19 years. No father's name. Hardly surprising. That would have been too easy.

Student Nurse? Now that was interesting. Lae had not known that. If I could not track her down through the records here, perhaps I could locate a university record? Immediately I recognized the futility in that endeavor. She could have attended one of many universities. I returned to the volumes in front of me. I needed something to take home to Louis, some part of her history that would let him know where he came from.

Several unproductive hours passed as I looked through the birth records for her mother—no child with the surname Rose and first name Jasmine was recorded. Searching the years on either side also turned up nothing. No *Jasmine Rose* was born in any year on either side of the age declared on Laetitia's birth certificate.

Slamming the dusty leather-bound volume shut, I placed it back in its correct place on the shelf, instantly recognizing the futility of doing so. How many people would seek birth, death, and marriage certificates in a deserted city?

Marriage. I pondered on that word for a moment. *Maybe... she married. Maybe Rose wasn't her birth name. Or...* It occurred to me that naming a child Jasmine if the family surname was Rose was a little unlikely. She also had listed no middle name on Laetitia's birth certificate. *Perhaps... What if her mother changed her name so that her family couldn't find her? Lae had no knowledge of any living family, so maybe her mother ran away?*

I cast my eye around, looking for the Deed Poll section. There wasn't one. A memory stirred in the dark recesses of my mind. Mum saying that it wasn't a requirement to register a name change in Scotland one day as she bemoaned her own difficult name. Wishing she had changed it before she moved to Australia, where it was so much harder.

I sighed, wondering what to do next. Such a waste to travel so far and find nothing. Feeling the need to learn about Lae's family, to provide that information to Louis, was burning a hole in my chest.

Finally, standing and cracking my stiff neck, I left the building and walked along Princes Street toward Calton Hill, the Nelson Monument, and National Monument of Scotland still standing proudly at the top. It was mid-afternoon, and the sun was setting.

Okay, what do I know? Lae's name and date of birth. Her birth location: Raigmore Hospital, Inverness. Her mother's name and age: Jasmine Rose, age 19 years. Nurse.

Only that wasn't her name.

Turning toward the Nelson Monument, I tried to focus. *What else do I have access to?* Death records were pointless. By the point her mother had passed, they likely wouldn't have been recorded. Not in time to make it into a leather-bound volume on a shelf. Marriage records appeared unlikely if there was no father listed, especially at the age of only nineteen, although not impossible. Checking every birth record for a Jasmine seemed a daunting task, but not as daunting as traveling to Inverness to seek a medical record. *Census then?*

Recognizing that the dark would likely overtake me soon, I returned to the reading room. I located the census data and looked at the books. Nothing before 1931. *Seriously?* Perhaps they were in a different space. I hunted around, and my eye caught sight of a plastic brochure holder displaying flyers coated in dust.

CENSUS DATA: We hold records of the census of the population of Scotland for 1841 and every tenth year thereafter, (with the exception of the wartime year of 1941 when no census was taken). Census records are closed for 100 years under the Freedom of Information (Scotland) Act 2002.

Closed for 100 years. Brilliant.

Looking out the nearest window, I estimated I had half an hour left of daylight, possibly a little more. After this, I would wait until tomorrow. Getting my pack close and ensuring that I could light the small gas burner I had taken from the camping store in Invercargill several years before, I checked it worked before returning to the volumes containing birth records. I could cook dinner in the dark, the light from the butane throwing off enough light for me to at least see what I was opening and eating.

Returning to the book I had discarded, the one I believed to be her mother's birth year, I touched the soft brown leather cover, the tissue-thin pages inside, yellowed with age, and squinted at the tiny black print in the dim light. Lae genuinely believed that her mother was Scots-born. Twelve thousand babies were born that year, according to the index. Sighing and getting myself comfortable in the leather armchair, I committed myself to my task. Tracing my finger slowly down the page...

Jasmine wasn't a common name, so by the time I reached the B's, I wondered if her name genuinely was Jasmine. Perhaps it was something completely different, and she had taken an entirely new name? Keeping a shortlist of names on the paper and pencils handily confiscated from the National Records main desk, I was almost nodding off by the C's and forced myself to get up and find the toilets. No water, but it wasn't like anyone would chase me if I didn't flush.

Returning to the darkened room, I realized I needed to call it a day, and placed the book carefully on the main table, open on the D's.

With little butane in the canister and no replace-ment, I heated the soup to a barely tolerable level and sipped at the tepid chicken and vegetables as I reviewed what I knew.

Lae told me her mum was Scottish, so she was likely born here. Immigrating when she was a young child would explain the accent but would throw a spanner in the works. The options now appeared to be that her birth name was not Jasmine Rose or that she wasn't born here. Either were entirely plausible options, but neither was a more straightforward pos-sibility. Finding immigration records would be dif-ficult, impossible if she just moved from England or Wales. Moving across the border was simple and didn't require any formal applications. Deed poll not being a legal record, there was no way of proving that she had just changed her name.

Ensuring the gas stove was off, I left the empty can and dishes for tomorrow. Feeling exhausted, I curled up in my sleeping bag, dreaming of Lae, her hair streaming behind her in the breeze. Shocked, I realized I had only once seen her with her hair blowing in the wind. The day we had visited my aunt's house. But now, she was standing on a rocky cliff, overlooking the beach, staring out to sea. Intently. What was she looking at? Peering past her, I saw a white yacht in the distance. She was waving happily.

Dawn light trickled through the windows, and I woke with a new determination to solve this mystery. As freezing as it was in this dark, dusty building, unoccupied for years, I gritted my teeth, pulled my sleeves down to cover my frozen solid hands, and set to work. My breath was visible in the frigidly cold air, partially obscuring my vision.

Carrying the volume to the window and dragging a comfortable chair into the daylight filtering in through the windows, I forced myself to pay attention to the book. Under no circumstances did I want to do this twice for fear that I could have missed something.

Page after page of tiny printed text blurred before me. Nothing.

Then I saw it. Blinking my dry, tired eyes, I closed them and looked again. I wasn't hallucinating. It was definitely there.

MacLEOD, Jasmine Rose, 13 March, Western Isles Hospital, Stornoway, Lewis.

It couldn't be. Surely not. But the year was correct. The name was correct. Of the 12,000 babies born in Scotland in that year, the law of averages said approximately half were boys. For the other half, Jasmine had been a relatively uncommon name. I had only seen four others, and none, Jasmine Rose. I wasn't sure Laetitia ever told me when her mother's birthday was. Closing my eyes, I tried to recall what she had told me. Memories drifted in and out. We were talking about flowers, wildflowers. I had brought her some machair wildflowers, those that grew near the coast, a posy of eyebright, lady's bedstraw, and native orchids. She had asked me if daffodils grew on Lewis; she liked them. They reminded her of sunshine. She told me she picked wild daffodils for her mother's birthday. Daffodils grew in the UK from late winter to early spring. So, a birthday in March... that would fit. My heart was pounding. If this was her... Laetitia's mother... she was from *Lewis*?

Standing to clear my head, I walked around the room, took a sip of my bottled water, and tried to get my thoughts straight. There was no guarantee this was her. It was all circumstantial, the dates, the name. She could have changed her name entirely and not just dropped her surname.

Heating baked beans for breakfast, I couldn't shake the feeling deep in my bones. This was her. Eating quickly, I cleaned up, a laborious task with no running water, and repacked my bag. There was no need for me to rush, but the feeling of invading this place permeated my skin. I was keen to move on.

Looking again at that entry—MacLeod, Jasmine Rose—I noted the names underneath.

Born to Angus Robert MacLeod, Engineer, and Amara Kalayani MacLeod, Lawyer, of Tarbert, Harris.

Other issue: None.

Amara Kalayani? Lae's grandmother was Thai? Closing my eyes, I could see Laetitia, standing in our kitchen, so tiny and lightly boned, her glossy brown hair flowing down her back. Her dark hair, and yes, the slightest hint of exoticism about her eyes. Not her coloring, but that beautiful, exotic look. She herself had assumed that her lovely almond-shaped eyes were from her unknown father. Instead, it may have been her mother, half Thai, who had transmitted those gorgeous Oriental features.

A thought struck, and I started looking through marriage records, beginning with the year Jasmine was born. Nothing. The year before. Nothing. Two years. I started thinking this was a wild goose chase. Then, there it was, two years before Jasmine was born.

Marriage.

MacLeod, Angus Robert and Siriporn, Amara Kalayani.

15 December, St Clement's Church, Rodel, Harris.

St Clement's Church. That sounded familiar. Had I been there? I wracked my brain to recall the churches my mother had taken me to visit. Had St Clement been one of them? Still, now was not the time. Mentally noting the name, I started looking forward in the marriage records. A year, two, three after Jasmine was born and was rewarded, if one can call it that. Five years after Jasmine's birth, and seven years after his first marriage.

Marriage.

MacLeod, Angus Robert and MacGillivray, Johanna Alice.

6 May, St Clement's Church, Rodel, Harris.

Jasmine's father had remarried and in the same church. Taken a new wife. Little Jasmine, only five. Is that what had kick-started her pattern of self-destruction, taken her down a road of teen preg-nancy and addiction?

Returning to the birth records, I searched again, this time narrowing the search to MacLeods. Wading through several volumes, I was ready to give up.

This is the final one, I told myself, flicking through the pages. I gasped as I read.

MacLEOD, Angus MacGillivray.

Father: MacLeod, Angus Robert. Occupation: Engineer.

Mother: MacGillivray, Johanna Alice. Occupation: Headmistress.

Other issue: Jasmine Rose, 9 years.

Slamming the volume closed, I choked on the cloud of dust it disturbed. Desperately needing fresh air, my head was spinning like a top. I walked across the Royal Mile, taking none of it in. I passed Holyrood Palace and through Holyrood Park to Arthur's Seat, picking a steep path and walked. I wasn't taking in the scenes of death and destruction. The pain in my chest matched the pain in my legs. Surely not. Holy fucking hell. No way. It could not be. That would be too cruel. Angus? Freyja's friend? Could he possibly be Laetitia's uncle? Half-uncle? Was a half-uncle even a thing?

As I walked, I stewed over what I knew. The facts were convincing. My hand shaking, I stopped, sitting uncomfortably on a large rock, and plucked the tiny notepad and pencil from my jacket pocket and started scribbling dates. Lae had turned twenty-eight the day she passed. Her mother was nineteen when she was born. She would have been roughly forty-seven years old, maybe forty-eight, had she still been alive. But her brother, Angus, was nine years younger, so thirty-eightish. The approximate age that I would have guessed Angus was. Surely not?

What was it that had he said? That he was originally from Harris but had traveled to Edinburgh for university and work and never returned? Fraser had told me that Angus was older than most of the settlers, but as he had been part of the scientific team, they had always accepted it. The only way to know for sure was to ask him, but goodness knew when that would happen. Both of us were a long way from Lewis, and heaven knew when we would meet again.

But I had found what I was looking for: Lae's family history. But now, I was more confused than ever. When Lae had believed her heritage was a mystery, that was hard. She wanted to know where she came from so she could tell Louis. But now that I genuinely believed she had a family, and from what Freyja had said, Angus was from a wealthy one, this just raised more questions than ever. *How did Jasmine go from a life of relative luxury as an old clan family of Lewis to living as an unemployed and sometimes violent alcoholic in a council flat in Glasgow?*

This triggered more questions as I walked. *Where to now? Back to Lewis?* I desperately wanted to get back to Louis and Katrin, missing them both terribly. But no. I needed to know more. When I returned, I never needed to leave again. Every person I loved was on Lewis. *What do I want?*

Closing my eyes, I pictured her. More time was what I truly wanted, but memories were what I had. When I thought of my family, I looked at my photos. Could I track down some pictures of Jasmine, so I could at least have something of her to show Louis? She didn't have any photos of her own family but had loved showing Louis mine. *What do I know?* They had lived in Glasgow. Maybe I could find her house, her school, find something of her? Some memento that showed him who she was. I had dozens of photos of my family. It only seemed fair that I had some of hers.

It made sense to travel overland to Glasgow. It had only been an hour by car. Probably less now that there was no traffic. Returning to the Records Office, I left most of my belongings. It wasn't like anything would be stolen. Besides, the boat I had traveled here was in the harbor, and I needed that to return home.

Emptying most of my belongings, I repacked my backpack with enough food for a day or two and a change of clothes. Outside, I hunted for a car. In case I found something I wanted to bring back, a motorbike wouldn't be big enough. I would also be exposed if it rained.

Several hours later, as I drove the tiny Fiat up Cathedral Street toward the imposing Glasgow Cathedral, I realized I had no clue of where Lae had lived. Likely there were quite a few council estates in the greater Glasgow area, and I had no way of knowing which she had called home. Her school, though. What had she called it? The Glasgow... *fuck!* I couldn't believe that I had come all the way here, only to find that I couldn't remember her school name. Putting my head on the steering wheel and setting off the horn, I closed my eyes and tried to focus on that conversation. What had she said again? She had won a scholarship to....

Academy! The Glasgow Academy. Praying that was correct, I used the car's GPS to track it down. Thankfully, it was listed: The Glasgow Academy, Colebrooke Street. Miraculously, the GPS still worked. Evidently, the satellites feeding it data were still transmitting.

Parking as close as I could to the main door, I looked up. It had been a prestigious school; that was obvious by the wrought-iron gates, a sweeping drive, and expansive lawns, now all dead and browned around an imposing and spectacular multi-storey sandstone building with columns and a sweeping staircase leading to the front door. Feeling irrationally guilty, I threw a boulder through the main entrance window, trying hard not to grin as I did so. Most students would relish hurling a massive rock at the main entrance of their old high school.

Once in, finding the enrollment files was relatively easy. A large room off the main office was marked *Archives*. Then I found the relevant year and surname.

Searching through all the R's for her enrolment record was a little more time-consuming as they weren't filed alphabetically. But in short order, I found it.

Rose, Laetitia. Wyndford Road, Wyndford.

I saw details of her scholarship exam and her perfect score as well as references from her teachers. Before I left, I searched for the yearbooks in which she would have appeared. I was rewarded with gorgeous images of schoolgirl Laetitia, looking much like a younger version of how I had known her. A more scared look, though. Studious, nervous, but still my lovely wife. Taking the books, I laid them carefully on the passenger seat, proud to have something to show Louis.

I reprogrammed the GPS, my mouth dropping as I entered the area in which she had lived. So near to the prestigious school geographically, yet in social terms, a million miles away. No wonder Lae had felt out of place. Burned-out cars littered the streets. Many more missing wheels and panels, in ruins, were propped up on old bricks. Every window was smashed. Doors were kicked in, never to be repaired, graffiti covering every surface. No trees or greenery had existed between the tower blocks, just slabs of concrete, even before the pandemic had struck. There were areas like this in every major city, and I had an idea of what her life must have been like. Getting off the bus in her posh uniform and walking through this. *Oh, Lae,* I thought sadly. *I can't believe you had to endure this.* How many times had she told me how *lucky* she was?

Parking the tiny Fiat between two unidentifiable wrecks, I looked up at the gloomy high-rise that had been her home, surrounded by scores of identical buildings, all with tiny windows and drab gray walls. Even from where I stood, it screamed cheap housing. *Barely a house,* I thought grimly. Fighting the urge to lock the car and pocket the key, I climbed the stairs to the tenth floor flat where she had spent her childhood, trying not to inhale deeply. The stench of rotting rubbish and decomposing bodies seared my nasal passages. The stairwell was filled with bags and piles of decomposing garbage, a narrow path barely navigable through the middle. The door to their flat was ajar, revealing the ransacked interior, although I realized quickly that, never having seen it beforehand, I couldn't prove that it had been looted.

Perhaps her mum lived like this after Lae left for university? Watching where I stood to avoid the crockery smashed everywhere, I grimaced at the food smeared, now dried out, and blackened on the benches. Surely not. No one living here would smash dishes all over the place.

It was a tiny flat, like all the others, I imagined, but I didn't care to find out. Standing inside the front door, I could see into every room: two small bedrooms, a bathroom, and a kitchen/dining/lounge room with brown fake wood cupboards and orange benches barely visible in the poor light. Filthy floors and tiny grease smeared windows so caked in grime that the city skyline was barely visible in the distance. Jasmine hadn't bothered cleaning after Lae left. Looking around the living space, I spied few belongings. Two mismatched prints on a wall were skewed but still intact. Fossicking through drawers, I searched for something, anything, that I could take home to Louis. There was very little here. Likely, that had always been the case. With little money, Lae and her mother didn't have much.

Stepping into Lae's room, I gasped in agony. Sitting on her single bed, which took up much of the room, closing my eyes, I could visualize a younger Lae, staring at the walls, lying in here dreaming of a better life. A life she had, for a time. A life cut short and in the most horrific of circumstances. Searching under her bed, I found a book. Just a novel, likely prescribed reading from school, but it had been hers. I knew she would want Louis to have it. Opening the wardrobe, I found her school tie hanging alone on a single wire hanger. Such a silly thing, but as I ran its silky fabric between my fingers, I felt her presence. It was the same tie she wore in the class photos, now in the car downstairs. Slipping it into my pocket, I turned and entered her mother's room.

They had stripped the bed clean, leaving a sunken, stained mattress, indicating that Jasmine had perhaps died here. Empty bottles of cheap whisky, vodka, and brandy littered the corners of the room. The brown carpet was sticky in places, but the wardrobe was empty.

Who had she been: Jasmine? How had she ended up here? If she was Angus's half-sister, how did he attend prestigious schools, leading to a fruitful career, and she end up here?

Slowly going through the drawers, I knew there was nothing left. What little Jasmine owned had been taken. Still, I made it to the last drawer and pulled it out, staring despondently into its empty depths. As I closed it, a thought struck, and I pulled it all the way out, getting on my knees to look underneath.

Rewarded, I could see, far at the back, a small, yellowed envelope, rat-eared and torn in places, propped upright against the back of the unit. Reaching my hand in, I withdrew it and opened it carefully, the paper fragile and disintegrating in my hands.

Photos. I pulled them out, looking at them, one by one. The first was an old photo, a wedding photo, likely Jasmine's mother and father. Her mother was undoubtedly beautiful, and they looked so happy. Standing in front of an old stone church, they smiled into the camera, the beautiful blue sky framing the scene. I squinted, looking at Jasmine's mother, Amara. Waist-length straight black hair and tiny next to the large brown-haired man beside her, she looked exotic in a long, simple white lace dress in front of the ancient church. In a second wedding photo, they smiled at each other. They seemed so happy, so in love. There was the hint of Laetitia about her. Not the coloring, but the bone structure, her size. Laetitia's grandfather looked like a kind man and very much like his son, Angus. His chestnut hair was similar in color to Laetitia's. My theory about Angus was correct then. I wasn't sure how I felt about that. Looking closely at the images, I recognized the church. It was on the south coast of Harris. I had been there once, many years ago.

Carefully unsticking the old photos not to tear them, I saw the next photo was another of Amara, wearing a gold dress, seated in an ornate blue chair, smiling lovingly at a tiny baby in her arms. Baby Jasmine, no doubt. Then one of another baby, a newborn, wrapped in a white blanket, lying in a clear hospital cot. This one was slightly more modern with white edging, and in the style of those my mother had of me. *Laetitia perhaps?* Filtering through the remaining photos, I didn't find many of Lae, but enough. School photos mainly, some copies of the ones I already had, but some from her primary school, depicting a skinny, scared-looking girl. But the last item was a clipping from a local newspaper, yellowed but still legible. A story about Laetitia and her scholarship to Edinburgh University. Jasmine had been proud of her then. That made me smile. If only Lae had known that. She never would, but Louis, he would have this. Finally, I could share these people with him.

Picking up Lae's book and the packet of photos, with the school tie neatly curled in my pocket, I returned to Lae's room, lay on her tiny bed, my feet hanging off the end, and fell asleep, dreaming of her.

CHAPTER 5

THE DIM GLOW OF morning light woke me, casting its dour shadows, even though the sun barely penetrated this dark, dank space. Her space. But she was here no longer. This had been her room but never her sanctuary in the way a child's bedroom should be— the place where you can dream. Imagine your role in a better world.

With a last scan of the dreary filthy space, I returned to the car, pondering whether to return to Edinburgh or head farther west to Kilmartin Glen. Temple Wood at Kilmartin was one of Kevin's suspected sites for a community and only ninety miles from here. I could drive that in around two hours, assuming there were no road blockages. Checking the fuel gauge, I noted it was three-quarters full. Sighing, I resigned myself to go. I had come all this way; it made sense to find out before returning home. Temple Wood it was then.

The gray stone structure loomed out of the dead brown landscape, still and silent. Even from the road, it was evident that there was no community here, no life. Parking the car, I walked into the center of the Temple Wood stone circle, closing my eyes and absorbing the ambiance. This, too, was a special place. I could sense it. There was a large, chambered tomb here, constructed of ancient gray stones, much like Newgrange and how I remembered Clava. Ringed with a stone circle, a passage marked the path of the sun at the solstice. *Why was this place not chosen as a site?* Closing my eyes, I could feel the serenity radiating from the stones, the specialness of this place sparking the atmosphere around.

"Makes you wonder why they didn't settle here, doesn't it?" a low Scottish voice asked from behind one of the enormous menhirs.

I jerked out of my trance and bolted upright, looking around wildly.

To my utter astonishment, Angus stepped into view. Behind him, I could see one of his crew members, Nate, lurking behind.

"Why are you here?" I asked a little tersely, feeling like I was being spied on.

"I could ask the same of *you*," he retorted quickly but not unkindly.

"Fair call," I responded, recognizing that it had been the element of surprise that had made me react as I had. He didn't appear to be offended. "I was in Glasgow. Kevin, from the community at Newgrange, thought Temple Wood might be an antipodal point. I was close, so I thought I would check it out."

"I am fairly sure it is," Angus admitted. "I'm just not sure *why* they didn't put a community here. The only thing I can think of is the lack of access to a fresh water source."

That was intriguing. "What is the antipodal point, then?" I asked curiously.

"A tiny island called Bollons Island, off the coast of Antipodes Island, near New Zealand. But they settled neither site."

"I can answer that," I replied. "The Australian teams deemed Antipodes uninhabitable. Do you know if they activated the portals?"

"I don't believe so, but I couldn't say for sure. It makes you wonder how many more there are out there, doesn't it? Waiting to be activated."

It raised many questions, I realized. *Why had they activated the Orkney portal, but there was no community at the other end?* According to Freyja, there was a settlement on the Shetland Islands too, but it wasn't one listed in the headquarters in Melbourne. *How many more people could they have saved if they had settled all the antipodal points?*

"Can we talk?" I asked, a little more abruptly than I had intended. "In private."

Not that I really gave a toss if his companion overheard me grilling him about his family, but I suspected Angus might. Freyja had a lot of respect for Angus, and he had been decent to her. I could try to be kind. Besides, Nate had helped rescue the women from Mousa. I had no quarrel with him.

"Is Freyja alright?" he asked quickly.

"She is fine. The baby, Katrin, too. Not that."

"What then?" he asked, dismissing Nate with a wave and settling himself on a curbstone.

"Can I ask a question?" I asked Angus tentatively as I sat, knowing the answer but wanting to hear his response anyway. Since his acceptance of Katrin, there was a newfound tolerance on my part. Not friends exactly—we could never be that. But I appreciated his role in ensuring Freyja was not the butt of community gossip.

"I guess," he replied tersely. "What?"

Inhaling deeply, I let it out as one sentence, not wanting to rabbit on. "Did you have an older sister? A half-sister, I mean. Jasmine?"

The most extraordinary series of expressions washed over his face—shock, concern, then utter confusion.

"How on earth did you know that?" he whispered. "She disappeared before I was even ten. Yes. Yes, Jasmine was my sister. Is she alive then?" he asked hopefully.

Shaking my head slowly, but deliberately, I watched his face fall. He cared then, a little.

"Let's walk," I suggested, standing. My back ached. I had been stuck in the tiny Fiat for ages, no longer used to sitting for long periods, and hadn't slept well on Lae's small rock-hard bed.

Angus nodded, recognizing my logic. "Meet you back at the dock," he called to Nate, who was lurking in the distance.

Nate, acknowledging the instruction, disappeared out of sight.

"Tell me about her," I asked gently, sensing that he was in shock.

"I haven't heard her name in nearly thirty years," he confessed. "Jasmine was my older half-sister. My father was married before, you see. He was from a respected family on Harris. The MacLeods of Harris had a long history, old money. Anyway, my father, also Angus, as all the firstborn sons were named, went traveling after he graduated from university in London. He was an engineer. He was expected to join the family business back on Harris. Building factories, being part of the community there. But he had loved city life and didn't want to return. My grandfather offered him an around-the-world trip before he returned. They thought it would knock the wanderlust from him, tame the rebellious streak. Only it didn't. He came home with a Thai woman. A stunningly beautiful girl, according to local gossip.

Your sister said once that your mother was from Lewis? Or maybe Freyja told me. Well, you may recall that life back then was a little more rigid. Hell, shops didn't even open on Sundays; you couldn't even get fuel! My father, returning to a conservative, well-heeled Presbyterian family with a Buddhist girl, likely didn't go down terribly well. But from what people tell me, he was madly in love and wouldn't hear anything against her. The family knew that they would need to accept her or lose him forever. They accepted her for a time. But they forced them to marry again in a Christian church, refusing to recognize their first heathen marriage. Then my sister Jasmine was born. Apparently, my grandfather softened, but my grandmother didn't. She refused to accept Jasmine as an heir to the family fortune, which put a lot of pressure on dad and his wife. Amara was her name.

Anyway, jumping forward a bit, Amara died when Jasmine was very young. Maybe a year old? I never learned how, but I always knew that it was under somewhat mysterious circumstances. Suicide? Someone taking a hand? I never found out. But something wasn't quite right, that was for sure. It was whispered about at dinner parties and community events my entire childhood. You need to understand that my family were very influential, employed many people on the island, so the police weren't likely to go charging them. They were above the law, I guess you could say. Not that it matters now. Then dad married mum."

Angus stopped. Stopped walking and stopped talking. Pausing beside him, I looked down and realized he was struggling with emotion—something I had never seen in Angus. As I waited patiently, he started again.

"Mum was local, the headmistress of the local primary school, and also from a respectable family. A MacGillivray. Another family that had been on Harris for generations. Wealthy landowners. The type of girl my grandparents wanted originally, I guess. After a few years, they had me, and I was ... well, spoiled is what I was. My mother fought to have me, and so I was their only child. Looking back now, I realize how badly Jasmine was treated by my mother and grandmother. They treated her like a second-class citizen. I became the heir, and she was, well, I don't know what she was. But it wasn't my equal. Grandpa had died, and my dad was CEO of the family business by this time and away an awful lot, the business expanding overseas. When he was home, he treated us fairly, but when he was away... things were different."

Angus continued quietly, "I am ashamed to admit that I didn't help matters. I was younger, spoiled, and the only boy. I wanted all the attention. As my mother's only child, she indulged me, and my grandmother encouraged this. I took every opportunity to blame Jasmine for things I had done. They were awful to her, I realize now. Much of it, my fault."

Recognizing that these memories must have been hard to dredge up again, I waited until he was ready to speak again, despite having a million questions.

"She moved to Inverness to study nursing when she was seventeen, and I became the only child. I admit, at eight, I was a self-centered little brat, and I relished it. The center of attention, getting everything I wanted. Then my father died. Completely unexpectedly. Had a heart attack on a business trip overseas and never came home. I went to bed one night, spoke to him on the phone as was my routine, and by breakfast the next morning, he was gone.

Jasmine came home for the funeral and was devastated, as we all were. But that was when the shift started. Not just exclusion. It became quite nasty. My mother blamed her for dad's death. Looking back, it wasn't her fault, but they excluded her entirely. Held family dinners that she wasn't invited to. Making her sit in the back row of the public funeral. She was eighteen by then and likely knew what they were doing. I was nine, had just lost my father, and didn't want to share the attention of my mother and grandparents with her.

The day before she was due to return to Inverness, she came home in a terrible state. She had been out walking, down to the church in Rodel where my parents were married. My mother had been particularly awful to her that morning, refusing to let her eat with us, so she went out for a walk. I sat at the top of the stairs watching, hiding, terrified. Her top was torn to shreds, her face dirty, bruises showing. Her hair was everywhere. Jasmine had gorgeous silky long dark hair that gleamed, but that afternoon, it was a bird's nest. I don't know why I remember that, but it had bits of straw and leaf in it. I could see it from where I sat, watching. I used to watch her brush her hair when I was little, but now it looked like someone had tipped the garden compost on it.

She told mum that one of the neighbors, a prominent and wealthy landowner on one of the neighboring estates, had attacked her. Raped her, I realized later, though, at nine, I didn't know what that meant. She was crying, sobbing, really distressed. I thought my mother would comfort her as she did me when I was hurt or upset. But my mother stood up tall and said, 'Well, you brought this on yourself, wearing a short skirt while out walking. You are nothing but a slut and deserved it.'

Jasmine protested and kept crying. Mum started screaming at her, calling her a slut and a whore. That everyone knew she had slept her way around Inverness. Jasmine cried that she was a virgin. I didn't know any of those words, and it intrigued me. I had never heard my mum speak that way. The way mum spat them at her. Well, I looked the words up in a dictionary afterward and was shocked. Finally, mum pushed her up the stairs, told her to shower and change and tell no one. She had shamed herself and her family. I overheard mum on the phone with my grandmother talking about what to do. He was respected, and they couldn't challenge him publicly. It would cause gossip, bring the family name into disrepute, especially so soon after the funeral.

The next thing I knew, mum had handed her a thousand pounds, packed her bags for her, and told her to leave and never return. She had shamed the family name and was no longer a MacLeod."

Exhaling, not wanting to interrupt, I watched Angus's face.

"Even at nine, I recognized this as serious. But I badly wanted to be the favorite, you see. My last memory of Jasmine was as she was being marched to the door, flanked on either side by my mother and grandmother. Tears were staining her beautiful, lightly tanned face, the pendant she wore glinting in the sunlight. Mum tried to take it from her, but Jasmine fought, screaming that she would never have that. She was curled up on the floor of our entrance hall, an old flagstone floor, my mother trying to pull it over her head. Finally, my grandmother told mum to let it be; it was worthless anyway. As she was fighting my mother, trying to stop her from breaking off her necklace, she spotted me up the stairs. She called out, sobbing, 'Angus! Tell them. You saw him attack me. Please tell them!'"

Angus paused. A long silence ensued, and I wondered if he had finished.

When he started again, it was in a half-choked whisper. "I saw the nasty old coot attack her. She was walking along the lane, picking flowers, and he jumped out at her from behind an old ramshackle barn. He was known in the district for being an old pervert, leering at young girls on their way to and from the bus stop. I saw him throw her on the grass verge, kicking and screaming. She dropped her flowers. I remember seeing them lying there, crushed, in the road. Broken. He hit her in the face, calling her filthy names. Words I didn't know, but I knew they were bad just from the tone he used as he slapped her. As she lay there, still struggling, with him on top of her, she looked up and saw me, hiding behind the tree. I saw her mouth the word *help* as he had his hands around her throat. But I was scared, and I ran. I said nothing, didn't help her. I just ... left her there. I was ashamed at my cowardice, so I looked my mother in the eye and said, 'I saw nothing. She is lying.' I watched as her face shattered, and they hustled her out the door, my mother and grandmother shoving her toward the car. I never saw her again."

Angus sat on a rocky ledge on a hill that overlooked the stone circle. Big skies, crystal blue as far as the eye could see. Rolling hills, the patchwork of brown paddocks, farms, and crofts. The tiny village in the distance, once settled, now quiet and still.

"I will never forgive myself for that."

Not wanting to justify his horrific actions, I tried for some comfort. "You were nine. You couldn't have known the consequences."

"But later, when I had the chance, I never looked for her. She was alone in the world. I could have tried to make amends. After all, she was my sister, my father's child, and he had loved her. But I didn't. I loved being an only child, the sole heir, all that it meant. They removed all trace of her from the house, and we never spoke of her again."

I didn't know what to say, so I said nothing.

"Actually, that isn't quite true," he said, thinking. "I heard whispers of her over the years, people in the town who said that mum was jealous of Amara, of Jasmine. That dad had worshipped them both so much, and mum couldn't stand it. That Amara had been tiny and elegant, like an exotic princess. She was from a very wealthy family, dad told me once, but they cut her off as she married for love. She had an arranged marriage planned, then she met dad, and they fell madly in love. They ran away and came back to Scotland together, thinking they would have a better life. The way I heard mum describe her, Amara was a whore from a dirty bar in Bangkok."

"How would your mum know?" I asked softly.

"Mum was from a local family, so she had seen Amara. They had invited her parents to the wedding as influential people in the district. Everyone said Amara was beautiful and very exotic in Harris. I recognize it now as jealousy, but at the time, well ... she was my mum, and I loved her. Didn't see the flaws."

"Amara was a lawyer according to Jasmine's birth certificate," I told him quietly, taking the wedding pictures from my pocket and showing him.

"Oh God," he said, confronted with evidence of the happy couple. "My father... he looks so ... *happy*. And Amara. Goodness, Jasmine looked like her."

Quietly I asked, "What was your mum like?"

"Mum was ... well, Mum. Strong-willed, dominating, a schoolteacher who always got her way. But I guess she wasn't a great beauty. Rather dumpy, I guess you would describe her. Still, she was from a respected family, and maybe dad was looking for something different the second time around. She looked after dad, and she idolized me. But I see now that she was positively evil to Jasmine. And I encouraged it. Honestly, I have thought about her, Jas, I mean, over the years. But I am ashamed to say that never enough to go looking for her. Too caught up in my own sense of importance. She was older and always kind to me, despite how the family treated her. She was gentle and kind. That is how I remember her. Quiet, gentle, and kind."

Realizing that Angus had ended his part, I continued the story, taking my turn to fill in the blanks.

"Jasmine was pregnant when she returned to Inverness. Likely from that … encounter."

"Oh, God!" Angus's head dropped into his hands. "What happened to her?"

"She went back to Inverness and had a baby girl."

"I have a niece?" Angus whispered.

"Had," I corrected, speaking with some difficulty. "That niece was Laetitia. My wife."

The chasm of frozen air chilled further between us as he took that in. For years, he had been so close to his niece, his sister's child, and didn't know it. Had even taught in the school with her for a short time. But never took the time to get to know her.

"Oh. My. God," he breathed, struggling.

I may as well finish it, I thought. Rip the band-aid off.

"Her mother raised Laetitia in a tiny, filthy council high-rise flat. 'The most undesirable part of town,' was how she described it, and now that I have been there, that is probably putting it mildly. Drug dealers, family violence, and rat infestations were common. Garbage filling the stairwells, likely syringes too. Jasmine was a non-functioning alcoholic. Spent her life intermittently ignoring or neglecting her daughter, occasionally beating her. Only Lae didn't know why her mother hated her so much. Laetitia was barely fed, shown no love, and didn't know where she had come from."

"Oh … my … god," he repeated, the shock plain on his face, "that poor kid. No wonder Jasmine hated her, blamed her. That is my fault too. My actions caused that." Angus sniffed. "I did that to her, oh God, and now it is too late to say sorry. She was the firstborn child, and she deserved a better life. My mother, no, *I* was to blame for what happened. I didn't step in, scream. I didn't tell the truth. I didn't go looking for her."

"Can I ask one more thing?" May as well go for gold. I wouldn't get another chance.

Angus, distressed at this trip down memory lane, nodded.

"Lae's mother, Jasmine, I mean, had a necklace. A blue pendant. You mentioned it."

Angus nodded. "A sapphire pendant. Dad bought it for Amara when they were first dating in Thailand. Amara had allegedly cherished it, and when she died, dad gave it to Jasmine. She never took it off. It was part of her. You never saw Jasmine without that pendant. Amara's rings went missing after her funeral, likely my grandmother's doing, but Jasmine was old enough to have the pendant, I once heard my dad say. Mum tried to take it once before, when Jasmine was a teen. Well, Jasmine stacked on a huge tantrum, and dad intervened, saying it was hers and no one else's. She took little when she left, but I am glad that she took that."

"That makes sense."

Angus' face dropped further as I explained that Jasmine had kept the pendant and the incident with Lae as a child trying to touch it. If only I could tell Laetitia that now. Why it had meant so much to her mother.

We sat there, together and in silence—both mourning our loss.

At one point, he whispered so softly I barely heard it, "I'm so sorry. Sorry I couldn't save her."

Finally, the shadows cast darkness over us. Angus looked over at me. "Your little boy. He is my great-nephew."

Staring out into the distance for a moment, I acknowledged, "I guess he is. That makes us family, in some small, removed way."

Lae's gentle spirit overcame me, and I knew it was for him—not me. I hugged him, impulsively, recognizing the spoiled little brat who hadn't done the right thing, but forgiving him nonetheless. He couldn't have known what would happen. Nor could he have saved Laetitia against so many men. Freezing at my touch, he relaxed within a few heartbeats, perhaps forgiving himself, just a little, for his role in destroying a life.

CHAPTER 6

SENSING I WAS BEING watched, my eyes shot open, and I blinked, taking in the room's dimness. Returning to the Records library for the night, I had slept soundly. Peacefully. Knowing Jasmine's story, as awful as it was, brought a sense of closure. I knew about Laetitia's heritage now and had photos to show Louis when he was older.

Slowly my eyes adapted, and I just make out the familiar shape, tall and slender in the doorway, illuminated by the dawn light. "Freyja? What are you doing here?"

"Well, I thought, you know, I have never been to Edinburgh, so just on a whim, I came here." The tone was flippant, but I knew her well enough to know that she was concealing underlying anxiety.

"You are nuts," I yawned, barely awake.

"Maybe. But I had to try."

"Try what?" I asked warily.

She sighed. There was no deception in Freyja. "I just thought if we spent some time together, alone, without the kids, your sister, the whole bloody community watching on, maybe we..."

"Could reconnect?" I interjected gently, sitting up, the sleeping bag falling off my shoulders, exposing me to the bitterly cold air.

"Possibly, maybe. Oh, not exactly. Cam, do you remember back to those early days on August? Keeping it secret made it more about us, didn't it? Our lives weren't played out in a public arena. It was something for us and us alone. I just thought if we could spend time together, without the pressure of others judging, maybe we could work out if there is still something there?"

"Frey..." I warned. This was a solo journey about finding Laetitia. Her background, her family. Only two days before had I visited her childhood home, her school—my meeting with Angus only yesterday. While I had that partial sense of closure, I wasn't sure I was ready to deal with anyone else.

"No, please don't. Don't speak. Please let's just spend some time together and see what happens. If you want space, I can give you that. If you want me to go, I will. I promise. But I have come a very long way to find you. Can we at least try—just for a few days? That is all I ask—just a few days. Can you give me that?"

Pausing, I looked away and considered. My next steps were to visit the community at Clava and learn what I could about the portals. *Would it really hurt for her to accompany me?* Finally, I replied quietly, "Yes, I can give you that."

"I mean it. If you want me to go, say so. I will leave."

I nodded, acknowledging. I had been alone for some weeks now. I felt peaceful after leaving Mousa, even more after learning of Lae's history. Perhaps some company would be a good thing.

"I assume the kids are with Sorcha?"

"They are. Leaving Katrin was the hardest thing I have ever done. I didn't think I could go when the time came. I don't know who cried more, her or me. Louis is fine. He was sad when you left, even more when I went too. But he is such a wonderful helper and so good to Katrin. He promised to take care of her for me. Asked me to give you a hug from him."

Smiling, I nodded. "I understand. It must have been important to you."

"*You* will always be important to me."

Holding my arms out to her, I held her apprehensively as I responded, "And you, me." Pulling back and gazing into her emerald eyes, I told the truth. "But Frey, I am a different person now. I lost you and found Laetitia. Then I lost her, too. I'm afraid that after that, I lost myself. I don't know who I am anymore or who I want to be."

Freyja nodded in understanding. "I will always be here for you, whoever you are."

"Well, you are here now. How about you tell me everything while I make us some breakfast?"

Settling into one of the comfortable armchairs, she looked at me. Shyly for Freyja. She was usually so self-possessed.

"Where do you want me to start?" she asked.

"The day you went through the portal?" I suggested. "I never heard that story."

FREYJA'S STORY

CHAPTER 7

"**WHERE ARE YOU, YOU** stupid bloody beast?" I muttered furiously, stomping through the mud. The perpetual drip of condensation made some lower parts of the forest permanently mud-soaked and more challenging to move through, the sun unable to penetrate the canopy to dry it out. Trust Fred to take off on the coldest bloody day of the year. It was freezing, and not having planned this little sojourn, I wasn't prepared for it. Expecting to spend my late shift in the warm vet sheds, I was only wearing jeans and a t-shirt covered with a light jacket. I was freezing and unprepared for an overnight expedition. Wishing I had brought my heavy coat or a rain jacket, the mud squelched up the sides and over the top of my boots, and I continued to curse him. Maybe Heidi was right. Perhaps it was time...

No. The simmering frustration and resentment at trudging through the forest in the middle of the night lessened as I thought of Fred, his big dopey eyes and gentle, kind nature. He was a gorgeous creature and the closest thing I had ever had to a pet. Sneaking cuddles occasionally, I wondered if the warm feelings I had for him would be similar to feelings I would have for my own child. I always felt stupid cuddling him but couldn't help it. Cam loved to cuddle, and I had grown used to it, despite not growing up in a touchy household. Cam often reassured me with a gentle touch or squeeze. My parents had rarely touched me, so it had felt invasive at first and had taken quite some getting used to.

Two days before, I had been shattered yet again, but I didn't yet have the heart to tell Cam that I wasn't pregnant. He knew how much I wanted this, to bond us, and was devastated when each month passed and it didn't happen. Accepting the night shifts, knowing he was working the days, I might be able to keep it from him, at least for the few days required. He would work it out soon, I realized with a sniff, when it became obvious. But right now, I needn't put him through any additional stress.

How on earth was I lucky enough to find the one man on the planet who loves me? Most women here don't like me. Di and Jacinda were the exceptions, but likely because they were friends with Cam first. Men appreciated my looks. I have always known that. Katrin or I could barely walk down the street without wolf-whistles. Since I lost her, I felt so alone, like no one really knew me. Not until I met Cam. He listened, cared, and understood. He was my equal, my partner, but never tried to control me. Many guys I dated were great to start with but either became controlling and jealous or resentful when other guys paid attention to me. Short guys usually had an inferiority complex, something to prove. Big guys were often gentler. Cam was bigger than me, physically larger and taller, and could force me physically if need be, but I never once felt that he would. That he struggled with his own demons meant that he never judged me for mine. He listened, understood, but never passed judgment. Not even on my parents. I was grateful for that. Despite how it appeared on the outside, like they were cold emotionally and had outsourced parenting, I knew they loved us. In part, it was cultural, teaching Katrin and me to be resilient. Independent from a young age. In part, it was our lifestyle. They gave us fantastic opportunities, the best education possible. They just weren't there emotionally. And I had not known any different. It had just been my life until I met Cam and realized there was another way.

Shining my torch around and realizing Fred wasn't in the gully, I began the long ascent, my stomach cramping slightly, and I wrapped my arms around myself, trying to warm up. The mild discomfort had never bothered me before. Now it did, but mostly as it was a siren blaring that I wasn't pregnant. Women complained about how painful labor was. How could I say that I would go through that, willingly, to have a child of my own?

When Jacinda announced she was pregnant, I thought my face would crack from the fake smiles, the congratulations, and the well-wishes. Not that I was unhappy for Jacinda and Jamie—I was thrilled for them—but at the same time, sad for us. Everywhere we turned, it felt like couples were announcing pregnancies or welcoming babies—except us. I knew it hurt Cam too, but he would never say so out of fear of distressing me. Dismissing the thought, I pushed through the cramping and up the hillside.

"Fred!" I called again, scanning the single powerful beam from my torch down the path and through the brush on each side.

An idea struck. *Perhaps he escaped the chilly night air and went into the cave?* Checking that no one was around, unlikely in the dark and at this time of night, I set a course for the cave, shivering. It was freezing and as dark as pitch out, only a few stars visible in the foggy sky beyond the dome. Frigging goat. The rope tied around my waist to tie to his collar slipped slightly, and I stopped to tighten it. Carrying Fred back down that steep path was not going to happen in the dark. I would drag him kicking and bleating if need be. Or just tie him to a tree until morning.

Approaching the straggly inaka bush, I smiled, remembering Cam and my first time here. He had been so taken aback by my advances that he had nearly drowned. The only man here who hadn't visibly lusted after me, he never treated me like an object. Not Cam. He acted like he didn't care what I looked like; instead, he cared about who I *was*. More than a year later, and he still treated me the same, with kindness and respect.

The bush pulled at my jacket as I shone the torch inside and called, "Fred?"

No response, but he likely knew that he was in trouble because I was unable to keep the frustration from my voice.

"Fred!" I called more forcefully. The name echoed down the tunnel, and I shivered in the freezing temperatures, grimacing at the thought of the long slippery walk back down the hill.

Should I? Just warm up before heading home to bed? The cramp in the arch of my frozen foot answered my question.

Squeezing down the tunnel, I wondered if I could still do this when I was pregnant. *Are hot baths safe for pregnant women?* I wondered how I would ask Nyah or Nalini that question, hypothetically, since there were no baths on August. There was no way I was sharing my knowledge of this place.

Stripping off my boots and socks, I walked over to the far wall and tipped the mud out of my boots. There was no point stepping in it when Cam and I next visited. Rolling up my jeans, warming my frozen feet would make the walk home easier. A solo visit felt decadent. I hadn't been here alone for over a year. *Maybe I should strip off? No pressure to talk...just a long hot soak* My skin was positively tingling with anticipation. Perhaps it was just being in the warm cave, my skin thawing from frozen after hours of searching in the dark and cold.

No, it was late. I sighed. I had been searching for hours. It must be almost midnight. I should just warm my feet and go. Slip into bed beside Cam. He slept so warmly that I would feel safe, nurtured.

I felt energized as I stepped slowly into the warm water, still holding my boots and socks in one hand. Not wanting to plunge in quickly and cause my frozen feet to heat too quickly, I wasn't paying attention to the feel of the cave. A fraction of a second too late, I sensed that something was wrong. Really wrong. Turning to get out, the whirlpool started, sucking, pulling me down under the water as the roar filled my head. Reaching for the rocks at the edge, I saw the world spinning out of control as it sucked me down, down, and under.

Spinning backward, my face pointed out of the whirlpool, I thought I was going to die. Fighting to retain control, to stay upright, my arms flailed to stop the whirling. Just when I thought I couldn't do it anymore, and I would surely die, it stopped. Suddenly. Like a tornado hitting a concrete pole. I fell forward, smacked my head with a sickening thwack onto the rocks, and the world went black.

CHAPTER 8

SLOWLY COMING TO MY senses, I could feel the blood as it dripped down my face and dried, crusted across my forehead and cheeks. The agonizing pain from my right temple seared through my eye socket, and I cried aloud as I clutched my head. Lying face down on the rock was impeding my breathing, and I tried to roll, the pain reverberating through my skull. Opening my eyes was excruciating, but as my thoughts took order, I realized I needed to move. My vision blurred from the raging headache and pain emanating from the wound on my forehead. I rolled as gently as I could until I hit grass and paused, panting from exhaustion, lying on my side, eyes away from the penetrating sun.

Feeling the grass beneath me and realizing that I couldn't be in our cave, I cracked my eyes open enough to let in the daylight. Through the blurriness, I could see several upright standing stones in a field, some nearby, some quite a distance away. Closing my eyes again, I knew I was dreaming. But what a throbbing headache for someone asleep. Reaching my hand to the tender spot on my forehead, I winced in pain as I probed the swollen, bleeding site. *Okay. Maybe I'm not dreaming. Where in hell am I? This isn't August.*

Patting my hand on the ground, I could feel dirt, damp coarse grass, the rock I had hit now at my back.

I lay there for what seemed an eternity, but no one came. The sun lowered in the sky, casting shadows across my exploded head. As the darkness came, I slept, fitfully, dreaming of being sucked in and down, then the exploding impact as I hit the stone as if fired from a cannon.

Dawn broke, and I could hear birdsong. I was within the dome then. But *where* was I?

Hours passed. Slowly, I inched my way to a seated position, clutching my shattered skull. Recognizing this for what it was, a significant head wound, I knew I needed to seek help.

Sitting for a while, I took in the vista. Water in the distance: lakes or ocean? I couldn't tell. Fields of grass in shades of green and brown. But alive. A ring of enormous standing stones but ones I had never seen. Not Stonehenge. These weren't capped, just a ring of ancient stones. Perhaps one of the many other stone circles, then. *Where am I?*

Staggering, I found my boots thrown clear of the stones and made my way toward what appeared to be a road. Roads led to buildings. Slowly, I inched my way along the road and found a house. Abandoned. That was clear from the moment I was within a hundred meters of it. Made of stone, but no doors or windows remained in the ancient structure. The antiquated thatched roof was collapsing, the garden overgrown. But the grass growing up the walls was alive. This wasn't right. There were no houses like this on August. Old homes. Abandoned. Looking back and up the hill I had descended, I saw the looming stones, ominous shadows in the distance, set in a field of green and purple.

Resting for a bit, I surveyed my surroundings. Fields, rock walls, and old roads, green meadows with trees, grass, and purple plants everywhere. But silent and deserted.

Steeling my resolve, I kept walking, slowly, to not jar my blisteringly painful head. Just as I thought I could move no more and rested on the grass verge, I heard a familiar sound. Stopping, I strained to listen. *Clip-clop, clip-clop.*

"Help!" I screamed, even though my head was about to explode. "Help!!!"

The sound stopped, and then started more slowly. Standing up and in the middle of the road, I waved my arms. *"Help!"*

A slightly balding man with chestnut brown hair on a large black horse, quite some distance away, gaped at me in astonishment. Slowly he approached but warily. Cautiously, he asked something, but I couldn't make it out.

"I'm sorry," I replied, in the gentlest tone I could muster, aware that I must look a right sight. "Can you please help me?"

Assessing the potential threat and concluding that a woman with a bleeding head wound was unlikely to accost him, the man dismounted and came to my side.

"What's your name?"

Now that I realized he spoke with a thick accent— Irish, maybe?—I tuned my ears to listen harder.

"Freyja. Freyja Jorgensen. Where am I?"

He looked around before responding, "Callanish or thereabouts."

"I'm sorry. Where?"

He looked at me suspiciously, hearing my speech. "You are not from around here, are you, miss?" he asked cautiously.

"No, I am Australian. From August Island, off the coast of Australia." I trailed off, wondering how I would explain who I was and how I came to be here without sounding like I was mental.

Visibly, he recoiled, taking a step away from me. "Australia!" he gasped in a strangled tone. "How did you get here?"

Cam placed a bowl of porridge in front of me, and I smiled my thanks, not breaking my story.

"But he helped me. A short time later, I found myself in the village, surrounded by strangers. As I dismounted the horse from behind the stranger, one pushed through and introduced herself as Morwenna. She steered me down a few laneways, and I ended up in the medical clinic where she cleaned and stitched my head wound."

"Where am I?" I whispered, and she looked at me, startled, thinking I had amnesia as she started firing off questions. All the usual questions. What was my name, my date of birth; where was I born?

Finally, I snapped. "I am not delusional, nor have I got amnesia. *I just don't know where I am!*"

"Lewis, Scotland," said the deep male voice of my mysterious rescuer from the doorway.

"Scotland?" I asked, equal parts incredulous and relieved.

"I can imagine that came as quite a shock," Cam smiled wanly. "It did to me too."

CHAPTER 9

CAM SAT BESIDE ME, handing me a cup of coffee. Instant, but still somewhat coffee-flavored. At least it wasn't International Roast. I doubt even I was that desperate. He indicated I should continue talking.

"From then on, Angus and I spent most of our time trying to work out how I had arrived here and planning how to get me back. People were kind enough, but I just wanted to get back to you. I never intended to leave August. I just wanted to warm my feet, find Fred, and come home to bed. Instead, I ended up half a world away and had no way to return. It was like a bad dream."

"I know that feeling," said Cam with a crooked smile. "Very well."

"Except that you found a reason to stay," I added, then realized how that sounded. "I'm sorry. I didn't mean for that to sound catty. I just meant that you met people and became part of the community."

"I did," Cam admitted slowly. "But for different reasons. I was ostracized on August, and I knew I could never return. When you disappeared, everyone thought I murdered you. They alienated me. I was alone. These people took me in, accepted me. Liked me. I was treated like part of the community. I always knew I would need to leave, to look for you. But," he hastened to add, "I never betrayed you or our vows. In the six months I lived there, I was not *with* Laetitia. That didn't happen until after I returned to Lewis the second time."

I nodded, accepting this truth and continuing the story. I paused. "Just for the record, I was faithful too. Nothing Heidi told you was true."

Downcast, Cam nodded. I continued.

"Angus and I spent all of our waking hours digging out his maps, textbooks, anything we could access to work out how I had traveled across the world—into a cave in the southern hemisphere and out of a stone circle in the northern. We barely left his house. He knew about the other communities, but he didn't know about the portals. Soon, he stumbled on the concept of antipodes, which fit. We started researching, looking for anecdotes, historical references, anything that could explain what happened. It was likely that I could travel back the same way, but there was no guarantee it was a two-way passage. By this time, it was still five months to the next solstice, and no matter how desperate I was to get back to you, I couldn't face that again. So, we briefed everyone on what we thought had happened and asked for volunteers. Three men wanted to come along, so we left.

One of the engineers, Nate, chose a small cruiser from Stornoway. None of the vessels in the harbor were capable of an around the world voyage, at least not in any degree of comfort or safety from the protozoa. So, we headed to Edinburgh, as Angus had lived there, and he knew the area well. It took us a few days. We followed the coastline. I could tell that it had once been spectacular, but now it was dead and brown. It made me remember all the times you had talked about your family, about your trips here. It was surreal. I couldn't quite believe that I was here, and you were on August. I knew you would worry about me disappearing like that."

"Worry doesn't even begin to describe it."

"I am so sorry," I said, unable to keep the despair from my words. "I never wanted to leave you."

"It wasn't your fault," Cam replied, sadness in his eyes as he recalled that distressing period of our lives. "I don't blame you. Keep going."

"We traveled around the north coast and down to Edinburgh. It was eerily quiet. I wanted to explore a little, and Angus wanted to show me. He liked me, I could tell, but respected that I was desperate to get back to you."

"Really?" Cam sounded dubious.

"Truly. I felt like half a person without you. Your honesty, your loyalty. You were always there for someone in need. Happy to lend a hand, to help. But you made me feel whole. For the first time in my life, I felt nurtured, loved. We shared a life. We shared everything. I told you things I have told no one else—then suddenly, in one night, it was all ripped away."

"I felt like that too," Cam admitted. "It was honestly the most awful time of my life."

"Angus showed me the Royal Mile, Edinburgh Castle, and the Palace of Holyrood. It was dead and still. I tried to imagine it as the bustling city you had described, but it was so bleak."

Cam nodded. "This isn't the Edinburgh I remember." He looked out of the window to the city beyond. "I mean it is. The buildings are the same. But it is so lifeless now."

"We found the headquarters Angus had worked at, but everything was locked down, and we couldn't access anything with no electricity. We managed to find the government warehouse filled with food and water. I knew the most about yachts, so I chose a vessel. We stocked it with as much food as it would hold and left. Angus had been part of the government task force, choosing and deploying individuals to the ground zero sites. He only knew of the one, Lewis, but knew that there were eleven others. Angus was born on Harris, raised there. His family were still on Harris, so he asked to be part of that community."

"I know," Cam said in a strange tone, making me look at him.

"How did you know that? Did he tell you? I didn't think you and he had ever spoken."

"Frey, I'm sorry to interrupt. But there is something I need to tell you," Cam said, still in the strange, strangled tone, like his words hurt him. He looked up. The morning sun was streaming through the windows, dust dancing in the beam of light. "Let's walk. It is freezing in here."

I cleaned up the breakfast dishes while Cam dressed and put his boots on. An awkward silence filled the room. The sunlight hit us in the eyes as we emerged from the room, like a butterfly exiting a chrysalis. Cam set a direction, and I kept up easily. We both had long legs and enjoyed walking.

"What is it?"

Recognizing he was struggling, I put a comforting arm on him, like he had done to me so many times. Comfort in touch, he called it. My parents were not the tactile type, so it had taken me a long time to get used to Cam's gentle ways. But four years with no touch, and I missed it.

Cam sighed but didn't look at me. "Angus is Laetitia's uncle."

"What?" I gasped. "He said nothing!"

"He didn't know. She didn't either."

"Is that what you discovered here?" I glanced back at the tall, imposing building behind us.

Cam nodded. "It is. Then, I met up with Angus in a place called Kilmartin Glen. I asked him, and he told me everything. Laetitia's mother was called Jasmine. She was Angus's half-sister from his father's first marriage. When Jasmine's mother died, he married again to Angus' mother. Jasmine ... ran away and had Laetitia."

"When did you see him? He visited Katrin and me, on Lewis, only a few weeks ago, just after you left. I just found him in the greenhouse when I went to pick some tomatoes for lunch."

"He said nothing about visiting you when I saw him yesterday."

"Maybe he forgot." I shrugged. "It was only a quick visit, just to see how Katrin and I were doing. Anyway, tell me about Jasmine. Why did she run away? The way Angus always described it, he had an idyllic childhood. Two loving parents, money, and opportunity. He never mentioned a sister."

"Well, he wouldn't."

As we walked toward an enormous park in the distance, Cam filled me in on the full story of Amara,

Jasmine and Laetitia, along with Angus's role in it. My mouth fell open with astonishment and disgust.

"Holy hell," I said finally, stunned by what he told me. "They treated her like that? That poor girl—by her own family! And Angus? He was that close to Laetitia all that time and never knew? He told me once that he felt terrible that he couldn't save his own family, despite being so geographically close."

"About that," Cam said and filled me in about the dome construction, Angus's knowledge of the escape hatches, and refusing to save the local residents. The news hit me like a blow to the stomach, and I felt physically sick.

"He let them die?" I croaked.

"He *watched* them die," Cam corrected tersely. "He was the only one who could have done something about it. He alone had the knowledge to open the hatches but did nothing. He could have saved his own family. Watching those people die came very close to destroying that community in the early days."

"Oh ... my ... God." I needed to stop. Standing still, I fought to breathe, unable to reconcile this with the Angus I knew. The man who had been my traveling companion for years. Had treated me with the utmost respect, even allowing people to think my child was his to save my reputation. Checking in on me. I couldn't believe it was the same Angus. Watching his sister raped and banished from the family. Never trying to find her. Then allowing innocent people to die when he had the power to stop it? His own family included?

"You said there were children?" I asked, half-choked, not really wanting to know. I already felt sick knowing that Angus had allowed dozens, perhaps hundreds of people to die. *Why?*

Cam was looking at me strangely. "There were," Cam acknowledged. "Babies, young children. Mike described it to me as, 'Mothers holding their babies up and begging those on the inside to save them.' They all died, every single one, because of him. He could have saved them all. But he chose not to."

Closing my eyes, I felt the waves of nausea overtake me, and my stomach gurgled, the porridge solidifying into a ball in the pit of my stomach. I could see it all too vividly—mothers clutching their babies, pleading with the people in the safe zone to save them. I knew without any doubt that I would do precisely the same thing to save my child, even if it meant dying myself.

"Are you okay?" he asked gently as I leaned up against a wall, trying to get a grip on my emotions. Detach myself. I couldn't change what happened. Despite my many years of experience in feigning indifference, I couldn't pull it off this time.

"Not really. I can't help but think: what if that had been Katrin? Or Louis? What if *we* had been on the wrong side of the dome?"

"There was a time when you would have agreed with him. Realized that there were limitations. Space, food, not to mention the introduction of potential illness had they let those people in. He was, after all, following orders."

Cam was right, and before I became a mother, I know that I too could have seen the logic in what he did. I could see Angus making that decision. Maybe, at some point, I would have made it, too. But now, it was different.

"They lived there. It was their *home*. They had children. There was space. There still is. There can't have been that many people. They could have quarantined them, taken steps to keep everyone safe. They could have saved them."

"Exactly."

"I can't imagine what it would have felt like to arrive on August and physically see the people we had displaced. Dying so we could live in *their* homes."

Cam was looking at me oddly, assessing me somehow.

"What?" I asked wearily as he supported my elbow and kept me moving. We slowly made our way into a once beautiful park filled with dead trees. The branches, now leafless, were blowing gently in the breeze. The sun was out and lighting the cloudless sky a brilliant blue.

"Is there more? I don't think I could take any more."

Not looking at me, Cam said in a low voice, "Once, you told me you knew why you were chosen and not others."

Recalling that day, I flushed with humiliation. Shrugging helplessly, I stopped walking and looked at my feet, unable to reply.

"I'm sorry," I whispered. "I felt like that. Once. But now, all I can see is a group of mothers desperate to save their babies. Mothers exactly like me. Prepared to sacrifice themselves if only their child could live. But they didn't live, did they?"

"No. They all perished. The babies and children too."

Unable to speak, I took several steps and sat down on a park bench, staring past the death at the city beyond, silent and still, a cityscape of buildings dark against the crystal blue sky. Closing my eyes, I felt the sun on my face. But even behind my closed lids, all I could see was Katrin, crying, screaming as I left her behind. And me, desperate to save her life.

"You have changed, Frey." Cam spoke so softly I barely heard it, like a whisper on the wind. Opening my eyes, I saw he sat next to me, close but not touching. Watching me intently.

"Maybe it is because I just left Katrin, and I feel horribly guilty. She cried her eyes out as I left, and I bawled all the way to Stornoway. But I keep seeing those poor mothers, helpless, with *their* babies, crying. Begging to save them. Wanting their children to grow up and fulfill their potential. To live."

"And that, honey, is how you have changed," he breathed. "Logic would have been your default position before. Now, you understand that family, love, and emotion play a role, too."

I froze, fighting not to show on my face that I had caught the endearment he had always used for me. *Honey.*

"I once called you weak for showing emotion," I whispered, not really wanting to remember that awful fight, the one that had led to me storming off and Cam being poisoned by Heidi. "I am so very sorry. I didn't understand ... then."

"But you do now?" he probed gently. "Now that you have a family of your own?"

"I do," I admitted, the mass in my stomach dissolving slightly as I spoke. "Part of me still understands the logic, the practicality of it. If Angus had saved his family, then he needed to let them all in, admit that there was a way out. That would have caused problems, too. People wanting to go or stay. Potentially introducing the protozoa by accident. But now that logic is kind of overlaid with a blanket of emotion, muffling it. I never felt that before. I would lay down my life for little Katrin," I admitted. Then I added, more hesitantly, "I love Louis like my own child. And you. My heart will always be yours."

Cam paused, gazing at me attentively. Then, cupping his enormous hands gently around my face, he drew me in and kissed me, passionately, with so much emotion in those lips that I felt my body soften and swayed slightly. Despite still being seated, I felt giddy, like we were first together, and my heart skipped a beat.

His soft lips were familiar, and mine knew his as well. My hands made their way around him, and we tasted, explored, and reconnected in a way we hadn't done in four long years. Despite the passage of time, the connection was still there, that bond we had felt from the beginning. He felt it too, responding to me naturally.

Running out of breath, he pulled back slightly, his breath still warm on my cheek.

"I have missed you so much," I whispered, terrified that this was it. He was going to stand up and leave me. Admit that this was a mistake.

"And I ... you."

He raised his hand and stroked my hair as I tried not to tremble at his touch. We sat touching, looking at each other. We had nowhere to be, nothing to do. Memories of that first night in the grotto fresh in our minds, we traced our hands over each other, remembering. We recalled we were the same, learning ways we were different, noting tiny changes like a scar. His large, roughened fingers traced my cheekbones and jaw, and my face pressed into his warm, familiar hand, ecstatic from his firm caress. As scared as I was, it had been so long, and my body hungered for his touch, leaning into him. His fingers traced the length of my neck, making me close my eyes in bliss.

I barely registered the chill as he lifted my top with one large hand, intermittently kissing, and ran his tongue across the still prominent cesarean scar on my stomach. He pulled my top deftly over my head, discarded on the ground in a moment of passion. Removing my bra, he expertly cupped my breasts, weighing them, making me close my eyes and tingle with desire. *Oh God, I want him. But does he want me, or is he just remembering her?*

His rough beard tickled my breasts, still enlarged from nursing Katrin. I saw the quirk at the side of his mouth as he realized this, but he didn't pause in his work. His hands were firmer now, rougher. Determined, he pulled at my clothes, and I was helpless to stop it. My desire for him was overwhelming, and I submitted willingly, silently praying it was *me* he wanted. Despite what conflicting messages my logical brain was sending, I wasn't going to stop now. My body was in no doubt about what it wanted—this I had sought for so long. My heart was pounding, butterflies in my stomach making me feel giddy as my skin warmed and molded to his touch. As his hands ran down my waist, making me flame, cupping my bottom as my jeans hit the dirt, I rose into his hands and sat astride him. *Now. I need you now!*

I tore off his top and kissed his chest, running my hands down his back: firm, dependable, and powerful. I unbuckled his jeans, and he slipped them off as he stood.

He lifted me effortlessly, and I felt like a feather as he carried me, wrapped around him, the few steps to a nearby tree and spread me under it, laying me gently on the dead soft mat of grass beneath. A slight moan escaped my lips as he entered, returning home. Arching my back, I rose to meet him, and we rode the waves together.

"I love you," I purred, sometime later without thinking. My heart stopped, regretting it as soon as the words had escaped my mouth. He was half asleep on his side but still half on top of me, keeping me warm in the cool air. A shy smile crossed his lips, his eyes still closed.

"I have always loved you, Freyja. Even when I was with another, as much as I loved her, I always loved you," he whispered tantalizingly in my ear.

Dying to know what he meant but not wanting to ask, I said nothing, not wanting to spoil this moment. But he knew me too well. Sensing my question, he propped himself on his elbow and looked at me directly.

"I wanted you from the first moment we met. That night I couldn't get the tablets for my migraine when we talked all night. I wanted you so very much. All the men on August were obsessed with you, so I thought I had no chance. You were well out of my league, so I didn't think about it. But I fell in love with you when you took me to the hot springs that afternoon, shared yourself with me. You made me complete. You changed my world. I was broken when I left Melbourne, leaving my family to die. I cannot thank you enough for making me whole."

Shifting his weight slightly, he continued, "Then shit happened, and we were apart for a year. More. It was the most awful year of my life, and for much of it, I didn't think I would survive without you. But at the end of that year, I learned you were pregnant and had moved on with another man."

Stirring, I wanted to speak, but Cam kissed me gently into silence and continued.

"I know it wasn't true, but at the time, I truly believed it. It hurt more than I can tell you. I felt like my heart had been ripped out. Knowing that you had fulfilled our dream with someone else. That he had given you what I could not. So, I returned to Lewis and married Laetitia. I had kissed her, once, before I left, but nothing more. But I knew there was something between us. After Heidi told me about you, I was shattered to the core. The wonderful memories of our time together were blackened, and I knew that the only place I could go was back there. I returned to Lewis and her. We married on the winter solstice, and eight months later, we had Louis."

Adjusting himself so he could see me better, he continued, "I will tell you about her, someday. But for now, my memories of Lae are for me. Frey, you need to know: Laetitia wasn't a rebound. I was completely happy for the second time in my life. I loved her, and she loved me."

My heart lurched as he spoke. *Is that it, then? Is it all over? Have I just made a complete and utter fool of myself? Again?* I tried to focus, listen to his words, but instinct told me to jump up and run away, mortified. My heart was frozen in fear.

"I was finally over you. Not that I didn't always feel love for you, but I needed to let you go to move on. You belonged to another, or so I thought. Then we had Louis, and we were happy. Then, Laetitia…" He choked on her name.

Still quelling the overwhelming need to run, I could see the pain emanating from him. I put my arms around him. "It's okay. You don't need to…"

Absently, he ran his fingers along the rippled purple scar that ran the length of my forearm, gently tracing it. I wasn't sure he was aware he was doing it.

"No, I need to finish. It has been more than a year now, and I came here so I could move on. Honey, part of me will always love Laetitia, just as part of me always loved you when I was with her. She knew that. I told her. Love isn't an emotion you can just turn off like a tap. Love has the amazing capacity to multiply, to include all the people in your heart. It isn't finite. But to be with her, I had to compartmentalize my love for you. Just keep it locked away in a small pocket in the back of my mind. Please don't ask me to forget her. I could never forget her, just as I could never forget you. But I need you to know this. Freyja, I truly love you. I have since that first day you kissed me in the hot springs. But you have changed. Over the past few months, I have watched as you have put your love into our child. I know it wasn't ever role-modeled for you, so it was hard. But you have learned compassion and how to care for another. I have watched as you have put both of our children ahead of yourself. And I love you for it. I need you to know: when I am with you, I am only with you. There are no others in our bed. When I make love to you, honey, I need you to know— it is only *you* I want."

My heart lurched, and feeling more relief than I had in months, I whispered, "That is all I needed to know."

Feeling the kiss on my lips, I fuzzily opened my eyes to see Cam kneeling beside me where I lay, smiling down at me, shadowing my face.

"Holy hell, I had forgotten what a goddess you are when you are asleep," he murmured as he nuzzled my neck, making me ache from wanting him again. "Did you know I used to lose hours just watching you sleep, wondering how on earth I got so lucky?"

Extricating my arms, I reached up and pulled his head down to my mouth, returning the soft, warm kiss. As my body awoke, tingling, I lifted my right knee and tried to roll him onto me, trying not to break the seal of our lips. Pulling back slightly, he gasped, "Honey, I want to, really I do. I want nothing more right now, watching you lie there, so beautiful in the dappled light. But we need to move. It is going to rain."

That made me wake fully and look past Cam's head at the darkening sky. He was right. We needed to move and now.

Seeking our scattered clothes from across the park, we ran for the nearest building, laughing as we tried to dress and run simultaneously. Reaching the building first, I picked up a plant pot, smashing the window to gain entrance, pushing past the heavy drapes, and barely making it inside before the downpour started.

"What is this place?" I asked rhetorically as shadows filled the gloomy darkness. The rain was pelting down and had blackened the sky, no light source penetrating the dark space. It was freezing in here, that cold, damp feel of a place long unused, and I shivered, pulling my arms into my jacket. Cam pulled a tiny keyring torch from his jeans pocket and shone it around.

We were in a home. That much was clear from the furniture I could see in the room we had entered. I could make out a beautiful wrought iron fireplace with painted tiles and an ornately carved timber mantle, dusty Chesterfield couches, a colored glass lamp, expensive rugs on the floors, and overladen bookshelves from floor to ceiling, making me sneeze from the dust coating. Thick drapes hung from both windows, blocking the view of the street. Heavily furnished, one would say. Stepping into the hallway aligned to the front door, the opening ran the length of the terraced property, lined with boxes, floor to ceiling. We had to turn sideways to squeeze past them, finally arriving in the kitchen. Thanks to the large windows and more modern conservatory, this was a sizeable well-lit space. Modern AGA cooker, large rectory table, and pews were all coated in dust. An expensive home, judging by the location and furnishings.

"A solid four stars on Trip Advisor," I quipped as I explored the space, making Cam grin. "Shame about the clutter and lack of heat. What is in the boxes?" I questioned Cam as he turned back to the hall. "Were they moving house?"

"I can't tell. There are no markings." Placing the torch between his teeth, he pulled the nearest box down from the stack and carried it into the kitchen. Taking the torch from him, I switched it off and handed it back to him as he placed the box on the table. I looked around for a knife or a pair of scissors with which to open the box. Grabbing a small knife from the knife rack, I carefully slit open the sides and top as Cam grabbed another box from the stack.

Opening them both, we were astounded to find well-stocked food packages, both identical, and enough to feed a family for several weeks: tinned food, packaged food, bottled water, and basic medicines.

"Look!" I pointed to the stamp on the far side of the box, barely visible in the dim light, the storm now raging overhead, rain pelting into the conservatory glass.

"Greenside Parish Church, Royal Terrace, Edinburgh" was stamped in faint purple ink on the side.

"Food parcels for the needy? Or parishioners, perhaps?" I suggested.

Cam nodded. "But how did they end up *here* in a private home?"

There were many possible answers to that, none of which we would likely ever get the answer to.

"There must be three hundred boxes here!" Cam gasped with astonishment as he shone the torch back in the hallway, illuminating the enormous wall.

"Um, there are more." I pointed out into the conservatory, where another neat wall of stamped boxes stood.

"Well, we know we are eating tonight," Cam said. "No need to travel back to the records office and risk the rain, although, with no capacity to heat it, we may very well be eating it cold."

The rain had set in with a vengeance, limiting what we could reasonably do. It bounced with force off the glass roof of the conservatory, making me feel odd. This was toxic rain, yet we were safe and not within the geodesic dome. We were trapped here, at least for a few hours.

"Let's explore," I said, heading for the stairwell. It surprised me to realize that it was a three-storey house.

Most homes in Australia were single or double-storey, rarely three. "It looks very old," I mused aloud.

"Georgian, perhaps?" Cam suggested.

"Six!" I exclaimed as we explored the family home, counting rooms. "Who needs six bedrooms?" There was no sign of the former occupants, thank goodness. I don't think I could have dealt with sharing their home, even in a storm with fewer more appealing options.

"Well, if you get fed up with me..." Cam said.

I didn't quite know how to respond to that, unable to read his tone. I had traveled all this way, leaving behind my baby, to meet up with the man I loved. We had reconciled, I think. But a lingering sense of doubt lurked in the recesses of my mind. *What if it this is a fling? What if he sends me home so he can continue his journey, his soul searching?* Cam processed his emotions so deeply. *What if he needs more time? Time to be alone?*

We reached the doorway of a large bedroom where enormous windows let in natural light, despite the pelting rain. I took the several strides necessary to reach the large king-sized bed. The white bedspread was covered in a layer of gray dust.

"Help me," I instructed, picking up one side. Obligingly, Cam lifted the other, and we carried it carefully onto the landing where we shook it, coughing and spluttering as we inhaled years of dust.

As we placed it back on the bed, Cam piped up, "You know, it would have just been easier to check the cupboards for clean linen."

Pausing, I looked at him and started laughing. Nerves won, and I sat on the bed, laughing hysterically. Watching me for a moment, the contagion struck him, and he started chuckling too.

Sitting down on my side of the bed, I laughed at my stupidity.

"I never even thought!" I gasped. "All these years with a single set of bedding, I never even thought to look."

The room went dark as his face blocked my view of the window.

"I love it when you laugh," he admitted, a little shyly, slowly stroking my hair off my face, picking out a small dead leaf. "You laugh with your entire body and like you don't care what people think."

Staring up into his face, I didn't want to admit that I was laughing from nerves, unable to ask what I wanted to know. I didn't need to. He kneeled on the floor beside the bed, and his lips met mine, searching. A question. *Do I want him?*

Laying back across the bed, I gently drew him down with me, his weight on his elbows, but the solid reassurance of his torso on mine. He knew my answer. Despite his warm body and physical presence, it was painfully cold in the room. I could see my breath on each exhale and shivered despite the close contact. Cam, feeling me tremble beneath him, sat up and pulled back the feather quilt. I gratefully rolled under it, slipping my boots off. Even fully clothed, I was frozen. My bones ached from the cold. The bed, unused for years, was almost damp from the chill. From beneath the quilt, I trembled as Cam hunted through the wardrobes for more blankets. Finding a pile, he gave them a shake and spread them on the bed, adding a reassuring weight. I watched as Cam slipped off his boots, jeans, and jacket to join me. His body was like a furnace, radiating heat that I couldn't get close enough to. Holding him against me, he kissed me thoroughly, waiting for me to warm up as my insides turned to jelly.

"Better?" he whispered huskily as my shivering slowed.

"Much," I oozed, feeling like melted chocolate as he slowly undressed me under the weight of blankets. We held each other, desperate to be close, daring anything to get between us. Forcing him to lie on his back, my weight atop him, I slowly kissed from head to toe, running my hands along his strong, muscled arms, legs, and torso, my long hair draping across his body, tickling him in places. Cam closed his eyes as I caressed, stroked, and deliberately ran my fingers over all of him. Breathing heavily, he let out a tiny moan as I ran my hands up his thighs, making him spasm.

"Oh God!" he moaned, barely able to lie still.

The delicious aroma of food woke me, and cracking open my eyes, I discovered Cam sitting beside me on the bed, watching. Feeling immensely self-conscious, I reached my hand up to check my hair. Birds nest, as I suspected. Making a slight noise of protest at being watched sleeping, I tried to smooth my hair and look slightly more presentable as I rolled to face him.

"Don't." He reached out and stopped my hand. "I love to watch you, all messed up but glowing. Knowing that I might have had a small hand in that."

Smiling faintly, I asked hopefully, "Food?"

"Soup."

Sitting up in bed, I started shivering as soon as my bare shoulders left the warm cocoon and hit the frigid air. Placing the tray on the bedside table, Cam lifted one of the red tartan wool blankets that had slipped from the bed and draped it around my shoulders before handing me the tray.

It was hot, and it was food. That was all that could be said for it, under normal circumstances. Canned soup is never exceptional, but when you are hungry and freezing, it is phenomenal.

"Oh, that is so good." I sighed as my belly filled, and I looked over to Cam. "Are you having some?"

"I ate while you slept. I didn't want to wake you."

"How did you heat it?"

"Found a gas barbeque outside that still had some gas in the bottle."

"Thank you," I breathed, feeling content as he cleared the tray, and I snuggled back down under the quilt.

Looking at the window, I estimated it to be mid-afternoon, but it was hard to tell in the dim light. A crack of lightning illuminated the dark sky.

"You shouldn't have let me sleep," I said in gentle rebuke. "Now I will be awake all night."

"Well then, we will just need to find something to *do* all night," he said, his eyes twinkling with mischief as he stripped off and slipped back in beside me.

As the storm raged through the evening and night, we reconnected on a deeper, more spiritual level. We talked. Really talked. About the kids, Lewis, and our lives now. I told him about my adventures, the wonderful places I had been, and the fascinating people I had met. My friend Luca, who had accompanied me and supported me through my grief of losing him. The differences but common resilience of each of the communities we had visited.

He spoke about his life on Lewis. The years he spent without me. He told me about letting me go that day on the hillside. He talked about finding his sister, his parents, and the communities on Bellcamp and Newgrange. People he had met on his journey. Sometime deep in the night, he turned to me, silently, and we made love again. Slowly, languorously, enjoying the connection we had forged.

CHAPTER 10

DAYLIGHT FILTERED THROUGH THE curtained window, casting a golden beam of light across the room. Feeling Cam stir beside me, I asked softly, "Can we go home? I miss the kids terribly."

"I do too," Cam admitted. "Leaving them was the hardest thing I have ever done. But I needed to."

"To heal?" I asked apprehensively.

"I guess. I feel like those men ripped Lae away from Louis and me, and we never got to say goodbye. When I left Lewis, I traveled up to the Shetlands and out to Mousa, trying to get my memories back."

"And did you?" I asked carefully, remembering that day. Cam's bleakness and despair. "Remember?"

"No," he admitted softly. "I remember one girl from Orkney, Alize, telling me what had happened, then I remember waking on the *Selkie*. Nothing in between. It is like my heart skipped a beat. I'm missing a piece of my memory. I don't regret what happened, you know," he said hurriedly. He rolled over to look at me. "It wasn't ideal timing. But Katrin—I wouldn't trade her for the world."

"I know." I was terribly conflicted about that time. I felt like I had taken advantage of him, that it was my fault. It *was* my fault. I knew that. He was fevered and thought I was her. But I had spent the best part of three years alone, pining for him and struggling with decisions I had made. When the moment had presented itself, I hadn't been able to stop it. But Katrin had been the result, and she was everything to me.

"What did you find on Mousa?" I asked cautiously.

"Nothing at all. The windswept broch, just like Lae had described from her history books. Only now enclosed with a tin roof and a solid door, which I assume they added. The houses the men had lived in. No trace of ... them."

"No," I agreed.

"What happened to them?"

Rolling up onto one elbow under the doona, I looked at him appraisingly. "Do you truly want to know?"

"I do."

"I gave the order to shoot them all," I whispered, emotionless, staring past him out the window and into the distance. I couldn't look at him in case I disgusted him. "Our choices were limited. Leave them there with the potential to retaliate against us or do it again somewhere else. Take them with us. Or kill them. One look at Isla, and I knew I couldn't take them with us. They would have raped those women a thousand times over if we hadn't made it in time. Beaten them, treated them as slaves, trapped on an island surrounded by infected water. They would have had children, been raised by those brutes, and likely equally mistreated. Imagine if they had daughters? I could picture clearly what they would do to them. I couldn't do it. They didn't deserve to live.

How did I allow them to be in such proximity to those women—again? We had no court, no jail. Besides, there was you—and Laetitia. In part, I did it for you so that you could have closure. It was in my power, so we killed them and dumped the bodies at sea. The women watched. They needed to. They needed to know, without question, that they were truly safe. I remember my mother talking about kidnap and rape victims she had worked with. The flashbacks, nightmares, and fear of reprisal attacks were always what kept them up at night. Stopped them from living their lives. Replaying what had happened, but fear of retribution if they spoke out, and it happening again. Never feeling *safe*. I could give those women some peace, so I did," I finished softly, remembering that day and the struggle I felt with vivid clarity. I remembered the hole Luca had pulled from when he saw the dark place it had taken me to.

"The women on Orkney told me you took care of it. But they were distressed, and I couldn't add to that by asking for details. Freyja ... thank you," Cam whispered. "Really. I don't think I could live knowing that the animals who did that to Lae were still out there, free to prey on others."

I turned to look back at him. "I just knew that I had to do it. There was no alternative."

"There is one more place I wanted to visit before heading home," Cam admitted.

My face must have fallen, as Cam added quickly, "I can go alone if you want to get home to the kids."

"No," I said steadfastly. "I am not leaving you again. We do this together. The kids are fine."

"Was it Di who offered to take the kids?" Cam asked suddenly.

"It was your sister. After you left, I spent more time at their place. Di is struggling with pregnancy, she is sick all the time, and the smell of food makes her worse."

"Hang on. You didn't tell me that part. Di is pregnant?"

"She is. It is very early, and no one else knows. Just a few weeks. But I guess congratulations are in order."

"Holy hell, another baby. Mine, I guess. But ... not mine. I'm not sure I know how I feel about that."

"It is a wonderful thing you did, giving them a child."

Cam shrugged dismissively. "You said that Di is unwell?"

"Poor thing. She is sick all the time. Not just morning sickness. She struggles all day. Not long after you left, Kat, Louis, and I moved in with them. Kat and I share a room and Louis shares with Sam. I arranged with the other vets to work early shifts, and Sorcha works late. That way, I could cook for us all—badly, as you know. But at least Sorcha could come home from work and have a hot meal, and there is someone there if Di is ill overnight and your sister is called out. Poor Di. She isn't even able to prepare food without feeling ill. Anyway, after a few weeks of this, your sister looks at me over the dining table one night and says, in that straightforward way of hers, 'I'm sick of watching you pine away over him like a puppy. Just go. We will watch the kids. Find Campbell. Bring him back. Tell him we need him here.' Go now."

Cam smirked. "Sorcha, direct? Well, it takes one to know one," he teased gently.

I flushed. Far too many times, I had been accused of being blunt. I just didn't see the point in wasting time or playing games. Better to be open and honest and not have people misunderstand.

"They had discussed it. Di just nodded and said, 'We have made arrangements. Go home. Pack a bag. We will tell the kids in the morning.' So, that was it."

"Ahh, so that is how you knew where I was. I told Di I was planning to go up to the Orkneys, then to Edinburgh to go to the National Records Office."

"She told me. You had been gone a few weeks, so I hoped I might catch you here. When I arrived in Edinburgh, I thought one boat looked familiar, but not knowing which one you had taken, I wasn't certain. Then, when I saw a single window of the Records Office broken, I knew you had been here. But I had a moment of panic. What if I had missed you altogether?"

You didn't, his kiss reminded me.

"Di is looking after the kids?" Cam asked when he pulled back, breathless.

"That was the plan. Di could stay home with Sam, Louis, and Katrin. Sam is old enough to help."

Cam's face fell. "Our poor gardens. What will we eat if Di can't look after them?"

"They will be okay. They have roped in some help."

"Thank goodness."

Quickly changing the subject, I asked, "Where is it you want to go next?"

"I want to visit the community at Clava Cairns. Back in Melbourne, Tadhg found evidence that the scientists set up their own communities. One on the Auckland Islands, not far from August. The other is at Clava near Inverness. One of the selection team from Melbourne now lives on Orkney. She told me some things which made me wonder. I just need to ask them questions."

"Yes, you told me about Clava once. Okay. Overland or by sea?"

Cam pondered that. "Car is faster. But then we would need to come back here for the boats. There is a harbor in Inverness, but I have no idea of the size or what might be available. As frustrating as it is, and it will take longer, it would make more sense to sail. That reminds me—how did *you* get here?"

"I brought one of the small fishing boats from Stornoway, one that was expendable. Taking it slowly, I made it to Scrabster, refueled, made it to Aberdeen, then around to here."

"Do you want to take both?"

I thought about that for a moment. "Two small boats are of little use. There are still a dozen or more in Stornoway plus more in Tarbert. We are probably better off taking one of the larger ocean-going cruisers from the harbor here. There were certainly plenty there. It is a better resource for the community on Lewis, just in case someone needs to get somewhere quickly. We should also try to source some more mountain bikes while we are here too. They are valuable, and everyone wants one, especially when you want to fetch a vet or doctor in the middle of the night!"

Cam nodded slowly, thinking. "Some spare parts too. There must be bike shops in Edinburgh."

"Almost certainly. The problem is—where? It isn't like we can Google it anymore!"

Cam furrowed his brows, then threw back the covers, making me shiver with the rude gust of cold air as he disappeared into the next room. A few moments later, he returned, holding a dusty telephone directory aloft, *BT Phone Book* emblazoned on the purple cover.

"It is a few years old," he muttered as he jumped back into bed, opening the directory and turning to B for bicycles, "but surely some of them are still there."

The storm had passed in the early hours of the morning, and the brilliant sun was reflecting off wet stone surfaces all around. Careful not to touch anything, I returned alone to the dock, reviewing the options available to me. Despite feeling so close during the night, now that we were up and moving, there was a slight distance between us. We dressed hurriedly in the frozen morning air while Cam repacked our bags, and he suggested that we split up. Cam left selecting a vessel to me while he tracked down the bike shops and returned to the Records Office for his bag.

There were dozens of beautiful, expensive craft here in all shapes and sizes. *What would be most beneficial for the community moving forward?* Angus had taken the *Selkie* when he left August again, leaving the Lewis community with no decent-sized craft capable of a long journey. Something biggish then—but not so large that it would be a struggle to moor in the smaller harbor at Stornoway or churn through fuel, which was now a limited resource. Casting my eye over the vessels, my mind flicked to the day before.

He told me he loved me.

My heart sped up a little. How I desperately hoped he meant it. I knew he loved Laetitia, but last night, we had bonded on a level I never thought possible. Younger and more inexperienced in relationships, we had been joyfully happy once. I prayed we could be that couple again.

Selecting a suitable vessel, a sleek modern 35-meter luxury yacht, I broke into the cabin and tried to start it. One of the few benefits of being a rich bitch was that I knew a bit about sailing. Finally getting it running, I went to fill the tanks before transferring all the food and stock from the small boat I had taken from Stornoway, pausing to run my hairbrush through my tangled hair in the mirror of the master suite. There were five bedrooms, or more technically staterooms. That should be adequate for any voyages.

Hearing a put-put sound over the sound of flapping sails in the breeze, I looked up to see Cam, his magnificent black hair flying behind him, chugging down the road on an electric bike. Laughing as my hair blew in the sea breeze, I asked why he had chosen an e-bike.

"Well, they take little to charge and can be charged from a normal powerpoint. Now that Di and Sorcs have algae bioreactors everywhere and we have excess power, I thought e-bikes would be a reasonable choice."

Considering this, I agreed. "You are right. Those algae are flourishing. It feels like every week they need to build new tanks. And e-bikes would help with the distances and the hills. How many are there?"

"A few dozen. Do we have the hold space?"

"Should do. We need to stock up on food. I can go to the warehouse Angus and I used last time. There was still plenty of food and water there."

"Okay, but later. Let me ferry these bikes while it is still daylight."

"I can do that after I finish here."

Leaving the bike on the deck, Cam headed off, and I re-boarded the *Eurydice*. I stood in the doorway of the master suite, looking at the large king bed. *Dare I be presumptuous and assume that we will sleep together? Or will he want his own space?* He said only yesterday morning that this was a solo quest, that he was seeking closure. But he had wanted me yesterday and all night. I smiled a little, remembering the night before, hugging my arms around myself. How close we had been, talking, holding each other. But now, in the cold, harsh light of day, things were a little more awkward.

Not wanting to sail in the dark, we cast off for Inverness early the following day. The hold and spare bedrooms were packed after a day of resource collecting: bikes, aquariums, and a range of food, water, and other supplies. Watching the city skyline of Edinburgh fade out of sight, Cam was quiet, pensive.

Desperately wanting to ask if he was okay but concurrently afraid of the answer, I stood beside him, just watching.

Finally, he said, "I have always loved this city. I always thought that one day I would live here."

"Is Lewis close enough?" I asked softly.

"It is."

Over the days we journeyed to Inverness, we made up for those lost years, never apart for longer than a few minutes. We piloted the vessel, ate, and slept together, always touching, catching up on the little things we had missed. We moored at night, traveling for only short periods during the day, taking regular breaks to enjoy being together.

"I can't believe I lived with you for the past year but didn't think to do this," Cam murmured in my ear as my hands slid over his taut, muscular stomach, down to his thighs, smooth at the top. We lay on the plush navy blue sofas in the main living area, views for miles through the floor to ceiling windows, offering a 180-degree panorama.

"It wasn't what *you* wanted," I replied instantly as I increased the pressure, massaging the tight muscles incurred from the steep walk up to the ruins of Dunnottar Castle that morning.

Cam exhaled deeply. "So my old candid Freyja has resurfaced. I wondered how long that would take," he taunted but kindly.

Sitting upright, I looked down at him. "You forget that I have been alone for four years. A year of living in hell—just wanting to get back to you. Finally getting back to August, hoping you were there but finding you were missing. Suspecting that you had followed me but with no proof. Then finding out that you had returned to August, for me, but had been lied to and left again. That was the worst. Knowing that you believed I had betrayed you. That cut me deeper than anything. I didn't leave the cabin for days, not speaking to anyone. I didn't eat, couldn't sleep. Finally, Luca forced me into the fresh air. He said I would suffocate, sitting alone in the dark."

Cam watched me kindly but said nothing.

"Because we had left Kerguelen early, I had promised the others that we could take our time after August. I thought you would be there, and I would jump ship there. But you weren't, and after Heidi's confession, I couldn't stay. But I needed to follow through on my promise of finding other communities in the northern hemisphere. They had come on this epic journey and not just for me. So, we traveled north to New Caledonia, up to Russia. Then, because it was winter, down and back around Australia to New Amsterdam Island and back to Kerguelen. Finally, we arrived back in Scotland. I had planned to stay, and the crew was going to head off to explore the UK. Then we learned you had married and had a child. Angus was fit to explode, let me tell you. I had talked him into an around the world voyage, and he is no sailor, only to find that you had left me. He wanted to kill you with his bare hands."

"Honey..."

Speaking over him, I knew I needed to get this out.

"We spoke that first night, and I couldn't accept that it was completely over when you kissed me goodbye. But the following night, I was watching you with her. That night at the community meeting. I could see from across the room that you were madly, deeply in love. You used to look at me that way. Once. I watched the way you gazed at your new baby. I thought my heart would turn to dust, knowing that it was finally over between us. There was no hope. We left again quickly because Luca was fearful for me, fretting for you. For my old life. Instead of exploring the UK, we changed the plan, and they took me as far away as possible. We traveled to Canada, Colorado, the Falklands. When we returned a year later, I thought I would be okay. More time had passed, and we both had different lives. I had been an integral part of the crew, valued and trusted. We only came back to refill the water tanks and rest landside for a bit. Then I heard from Di that Lae was pregnant again. I was so jealous I could barely see straight. You had it all—your sister, a wife and child with another on the way, and now, our best friend too. I knew I needed to find a way to move past it but leaving wasn't the answer. When they cut Angus and Lae was taken, I knew I needed to help. Maybe then you and she could find a way to include me in your lives, even just a little. Maybe that was how I could move on, find someone else, and live my own life."

I took a deep breath and continued. "But then things happened. We lost Lae, and Katrin came. You were mourning her. I knew that. We co-habited like ghosts for all those months, and I was terrified that was all we had left. You treated me kindly, like a friend, but nothing more. I cried myself to sleep most nights, wondering if that was all we had left. Wondering if I wouldn't have been better off terminating the pregnancy. How would the baby end up if we brought a child into a dysfunctional, distant relationship? A cordial friendship at best. I knew that life was trying to break me, swallow me whole. But I tried, I really tried to make the best of it. Waiting for a sign, a tiny glimmer of hope that you still cared for me. But each night, you went off to bed, alone. I could hear you crying out for her in your sleep as I fed Katrin in the night, and I knew you would never be mine again. Your heart would always be hers."

"You considered ending the pregnancy?" he asked softly.

"I did," I admitted. "Something I desperately wanted for so long. Ached for with every waking breath. But when it happened, it felt so *wrong*. Di was wonderful, non-judgmental, and supportive. But your sister, she was arctic. She blamed me, made it blatantly clear that Katrin was my fault, and I had taken advantage of you. She was right, of course."

"That isn't fair. It involved two of us. Sorcha... she is my sister. She was protecting me."

"That is why I was surprised when it was Sorcha who told me to come and find you. Told me we were meant to be together. That we needed time alone, without the kids or the community, to see if we could find our way back to each other. She said that you needed me, and I needed you."

"Really? Sorcha said that?"

"She did. She really loves you."

Cam grinned sheepishly. "She does. But really, you were alone for four *years*? There were four other men on that yacht!"

"You were the only man I have slept with in those four long years," I said, in a voice so low I wasn't sure he could hear me over the crashing waves and wind battering the yacht outside. "I yearned for you. It was only ever you."

Cam lifted my chin and looked into my eyes, his own so clear and blue behind the dark lashes, like the beach of a tropical island. Intensely he watched, not interrogating but searching.

"I am sorry you were alone," he said finally. "I thought—no, I hoped, that you were loved, that you were happy. That you had moved on, forgotten me."

"There were times when I hated you," I confessed. "Especially when I knew you had a child. I have never been jealous in my life until then. The only thing I had so desperately wanted, and you had it, without me. If I hadn't visited the springs that night, maybe Louis would have been ... ours. Then when we had a child, we weren't together. It was beyond cruel. Giving me what I had wished for, every single day, but with a backhander. Here is the child you wanted, with the man you wanted, but he no longer loves you. I admit: I struggled with her in the early days, wondering if I wouldn't just be better off giving her to you to raise and leaving again."

"That was never it," Cam breathed, stroking my back. "It wasn't that I didn't love you. I never didn't want Katrin, but the circumstances were cruel for me too. Laetitia and I fought that day. It was her birthday. We so rarely argued, and I don't even know how it happened, but we fought. It was about something trivial. She was always fearful that I would leave her for you. She stormed off, and I didn't go after her. I thought it would blow over. Then ... she was gone. Our child dead. I lost them both in a single day. I never got to say sorry. Goodbye. I love you. The last thing she said to me was in anger, and that was the part that haunted me for so long. If only I had gone after her, stopped her from leaving...

Then Kat came, the replacement for the child I had lost, and I didn't know how to deal with it. Lae was dead. Our baby too. But almost immediately, I had a new child. It was wrong, but I realized I was *happy*, and that was what made my stomach rot. I realized that Louis and I were content, with *you*. The four of us were a family. Laetitia's greatest fear, that I would leave her for you, had come true. That is why I left."

"Is *this* what you want?" I asked in a small voice, terrified of the answer. I steeled myself for the reply. Bracing my backbone, closing my eyes, I listened.

Silence echoed through the open room. My heart squeezed and my stomach sank. Tears filled my closed eyes, and a lump rose in my throat. *Maybe I can make it to the bathroom before they spill, and he sees? But where can I go on a yacht off the coast of Aberdeen?*

"What the bloody hell have we been doing?" he gasped finally, laughter overtaking the incredulousness. "Jesus Christ on a piece of toast, Freyja, I've barely had my pants on in a week!"

Insecurity was a feeling I was not familiar with, and I didn't like it one bit. "Don't laugh at me!" I tried to be forceful but couldn't pull it off, the tears spilling despite my willing them not to.

"I am not laughing at you, my darling. I am laughing because I am astounded that you, of all people, can't see how utterly happy I am—with *you*."

"Really?"

"And everyone thinks I am the one who can't read emotion!"

I slapped at him, but he dodged, and I missed. Instead, he caught my swinging arm, neatly flipping me onto my back. Pinning me in place, he hovered above me, his hands gripping my wrists above my head.

"Mine," he pronounced.

CHAPTER 11

"TELL ME ABOUT THIS," I asked, playing with the necklace around Cam's neck as we lay in bed, quietly absorbing the silence. "It is old, isn't it? But you didn't have it before."

"It belonged to my father," Cam said, watching as I turned the doubloon so that the light hit the silver and black molded pattern. As he told me the story of where his father had bought it and its history, I looked more closely, then let it fall back onto his chest.

"I wish I had something from my parents. I didn't think to grab anything before I left. I took photos, as you know, but not a keepsake."

"Did you get your photos back?" he asked kindly.

"I did. That was what I was looking for when Heidi made her move on me. Tried to throw me on our bed and kiss me. I may have broken her nose," I admitted, a little sheepishly.

"Where are the photos now?"

"Di had taken them, kept them safe. Just in case I came back. They are in our house on Lewis. Under my bed."

Many times we had looked at those photos—my family, his family. I could picture them, each one carefully chosen to remind me of a fond memory. But it was the reference to our house and my bed that made me fall silent, wondering if he would comment. *Has he thought ahead to our lives when we return to Lewis?*

"What would they think of me? Of Katrin?" Cam asked, breaking into my thoughts. He hadn't asked me about my parents much, recognizing that many of my memories were painful.

I thought about that for a moment but decided honesty was best.

"I hate to say it, but they would be judgmental," I admitted. "They would think you were not of the same social standing as me. All that money and yet they still couldn't see that people should be judged by their actions, their values, and character, not by their education or income."

"I thought your dad worked in international development. Isn't part of that line of work to be tolerant and accepting?"

"Oh, they were—when it was in relation to others. They supported charities, especially getting girls in third world countries a good education. Much of my father's work was assisting the poor, the marginalized. My mother did work for victims of violence and abuse. But all those rules went out the window when it came to their daughters. You needed to be of an excellent family to be associated with Kat or me. The crazy thing is, I suspect that they would have loved for me to have a rich, well-educated black or Asian husband. It wasn't about culture, religion, or nationality. It was just downright snobbery."

"You are telling me they would think of me as your bit of rough and not husband material?" Cam teased, but I knew the look. My words had stung, despite not intending them to. Hurting him was the very last thing I wanted to do.

"Let me put it this way: my parents were rich, well-educated elitists. They raised Kat and me to value letters after your name on a business card and to know how to namedrop at parties, behave at posh restaurants and art gallery openings, and wear designer clothes. I knew as soon as we spoke that night that you were different. You didn't judge me for where I came from, for what I had, but for who I *was*. I wanted to be like you, Cam—that person who everyone knows, without question, will help them out when they are in difficulty. The person who always has a kind word. The person who doesn't judge."

"How would they have treated our Kat then?" he asked softly.

"Oh, they would have spoiled her, insisted on paying for everything, and thinking money would buy her love. They would have tried to mold her in their image with private schools, fancy clothes, horse riding lessons. Taken her on overseas holidays, flying first class and staying in posh hotels."

"Oh." The air left him like a deflated balloon.

I could see from the look on his face that my words hurt him, leaving him feeling inadequate.

"But *I* wouldn't have it any other way," I finished. "You, Campbell Mackintosh, are my dream man: honest, ethical, and caring. You care more for those you love than you do for yourself. I know, without question, that you would do anything in your power for little Kat. You would place her needs ahead of your own, and that makes you a true father."

"That is nothing special. To me, that is what a father is." He shrugged. "Once you have children, their needs need to be placed ahead of your own."

"Did you ever think that perhaps Katrin wasn't yours?" I asked, a little cautiously.

Cam responded instantly, and I knew he spoke the truth. "I never questioned that she was mine. I don't remember that night, I readily admit. It shocked me. I was devastated, feeling that I had betrayed Laetitia, especially so soon after her death. But I trusted *you*, Frey. You have never lied to me. I thought about not being part of Katrin's life ... for about two minutes. I realized she didn't ask for this situation any more than any other child brought into the world. She was the innocent, and it was my job to be the adult. So no, I never questioned being part of her life. I guess it just took me longer to reconcile with *you*."

"And have you? Reconciled with me?"

Rolling his eyes, he turned to look at me. "Freyja Jorgensen, I told you once that I would commit to you as long as love lasts."

My heart froze.

"Well, it still lasts," he whispered as he ran his hands up the smooth inside of my thighs, making me tingle with desire.

CHAPTER 12

"WHO DOESN'T KEEP SPARE spark plugs?" I knew I was ranting but couldn't help it as I slammed every cupboard door in the main cabin. "Seriously, who keeps a ten-million-dollar yacht but doesn't keep a bloody spare ten-dollar spark plug?"

Poring over the map at the dining table and ignoring my tirade, Cam said, "I hate to suggest this, but..."

"What?"

"Well, it seems to make more sense for us to split up. Just for a few hours!" he rushed to say before I could interrupt. "I need to go to Raigmore, near the golf course ... here." He pointed to the map. "Then you can keep heading into Inverness proper and refuel, get your spare parts. I..." He paused, considering the impact of his next words.

"What?" I asked cautiously.

"I want to stop by Raigmore Hospital."

"A hospital? Why?" I asked, perplexed.

"Laetitia was born there," Cam whispered. "I just want to see if there are any records. Of her birth,

Jasmine's medical records. Anything that can help me tell Louis about her history. When the time comes."

At the name of the woman he had left me for, a stabbing pain penetrated my heart, but years of experience permitted me to maintain a cool demeanor, not letting emotion show on my face.

"Sure," I said with as much nonchalance as I could muster. "A couple of hours? It could take me that long to find the parts I need and fit them. Then we can rendezvous at Clava? That is it, there on the map, isn't it?" I pointed to *Clava Cairns: Bronze Age Burial Site* in tiny font. "What is it, about ten kilometers?"

Relief washed across his face for not engaging in a debate over his mission. "It is. We can each take an e-bike. It won't take long. The site is an antipodal point, so it will be within the dome. It can't be hard to find."

"Fair enough." Deep down, I didn't want to be apart but recognized the logic in getting our tasks performed to rendezvous sooner. The sooner we arrived at Clava, the sooner we could leave, and I would do anything to get back to Katrin. I never thought I would miss someone so much, especially someone who couldn't even speak. I couldn't give a toss about Clava, but it was important to Cam.

I should get as many spare parts as I could, I mused, noting down the part number on the spark plug. The *Eurydice* was a modern and highly useful vessel. Not that I wanted to travel anymore. I had spent several years traveling the world, visiting other communities, meeting people. But now, I wanted nothing more than our children, Cam, my home, and my bed. Thinking of home made me consider our living arrangements. *What will happen when we get home? Will we share a room? Or will he want to keep this a secret? From his sister and Di?* Surely not. We all lived in such proximity that they would work it out fairly quickly. Besides, it was they who sent me to find him. But other residents? He was loved by all, but Laetitia had been, too. As far as I was concerned, we were together. Damn. I wasn't good at game playing.

But is he happy? That niggling little voice pricked at me. He seemed to be. There was no deception in Cam, but he was still grieving Laetitia. His visit today was evidence of that. Refocusing my efforts, I located the hefty manual and started noting spare parts codes.

Pedaling down the road on the B9006, I paused, checking the street signs. Most were in a state of disrepair now after six years with no maintenance. Many signs were illegible, obscured by a layer of dust thrown up from the barren landscape. It was hard to keep track of precisely where I was. I thought about what Cam may have found at Raigmore. *What is he looking for?* He knew who Laetitia's mother was. Her uncle, too. Had even found some photos. *What more does he need?*

The e-bike chugged along, making an estimation of distance difficult. Stupidly, I had forgotten to set the trip computer before leaving, not being familiar with e-bikes. It was faster than walking but slower than a car. Had I traveled eight kilometers yet? Slowing the bike, I came to a stop, noticing a slight movement in the forest to my left. The pine trees were dead and rattling in the wind. Berating myself for feeling skittish, I looked down at the screen to return to level one. There was no point in stalling it or falling off. I heard a high-pitched whistling sound, then heard before I felt the resounding thud as something hard struck my temple, and abstractedly watched the dirt of the road come up to meet me.

I awoke with a cracking headache, cheek down in the dirt. Fighting to focus in the dark, my immediate thought was that I had taken off too quickly and fallen off the bike into the road, knocking myself unconscious. That myth was dispelled a moment later when I realized my hands were tied securely behind my back with what felt like coarse rope cutting painfully into my wrists. Panicking, I pulled, and the rope gave a tiny bit, but the knot held firm. Struggling to open my eyes, I closed them, trying again as they watered, slowly becoming accustomed to the gloom. Inhaling the dirt from the floor, I realized I was in a shed and the stench was overwhelming. Something was dead and rotting in here. Trying not to gag from the overpowering smell, I tried to look around, realizing that I was in danger. Surely this wasn't Clava?

What happened?

I forced myself to focus. I was riding; I had stopped, looked down at the screen. Wincing as the throbbing in my temple reminded me of the crunching impact. I feared it was in the exact location as the skull fracture I had sustained coming through the portal several years before. The agonizing pain was the same, making me feel nauseous, and the pain was radiating from roughly the same location. Great. Unable to check the wound with my fingers, I grimaced, trying to pinpoint the source of the pain.

Struggling to sit up, the movement made my head swim, forcing me to lie down again and close my eyes against the wooziness. Just in time, too. I heard voices, male voices, coming closer. I prayed I hadn't disturbed the dirt, alerting them to my movement. Relaxing my eyes and slowing my breathing as the door swung open, instinct told me it would be better to feign being unconscious. Desperately wanting to crack an eye open, I didn't dare. Getting the upper hand here may save my life. I felt the light strike my face from the open door, fighting to stay calm and still.

"My, she is a pretty one, Geoff. You did good. I'm going to enjoy this," a sleazy Scottish male voice oozed in the darkness.

An unintelligible grunt responded.

"Can we take her now?" The slightly lisping older male voice leered close to my face as I felt a hand suddenly plunging into the top of my jeans, and stubby fingers started rubbing my crotch. Trying desperately hard to stay relaxed and ignore it, I deliberately slowed my breathing. *Breathe, Freyja, breathe.*

"God, she is warm, Geoff. Wet. Let's do it now."

"Nea, she can wait. We need to space them out. The other is fresh too."

Geoff, whoever he was, spoke with a markedly uneducated Scottish drawl.

"Aww, Geoff, it's been ages," the first man whined. "Look at her. Such pretty hair, fine skin. I can't wait to have some fun with that."

Slowing my breathing, it took every ounce of self-control not to flinch as the disgusting, foul-breathed, spiky bearded creature licked the full length of my cheek with his fat, sloppy tongue.

"I'll bet she makes some noise. I do love it when they make noise."

"Aye, and I said, she can wait!" the second voice snapped. "There is no rush. She isn't going anywhere. Besides, she doesn't look like she will put up much of a fight. She went down easy enough."

That's what you think. I seethed inwardly, battling to continue feigning unconsciousness. What I wanted was to do was vomit on his shoe and punch him in the nose so hard that he couldn't breathe. In my current condition of restraint, that wasn't a likely outcome.

Shuffling footsteps left the room, kicking up dust and making me want to cough. Fighting to remain still, I heard the sickening thud of a bolt being drawn into a lock.

Fuck. They weren't taking any chances. After hearing the lecherous manner in which the first man had sneered the word *fun*, my heart had gone cold. Fun for them sounded like it would be decidedly not enjoyable for me. I needed to get out of here, and now.

Cracking my eyes open, I glanced around the space, straining to focus past the throbbing headache. Shuddering, I used my shoulder to wipe the residual vile-smelling saliva, still wet on my cheek. I was definitely in a shed or barn. Piles of crap and old farm machinery blocked most of the light from the high window, but a single shaft of sunlight streamed in from under the door. Good, so it was still daytime. Likely I hadn't been unconscious for too long then. The floor was dusty, compacted earth and scattered with mud, old straw, and bits of rubbish. An ancient rusted corrugated iron roof was held up by solid timber sleeper walls, further supporting my theory of a barn. At least it was watertight. Testing the bonds on my arms, I found there was no way I could break the rope. If nothing else, these sick bastards knew how to tie a knot. Thank goodness it wasn't cable ties, I thought abstractedly.

Unless I could cut the rope. I started looking around the room for something that I could use to cut: buckets, shovels, pieces of old farm machinery. *Ugh, that disgustingly awful smell.* Something had died in here, and not that long ago. I thanked my lucky stars that they hadn't gagged me; vomiting into a gag would likely have suffocated me. I moved slowly and quietly searching for something to cut the bond.

Cardboard boxes, piles of old newspaper, bales of straw, rags, and pieces of ancient wood were piled up around the room. In the darkest corner, I could just make out a large mound. Hay bales? An old car wreck, perhaps?

My temple was throbbing like a jackhammer. I silently blessed the darkened space. I doubt I could have dealt with bright light along with all of this. But not being able to see well was making things difficult. Not wanting to use my mouth for fear of what feral germs existed in here, I tried to stand side-on, pulling rags and newspapers down with my bound hands. Surely there was something in here I could use. An image of watching old episodes of MacGyver crossed my mind, making me smile despite the situation. Luca popped into my mind. Solid, dependable Luca. He had taught me many valuable skills. *What would he do?*

Focus, Frey, focus. I told myself. *First, cut the rope tying your wrists. If you can do that, then you have a fighting chance. You are a sitting duck unless you can defend yourself.* Doubling my efforts, I pulled more rags, empty cardboard boxes from the pile. Nothing sharp. *Fuck!* I seethed silently, terrified the men would return. If they did, I would not get across the room and into the same spot again fast enough and not without making some noise or throwing up dust. Besides, I didn't think the fake unconsciousness trick would work a second time. I had to move and fast.

The sun was setting, shadows were cast across the room, and no light penetrated the room. My eyes strained against the dim light. I moved to one wall. Something. Anything. I did not want to see what this fun entailed, under any circumstances. The look on the women's faces when we had rescued them from Mousa flicked into my mind, and I bit it down. *No.* There was no fucking chance on this earth that I was going to be a plaything for two filthy feral beasts under any circumstances. I would fight and fight hard. They did not know what they were up against.

Gritting my teeth, I used my feet to feel around. Bales of hay, an old wooden wheelbarrow. Some old broken shovels. Nothing I could use to cut my bonds. *Fuuuuuck!!*

No. Don't lose your cool, Freyja. Think. It doesn't need to be anything significant—even a nail. The important thing is to move fast, in case they come back.

Sifting through the rubbish on the floor, I made it to the corner, and bile filled my mouth as the smell overpowered me momentarily, forcing me to turn away. A faint blue light from the high window illuminated the scene. Looking around wildly, I needed something, anything, to cut this rope. If I could cut the rope and climb high enough, then maybe I could break the window. Not being able to climb meant I was limited. I needed the use of my hands first.

My feet kicked it first and turning around, I used my bound hands behind me to feel. An old car? No, an old, rusted tractor, tires and seat missing, the rusted wheel arch barely protruding through the piles of rubbish. Using my hands behind me, I knocked down the garbage and broke off the loosened rusted parts, searching for a sharp piece. Pat, pat, argh... *There!*

Finding a sharp edge, I awkwardly started sawing. Unable to get clear access, I knew from the pain emanating up the inside of my arms that I was slicing my inner forearms as much as my bonds. I didn't care; I was struggling to focus, trying to stay in one spot. Working blindly, I was unable to see what I was doing, both due to the darkness, and that those fuckers had tied my hands behind me. Pulling against the bonds, I felt it give a little but not enough.

Voices. Fuck! There were voices. They were coming. Sawing as hard and fast as I could, I tried not to breathe loudly, especially as the pain radiated up my arms and drops of blood dripped onto the dirt floor. Tugging, slashing. After what felt like an eternity, the bond snapped with the cord still wrapped around my wrists. But I could move my arms at last. I could bring my arms back to my sides. Cracking my neck, I felt invigorated with renewed energy.

The voices passed close by but didn't enter. I could have sworn they would hear my heart thundering out of my chest. *No. I will not allow fear to paralyze me.* Choking down the emotion, I used anger as my motivator. Remembering the appalling breath and sloppy tongue licking my cheek, the grubby hands down my pants, and realizing that there was far worse to come, I shuddered and used my freed hands to untie the rope from my wrists. Rubbing my wrists firmly to return circulation to my hands, I could feel the blood smeared down my arms and hands, making them sticky as it dried. I had no time to worry about that now. I needed a weapon.

Tiptoeing to the wall, I tested the shovels. One had a wooden handle, so brittle that it would shatter on impact. The second seemed solid and intact. I tested it on the ground. Good. Perhaps I could use it to dig my way out.

Moving as far as I could from the voices I had heard, I tried to dig against the wall, realizing the futility of this within seconds; the ancient dirt floor was rock hard. Testing it with my fingers, I realized the blade was blunt. It would take something a lot sharper than this to cut through the floor.

Another hunt around the barn proved fruit-less. There were no tools, nothing better to use as a weapon. Trying to quell the rising panic, I returned to the shovel. Maybe I could sharpen the blade? Heading back to the rear of the barn, I paused to shake the foul stench from my nostrils. Working quickly, I wrapped the blade except for the tip in grimy rags and filthy, appalling smelling cloth. Scraping the edge of the shovel blade against the sharp rusted tractor edge, I tried to muffle the sound as much as possible. The noise was deafening to me but hopefully not too evi-dent outside. Running the tip over the metal tractor wheel arch, I scraped as hard as I dared. But once I had started, I knew I needed to finish. There was no point in a half-finished job. After half a dozen passes, I knew it was highly likely that the noise I made had attracted attention. Moving quickly, I returned to the open space where they had thrown me upon arrival. It was a good choice, and just in time. The voices, low and the words unintelligible, were coming closer. Had I stayed at the back of the shed behind the piles, I would not have heard them and would have been trapped.

Standing behind the door, I waited for them to enter, the slow trickle of my bloodied arms pit-patting audibly on the dirt floor. Wiping them quickly on my jeans and grimacing at the pain of the cuts being scraped, I hoped they wouldn't hear the muffled dripping.

The heavy grinding of the bolt sliding made me tense my shoulders, still sore from having them tied behind me for hours. Rotating, I tried to loosen them, focusing all of my attention on the doorway and what I needed to achieve. *Game On.*

"Awake yet, my pretty, pretty? Ready to have some fun with Joey?" the man drawled through the open doorway in a slow, mocking tone.

Everything happened quickly after that. One man entered, and I managed to swing in the moonlight and get a solid blow on the back of his head with the shovel blade. The impact sent him sprawling. The second one caught me off guard, pushed me hard in the back, and fled. Sent flying, I staggered to my knees but managed to reach the shovel lying in front of me before my abductor did. Lifting it with as much force as my limited range would allow, I caught him square under the chin, sending him stumbling heavily into the wall. He bellowed with fury as he came at me again. Only having time to lift the shovel as a shield, he didn't see it in the dim starlight and ran full pelt into the end of the blade. The momentum of his running hit the blade's edge while the handle pushed into my stomach, my hands grappling to hold it in place as he forced me backward. I was taller and likely stronger, and I used all of my strength to dig my feet in. *It is like surgery on a cow,* I thought abstractedly. There was some resistance as the edge pushed into his skin and muscle, then a pop as it penetrated his abdomen, and the blade achieved its target. He dropped like a stone. I stared spellbound for a second at the blood gushing from the man's wound, the shovel sticking upright as the black pool spread beneath him, now illuminated by the starlit night visible through the open barn door. His eyes were open in shock, his mouth moving silently, like a fish gasping as he took his final breath.

Retrieving the shovel from his abdomen took some force, and I needed to use my foot to push the body off. Glancing down at him, I poked him with the bloodied shovel, confirming he wouldn't be coming after me. *Good. One down. But how many are there?*

Still holding the shovel in front of me, I cautiously left the barn, listening carefully in the night air for his companion. Waiting for my eyes to adjust to the gloom, I skirted the outside of the shed, my back to the wall, my eyes now adapted to the dark. Scanning, I listened for any trace of the second man. I could make out a small window a hundred meters away and a chimney barely illuminated in the dim evening light. A house, most likely. *Best avoid that.*

Heading around the back of the barn, I saw several other sheds and outbuildings, the forest only a few hundred meters behind. Resisting the gut-deep urge to run, I paused, Luca's guiding words coming to me. *First rule of battle. Defend yourself.* I needed a better weapon. The shovel was far from ideal, especially if they were hunting me. It was only good if there was only one man left, and I was in close range. Even close range was dangerous, especially if they had a knife, or worse, a firearm. The worst part was not knowing how many of them there were. The man who ran would definitely be after me. They wouldn't just let me escape. There would be nothing useful in a dead forest with brittle branches. No, I needed to arm myself with something better.

The closest shed loomed dark and silent in the night sky, with just enough light from the moon and stars to see the outer walls. Slowly pushing the creaking door open, I could make out dark shapes, but not enough to see what they were, and not enough to find a useful weapon. *Damn. I need a torch.*

Turning to go, I thought I heard a soft moan.

Freezing, paralyzed with fear, I stood in the doorway and paused. Unsure of whether to enter or run.

"Frey..." he moaned in agony.

Dropping the shovel in the dirt and feeling with my hands in the darkness, I reached him in two strides. Cam was hanging, his arms outstretched, strung up above his head. *Damn.* I couldn't feel how he was hanging with him taller than I could reach. His weight was pulling him down, his feet not quite touching the floor.

"Fuck, fuck, *fuck!*" I muttered, frustration rising. "I can't *fucking see!*"

"Torch ... front ... pocket," he gasped. Fossicking around in his jeans pocket, I pulled out the tiny key-ring torch and switched it on. Even with the weak light it threw out, I froze momentarily when I saw him, shirtless, hanging from a filthy silver butcher's hook suspended from the roof, his hands and feet bound. A deliberate and vicious gash stretched from hip to chest, so deep in places that I could see muscle as the wound gaped sickeningly. Dried blood stained his face, skin barely visible, his eyes blackened and swollen. His bare chest and jeans were soaked in blood, clearly his own. Even his boots were blackened from the dripping blood.

Forcing myself not to react, I tried lifting him from his lower legs but struggled with his heavier weight, unable to lift him up and off the hook. Anger surged through me. I had not come all this way and reunited with my husband to let him die now. Fueled by fury, on the third attempt, I managed to lift him high enough to get his trussed wrists off the vicious hook, leaving it swinging violently in the dark.

He collapsed to the floor, half on top of me, and I stumbled, slipping on the blood-spattered floor, landing painfully on my knees, but managing to hold on to the torch. It only gave off a small beam of light, but what it illuminated was more than enough. I was sitting on the floor of a butcher's room filled with saws, knives, and drills. All were coated in varying shades of blood. Vats of yellow rendered fat lay in one corner, chunks of aged meat hanging from the other hooks. The walls, floors, and benches were all stained brown. And the smell. The overpowering stench of death, the same odor as in the barn.

Springing into action, I dragged Cam by the feet, out the door, and into the crisp night air. I pulled him as far as a nearby tree, propping him up.

"Cam? Can you hear me? Are you okay?" I hissed into his ear, not wanting to draw attention to us in case they were out here, searching.

Grimacing, he groaned, barely conscious. "Untie me."

I scanned the yard cautiously, but there was no sign of life. "Can you keep watch? One got away."

Cam perked up slightly at that. Leaning forward and holding the tiny torch in my mouth, I strained my eyes against the dark to untie the knots. Bloody hell, these assholes knew how to tie a knot. Unable to see clearly, I cursed and seethed. Taking the torch and dashing back to get a knife from the shed in which they had hung Cam, I returned, weapon in hand. I hacked at his restraints, and after what seemed an eternity, he was free, rubbing his wrists and swollen forehead.

"Can you stand?" I hissed. "We need to move. *Now*."

Forcing himself upright, he could. Barely. Struggling from his mistreatment and using each other as support, we struggled into the woods and away from the barn.

"Where are we going?" Cam whispered in my ear as we dodged fallen trees.

Sluggishly, hindered by his injuries, we limped deeper into the forest. Dead as it was, at least it was dark, the unfiltered starlight barely penetrating the canopy. With the dead leaves and branches cracking underfoot, we made some noise, but at least we could also hear anyone following us. I headed for a small cluster of pine trees grown together in a tight circle. Leaving Cam leaning against a large oak tree for a moment, I pushed my way through the dead branches into the center and, shining the tiny torch around, and found a small space, just big enough for the two of us.

Good. That will do for now.

Pushing my way back out, I reached for Cam. "Come on. We will be safe here. They will look out on the main road, and we can't see in the dark to travel overland. Best to hide now and move in the morning."

Cam followed me in, still moving painfully from his wounds, and I carefully rearranged the branches to camouflage the entrance.

"Did they have dogs?" Cam whispered in my ear.

Shit. I hadn't thought of that.

"Unlikely," I whispered upon consideration. "I didn't hear any. Besides, how would you keep them safe all these years?"

"How did *they* survive all these years?" Cam replied in a voice thick with pain.

"I have absolutely no idea. Why did they leave you?"

"They strung me up and were taunting me, joking about where to start. What would make me scream the most, losing an eye or a finger? They said they liked it when people screamed. It made the meat more tender." Cam groaned, trying to muffle it, evidently in agony.

I cringed in the dark, hoping Cam didn't sense my movement.

He spoke again, slowly, the pain affecting his thought processes. "One beat me around the head ... then cut me across the chest as slowly as he could. It took an eternity as he pushed the blunt blade in and drew it down. I did my best not to make any sound, even though it hurt like nothing I can describe. He put his fingers in the wound and started running them down the inside of the cut, scratching with his nails. He was toying with me, treating me like a hunted animal. He said he wanted to take his time, make me a piece of art. They had just picked up a hand drill and started on my face when we heard a metallic scraping sound. They went to check it out and didn't come back. Frey, are *you* okay?"

"Fine." I would never admit that I didn't feel it. My head was throbbing, and my wrists were aflame with scratches and cuts, likely infected. I would deal with them but not now. He was in far worse shape. I had no right to complain.

"That sound you heard was me. Sharpening a shovel. I got one of them. How many were there?"

"Only two, I think. I only saw two."

"Same. How did they get you?"

"Slingshot." Cam stopped to rub his head. "With a rock. Fucking knocked me out."

"Me too," I admitted, touching my wound gently. It was hurting more now that I had calmed down. The anger fueling me had blocked the pain temporarily.

Cam kissed my forehead, taking me by surprise. Silence rose between us as we sat, holding each other tight, listening. His chest still oozed blood, much of it soaking my t-shirt, leaving my clothes sticking to me. Not quite protected by the dead trees, I concentrated on the sounds of the night, the wind rattling through the trees, listening carefully for the sound of footsteps.

Feeling Cam drooping beside me, I whispered in as soothing a voice as I could manage in my heightened state, "Sleep now. I'll keep watch."

"But..." he protested weakly.

"I'll wake you in a few hours," I promised. "I am okay for now. We are a team. We will get through this."

Squeezing me gratefully, I felt Cam's head relax on my shoulder as he fell into a fitful sleep, the pain barely numbed. Placing my arms protectively around him, I vowed we would indeed make it through this. I would not abandon our children. Feeling his blood-soaked clothing and now mine, I worried about how much blood he had lost. That would weaken him and make our movements slow going.

Not a bloody chance. Anger rose in me again as I pictured what they had done to him, based on his description and what little I had seen. *A hand drill?* Thank goodness I couldn't see in the dark and by the poor light of his tiny torch. I kept the knife in my hand and gripped it tighter. Anger was better than fear. I would not cower from these filthy, sickening excuses for human beings. I would survive, and so would Cam. In the years we had traveled together to unknown places, Luca and Jakob had taught me a lot about self-protection and battle strategy. We had succeeded on Mousa. We would here too.

Remaining angry kept me awake and focused as I plotted our next steps. We couldn't just make a run for it. We were too exposed. Even if there were just one of them left, he would look for us. Potentially he had a gun or a vehicle. We would never make it back to Inverness or even Clava. No. Better to do what we did on Mousa and strike at dawn, hoping they were asleep. There was no way the one in the barn had survived that impact. That was one down. There was at least one other. I had only heard one other voice, and Cam had only seen two. Maybe, just maybe, we were in with a chance.

As the tiniest sliver of light lightened the edge of the morning sky, I gently nudged Cam awake, careful to avoid his wound. "Honey, you need to wake up. Now."

He was alert in an instant, not sleeping soundly. Just resting. "What?" he whispered, panicked. "Are they here?"

"No. We need to go. Follow me."

Creeping through the dead forest, watching where we put our feet, we traced our steps back to the barn, the light barely illuminating the trees.

It didn't take long to reach the clearing, the barn to the left, and the house beyond. The waft of death hit me from the open barn door, the smell making me shudder with disgust. Cam, thinking me cold, put his arm around my shoulder, but I gently removed it.

"Stay here," I hissed, taking Cam's tiny torch and moved as quickly and quietly as I could to the barn, peering inside, returning to Cam.

"He is gone!" I tried not to let Cam hear the panic in my voice. I was positive I had killed him. Judging by the significant pool of blood soaked into the dirt floor, he had not survived. *But what if...*

"We need to leave, now!" Cam whispered. "It is too dangerous."

Shaking my head made me dizzy, so I spoke curtly. "No." I was adamant. "We complete the mission." They would pursue us, and we didn't know the area. They had a decided advantage.

Cam sighed. "Okay, but I need a weapon too."

Casting about, I looked for a weapon, anything. I wanted to strike. Now. Dawn was close. We didn't have time to search the sheds again. I scanned the forest floor. *There.* A solid tree branch about three inches thick and three feet long. The perfect club.

"Can you wield that?"

The look of grim determination on Cam's face in the pink dawn light made me smile.

"Let's go."

Tiptoeing toward the main house, we stopped and listened as we reached the porch. Nothing. We waited and carefully tuned our ears to any sign of life. Outside of the dome, there were no sounds of animals starting their day, just the sound of wind through the dead branches.

Looking over my shoulder, making sure Cam was ready, I caught his eye and nodded. It was time. The club balanced on his shoulder, I opened the door as quietly as I could. The creak was deafening as the hinges swung open, and I heard movement in the back end of the house.

There goes the element of surprise, I thought grimly.

Cam stepped through the front door, crossed the room silently, and stood to one side of the far doorway, currently closed, the club braced on his shoulder, ready. The knife squarely in front of me, I stepped in behind him. As my eyes adjusted to the dim light, I could see that we were in a living space of sorts. A combined kitchen, dining, and living room, filled with junk — old boxes, rags, broken pieces of machinery, many of the windows blocked by piles of rubbish. The filth and stench made me gag, but I swallowed it down as I waited. The inner door swung open and revealed a scrawny, middle-aged man wearing filthy, torn clothing, little better than blackened rags and soaked in fresh blood. A quick scan revealed it was not his own.

He grinned when he saw me, like I was a prize he had won at a fair. As he smirked, I realized he had no teeth, his face so filthy from years of grime that the wrinkles that deeply lined his face were filled in with muck. His hair blackened, greasy and matted, hung in a single dreadlock down his back. He looked like he hadn't bathed in years.

He took one step toward me, still smiling mockingly. He opened his mouth to speak. The look of shock that replaced the grin was almost comical as Cam brought the club down on the back of his skull with an audible thunk, splintering the dead timber. The reverberation shuddered up Cam's arms, making him jerk violently as the chips fell. The piece of filth dropped but was still conscious. He lay amid the muck that coated the rancid floor, which had never seen a mop in its life. Standing over him with the knife, I gestured for Cam to check the other rooms. Grabbing a dirty knife from the kitchen bench first, he did, returning within a moment.

"Empty."

With the knife poised on the filth demon's blackened neck, I barked, "Where is the other one?"

He grunted, and for a moment, I thought he was going to fight me. Then I realized he was crying.

"Where ... is ... he?" I bellowed in the most menacing tone as I could manage. My voice resounded around the small, dank, and putrid room. The light was barely penetrating the layer of scum built up on the windows.

"He ... dead," the sticky, grotty piece of excrement mumbled, barely audible.

"Where is he now?" I snarled, a little quieter. Luca had taught me that tone was everything, not volume.

"Out ... back," he mumbled through foul breath, making me recoil slightly as the odor of feral rotting teeth stumps hit me for the second time.

I gestured at Cam, and he quietly left, heading back out the door through which we had entered. It was a tiny home, just three rooms: the main room, in which we were standing, a bedroom with two single beds, and a disgusting bathroom. I could see both from where I stood over him. The inhabitants had not showered the rest of the house with any more attention than this room.

Not wanting to speak to this monster but struggling with the silence as he lay on the floor, his face hidden, I barked, "Who else lives here?"

He flinched at my tone, carefully replicated from Luca's military tone, and mumbled, "Just me and Geoff." His voice was thickly accented and uneducated. Slurring and unable to enunciate words properly. *Drunk? Or maybe just a little simple?*

"Who is Geoff?" I demanded in a tone that indicated I had better be taken seriously. Just for good measure, I pushed slightly on the knife tip I had placed on his neck, white edges showing alongside where the tip of the dirty blade applied pressure. A drop of blood pooled on his blackened neck.

He cowered, his head shrinking into his filthy collar, and responded, "Me ... brudda."

Not taking my attention from him, I glanced around the room. The table, bench, and floors were covered in filth, grime, dirt, and unidentifiable substances. Piles of putrid dishes covered every horizontal surface. Boxes of empty beer bottles and general rubbish were strewn everywhere. Wondering if it had ever been cleaned, I wondered how on earth they had survived. *What did they live on, out here in the open? Without water?*

Cam reappeared at the door, his face as green as the algae in the bioreactors on Lewis but with a grim determination in his eyes. I looked at him, slightly surprised. Maybe Geoff's body was a bit gruesome?

Cam took two steps across the room, and without removing my hands, pushed down with all his strength on the knife. Frozen, I stood there as he withdrew it from the man's neck and repeated the maneuver.

"Stop!" I bellowed, getting my hand out from under his and blocking the knife. The first strike had hit the carotid. That was where Luca had taught me to place a knife long before Mousa. I knew what I was doing. Blood sprayed in an arc, hitting the wall behind.

Cam's eyes were wild, dark, and unreadable. The man on the floor was dead, beyond a doubt. A pool of fresh blood was spreading across the filthy floor, flecks of dirt floating to the glossy, dark surface. His eyes rolled back in death.

"What is wrong with you?" I snapped.

Dropping his knife on the sticky, blackened floor, he left the room, and I followed, floored by this change in the man I loved. I walked around the back of the house to where there was another small shed, this one spattered in mud. It wasn't mud, I realized as I got closer, and the rising orange dawn that lit the sky revealed sprays of congealed blood. Old blood. The stench hit me then, and I pulled my blood-soaked top to cover my nose and mouth as Cam pushed the creaking door open to display what was inside.

I looked once, paused, then away. In that second, I had taken in enough of what lay beyond. The shed contained benches and shelves, all stained dark red-brown, splatters up the walls. The windows were caked in filth and sprays of blood. Saws of all shapes hung from hooks above the bench, used to mutilate the carcasses that the shed still held. Racks of meat, large wooden tubs filled with congealed blood, a layer of scum on the top. A rack contained knives, axes, and saws, a variety of sizes, all filthy but laid out neatly like a workbench. Each one was stained in the same shade of red-brown.

As I left the shed, I noticed the pile of bones stacked behind, bleached white and stripped clean, evidently boiled. Human bones. They had arranged the skulls in a playful pyramid. There must have been sixty of them, all stacked neatly, facing the same direction, grinning at me in open-eyed silence. Beside them was a neat cross-hatched stack of femurs, various shapes and sizes looking like a giant Jenga puzzle.

Glancing over at Cam, I followed his gesture inside the shed to the body of Geoff, seated on the floor and propped up against the far wall. His withered body was naked, the shovel wound in his abdomen caked in dried blood. His arms and head were already removed, sitting on the bench. His eyes were open, looking at me from the bench-top, puzzled.

Turning, I walked down the path toward the road, and Cam caught up with me.

"I'm sorry," he mumbled. "I couldn't let you be in the same room, sharing air with that ... thing ... any longer. Not when I saw how... how many...."

Understanding, I nodded, unable to speak. Monsters. Both of them. That was what they would have done to Cam and me, too. Inflicting a slow, excruciating, torturous death to derive a perverse sense of pleasure. Then ... ugh. I shuddered. *What on earth would drive someone to cannibalism?*

As we exited the wooden gate, falling off its hinges, I looked at Cam. Did he still want to go to Clava?

Gazing first at his blood-covered bare chest and jeans and then over at my blood-soaked attire, he sighed. "We might get a better reception if we clean up first?"

Slowly walking up the road back to the harbor, I played and replayed the grisly scene over in my mind. "How long do you think they had been there?" I asked Cam quietly, some distance down the road.

"Years," he replied.

CHAPTER 13

AS WE BOARDED THE yacht, still unable to speak about the horrors we had observed, I stopped to strip off my clothes and throw them overboard. Just shedding my blood-soaked clothes made me feel slightly better, although I desperately needed a shower. Blood from my wound caked my hair, my skin sticky and stained pink with Cam's blood. I closed my eyes, envisioning the bliss of a long, hot shower. A simple wash using bottled water like we usually did would not cut it.

"You were amazing," Cam breathed without warning into my ear, making my insides quiver. "You were all, 'take charge, make the plan, execute the plan'—my warrior goddess. You saved my life, Frey. Again."

As he kissed a rare blood-free spot on my neck, I brought my arms up to his head to brush back his fringe so I could see the drill wound beside his eye. Halting, he grabbed my wrists and pulled my arms into the sunlight.

"What happened?" he gasped, holding my arms up to the light. "Did those freaks do that to you?"

"No," I admitted, thinking for a moment that Cam might go back to that house of horrors and kill them all over again just for hurting me. Turning my arms over in sunlight and examining them properly, with the blood streaks and crisscross cuts all up my inner forearms and hands, I thought it looked like someone had been playing with a razor blade, haphazardly slashing at my arms. The most painful ones, I realized as I looked at them, were on my right arm, where they crossed the old scar, the one I had received from Heidi.

"I did that trying to cut my bonds loose."

"Bloody hell!" Cam was more distressed than I was. "You are a mess!"

"It isn't as bad as it looks," I soothed, noting as I did that some needed suturing, my skin flayed open in a web of open wounds.

"Well, it looks bad, Frey. We should clean those cuts and..."

"You can do it for me," I sighed. "But later. All I want is a shower."

Cam fossicked around in his back jeans pocket, pulling out a small white envelope which he lay carefully on the table beside the tiny torch before tossing his blood-stained clothes overboard. Diplomatically ignoring this, I carefully checked the deep gash wound across his chest. *It is like a red military sash from hip to shoulder,* I thought abstractedly.

"I must stitch that," I said cautiously. I had sutures in my first aid kit but no pain relief or antibiotics.

"Later."

We left our boots on the deck. We knew we might be unable to replace those, but not able to deal with cleaning blood off them right now, blood that once belonged to the pair's many nameless victims.

"You know we can't shower. We can't trust the water in the tanks," he said, reading my thoughts.

"I know," I replied, unable to keep the note of disappointment out of my voice. "We have a room filled with bottled water. Would it be okay if we use some of that?"

Placing the plug in the bath, Cam scooped me up effortlessly and lay me in it. Handing me a tumbler of whisky, I sipped as he carried several of the large containers of water I had sourced in Edinburgh to the galley. I watched, relaxing as he heated pot after pot and started pouring it onto a cloth and slowly cleaning my skin. Hot, safe water. My face, neck, and all the way to my feet. It was blissful to feel warm, clean, soothed. I hadn't been immersed in steaming water since the grotto. Slowly and carefully, Cam washed my hair, massaging my scalp, and gently rinsing the blood away. He paid special care to my arms, gently wiping all traces of dirt away from the cuts, flinching as he saw the corners of skin lift from the X patterns I had created.

"We will need to disinfect those," he breathed into my ear.

Feeling a little giddy from the whisky and heat, I giggled, startling him. "Antiseptic in my first aid kit."

As Cam finished swabbing all of my arm wounds, he looked carefully at my head. Fossicking around for a mirror, he held it up to my face. "Does it need treatment?" he asked worriedly.

Forensically, I checked my wound, wincing through the pain, probing, testing. Sighing, I said, "Probably—just one or two stitches. I need to be careful that it hasn't affected the skull fracture from a few years ago. They hit me in the same spot. That could cause complications."

Cam looked alarmed, making me smile.

"I'm okay: concussion most likely, but not brain-damaged. Well, at least I don't think so."

Getting out of the bath, now ringed red with blood and a layer of grime lying on the base of the white porcelain, he dried me carefully with a fluffy white towel found in the cupboard.

"Ahh," I moaned in ecstasy as he dried my hair. "Please tell me we can take this towel home. I have not used a towel this good in *years*."

Opening the top cupboard so I could see, he said with a grin, "You can take all of them, my darling."

Turning to look into his eyes, I said, "Your turn."

Cleaning the tub and repeating the process, heating water and pouring it into the bath, I washed and tended Cam's minor wounds first. Like me, they had hit him with a slingshot, and he had fallen from his bike into the road. Because of his larger size, they had given him a good whack across the back of the head for good measure before they had dragged him to the shed where they had strung him up. But most of those wounds were comparatively minor. A thorough clean and they would be okay. The chest wound was a different story. After a comprehensive assessment, I pronounced he would require stitching to his chest, forehead, and the wound beside his eye.

As Cam dried himself off, I gestured toward the dining table where I had laid out the first aid kit. Surrounded by large windows, it was well lit, and I could have my equipment to hand. Handing him the bottle of whisky and forcing him to drink, I stitched his chest wound first. It was nasty, deep, and evidently made with a filthy blade.

"I think we both need a tetanus shot," I muttered as I did my best to disinfect the wound. It was deep, and he kept holding his breath as I hurt him, wiping the dirt out as I worked.

"I'm sorry," I kept saying as he tried hard not to flinch at the insertion of each needle movement. "Drink more. It will numb the pain."

Fifty-three stitches later, and he looked like a pirate, dark hair wet down his back. The wound was looking like it had been inflicted with a cutlass. His black eyes were now carefully tended, but several stitches were holding the deeper wounds together. I carefully re-threaded the needle.

"Now you need to do mine," I instructed, rolling my arm upright on the table I was using as a surgical bench. I took a good mouthful of the whisky.

Cam went white. "I've never..."

"Oh, it's easy enough. I can talk you through it. Sewing is sewing. You just need to use a little force. It is kind of like pushing a needle into an orange. There is a little resistance at first, so you need to apply more pressure, but then it is just like sewing fabric."

Cam's hands were shaking so hard that he only managed to finish one stitch before dropping the needle and thread. "I can't do it, Frey. I can't hurt you."

Taking another swig of the whisky, I got Cam to sit in front of me with the hand mirror and carefully stitched my forehead first. Trying not to screw my face up as I grimaced with the pain, I was pleased with my resultant handiwork. Three neat stitches. Laying my left arm on the table and continuing to self-medicate for pain relief, I managed a reasonably

neat job, despite feeling slightly woozy by the end—
eight stitches in total. Being right-handed, stitching
my right arm was somewhat more challenging, and
this was the arm with the worst damage as my right
inner arm had been tied facing out. Instructing Cam
on where to insert the needle and finishing off myself,
we managed not to entirely ruin the job. Not as neat
as I would like, I surmised, but not too bad, although
it looked much like a spider's web. Now I just hoped
it wouldn't get infected.

Completely drunk but unable to eat, we went to
bed, the stench of death still searing my nostrils.

"Did you find what you wanted? At the hospital?" I
asked shyly as we flopped onto the bed and pulled up
the cool cotton sheets.

"I did. And I will tell you about it, but not now."
Deftly rolling me on top of him, he held me at arm's
reach and sighed. "Oh God, I love you, Freyja. If something had happened to you..."

"I'm okay," I soothed. "Be careful of those stitches!
I'm too drunk to do them again."

Ignoring me completely, he kissed me, effectively
ending the conversation. Running my fingers through
his thick wet hair, fueled by alcohol and the desire
for oblivion for a time, I kissed him all over. The pain
numbed. All I wanted was him.

"Let me..."

"No, it is my turn," I demanded forcefully. Slowly,
tantalizingly, I tortured him with my hands, my
lips, my hair.

"Please..." he begged, gasping.

"No," I replied firmly. "Not yet."

His head lay on the pillow, and I could see he
was torn between torture and ecstasy as I aroused

every inch of him. Pleased with myself, I took my time, taunting.

"Now!" he pleaded.

Sighing, I yielded and squealed as he flipped me over like a man possessed.

"My turn," he growled softly in my ear, dangerously close to the point of no return.

I moaned in delight, making him smile as I writhed and squirmed beneath him.

"Tell me what you want?" His breath was husky in my ear.

"You. Now," was all I could manage as he split me like a ripe apricot. My head rolling back on the pillow, I moaned with pleasure, forgetting the horrors of the past few days.

CHAPTER 14

"**DID YOU MEAN IT** about getting a tetanus shot?" Cam ran his fingers gently along the crisscross pattern of cuts along my arms. "How long has it been?"

"I got a booster before we left Melbourne. That was what, nearly seven years ago? I'm fairly sure they are active for ten years."

"Regardless, some of those look nasty. Did I ever tell you about the woman from Bellcamp who died on our trip back to Australia from tetanus?"

Looking closer, he was right. It did. The edges were red and inflamed. So was his chest wound.

"Perhaps antibiotics too? For both of us?" I suggested. "And no, you didn't. It was Di who told me about her. 'The stuck-up cow,' Di called her," I said, to change the topic.

Cam grinned at Di's nickname but didn't continue that line of conversation. "What did you cut it on? You never told me."

"A rusted wheel arch," I confessed softly, not really wanting to discuss it.

"On *what*?"

"It was the only thing I could find that was sharp," I said as casually as I could. "They had checked on me once. I knew I didn't have much time. I was fearful they would come back."

"Did they... did they hurt you?"

Banishing the memory of Joey's hands molesting me, I lied. I didn't need to tell him about *that*, not after what they had done to him.

"Only my head," I admitted, gently feeling the lump behind the bruise and stitches. "But I don't think my skull is fractured this time. My head is a bit better today."

Cam kissed it. "Bloody slingshot hurt."

"I was desperate to cut the ropes around my wrists," I confessed, "so I didn't care what damage I did to myself. I heard them say they wanted to have fun with me. I didn't care for the tone they used."

Cam shuddered. "They are gone. They will never hurt anyone else. Thanks to you."

Not wanting to relive awful memories, I fell silent, trying to banish the feeling of being bound and feeling helpless.

"What is it?" Cam asked, looking at me closely.

Relenting, I explained, "All the time I was locked in that shed, tied up, all I could think about were those beasts on Mousa, kidnapping those women. I thought being starved, beaten, and raped daily was the worst cruelty imaginable. Now ... I think we have a new contender."

"Prolonged torture and cannibalism? But in your case, likely rape too."

"Are you certain?" I asked miserably. "About the cannibalism part?"

"Positive. I saw the cooking pot, and the rendered fat. Dried skins were hung in one of the sheds. They were unmistakably human. Goodness knows what for. Cages too."

I shuddered, thinking of all those skulls. Each one had been attached to a person at one point.

"Should we search for clothes before we head to Clava?" Cam asked after a pause. Neither of us wanted to dwell on the previous day. "Not that I mind you naked, that is." Cam blushed at his forthright comment. God, he was sweet.

"We should try. I have very few clothes left, and my boots are likely ruined. Yours too."

"I passed the main street after I left the hospital." He trailed off, clearly not wanting to talk about the hospital. "It didn't look ransacked. Well, the Tesco looked like a bomb hit it, but the clothing stores looked intact."

"Did you find what you wanted?"

"I did. Medical records, which told me nothing. But a photograph."

Reaching across to the bedside table, he opened the envelope he had retrieved from his back pocket the day before and handed them to me. The envelope was crumpled and blood stained after our misadventures, but the contents were intact. A single photo. A scared-looking girl with long dark hair, holding a blanketed bundle.

"A photographer used to take photographs for the local newspaper, but there was a note that Jasmine refused to have it published. The photo ended up on her file waiting for her to collect it, but she never did. It sat there all this time."

Cam had told me Jasmine's story, and I fully understood why this terrified nineteen-year-old girl, alone in the world, wouldn't want to have her photo published. With as much enthusiasm as I could muster, I smiled and said, "Louis will love it."

Dressing alongside him in the tiny bedroom, I realized I was still slightly nervous with him. Silly, considering how well we knew each other. But part of him was still distant, secret. The years of his life that he had spent with another woman, happy and raising their child. The baby in the photo he had just shown me. The part of his life where I had been alone, fretting for him, but never admitting it.

Carefully putting on my only remaining t-shirt and jacket, I carefully pulled it over my torn arms. The short sleeves exposed my arms, which looked like I had slashed at myself maniacally with a knife, with not enough dressings to cover them. I hoped he hadn't noticed. Doing up my cargo pants, I joked, "These are my last clothes, so no mess today, okay?"

Grinning, he kissed me. "I promise."

After a breakfast of porridge from the stash of oats we had found in Edinburgh washed down with coffee, we visited the clinic at the hospital first. Although slightly out of date, the tetanus vaccines were easy to find and were better than nothing. Antibiotics, too, although there was no morphine or other pain medication. I found an intravenous antibiotic, and after jabbing us both, we took what little remained. It wouldn't hurt to have a stash, anyway.

After our medicinal raid, we headed for the high street where Cam believed the outdoor shops were. Smashing the window to enter the largest, the look of guilt on Cam's face made me laugh aloud. Smiling, he responded, "After all the times I have done this, you would think I would be used to it."

"But you never do?" I teased.

"I don't think I ever will," he admitted. "To be raised with the values of honesty, integrity, and acting ethically makes it hard to break and enter. Steal other people's property."

"Honesty wasn't a value that was respected in my house," I stated.

"What was then?"

"Achievement, commitment, excellence, resilience, education. Values to do with the person, I guess, not how they treated others."

From the look on his face, I could see that Cam found that strange and was uncomfortable for a moment. "You have come a long way," he breathed, and I recognized it for the compliment it was.

I pulled several pairs of pants off the rack in my size. It had been years since I had been in a change room, curtained and mirrored. After having Katrin, my shape had changed slightly, I thought. A pronounced purple bruise was visible, like a stripe across my stomach, where the shovel had pushed into me with some force.

Watching me as I was pulling off the third pair, Cam exclaimed, "Don't rush. I'll be back in a few minutes," and disappeared out the broken window.

Standing in my underwear in the change rooms, I was speechless. *Where is he going in the middle of an abandoned city?*

Returning to the rack, I searched for loose long-sleeved tops and warm down jackets. While the winters weren't as harsh under the geodesic dome with no snow, it still got bitterly cold, especially when tending livestock in a freezing paddock. Returning some twenty minutes later, looking exceedingly embarrassed, he held out some chocolate as I sat on the floor with my new pile of clothes.

"Chocolate!" I gasped. "I haven't had chocolate since, since... you remembered?"

Cam smiled, looking down at his feet. "Come on, boots next. Let's get some stuff for the kids too, for Christmas."

"Did you see our bikes? At the farm?" I asked suddenly, realizing that I had been riding one. The prominent lump on my temple, woolly-headed thinking, and dull ache were a semi-permanent reminder of the nightmarish events of three days before. Cam stopped dead in the street, his arms laden with bags. "I didn't, you know. I was so desperate to get away that I didn't even think to look. There must have been more sheds. Do you want to go looking for them?"

"Not a chance in hell." I enunciated each word slowly. "Nothing, I repeat, nothing would ever make me go back there. I have never been so completely terrified in all my life."

"Even more scared than the portal?" Cam asked cautiously.

I considered that before replying. "The portal scared me as I didn't know what to expect. One minute I was thawing my feet in a place where I felt safe. The next I was being sucked into a black hole. At the farm, when they had tied me up in the barn, I had time to consider all the possibilities of why they were keeping me captive. Though I must admit, cannibalism wasn't one I thought of."

Cam shuddered and changed the subject. "We found a lot in Edinburgh, but should we find more bikes?"

Thinking about it, I said, "I think we should, with those trailers for kids too if we can find them. I also want to ride out to Clava if you don't mind. We have a better chance of getting away if there is anyone else out there. I was stupid last time. I thought I saw something in the woods, so I stopped. Not that I think the Scottish countryside is filled with raving cannibalistic nut jobs, that is, but ... just in case."

"You know," Cam said conversationally as we started back up the street, "I traveled across Victoria and New Zealand, and I didn't see any other people alive. It makes you wonder how they survived so long, doesn't it? I mean, with no water, that meant no vegetables or other crops. How did they stay alive?"

I shuddered but remembered the rotting stumps of teeth in Joey's head.

"They likely had scurvy if all they ate was meat, lots of other forms of malnutrition too. Maybe they came into town and raided shops and other homes. But the bulk of their diet was..."

"Meat," Cam finished gently. "Beer too. There was an enormous stockpile of it in one outbuilding. But where were they getting the meat supply? We weren't their first. There was a pile of skulls beside the shed and another enormous pile of bones alongside the far side of the house. Cages where they held people captive, awaiting their turn. But now there is no one left, no animals either."

"More," I croaked. "Why didn't you say something?"

Pausing, Cam contemplated his answer.

"What is it? You can tell me," I said, feigning confidence I didn't feel.

He was silent for a long time. Then finally, he said, "There were children's skulls among them, babies too. That was what made me need to get him away from you. I... I wanted to spare you."

Tears welled in my eyes, and I blinked them away angrily. We were in no danger now. I wasn't some emotional, mushy, girly-girl. But despite fighting it, emotion overcame me. Behind my closed eyes, I could see Katrin's tiny skull that fit perfectly in my hand as she gazed up at me, total trust in her cool green gaze.

"Babies?" I croaked, unable to get the word out. "How do you know?"

"I saw the skeletons. That is what made me... I knew that there was no redemption."

I felt the shudder up my spine as I hit the concrete footpath. Cam's arms around me anchored me to the earth as I sobbed, my heart breaking for those poor children. Children like Louis and Katrin. My children.

"You don't need to come," Cam soothed eventually. "Please stay here, on the boat, where it is safe. I won't be long: two days max."

"No." I lifted my head, determined. "I won't leave you again. Bad shit happens when we are separated. Promise me we will never be separated again."

"I promise," he replied, kissing me until I believed it.

CHAPTER 15

WE DIDN'T LEAVE FOR Clava until the next day, an afternoon shower putting an end to our plans. We enjoyed a much-needed afternoon spent in solitude before facing people again. On the deck under the fixed awning, ensuring we were well away from wind and rain, I tried to read one of the books I had taken in Inverness. But something was amiss. Glancing over at Cam, I saw he was staring out to sea over the book he held on his lap.

"What are you thinking?" I asked, trying to sound confident. I wasn't sure I wanted to know the answer.

An uncomfortable silence rose as he continued staring. Just when I thought he hadn't heard me, he spoke. "I'm thinking: I wonder how many people survived the virus. For weeks, months, years. May still be out there."

Placing my book down on the small table between us, I asked, "More survivors, you mean?"

"I guess..." He was lost for an adequate description for the two monsters we had encountered. "Surely they aren't the only ones? After all, my parents lived

for years. Those feral brutes on Mousa survived too."
His voice drifted away like a leaf on a breeze.

Recognizing the underlying issue, I stood, purposefully took his book, and placed it on the table. Straddling him as he sat on his chair, my eyes only centimeters from his sparkling blue ones, I ran my fingers through his now clean hair, gently touching his facial wounds as he winced. Like my own wounds, the pain was a constant reminder of the previous days. The rain pattered down overhead onto the canopy. Looking into his eyes, I could see that he was tortured, conflicted.

"Campbell, where there is life, there will always be good and evil."

"I took a life," he whispered, shaken by the memory. "Does that make me as bad as them?"

"So did I. Do you think that makes *me* a bad person?"

He looked surprised at that. "I could never think of you as bad."

"I have taken lives. The man in the barn, that was self-defense. I won't lose sleep over that. He would have done far worse to me if he had the chance. But the men on Mousa? I ordered their execution. I didn't pull the trigger myself. But I made the call, and I stand by it. But now I need to ask: do you think I am evil?"

"Never. They were monsters."

"What makes you think the life you took makes you evil?" I asked.

Unable to answer, he looked away, unhappy.

"If it makes you feel any better," I continued, more gently, "it took months for the nightmares to stop about Mousa. Wondering if I had managed it badly. If there had been a better way. Logically, I knew. They had killed three men plus Laetitia without a thought, gutted Angus and left him for dead, kidnapped eleven women, and would have subjected them to goodness knows what. It was a violation and pre-meditated. I knew these were not good people. But even so, I struggled with it. I was plagued with guilt and constant nightmares. What gave me the right to take their lives? Who appointed me judge, jury, and executioner?"

"How did you reconcile it?"

"Luca saw I was struggling and sat me down. He told me that as part of his military training, he needed to accept that he would, at some point, take lives. Saying it was 'Just following orders' is a cop-out. You always have a choice. It is never easy, but you need to weigh it up. Does taking that step make the world a better place? Can you look at yourself in the mirror if you do it, or if you don't do it?"

Silence filled the void between us. Despite being so physically close, he felt distant, not connected to me. He wasn't here with me. It scared me. I knew what this felt like, questioning your actions. He was standing on the abyss. I needed to pull him back.

Finally, I asked in a low voice, "So, what do you think? Did killing those monsters on Mousa make the world a better place? Did I do the right thing?"

In answer, he raised my new black t-shirt and dropped it on the deck, running his powerful hands down my sides and back. I arched backward with the bliss of being touched. I could feel his chest thundering beneath me. Unhooking my bra and discarding it, he took one breast into his mouth, then the other. It was exhilarating, the feeling of being nurtured, loved after so many years alone.

"They are bigger now," he murmured, as he appreciated them in the light, kissed them, and worshipped them. "You are so beautiful."

Running his hands down my belly to my hips, he pulled me toward him, grinding me against him through our clothing. Lifting his shirt over his head, we joined in a kiss, our bare chests enjoying the skin-on-skin sensation as my breasts flattened against his wounded chest as we tried to get closer, *be* closer, and bridge the chasm that his anxiety about his actions had created. Finally, he stood, my legs locked around his hips, and he lowered me to the deck, able to see the rain lightly patter on the roof overhead. Slipping off my pants, I watched as he undid his own jeans, his dark hair glinting in the setting light. The laceration was still raw, vivid across his chest.

"Careful," I wanted to say but didn't. No, I wanted him hard, and I wanted him now. I needed it, to feel alive after all that death. He was watching me.

"Now," I urged.

"No. I want to watch you." He placed one of my own hands on my mound and moved it up and down. "Do it," he implored. "I want to watch how *you* like it."

A warm pleasurable sensation rose within me as I moved, stroking, touching, taking my time. Moisture aiding my movements, I writhed, feeling self-conscious, knowing that I had an audience. Closing my eyes as I drew near, the warm tingling sensation started, and I felt him fill my depths, and I clamped down on him, cascading into oblivion.

Some hours later, I woke, still on the deck, covered in a blanket, to a sky filled with stars.

"You did the right thing," he whispered into my ear as he felt me stir.

"So did you."

CHAPTER 16

THE SUN ROSE THE following day, clear and cloud-free. Realizing that we couldn't delay this any longer, we took two new e-bikes, freshly charged, and following the map we had taken from the outdoor shop, tracked a different path to Clava. Like all the communities, it wasn't hard to find a looming dome, visible from a distance. The difference here was that the lower section, almost three meters off the ground, wasn't transparent like all the others, rather a milky opaque, impossible to see through. Looking at each other, perplexed, we could tell it was patently still a dome, so we started hunting for a hatch, Cam walking one way and I the other. It didn't take long. While slightly harder to find, the access hatches still worked the same as every other community we had visited. Hiding our bikes in some shrubbery on the green side, we walked roughly toward the center, the highest point of the dome arching high above.

While we had no knowledge of where the community here was or in which direction to head, once inside, it didn't take us long. The noise of civilization traveled quite a distance, and we could hear them long before seeing them. Modern brick duplex buildings with neat gardens in carefully laid out streets greeted us, a world apart from the dull gray prefabricated dorms we had lived in on August. The residences there had been functional dwellings. These were proper homes with pretty porches, flowers, and lawns, streetlights, and paved streets—luxuries they had denied us. Noise blanketed us. After the relative silence of August and Lewis, here the sounds of motorized scooters, small electric cars, and industrial noises made Cam and I look at each other in astonishment. Feeling like we were stepping back in time, it was like being back in the Australia of our childhood.

Unsure what to do, we stood and watched, waiting for someone to approach us. A man exiting a nearby house turned toward us, on his way somewhere, oblivious to our intrusion.

"Derek?" Cam quizzed as he neared us.

Screwing up his face, Derek blinked at us. Then enlightenment brightened his face. "Ahh, from Offshore One. How are you?"

"Fine," Cam answered cheerily. "It is Derek, isn't it? I'm Cam. This is Freyja. You were my guide."

"Yes, I remember now. I did a few others after yours. How is life on Lewis?"

"How did you know that?" Cam fired back rapidly.

"Oh, we set up satellite surveillance over all the communities. But on Offshore One, the entry point was in a cave, so we couldn't see when you," he nodded at me, "traveled, but we saw you arrive on Lewis. We were so excited. It is thrilling for us every time a community finds its pair. Then we saw you," nodding at Cam, "go after her. We were pleased you worked it out too. Some communities still haven't made the connection."

"Do you watch all the communities?" Cam asked curiously. "The inland ones too?"

I knew his friend on Orkney had told him about satellite radios. But knowing they had seen us as well came as a surprise.

"Well, yes. We have amazing technology at our disposal."

Sensing Cam about to fire up and trying to stay calm myself, I asked, using as balanced a tone as I could manage, "So, you spied on us?"

"Oh." He looked quite taken aback. "I wouldn't call it spying. No. Rather … it was observing. Monitoring. Keeping an eye on you. Just making sure everything was okay."

"But it wasn't okay," Cam interjected in a slow, flat tone. "My wife went missing, and I spent six months in every shade of hell looking for her, presuming her dead. She came through the portal with a potentially life-threatening head wound. The community on Lewis. They watched the former residents die, all while you sat here and *observed*. In one of the inland communities in Victoria, a quarter of their people died in their establishment phase. What value is watching, I ask you, when you don't *do* anything?"

"It isn't part of our remit to interfere." He looked quite taken aback at Cam's comments, not aided by the fact that Cam stood almost five inches over him. "Our job was to help you establish safe communities, and we did that, didn't we?"

"'Part of your remit,'" Cam echoed in the same slow, flat voice. "The lives of your fellow man, all of whom you placed in those communities, but it wasn't your remit to interfere? Help, I think you mean. Assist. Were we some experiment to you? A test to see how it would all work out?"

Backpedaling rapidly, Derek exclaimed, "Of course not. You misunderstand. We could see, not hear. We didn't know everything that went on."

"I just need to ask one question." Cam's voice was gentle and calm, but knowing him so well, I sensed the underlying tension. The snake ready to strike. "Just one question. But you need to promise me the truth." He looked into Derek's eyes. Calmly. Cam's cerulean blue eyes did not betray the turmoil I knew lay underneath.

Nodding, Derek consented. "Of course."

"When the men came to Lewis last year. In the fishing trawler. Could you see that?"

"We don't watch *all* the time," Derek started to say.

"But you could see it?" Cam pushed, gently.

"Yes, we saw the footage. It quite surprised us. We didn't know there were other people outside of our biospheres."

"I've heard enough," I announced, and gripping Cam's arm, steered him away.

"Mackintosh?"

We had barely taken a dozen steps away from Derek, who had turned in the opposite direction and fled, when a middle-aged man approached us both.

"Ashton?" Cam queried.

He looked familiar. I had met him before. *But where?* Cam certainly seemed to know him.

"Wonderful to see you! How are you?" the older man gushed.

"Fine," Cam responded curtly. "I'm fine." *No thanks to you* being the undercurrent, but Ashton didn't seem to detect it.

"How on earth did you both get here?" he asked in amazement.

"Boat." Cam shrugged.

"Well, of course. We saw you travel through the portal, several times, in fact. But we didn't know you would find us *here*."

"My mother was from Lewis originally. She bought me to the Clava Cairns several times. I thought if Callanish was a portal, Newgrange too, then perhaps Clava was as well," Cam explained nonchalantly.

Noting that Cam had not mentioned breaking into the government facility in Melbourne, nor his conversations with his friend on Orkney, I played along.

"We'd love to see the site," I gushed, hoping I wasn't overdoing it. Acting wasn't my strong suit. "Cam tells me that the cairns are positively amazing!"

"Of course! We'd love to show you." Ashton looked at Cam carefully. "I recall your mother was from Lewis. That was one of the reasons you were one of our first chosen candidates. You had all the technical skills, agriculture, resilience, lifestyle, it was just..."

A look of horror crossed Ashton's face as he realized he had painted himself into a corner.

"My Aspergers?" Cam guessed, putting him out of his misery. "It's okay. She knows."

Ashton looked relieved. "Your skills in sustainable agriculture were first class. It was just your social skills we were worried about, but we took a chance. Looks like we made a sound choice. After all, it is you who found us. It was difficult when we couldn't contact you."

"Contact us?" I asked cautiously. I remembered now where I knew him from, the assessments and departure briefings in Melbourne.

"Oh yes, you wouldn't know. You didn't end up with a broadcast engineer on your site."

"A what?" Cam asked incredulously.

"Is that part of Angus's mission?" I asked, thinking of the satellite radios Illyria had told Cam about. *Maybe he is distributing them?*

"Angus? MacLeod, you mean? Oh, that's right, you traveled with him, didn't you? Did he tell you about his mission then?"

Ashton looked quite taken aback at my question, and even now, was flustered. I sensed it but couldn't work out why.

Not answering the question, I said, "You mentioned a broadcast engineer?"

That was safer ground as his face relaxed. "Yes, we sent a broadcast engineer upon settlement to each site. Someone who was in contact with us and who had the skills to establish broadcast systems when they felt the community was established enough that it wouldn't undermine the sense of cohesion. That person alone was entrusted with the knowledge. It was their role to judge when the fledgling society was ready. We didn't want to affect the stability of the community. If people knew too early, they would not put effort into establishing their new lives. It would be seen as temporary. It had to be done this way."

Logically, that made sense; those early months on August, we had worked hard to form a community.

"You said there was an engineer on every site?" Cam asked cautiously.

"Each one settled from Melbourne, yes."

"What about August? Ruapuke, I mean. Who was your person there?"

We had both known every person on August. It was not a pleasant feeling to suspect one of them of being a spy.

"Ahh, Offshore One. Well, no one. The engineer was one of the two that bailed on the day of settlement. So you didn't get one. We tried to think of a way but realized that we couldn't exactly drop someone new without arousing suspicion or letting on that there were access points. We also thought there were enough people there with tech knowledge that you could work it out for yourself."

"Who was the engineer from Bellcamp? Campbell Island, I mean," Cam asked.

"Why, that was Daniella."

"That rigid prude? Seriously? She was an engineer?"

"Oh yes. She was in contact with us, waiting for the right time. But something must have happened. We stopped hearing from her nearly two years ago."

"I'm sorry," I interjected, never having met this woman, but had heard Di's highly unflattering description of her. "What do you mean by, 'she was in contact?'"

"We had weekly check-ins with each engineer to see how the communities were faring."

"What were you waiting for?" Cam asked.

"We established a community maturity model and an index, by which we judged the level of development within each community. When it was the right time, we would instruct the engineer to implement a communication system with other safe communities, and eventually, with us."

"You established a spy, you mean," I asked coldly. I was starting to see a pattern forming here.

"Well, no, I wouldn't call it that."

"What would you call it then? Someone who had the knowledge that there was the ability to make contact with other communities and didn't tell us?"

"Not until you were ready. It was for your own good."

"And Lewis? Newgrange?" Cam asked. "What about those communities?"

"They were different. We had no control over the people who they sent there. That wasn't our call. Different governments had different priorities. Ours prioritized saving as many people as possible, but second, to assist them in connecting with other communities when the time was right. We worked with those governments to reactivate the antipodes, but who they sent was their call. We wanted a contingency just in case you couldn't travel or didn't find the antipodal point. Our communities were far more remote. We wanted you to form a network with other established communities when the time was right."

Part of me could see the logic in this. It was true. If people had known in the early months, even years, that there was a way off the island and that there were other settlements, people wouldn't have invested the time and energy in building a society: establishing friendships, relationships, and having children, creating social activities and networks. The adage 'The grass is always greener on the other side of the fence' rang true. I knew this from my father's development work. People often thought it was safer, cleaner, *better* in another place. People would always want what they didn't have, would covet what they thought other people had. All societies had their challenges.

None were perfect. I knew this better than most. In Melbourne, I came from a wealthy family, had an excellent education, a lovely home, and unlimited opportunities. But I found genuine friendship and happiness when it was all stripped away to bare bones, and we worked together to survive.

Cam had just finished filling Ashton in on what had happened to Daniella. The look crossing Cam's face as Ashton was now explaining about the radio network they were establishing across all communities considered mature enough was enough to indicate that he, too, was finding this hard to swallow.

Recognizing that it was time to interrupt, I asked as sweetly as I could muster, "Mr. Ashton, could you tell us where the cairns are? I would love to see them."

"Oh..." He looked startled at my interruption but politely answered the question. "If you head down this street and turn left at the intersection, you will find signs. It is about five kilometers. Inside the geo, of course."

"Geo?" I asked blankly.

"The geodesic dome." Ashton puffed his chest with self-importance.

"Oh, we just called it the dome."

"You are lucky you made it here safely," he continued. "There is something out there..." He waved, encompassing the area beyond the community. "It has taken a few of our people. We can't work out what sort of animal it is to have survived the outbreak."

"Ahh..." Cam filled Ashton in on the farm and our gruesome discoveries.

Ashton looked more and more ill as Cam supplied the gory details: the torture shed, the butchering shed, the meat racks, the skin preserving, and the piles of bones. Giving him directions to the farm, Cam then turned to me and linked his arm into mine.

"I'll arrange somewhere for you to stay," Ashton offered graciously, barely recovering himself. Considering what Cam had just told him, that his colleagues had likely been tortured and eaten by two psychopaths, I thought this was exceedingly generous.

"Thank you," I said kindly and meant it. Despite how we felt about being spied on and desperately wanting to get home, it was apparent that there was much we could learn here, and we needed to stay a few days to maximize our knowledge.

Ashton escorted us to a small white two-storey cottage with a black slate roof, red door, and window boxes filled with flowers. It looked like something out of the Swiss countryside, lush green pastures visible from the windows, just no snow-capped peaks in the distance. Inside we could see a neat, well-equipped kitchen, comfortable living room, and the main bed-room containing a four-poster bed, the floral bed-spread currently crumpled, suggesting that we wouldn't be alone. He escorted us upstairs and ges-tured us toward a small room with two single beds, currently unmade, but opened a wooden chest with clean sheets and bedding at the foot. There was a small modern bathroom on the other side of the landing.

"We use it for guests from Auckland," he said by way of explanation. "Some of our team travel each solstice. We have several properties serving as guest quarters. Do you need help to get set up?"

After we assured him we were fine, he left, still looking grim after Cam's detailed description of the farm.

As we finished making the beds and were contemplating taking a walk, our new roommates returned home, effectively putting an end to our explorations. My head still not entirely recovered, and my arms throbbing from the stitches and swelling, I wasn't disappointed at not traveling any farther.

Jorja and Bridget were here on assignment from Auckland, both originally from Australia. While they were pleasant enough, I couldn't get past the distinct feeling that we were being tested, and that everything we said was likely going to be recorded in a briefing paper somewhere. Cam's slightly chilled tone reflected that he felt the same. But he was polite, telling them about their mutual friend Illy on Orkney and the business model she had set up, bartering goods around the island.

"Have you seen Angus lately?" I butted in during one interlude. "He is a great friend. I accompanied him on his mission for a few years, you know."

The women looked at each other in astonishment, taken aback at my comment. That was interesting. Something was up. But they answered respectfully enough. Yes, they had seen Angus a few months ago when he had visited Clava. No, they had no idea where he was now but to send their regards. It was all a little too rehearsed, too polite. My spider-sense was tingling.

Invited to join them for dinner, we had no way of escaping without being rude. With nowhere else to go, and no food of our own, we smiled our thanks, disappearing into our room for a shower and a change of clothes before we ate.

Running the shower, my mouth fell open when I saw the steam rise and realized that it was hot and had some serious pressure. After years of drip-fed showers, barely lukewarm and limited to a few minutes, I was conflicted—in heaven at the idea of stepping into the cubicle and simultaneously angry that we hadn't been afforded the same luxuries. Beckoning to Cam to be quiet and strip off, we stepped into the shower together. Noise from the running water and extractor fan was sure to drown out any conversation.

"Feel like you are in the Stepford Wives?" Cam whispered as he nibbled my ear.

"Very much so," I replied as quietly as I could. "There is something odd going on here, and I am feeling very uncomfortable. Some of it has to do with Angus, that is for sure."

"It could be nothing," he breathed into my ear between kisses on my neck. "We are outsiders. It could just be that they are wary of strangers."

"But we aren't strangers," I countered. "They chose each of us to place on August."

"Yes, but they placed us on August," he continued as he ran his hands down to my waist. "They never thought we would end up here. Maybe it is just guilt— the houses, showers, technology. They have a lot more than we do. Maybe they just don't want us to be resentful."

I considered that, a little distracted. It was a fair point.

"That bruise is getting worse," Cam noted as the water ran down my stomach, and I flinched as he touched it. "Are you sure you are alright?"

I glanced at the deep purple stripe across my belly and nodded dismissively. "Come on. We had better wash up and get out. Jorja and Bridget will wonder where we are."

"Enjoying this shower is where we are."

Cam stretched his neck languorously and washed his hair and mine. Using the white face washers left out for guests, I gently wiped the dried blood from his chest wound. It was taking on a greenish tinge around the edges.

"We need to get that looked at," I noted, concerned. "It is looking infected."

Lifting my arms, I noticed a few cuts that also looked a little nasty. "I should probably get mine checked too."

Rinsing my hair, Cam whispered into my ear, "Here we are, in the best shower I have had in six *years*, and you want to talk about infections? Could you please stop being so bloody pragmatic and kiss me?"

We were late for dinner.

Entering the dining room, we followed their gestures toward the table. We sat down, embarrassed as they served us several courses of delicious Thai food on beautiful blue and white China plates with a fabulous sticky rice pudding with coconut for dessert.

"I haven't had coconut for so long!" I gushed, savoring every mouthful.

Cam and I felt very underdressed for the occasion, although Bridget and Jorja were wonderful company. They talked about life in Australia, their families, places they had been. Not mentioning their work here, though. A few years older than us, they were witty and intelligent, and as the wine flowed, I let my guard down and enjoyed myself.

We were a little surprised to find an automatic dishwasher but said nothing, chatting away as we loaded the dirty dishes and sat down to a cheese platter with a bottle of dessert wine. While we made cheese on Lewis, it was nothing like this, and we raved about the quality.

Finally excusing ourselves to go to bed, we smiled until we closed the door. Cam opened his mouth to speak, and I leaned in for a kiss. "Not yet," I whispered into his lips. "I don't feel safe."

He pulled back and looked at me, but leaned in for a further kiss, simultaneously taking off my top and dropping it on a chair. Leaning past him, I flicked off the light switch, plunging us into darkness. The lights from outside were blinding when compared to Lewis. At home, the only outside light was the glow of the night sky, filtered by the geodesic dome fabric, and the occasional lantern fueled from biogas or the biophotoreactors. Here, there were streetlights and full-powered electrical lights in the adjoining houses, glowing past curtains and blinds. Closing the curtains firmly, we undressed, pushed the twin beds as close together as we could, and jumped into bed. The mattresses didn't quite touch and being smaller, I kept falling down the gap, giggling.

"Do you feel like we are the poor cousins?" I whispered into his ear as he made room for me in his tiny single bed. I still could not get over the feeling of being watched.

"Very much so."

CHAPTER 17

THE PLEASANTRY CONTINUED OVER breakfast, and mid-bite of a fresh, flaky, buttery croissant with raspberry jam, I asked Bridget directly what role she played here.

"Communications," she answered without pausing.

"Communicating what?" I asked.

"Originally, it was my job to broadcast to the new communities. The Offshore communities. We didn't do it for the ISO one, the ones in Australia. Did you know there were some on the mainland? Anyway, for the Offshore communities, it was to give them a small update on how the world was faring. We knew people would worry, would want to know. That could affect relationship-building in their new society. It was all carefully structured to give enough information so that people knew they were safe, lucky to have been chosen, but without giving away too much, making them regret their decision. For the ISO ones, they knew. Most of those weren't set up until May or June. By then, the world was falling apart. Even we were mobilizing by late June after we had finished setting up the ISO sites. Now, my role is to assist the communities in contacting each other, forming relationships, and facilitate trade."

"Maybe you can answer a question of mine then," Cam said through a mouthful of pastry. "Frey and I were both posted to August, Ruapuke, I mean. Offshore One. We left in February. They posted my sister to Kiewa, and she told us they were installed in June."

"That's right," Bridget confirmed, looking slightly taken aback at Cam's knowledge. "Kiewa was one of the last."

"If you also left in June, why was it that the last broadcast we received was in December?"

"The last months were made from Auckland Island," she admitted. "It was all to promote cohesion. If we had told people only two or three months after they had arrived that the world was disintegrating, people were attacking each other, unable to access food, and starving, it wouldn't have helped the community become unified, work together. Everyone would be focused on those they left behind. It was better, well, we thought, for you all to focus on strengthening your new society, not worrying about the fate of the world."

After taking another delicious bite, the raspberry jam dripping on my plate, I could see the logic in that and said so.

"We tried. We really did. We knew that the best chance of survival was for the group to bond, interconnect, and work together. Pair up and start families. We knew that personalities, politics, would get in the way at some point. But we sought to ensure that religion and culture didn't."

Cam nodded. "I have to admit, religious and cultural differences were never an issue on August, Lewis either. The community accepted everyone as an equal. There were never disputes along those grounds."

"What happened in December?" I asked curiously. "That you stopped transmitting?"

Bridget paused, her cup halfway to her mouth, and laughed. "I forgot! We had been busy setting up on Auckland. Then one community discovered the portal on the summer solstice, and we were ecstatic, celebrating. People knew they weren't alone. This was what we had wanted all along. It would promote communications, sharing of skills and resources, trade. So, the day slipped past. We were hoping to keep you connected for at least a year. But then, when I forgot that one, we discussed it and realized that we couldn't try again. We had to let you go and see what you would all do."

Jorja had been sitting quietly, listening to Bridget, nodding agreement in parts.

"What about you, Jorja? What do you do?" Cam asked, finishing his coffee.

"I'm on the medical team."

"Ahh!" I rolled up my sleeves and displayed the nasty cross-hatching of scars that webbed my lower arms. "I suspect I might need some treatment. Cam too."

"What on earth happened to you?" Jorja asked, concern evident in her voice. She took my hand from across the table and tilted her head, trying to look at wounds in the shadowed room. "You look like you have been whipped!"

"Close." Taking a large gulp of coffee, we explained about the farm, the brothers, and their recreational activities.

"I had heard that people from here had gone missing when they were outside the geo," Bridget said in a hushed voice. "But cannibalism?"

"We saw it with our own eyes," I assured her. "Look at what they did to Cam."

Cam obligingly lifted his t-shirt, and I pushed his long fringe out of his eyes, displaying his war wounds. They both gasped.

"I noticed Cam's eyes yesterday," Jorja admitted. "But I didn't want to say anything. You hadn't mentioned it, so we assumed you didn't want to discuss it."

"It is all a little too fresh," I admitted. "But I think we need antibiotics. Some painkillers, too, if you have them."

"Freyja saved my life," Cam said quietly, dropping his t-shirt and raising the refilled steaming cup. "They trussed me up like a turkey. They wanted to make a piece of art from me, they said. This wound here," he pointed to his temple, "they made with a drill. Freyja stopped them."

As I blushed furiously, the women turned to me in astonishment.

"Did you know that ten people from Clava have gone missing the past two years?"

"Judging by the number of skeletons we saw, they had other sources too," I said dryly.

"We need to tell Ashton!" Jorja blurted, horrified. "He will need to know! Send a team."

"He already knows. We told him yesterday," I said. "We gave him directions. They can find the place and verify what we have said."

"Well," said Jorja, standing up. "If that is taken care of then, you two are coming to the clinic with me."

Standing, I picked up my plate as Cam finished his last bite of rhubarb and custard Danish.

"Don't worry about it," Bridget fussed. "I can clean up. Go to the clinic. Get treated."

Clinic was an understatement. It was small but likely the best-equipped hospital I had ever seen. Everything was pristinely clean, the space well-lit, white, and spacious. Machines sat quietly in alcoves built into the walls, opaque plastic covers over them. The facility was purpose-built. They had spared no expense in setting up this place. I looked around in amazement. I had seen nothing like it, either on any of the communities I had visited or in Melbourne.

Jorja didn't seem to notice our astonishment. "Who wants to go first?" she smiled at us.

"His wounds are far worse," I said, lifting my chin at Cam. "Mine are superficial and can wait."

Helping Cam out of his top, she sucked her breath in when she saw the wound up close as he lay on the bed, the bright light overhead illuminating the horrors beneath.

"They weren't mucking around," she muttered under her breath, poking at the wound in places. She glanced up at me. "Did you really stitch this up with no anesthetic?"

"We don't have any," I confessed. "No antibiotics or pain relief either. We ran out a few months ago."

Jorja nodded, only half hearing me as she worked her way down the wound. "When did you say this happened?"

I counted silently. "Nearly five days ago."

"Why didn't you say something yesterday?" she asked incredulously. "I would have helped."

"I didn't know you were a doctor yesterday," Cam pointed out logically, making her laugh.

"True enough, although this isn't my specialty. Did you want me to call an emergency physician? I mean, I have a generalist medical degree, and I can do stitches, but anything else, and you might need someone more specialized."

"It's fine. Happy for you to do it." Cam smiled.

"Well, in some places, this incision has cut through the muscle, so I am going to need to reopen it and place some dissolving stitches in first, then sutures at the skin level. Shame as you were just starting to heal too. But better to be on the safe side."

"How on earth did you do this without an anesthetic?" Jorja looked at me, the amazement clear on her face. "I am intrigued how you kept him still enough."

"Drunk." I shrugged. "We didn't have a lot of options. Sorry about my messy stitching. My stitches have always been for animals. They don't seem to mind as much."

As I held Cam's hand, Jorja injected him with morphine for the pain and a local anesthetic. We chatted away through the procedure, this time conducted in a sterile environment. It was a world apart from the dining table aboard the *Eurydice*, medicating with whisky. Checking Cam's head wound, she swabbed it with antiseptic but deemed my stitches adequate. As she finished with another tetanus booster and antibiotics, I felt a little proud as she turned to me, Cam's treatment complete.

She checked my head wound and, aside from a swab with antiseptic, left it alone. Prodding my stomach, I could see the concern in her eyes. After much nagging from them both, I relented, agreeing to have an ultrasound. Fortunately, the impact of the shovel handle missed most of my internal organs. Although there was some internal bleeding, the verdict was that surgery wasn't required. Relief washed over Cam's face.

As I lay with my arms underside facing up on the crisp white sheet, a stranger scrutinizing each individual cut, I realized how much of a mess my arms were. It embarrassed me suddenly, studying the lattice of cuts and tears, the patchwork of uneven red blotches and slashes.

"How on earth did you do that?" Jorja asked, confused.

Realizing that it looked very much like a haphazard suicide attempt with a razor blade, I explained they tied me with my hands behind my back and left me in a dark shed. In a rush to free myself before they returned, I had tried to cut my bonds hurriedly, not paying any attention to what I was doing to myself.

"She escaped, and she saved me," said Cam, laying a hand on my shoulder. "Those wounds saved both of our lives."

Jorja nodded and injected a local anesthetic. She started deftly swabbing my right arm as pride from Cam's words surged through me.

"That one is worse," I admitted. "I am right-handed and struggled to stitch with my left hand. That one was also on top of the other when they were tied behind my back, so it copped the worst of it."

"I think we need a plastics consult," she said, not looking up. "I am a little out of my depth here. We have a plastic surgeon on Auckland. I can call him."

"No," I countered softly, making her head jerk upright.

"Sorry. What did you just say?" Jorja asked incredulously, looking into my eyes.

"I don't want a plastics consult," I responded quietly but firmly.

"Why not?" she asked, stunned. "Your arms are a mess. I can stitch them okay, but only a plastic surgeon can minimize the scarring, check for nerve and ligament damage. It is only a few weeks until the solstice. You could spend them here, and we can radio ahead and ask him to travel."

"Thank you, but no. I want to get home to our daughter."

"We could send someone to get her, then she could be with you," Jorja said, without looking up. "Your son too," she said, glancing at Cam.

I felt rather than saw him freeze.

"Jorja, you have been so kind, truly," I said in the most sincere tone I could manage. "I appreciate everything you have done for us. I know my arms are a mess, and I am aware that I will be scarred for life. But, every time I see them, I will see how close I came to losing everything: Cam, my children, my own life. I know it sounds strange, but maybe it will make me more grateful for what I have."

"Are you sure you don't want them fixed, honey?" Cam asked, with so much tenderness in his eyes that I knew, in that moment, no matter what else we faced, we would face it together. "I can get the kids—bring them back here."

"No. I am okay. Let's just clean them up and stitch them."

Jorja assented, and Cam didn't take his eyes off my face during the entire procedure. He didn't need to say it. I knew he didn't see them when he looked at me. I knew without a doubt, no matter what had happened over the past four years, we were together now.

Sent on our way with bandaged arms and chest, we went for a slow walk, desperate for some fresh air after the confines of the clinic, both of us light-headed and somewhat nauseous from anesthesia and morphine.

"I never mentioned Louis, did I?" Cam said under his breath. "Or am I being overly suspicious?"

"You did not. Perhaps Angus did? Didn't Bridget and Jorja say that he had been here relatively recently?"

"That is true. But why would he discuss Louis, of all people? I wouldn't think he even knew Louis's name."

"He knows. I mentioned it."

"You?"

Sighing, I knew I needed to tell him. "That night, after the town meeting, where we told everyone about the lists? Well, I held it together for the meeting ... but behind closed doors was another matter."

"Oh, honey, I never meant to rub your nose in my happiness. Laetitia was distraught when you returned. She needed people to see us together. To tell the truth, I never even thought of how it would affect you. It had only been the night before that I learned you weren't with Angus, that I had been lied to. We had been apart for two years, and much of that I spent believing that you had moved on with him."

"I watched you with her, gazing at your tiny baby with so much love. For the first time in my life, I couldn't see the path forward," I confessed haltingly, the darkness of that time threatening to engulf me.

"I know how that feels, honey. When you disappeared, it hurt to breathe. I couldn't put one foot in front of the other. So, what did you do?"

"Got absolutely shit-faced drunk!" I snorted. "Bitched about you and her. Cried about Louis. But then … Angus tried to kiss me."

"He what!"

"It's okay. Nothing happened. I told him I couldn't, not then."

"Not then, or not ever?" Cam asked suspiciously.

"To be honest, I don't recall. I was steaming drunk. But my recollection is not *now*."

"The implication being that he was in with a chance, at some point?"

"Maybe. I really don't remember. In a moment of clarity, I would have told him no. I had no feelings for Angus. But drunk, distressed? I may have inadvertently led him on."

"Well, that possibly explains why he hates me so much. Now that we have a child together."

"I'm so sorry, Cam. I never meant to drag Louis into this."

"You didn't. Louis is fine at home. You did nothing wrong. But what is the real reason you didn't want to see a plastic surgeon? Not that I mind," he hurried to add. "It is entirely your choice. I will always love you, just as you are. I don't care about a few marks."

"I know that, and I can't tell you how much that means to me. It is two things. The first is what I said to Jorja. We came so close to losing our lives the other day and everything that means. I have so much to lose: you, Katrin, Louis, even your sister and Di. I have come to love them all like family, and we so very nearly lost all of that. Left our children without parents."

"But do you want a permanent reminder? Of that place?"

I thought about that for a moment. The images of death, blood, and bone were all too fresh, along with the vats of congealed blood, rendered fat, and aged meat ready for stewing.

"The thing is, to me, it isn't a reminder of the horrors, those poor people. I will never forget what we saw there. Time won't erase those memories—those poor people who fell victim to them. Every time I hold our children, I will thank my lucky stars that it wasn't them. But this isn't about that. This is a reminder. We *survived*."

"I get that. But do you need a physical reminder?"

"I think I do. For many years, I placed importance on the wrong things. Took for granted what I had. In that place," I shivered, "I came so close to losing everything that matters to me."

Acknowledging my words, but I could tell, not really agreeing, Cam asked, "You said there was a second thing?"

Sighing, I sat under an enormous tree, Cam settling beside me with our backs to the trunk.

"A close friend of my parents was a plastic surgeon, an expensive one too. He had consulting rooms in Toorak and only operated on the rich and famous. Arrogant, opinionated fuckwit, I realize now, but at the time, he was someone we saw a lot. Once, when I was about fifteen, and Katrin was thirteen, he came over for dinner with a group of other people. My parents would arrange a private caterer and a sommelier so they could entertain. They expected Kat and I to sit quietly and let the adults talk. Somewhere during the main course, he was making them all guess who had work done. People they knew. Famous people. A lot of wine had been consumed by this point. Then he made an off-the-cuff comment that if Kat ever wanted work done on her nose that he would look after her."

"Katrin's nose? I've seen photos of her. She looked exactly like you. Your nose is perfect."

"So was hers. She went bright red as everyone at the table scrutinized her. Mum and dad laughed and brushed him off, and the conversation moved on. But after that, I occasionally caught her looking at herself, really studying herself in the mirror. Critiquing herself. That comment, no matter how many times I told her he was a jerk and just trying to drum up business, really hurt her. She never forgot it. She was a kid, barely thirteen. She hadn't even grown into her face yet. But one thoughtless remark from an asshole made her question her self-worth for *years*. She never saw her own beauty. Her self-esteem plummeted, and she never recovered. I have often wondered if that single remark, at a time when she felt gangly, pimply, and ugly, led to her experimenting with drugs. That started soon after. Only it took me years to connect the dots."

Cam's arm came around me as the recollections of that night, finding her unconscious in the bathroom, returned to haunt me, Katrin's body lying there, lifeless, never to recover.

"Do you have a thing against plastic surgeons?" he asked, concerned.

"Not exactly. Not if it was a burn or an accident. Reconstructive stuff. I totally get that. But I can't help but think the pure vanity aspect of cosmetic surgery summed up everything wrong in the old world. You didn't like your nose? Get a nose job. Flat-chested? Get a boob job. Your life will be better. You will be more attractive to men. Feeling fat? Get liposuction."

Cam mused, "I never knew anyone who had purely cosmetic surgery. Reconstructive, yes. I had a friend at uni who had cancer and lost both breasts. She had them reconstructed, but it wasn't cosmetic. Also, I suspect it is different for men."

"Oh, not where I grew up," I assured him. "Men didn't speak about it as openly, but they did it too. You should have heard the stories on a Saturday night at the yacht club."

"Really?"

"Oh, absolutely. Men aren't immune to vanity. Nose jobs, lipo, hair transplants, even making certain parts of their anatomy bigger."

"Seriously? That is a thing? But even so, I don't see why..."

Exhaling, I tried again. "Cam, I have tried really hard to move away from everything that I *was*. Everything I was raised to value and expect. Please. Don't fight me on this."

My world went dark momentarily as he pulled my face into his chest, and I realized my eyes were wet.

Breathing in his clean, masculine scent, I barely heard his words. "You are nothing like them, Frey, because you chose not to be. You are truly one of a kind."

CHAPTER 18

ASHTON GREETED US OUTSIDE as we approached the main office complex. A three-storey white box-shaped building with clean windows all around, it wouldn't have been out of place in any city.

"Are you okay?" I asked kindly.

"Yes, yes. Fine." His tone was friendly enough, but it was evident that he wasn't.

"Did you send a team to the farm?" I guessed, and the look on his face, a mixture of relief and disgust, answered.

"I was skeptical of your comments yesterday, although I couldn't see why on earth you would make it up. We sent a team at first light, and…" He trailed off.

"It is quite horrific, isn't it," Cam noted, a note of calm underpinning his words.

"Horrific doesn't cover it," said Ashton bluntly. "I had an update, just as you were arriving. Live feed. The teams have discovered pits filled with bones. We haven't been able to examine them yet. That will need to wait until we get some forensic equipment out there, but on preliminary examination, it appears that some are well over a decade old."

"*A decade*?" Cam and I said in unison, staring at each other, shocked.

Ashton just nodded, clearly still shaken.

"I have to ask, if your people went missing, why didn't you just use the satellites?" I questioned, testing the information Derek had given us the previous day.

Pulling himself from his maudlin state temporarily, he responded, "We have at various points. But satellites are in orbit, so it takes time to reposition them. We watched this area for months but saw nothing. Our primary purpose is to watch over the other communities, keep them safe. We only have a few satellites, so when we saw nothing, we felt that wasn't what we should use our resources for. It had been years between people going missing. They could have just been accidents."

"You didn't go looking for them?" I asked curiously.

"We are scientists and engineers. We didn't think to bring military personnel or police with us. We just didn't feel equipped."

"But ten people?"

He looked surprised that we knew that. "Over the course of the six years we have been here, we have lost ten people, in small groups of two or three. Scientists mainly, assessing the situation outside, tracking our potential for resettlement. Honestly, we thought the first group or two had become infected and just hadn't made it back before it rained. We all knew the risks. After the third group didn't return... that was when we got suspicious. I lived here by then. It was a beautiful fine day with no rain at all. That was when we realized that it likely wasn't the protozoa. So, we tasked the satellite and watched. But saw nothing. Months passed. We prohibited everyone from leaving the protection of the geo and have had no problems since."

"But Illyria left," Cam noted quietly.

"That was her choice," Ashton confirmed. "She wanted to return to her roots, so we wished her well. She had a radio with her, checked in at various points along the way. We knew she was safe."

"Angus visited here too," I pointed out. "He had no issues getting here or away."

"Also true," Ashton acknowledged. "We suspected an animal of some kind. It was only this morning that we learned the truth."

As we approached the double glassed front doors, Ashton switched to official mode and gave us a detailed tour of the office, introducing us to various people, all of whom seemed genuinely pleased to meet us. With large meeting rooms with projector screens, computers, and offices, it looked very much like a corporate office, a typical workplace.

Everyone looked busy but happy. There were lots of conversations going on, laughter and cheerful chatter—people who knew each other and enjoyed working together.

Ashton escorted us through the medical clinic we had visited that morning, pointing out all the equipment and machinery. Rooms of MRI, CT scanners, x-ray machines, all covered, linked up to computers. A walk-in fridge with enormous glass doors and shelves were covered in medications. It was a world away from the basic medical clinic we had on Lewis.

"Sorcha would fit right in here," Cam murmured to me as Ashton greeted Jorja warmly and introduced us to two of the technicians, Dale and Kalyan.

I nodded my reply, not wanting to seem overly enthusiastic.

Entering the veterinary clinic, my eyes popped when I saw the array of world-class equipment. *If only I could work in a place like this! How much more efficient could I be?* Eyeing off the glass cupboards filled with equipment, vials, and manuals, I thought every diagnostic tool ever invented was here: ultrasound machines, 3D printers, and ground-breaking technology, the likes of which I had seen only in industry journals. This was better equipped than any high-class veterinary clinic I had ever visited in Melbourne. My parents, being well connected, had ensured that I had done my placements at elite clinics, pulling strings with their friends and acquaintances. But this... I was speechless.

Ashton continued talking as we walked through, pointing out items of interest. Itching to open all the cupboards and drawers, I forced myself to pay attention to what he was saying. Something about prosthetics and 3D printing. Our surgery capabilities were far more rudimentary on Lewis, August too. We couldn't afford to waste time rehabilitating most creatures, so if they were injured, they were usually euthanized and used for cooking. I had never told Cam; he would be most upset. It was the principal reason I had asked him to allow Fred the goat to be rehabilitated at our house, knowing he would never deny me anything that I asked. Heidi would have slaughtered him otherwise, used him for a meal, and had after I left.

Shown outside to an enclosed golf buggy, Ashton escorted us around the outer areas of the community, pointing out places of interest, a chain of linked but separate scientific laboratories, an enormous library, shops where residents could get food and supplies, even a cinema.

Cam's eyes popped as we approached the enormous vegetable gardens and orchards, all in temperature-controlled, purpose-built greenhouses set on timers. Some were the size of warehouses. I could tell from the look of ecstasy on his face that he was dying to touch the plants, imbed his fingers in the soil. I had to turn away so he wouldn't see me grinning. This was his idea of heaven. I would never see him if we lived here.

The school was a remarkable place and a world away from the tiny, repurposed house where Lae had taught in Garynahine. It looked much like the schools we had attended ourselves, with interactive whiteboards, neat desks, and colorful displays on all the walls. *Well, that I attended*, I corrected. Cam had never told me about his schools, state schools, but surely they couldn't have been so different. The school on Garynahine was rustic. There, the children learned from the teacher and what books we had. Here they seemed to have access to everything. Large windows flooded the room with natural light, and the children seemed engrossed in their work.

"What do you think?" I asked as Ashton went to ask the teacher something.

"I think we are neglecting our children's education," he replied. "Look at those bookshelves!"

He was right. Now that we lived out of the main village, we needed to fit education for our children around our work in the limited daylight hours. Many evenings Sam and Louis had nodded off during their lessons. *Maybe they would have a better life here*, I considered. *Other children to socialize with, and we could work, knowing that they were safe.*

"They seem happy," I admitted, scanning the room of silent children reading.

Ashton returned at that point, effectively ending the conversation.

"Let's have some lunch, shall we?" he suggested as we climbed back into the buggy. I was still full from the croissants for breakfast, combined with the wooziness of the anesthetic, but didn't object. We might learn something useful, and then we could be on our way home.

"Sushi?" I gasped when confronted with an enormous platter in the private dining room back at head office.

"Oh, do you not like sushi?" Ashton exclaimed. "I can arr..."

"No. I *love* sushi," I gushed. "I just haven't had it..." *For nearly seven years* was the part I didn't finish as I placed the first piece of salmon nigiri in my mouth. Closing my eyes as I savored the flavors of fresh wasabi and salmon, washed down with sake, I was in heaven.

Cam, who had been to Japan several times, also looked supremely happy as he ate, beaming across at me. The food here was phenomenal, fresh, diverse, and the best part was that I didn't need to make it.

After we ate far more than we should, Ashton showed us to a meeting room, coffee and fresh cakes arriving within minutes. They were delicious. I was seriously considering staying here for the food alone. The look of bliss on Cam's face as he bit into a chocolate brownie proved he was also enjoying the culinary delights. Keeping my face neutral, I thought of all the times he had saved his dessert for me, telling me he didn't have a sweet tooth.

"Would you consider joining us?" Ashton asked without preamble. "Our role here is to help all the communities, to ensure the survival of humanity. For now, that is within our geodesic domes, but later, it is about resettling the planet. We need to keep the skill levels up, so that is possible. Freyja, you have exceptional veterinary skills and could help many of the communities breed livestock and deal with unexpected issues. You have proven to be tenacious, resilient, and a leader in times of adversity. You would be a genuine asset here. Cam, you have proven to be our best specialist in food diversity and security. Some communities have struggled to produce enough nutritious food, especially during winters. Your greenhouses and planning schedules have proven to be first-class and tailored to the local conditions. Across all the communities you have visited, you have trained and mentored others. Both of you are an asset to the program and could help many people."

"We..." Cam started, but Ashton cut him off rapidly.

"Your children too and your family. From what I hear, your sister saved Angus's life and is an outstanding physician. They would all be most welcome here. We have excellent schools for the children. We can give them opportunities. Just let us know what you need, and we will make it happen."

Cam and I looked at each other, not speaking. Ashton had pinged the one thing that would make any parent consider a move, offering better opportunities for their children. Cam looked at me expectantly. *Is this what I want?* I knew he would follow me.

The ease of life here was partly what made it so attractive: vehicles, dishwashers, fantastic food. I would even move just for the daily hot showers. It was so much like home. As I reached for a miniature raspberry cheesecake, a twinge on one of the new stitches on my right forearm made me look down at the white bandages I now wore. Looking across the table at Ashton, I smiled as charmingly as I could.

"We very much appreciate the offer..." I started before he cut me off.

"Take some time. Discuss it. Let us know what we can do."

"Do you want to talk about it?" Cam whispered as we ambled out of town.

"Not really," I replied. I was horribly conflicted. I knew he would let me decide for us all. I struggled with washing dishes, cleaning bathrooms, and performing menial tasks. Not that I didn't recognize them as necessary—I did. But I would just much rather be doing something else. Having dishwashers, flushing toilets, and a catering team would make life easy. *They said our family could come. Sorcha would undoubtedly like it here,* I thought. It surprised me she hadn't been offered a place here to begin with. Strong, forthright, and brilliant, she would have slotted in here seamlessly. But she had asthma, I remember Cam telling me once. I had never seen her have an asthma attack, struggle to breathe, but I knew from Di that she still had them. I had never seen any sign that Sorcha wasn't an iron giant. But maybe that was why she ended up in Kiewa and not here.

We walked in silence, both of us considering the possibilities.

Two of Jorja's colleagues, Magali, an oncologist, and Nasir, a pediatrician, joined us for dinner and again proved to be delightful company. Magali was friendly, chatty, and entertaining. Nasir was quiet and reserved, happy to let Magali speak for them both. Delectable pasta and several bottles of wine later, I never wanted to leave. Sneaking a look at Cam, I watched him laugh uproariously at a joke Magali told.

She was hilarious with her strong French accent, telling stories of her misunderstanding English expressions and mispronunciations. She had just finished telling a story of calling out to her friend's children to watch out for the cycle path, and wondering why everyone started screaming, turning to stare at the crazy French lady warning them about someone with a knife.

Cam was trying to get her to repeat indigenous Australian place names like Wangaratta and Mooloolaba, making us all laugh as she tried to wrap her tongue around them.

Maybe... just maybe life here could be an excellent choice?

As the small hours of the morning came upon us, Nasir and Magali made their excuses and left. Jorja and Bridget insisted we leave the cleanup for the morning.

"I'm exhausted." Jorja yawned. "Do you need some pain relief to sleep?"

The liberal amounts of wine had numbed the pain nicely, but I smiled and reached out my Michelin man arms, accepting the small glass bottle of codeine pills.

They would come in handy later. Heartily wishing them both goodnight, we escaped upstairs to our room.

"Are you in pain?" Cam asked, his concern bubbling over as we closed the door.

"Not at all." I giggled in his ear, though my arms were aching. "I just thought we could stash them."

Waking early, I could hear the dishes being clattered in the kitchen. Leaving Cam to sleep, I pulled on my jeans and top and tiptoed out barefoot, finding Bridget in the kitchen, cleaning up.

"Wow!" I said, surveying the carnage. "Big night."

"It was an amazing night!" she gushed. "We love having you guys here. I wish you would stay."

"Part of me wants to," I admitted. "But we have children, family on Lewis. We can't abandon them."

Bridget nodded in understanding. "How are your arms?"

They were throbbing terribly this morning, the aftermath of being poked with needles and stitched properly, the anesthetic and morphine now having worn off.

"I'm fine," I said, clearly not convincingly but began scraping plates to avoid further questioning.

"Bridget, can I ask a favor?" I asked as I made my fourth trip back to the dining room to collect glasses and plates.

"Sure. We are all friends here."

"I don't suppose you have access to maple syrup?"

She smiled. "How much do you want?"

CHAPTER 19

EACH DAY IT FELT like someone wanted to meet with us, show us something, so it took us some days before we finally traveled to the Clava Cairns, armed with a packed lunch, courtesy of Bridget. En route, Cam and I reviewed what we knew: mostly knowledge he had gained from Kevin and I a little from Angus. We knew this site linked to the Auckland Islands, south of New Zealand, the second community settled by the science teams and likely as highly resourced as this one. They would have a life of comparative ease, especially when compared to August and Lewis.

Cam had been to this site several times, but many years ago. "You are going to love it," he promised.

"Wow!" I enthused as we approached. The site held a calm, magnetic pull. Tall ancient trees encircled the area with hand-crafted stone walls forming a boundary. From the old wooden entrance gate, open on its hinges, we could see the line of three ring-type chamber tombs, with rounded bleached-gray stones stacked high around the outside. As we approached the first large chamber tomb, a heaped circular pile of rocks with a passageway up the center, I stopped to touch the cleaved stone within the stone circle that encircled the first chambered tomb.

"Wow!" I repeated as I did so, feeling that the word was woefully inadequate to describe the sense of tranquility, the overwhelming serenity about this place. But in the moment, I could not come up with more detailed adjectives.

We were alone and wandered through the site, peaceful and still. The magnificent fall trees scattered around the perimeter, dropping their final bronzed leaves. The golden colors formed a blanket over the ground, making delightful crunching sounds as we walked.

Cam chose a shaded grassy spot and spread out the blanket, unpacking the goodies Bridget had sent: fresh bread rolls, an array of cheese, fresh fruits, and yet more cake. Goodness, it was amazing we hadn't stacked on the kilos with all the pastries, cakes, and biscuits they had served us since we had arrived.

"Which other sites are like this?" I asked, lying back between bites, gazing through the tree canopy to the sky beyond the dome.

"Newgrange, to an extent. That is one tomb and far more ornate. It is enormous but has a similar design, a circular stone ring that you can walk into, with a circle of upright menhirs around it. These would have had roofs at some point. Newgrange is still enclosed. But I have always found Newgrange less tranquil than here. I know there are others in that same region in Ireland, but I haven't visited them. Then there is Temple Wood at Kilmartin Glen. That is smaller than this but the same basic design: two stone circles you can walk into. The more intact one has a stone circle inside the rocks, but it is much flatter. See how these still have distinct walls? Well, the one in Kilmartin is almost ground height. The rocks have been plundered. Makes it hard to work out what it looked like originally. That site wasn't settled. Angus thought because of lack of direct access to fresh water. He admitted it had a portal, though."

"What about the Orkney sites?" I asked, reaching for my second piece of carrot cake. After this, I really must stop eating. While I had been to Orkney on our rescue mission, I hadn't lingered to see archaeological sites.

"There are several within the community itself. There is a ring of standing stones at Stenness, much like Callanish, but without the chambered tomb. There is a prehistoric village at Skara Brae, but the portal is in a chambered tomb at Maes Howe. Illy took me to see them."

Not wanting to linger on the subject of the mysterious Illyria, I reluctantly packed up the remains of lunch so we could continue to explore. Cam, snaffling a last piece of cake, headed toward the center ring while I, turning under the trees, discovered a low, almost buried, simple stone circle in the ground.

Squatting to touch the ancient stones embedded in the earth, I called, "Where is the actual antipodal point?" Cam pointed toward the northernmost cairn.

"The one at the end. See how they run in a line, north-east to south-west, and the openings are faced south-east—the direction of the winter solstice light? I have never been here on the solstice, but apparently, the morning sun aligns with the passage illuminating the center on the winter solstice. It is the same as Newgrange. If they were burial sites, then the insides would be completely lit for a few minutes but only on the solstice. Makes sense now that we know what they are."

Slowly, we made our way through the ancient site, soaking in the history.

"Kevin called them temples, and I think he is right," Cam mumbled as I joined him at the middle cairn, not wanting to disturb the sense of overwhelming peacefulness. I understood. There was something mystical about this place. I could envision it shrouded in mist on the solstice. I longed to build a house here and stay forever in this incredible place.

Nearing the northernmost cairn, we progressed slowly. Even though it was a few weeks until the winter solstice, we were apprehensive. Neither of us wanted to repeat our experiences. As Cam entered the passage, I tensed behind him, unsure what I would do if that roaring vortex started unexpectedly. Grab him and try to pull him clear? Or jump after him, leaving our children behind? But he stepped into the circle, and it remained calm and serene, the magical feeling enveloping us as we entered.

"See?" Cam said teasingly as he planted a kiss on my cheek. "Nothing to fear." He turned to keep exploring the inside of the ring.

No, that won't do at all, I thought impulsively and thrust my hands behind his head, pulling his mouth to mine and holding him in place. His arms came around me and lifted me slightly to his height. Frogmarching me to the edge, he pushed my back against the inner ring of gray stones as he continued what I had started. Fueled by an external force, his hands untucked my t-shirt from my jeans, and despite the hard, gray rock gouging uncomfortably into my back, I let out a tiny moan as he lifted me, and I wrapped my legs around his waist. Smirking, he recognized the sound as one of encouragement and worked his way down my neck. With the expertise of a man who had done this many times, my bra was off and on the ground before I could blink.

"Your stitches," I breathed into his ear as he started on my breasts, already tingling with the attention. "You will burst your stitches."

In one deft move, he had flipped me, laying me gently in the center of the ring. I felt the blanket of leaves crunch as my now naked body reclined on them, gazing up into the sky. As his head dropped lower, past Cam's larger form, I could see the clouds drift across the blue sky beyond the dome, the sunlight filtered by the fabric. I felt surprisingly hazy, like those clouds, floating. The central ring was just wide enough for the two of us to lie down; it felt naughty, decadent, but oh so thrilling to make love in the middle of an ancient site, a place that was revered by generations of people, and the very real risk we could be seen at any moment.

"Aren't you afraid of being seen?" I purred in his ear.

"You used to love taking risks," he whispered back, nibbling on my earlobe. "Remember all those times we met in secret on August? In the greenhouse? The orchards? Behind the sheds? Even in the meeting hall late one night, if I recall correctly."

I didn't know what I felt, just warm and light-headed. Perhaps the morphine was still in my system. Excited—yes. Terrified of being seen—absolutely. But oh god, I wanted him, and that desire overrode everything else. As Cam kissed my thighs, my eyes closed, and my head rolled back with ecstasy, focusing solely on the sensation. I no longer cared who could see me, it surprised me to realize.

His hands were everywhere, stroking, kneading, but it was his tongue that made me tingle. Each time he brought me to the brink but stopped just before I could climax. Teasing, taunting. Finally, I could stand it no more. Using my knee, I flipped him deftly and sat astride him, facing the ancient stone wall.

"Make that little whimpering noise," I whispered breathlessly in his ear. "I do so love it when you do that."

"I ... don't ... whimper ..." he breathed as my hands dropped lower, stroking, caressing. So he wanted me and badly.

"Oh yes, you do," I advised as I ran my finger gently over his chest wound, now covered in a less than clean white dressing. It would likely need replacing after today's adventures. That could be difficult to explain. "Let me show you..."

Lying in the bed of leaves, now feeling heavy and boneless, trying not to drift off to sleep, I asked, "What's that?" gesturing feebly with my chin. I didn't have the energy to lift my arms.

"What?" He glanced in the direction I was motioning, barely awake himself.

"On that bottom stone, it has circles carved into it."

"The curbstone, you mean? They call those cup marks. The curbstones are those with the random spirals and double spirals engraved on them at Newgrange. It is thought that they were carved before

the site was built around them, not carved in situ."
Cam spoke slowly, dreamily. Much how I felt, still
pleasantly hazy.

Lying on my side, I stared at the pattern; it looked
so familiar. The pattern floated in and out of focus,
gently pulsating.

Cam curled up behind me, stroked my hair, gently
pulling out pieces of leaf and twig.

"They aren't random," I said finally, still
feeling dreamy.

"What do you mean?"

"That is a constellation," I pronounced. I was
reasonably confident. "And specifically, Carina. See
the nine holes? Carina means keel in Latin, like a
ship's keel."

Cam lifted himself onto one elbow to look more
closely. "I can see the cup marks, but I don't know what
I am looking at. I know nothing about constellations."

"My father was an amateur astronomer," I admitted,
rolling onto my back to look at the sky beyond. "He
taught Katrin and me about the stars, especially when
we were out sailing at night. What is interesting about
this one, though, is that it is a southern circumpolar
constellation."

"What is a circumpolar constellation?"

"There are seasonal constellations, the ones that
our ancestors depended on as indicators of changes
on Earth, but circumpolar constellations are the ones
that, although their positions change with time, they
seem to travel in a circle centered at the sky's pole. The
three southern circumpolar constellations are those
that are always visible from southern hemisphere
locations, rarely from the northern hemisphere."

That got his attention. "What you are saying is that those holes in the stone are marking a constellation usually only seen in the southern hemisphere?"

"I think so."

Realizing what that meant, we turned to look at each other. All these millennia, there had been a roadmap. If only we had known where to look.

CHAPTER 20

FINDING COHABITING WITH ANOTHER couple not entirely to our liking, we had taken to sharing long morning walks in the woods where we could be alone. Cam was quieter than usual this morning. Something was on his mind.

"What are you thinking?" I asked softly.

"Honestly, that life here could be good," he admitted, looking up at me from where we lay under a large oak tree.

"You don't have concerns?" I propped on my elbow, closing my eyes, enjoying the sunshine on my face.

"I do, but there are obvious benefits. Especially if Sorcha, Di, and the kids can all come. You don't think this is a potentially better place to raise children?"

"I do," I confessed. "The opportunities here, for all of us, are amazing. Though, with all the food, we will need to incorporate more exercise into our routine." Breakfast this morning had included pancakes with maple syrup, and I had barely been able to drag Cam away from the table. I had never been an enormous fan of pancakes, but even I had to admit that these had been delicious.

"Oh, if it is more exercise you want..." Cam neatly rolled me onto my back, coming up on top and using his weight to pin me down.

"*I* only had one pancake," I teased. "*You* had four. It is you that needs the exercise. Besides, we need to go. Ashton is expecting me."

"He can wait a little longer. You can tell him we were exercising."

"You mentioned that all the communities had satellite radio?" I broached the topic with Ashton, somewhat cautiously, later that morning. Cam had gone to a different room in the head building to advise on food security, crop diversity, and seasonal planting, leaving me to meet with Ashton alone.

He nodded. "Most now do, but not all. But that is certainly the plan—to have all communities able to contact us and each other. In case of an emergency, you know."

If only we had been able to radio ahead to Orkney to let them know about the raiders, I mused but then equally quickly realized that this would have resulted in a very different outcome for me personally and the existence of our daughter.

To cover my conflict, I asked, "Will you provide us with one then?"

"Of course!" He laughed. "We were just waiting to see who would transport it."

Cam and I had given no indication that we would stay, but with a pang at leaving this place, the easiness of it struck me anew.

"To be honest, we haven't decided," I admitted. We both recognized that we could start again here with no awful memories, his loss of Laetitia, questions over Katrin's parentage. Me, well, I could settle anywhere. I didn't have friends on Lewis as Cam did. They respected my skill here. I had been consulted on various issues. The idea of staying was appealing. Life was just simpler here, without many of the challenges we faced on Lewis.

"You know we would love to have you. Angus said you would be an asset to the team here."

I perked up at that. "He did? You were discussing me?" It came out blunter than I had intended, but he didn't appear at all perturbed.

"Oh, not exactly. But Angus mentioned you had left the crew and that he missed you. But equally, he recognized that there was no life aboard a yacht with a baby—especially when traveling across infected waters and with no way to protect her. But here, we have exceptional schools and care facilities where your children will be safe and very well educated. We can support you—all of you."

While that was true enough, and as a parent, I desperately wanted to know that my children were safe, it left me wondering exactly what Angus and Ashton had said about me. I had heard enough from Cam to know that there was a side to Angus that he had kept very well hidden.

Neatly dodging the question, I spent the next few hours learning about radios, which communities were connected, and the transmission protocols.

Ashton was intelligent and friendly, and as the day went on, I relaxed and enjoyed his company. Copious cups of tea and biscuits were provided. I learned a great deal about each of the communities, including those excelling and how they were helping each other. I felt quite optimistic about the project, the support that the communities were being provided, and the resources allocated to them.

A shadow darkened the doorway, and I looked up to see Cam smiling down at me. "Finished?" he asked.

"We are," Ashton beamed at him, then at me. "Same time tomorrow?" he looked at me expectantly.

"Absolutely."

Over dinner, Cam noted the accomplishments of the different communities.

"It is innovative stuff," Bridget gushed. "Considering the limitations we have, we have come such a long way in such a short period."

"You have," I admitted. "What I saw today impressed me."

"Me too," Cam said, beaming. "Many of the communities are doing amazingly well. The crop diversification is immense. I can't tell you how thrilled I am that so many species and varietals survived. I can't wait to share those resources between communities."

I smiled, knowing that this was Cam's area of interest, but honestly, I struggled to understand how one species of tomato differed from another. They all tasted the same to me. Not that I would ever tell Cam that.

"An interesting day." Jorja smiled. As a doctor, I was reasonably sure she was like me: she ate food and enjoyed the taste but didn't give too much thought to what it was.

"It really was." It was his tone that made me look over at him, a pensive look on his face.

"What?" I asked guardedly. I knew that look. He was stressing over something. But as soon as I had spoken, I regretted it.

"I asked the biology teams why there was life on Mousa."

"And?"

"They didn't know. They hadn't seen it before. So, they repositioned the satellite, and we looked. It is such a tiny dot from space. But when they zoomed in, I could see the broch. The houses..."

"Oh, Cam. I am so sorry." I was aware of the looks Jorja and Bridget were giving us but frankly didn't care.

"Don't be. It thrilled the team. To know that somewhere outside the communities, there was life. The noise in the room hurt my ears. They were all so excited. They are planning an expedition up there to find out why. Why is there still life on Mousa when there isn't anywhere else?"

"Do they have a theory?"

"Many. But no facts."

"What do you mean, life on Mousa? Is Mousa a place?" Bridget asked cautiously, recognizing a backstory here, but diplomatically not wanting to pry into a sensitive matter.

"It is," I said with as much lightness as I could muster. "A tiny island just off the coast of the Shetland Islands. We visited there once. It isn't under a dome, a geo, I mean. But there are grass and shrubs and small trees, all still alive. We couldn't work out why."

Cam flashed me a look of gratitude. Neither of us wanted to share that particular story, but I had forgotten about the greenery on Mousa until now. We had spent less than a few hours there all up, and I was focused on other matters. But Cam... it had been on his mind, unable to let it go. My heart lurched as I wondered what else he was stressing about from that time. But he did not show it as the conversation moved to Bridget's day and her discussions with the Falklands, which was engaged in a unique breeding project for penguins.

"Do they have puffins?" Cam asked out of the blue.

Bridget blinked at the random question but recovered her composure quickly. "No... I don't think so. Why?"

"I've never seen puffins in the wild but always wanted to. I was just wondering if they had survived. As a child, I loved their comical clown-like beaks and big orange feet."

"I'm fairly sure they are a northern Atlantic bird," I added. "Northern Scotland, Iceland, that region. I did a research project on them when I was studying for my degree. I had aspirations of being a zoo vet at one point. Do you want me to ask tomorrow?"

"No, that's okay. I was just wondering."

Preparing for bed, I gazed wistfully out the window, across the shadowed street glowing with lights.

"Goodness, it is getting dark early. I feel like I am losing track of time."

"I was too, until today. It is nearly Christmas. Can you believe it! Where did that time go?"

"What is the date?" I asked, suddenly panicked.

"13 December. I saw it on the screen today when we were talking to the community in Toulouse."

"No!" I gasped. "We can't have been here that long! It can't possibly be."

"Sorry, honey, it is. Did you forget something?"

"It was her half-birthday. Katrin. She was six months old on 28 November. How could I possibly have missed it!"

Sheer horror must have been plastered on my face as Cam was at my side in a shot, his comforting arms around me.

"It's okay, honey. We will be home in a few days. She won't know."

"Katrin wasn't quite five months when I left," I whispered. "I promised her I would be back for her half-birthday. Oh god, I am such an awful parent. I need to get back to her, Cam. Now. I need to leave now." I started casting my eyes around the room, searching for the small daypack I had brought with my single change of clothes.

"That was exactly how I felt when I traveled back to Australia to find Sorcha," Cam admitted, his arms pulling me in and turning me to face him. "Louis was just four months old when I left and seven when I returned. I will never get that time back."

"I promised. I can't believe that I broke my promise!"

"It is late. Sleep now. Tomorrow. We will leave first thing tomorrow."

CHAPTER 21

RISING EARLY, PACKING OUR few belongings, and preparing a quick breakfast, we contemplated leaving a note explaining our departure. Feeling that was a little inadequate, we were most relieved when our housemates emerged, sleepy and rubbing barely awake eyes as we finished our toast and coffee. We broke our news gently, expecting accepting smiles. Instead, they astonished us when Jorja and Bridget were utterly shocked at our sudden announcement, appearing both concerned and distressed. Hugging them goodbye, the scene was far more emotional than we had expected.

"But we won't see you again," Bridget wailed. "We are returning to Auckland in a few days. Can't you stay just a little longer?"

"We really can't stay. We want to get home to the kids before Christmas. We can talk. We have the radio," I said in explanation.

"But isn't the same! Who will laugh at my awful jokes now?" Bridget exclaimed, half laughing, half crying.

Recognizing that the Clava residents had been most gracious in accommodating and welcoming us, we knew we couldn't just leave. After finally escaping the house, we attempted to find Ashton and thank him for his hospitality. Both of us knew that a permanent move here could be a good one. It felt like every person we had met here crossed our path to say farewell and ask us when we were returning. Kind proposals abounded; they offered us a chaperone, a faster ship, basically anything we wanted. Without giving a definitive answer, but just saying we wanted to get back to our family, we departed a little before midday.

It wasn't until two days later, back on the yacht, sailing around the northern coastline as fast as we dared and talking about our experiences, that we remembered some of our initial regrets.

"It is the strangest thing," I said to Cam. "I had doubts initially, but those faded the more time we spent there. I saw the benefits in what they were doing, the positives. But now that we have left, that sense that something wasn't quite right has returned."

Despite our doubts, we both knew that our hearts were in Lewis, and as we rode our new bikes on the last leg, we paused atop the hill that overlooked our home. We gazed over our tiny valley, our own home nestled at the end, tucked in among the rolling green hills on three sides. Sorcha and Di's home nearby glistened in the daylight, but now there were two new houses—both nearly half a kilometer away from our own, one almost complete, the other in planning stages. We could see pegs marking the boundaries and some stumps showing the proposed floorplan. A large shed glistened in the sunset, next to the new house and a newly doubled greenhouse.

"Houses?" Cam looked at me in surprise. "Who are they for?"

"Well, Fraser, Isla, and the girls live in the closest one." I beamed. "The shed is the new vet clinic. Isla and I decided before I left that we should share the load with all the kids, and it is easier if people come to us. The community agreed, so a clinic was built here. We will still need to travel to see larger livestock, but they can bring smaller animals to us for surgeries and such."

"A clinic? Fraser?" Cam babbled.

"That was the help we roped in before I left when Di was unwell. I moved in with Sorcha, and they stayed at our house until their home was built. Fraser now works in our greenhouse with you. The builders have expanded it so we can still provide food for others, and you no longer need to travel to Garynahine as often. Much of the stock and one greenhouse was transplanted here and joined to expand yours. Di has taken over the children's education, all six of them, plus the baby when they come. They still need Sorcha at the medical center. I hope you don't mind. It was a risk, I know."

"Mind? Why would I mind?"

"Well, because of me and Kat," I responded cautiously. "You moved away to avoid town gossip, and now I have invited people to live here, in your place. Without consulting you."

"Moving away from Fraser and Isla, keeping this from them was one of the poorer decisions I have made," he confessed. "The timing wasn't great, but now I don't care if they know how much I adore you both. Who is the other house for?"

"Ahh, that is a surprise."

"Kicking me out already?" he asked, a mischievous twinkle in his eye.

"Only if you fart in bed," I teased.

"You realize we will need a bigger bed?" Cam said as we surveyed the stillness below. "Both of them will probably want to sleep with us for at least a few weeks."

Smiling, I admitted, "Is it wrong to confess that I have very much enjoyed having you all to myself? But it is time to come home. I have missed them both terribly."

"You know, this will be the first Christmas we get to spend together," Cam said longingly, looking over at me as he prepared to descend the hill.

He was right. On our first Christmas together, Heidi had poisoned him and left him hospitalized. By the second, I was gone. Part of me was fearful that something would spoil this one as well.

"Nothing will stop us this year. I promise," Cam vowed, leaning over and kissing me gently.

Before I could respond, we heard shouts in the valley below.

Sorcha and Di, with Sam and Louis tagging along behind, were now racing up as fast as they could. Louis was running as fast as his little legs could manage. Katrin was bouncing along in a sling on Sorcha's back, Sorcha's long red hair flying behind her and flapping in Kat's face.

Dropping our bags and bikes, we ran down the hill, struggling to pull up before we plowed headfirst into our family, knocking them flying. Hugging first the children, then Sorcha and Di, it was impossible to distinguish a single voice amid the happy, excited chatter of reunion.

216

"Thank you *so* much for watching the kids," I said excitedly as I hugged Di.

Di peeked around me to where Cam was greeting his sister. "Does that mean...?" Di asked me eagerly, not wanting to be overheard.

"It does. Mission successful." I couldn't keep the joy from my face, nor my voice. I was ecstatic to be home with my family and the man I loved. Di squealed, hugging me tightly. Finally able to extricate myself, I turned toward Cam in time to hear, "I am so thrilled for you both!" Cam was hugging Sorcha hard. Goodness, they looked alike. Despite the different coloring, they were so similar, their height, their features. They were so clearly family.

Reaching Sorcha in two strides, I also hugged her. "Thank you," I whispered, feeling choked. "You have reunited my family. I can't tell you what it means to me."

"Thank *you*," she said breathlessly, looking between us both. "For finding me. You both had a hand in that. For introducing me to Di, for bringing me here, and now ... this ... gift." She gestured toward Di's stomach. "Thank you. With all of my heart. Thank you."

"It is my absolute pleasure. You saved my life. It seems right that I can give you one. But you know, nothing says thank you quite like not telling embarrassing stories about your little brother in public!" Cam said pointedly.

Sorcha laughed. "I'll try, but no promises!"

Scooping Louis up into his arms, Cam told him, "There is going to be another baby. What do you think about that?"

"Ugh," he said, wrinkling his nose with disgust. "Babies smell and they cry too." Then, thinking about it for a moment, he asked cautiously, "Can it be a boy this time?"

"Maybe, son. Maybe."

CHAPTER 22

FRASER, ISLA, AND THEIR three girls came to greet us as we arrived in the clearing between the houses. Cam expressed his delight at learning that they now lived here. They said nothing, but I saw them watching covertly as he touched me gently, helping me with the bags.

Pregnancy did not agree with Di. Initially bed-ridden for weeks, she was finally up and mobile but regularly overcome with waves of nausea, forcing her to seek a quiet corner in which to sit. She was per-petually exhausted and had lost a lot of weight since I had left, which I wasn't entirely convinced was due to her pregnancy.

Watching her furtively as she helped Cam in the greenhouse a few days later, I was suspicious and concerned.

"I'm so sorry. I feel like I am letting you down," I heard Di say, sounding weary.

"Do you want to go home?" Cam asked kindly. "I can do this. Really."

"No," she responded through gritted teeth. "I want to be useful. Give me something to do standing up. Bending over makes it worse."

"How about you weed the tomatoes over there?" He gestured with a toss of his head to an overgrown patch of seedlings. "You could stake them if you like. Then finish choosing the vegetables for Christmas. We likely won't have time tomorrow with the Christmas Eve celebrations in Garynahine."

I stood watching as Di smiled gratefully and moved to the waist-height bed Cam had indicated. Watching her move, she looked more uncomfortable than she should. She wasn't even that far gone, barely twelve weeks. Not that I was an expert on pregnancy. The total of my expertise was my one pregnancy, and at the time, I hadn't focused on my health. But I hadn't struggled the way Di was. I was barely showing at twelve weeks, just tired. Even though my medical training was on animals, not humans, I was concerned and made a mental note to speak with Sorcha when I had the chance. When animals struggled in pregnancy, it was usually an indicator that there was something wrong. The problem was, in the few days we had been home, I rarely saw Sorcha alone. There was always Cam, children, or Di around, and I didn't want to alarm any of them unnecessarily.

Picking up the wilted lettuce leaves to take to the chickens, I asked Di gently as she passed me, "Are you sure you are okay?"

"Quite sure," she responded unenthusiastically, without turning to look at me. "I just didn't realize that growing a person would be so exhausting. I hear they are worth it, though."

"Oh, they are. They most certainly are." I smiled at her as I left.

The entire community was thrilled about our return, and on Christmas Eve, they called a town meeting to hear what we had learned, followed by a Christmas celebration. Di, feeling unwell, had stayed behind with the children. But Fraser, Isla, Sorcha, and Cam accompanied me. I did most of the talking, explaining about the communities, radios, and satellite surveillance. A hushed silence fell over the room as we raised this. It was Josh who finally asked, "Did they see them come? Last year?"

"They did," Cam replied, with a decided edge to his voice. "You can imagine how I felt learning that."

Silence filled the space.

"What about at the beginning? The residents here. Did they see that?"

It was Mike, the horse handler. I could see the tortured look. Cam had been right about Angus nearly tearing the community apart.

"To be honest, I don't know," Cam addressed Mike directly but also the group at large. "I didn't ask that explicitly. But I would imagine so. I don't think the satellites are a new thing."

A sense of indignant murmurs filled the room.

"But," Cam continued, "they have given us a satellite radio so that we can contact the other communities. There is an impressive network in place. Communities are helping each other, sharing information, and giving advice on similar issues and challenges. The problem is, I have little knowledge of radio broadcasting, nor do I have any interest in it. Freyja was given the briefing, but as her veterinary work requires her to move around, and sometimes unexpectedly, we realize we aren't the best choice to monitor the transmissions. To be most effective, it requires someone based in one location but who has access to everyone else. With the time differences, some transmissions will be overnight, our time. I realize I haven't made it sound all that attractive, but we were wondering ... does anyone want to volunteer for the job?"

People started glancing around the room in that way when no one wants to do something. After hearing that we were being watched, I wasn't surprised. They had taken that news well, and to be honest, better than I had expected. To my immense surprise, Aidan put up his hand.

"I was a radio hobbyist back in Kingussie. Had a little setup out back of my house. I have a fair idea of what to do. I am happy to take it on."

Cam and I looked at each other in confirmation. But with no other takers, the community appointed Aidan as the official spokesperson for Lewis. Aidan still managed the fields of wheat and corn and operated the mill but could easily monitor a radio signal. Still single, he had no one to disturb, and nearly everyone visited him weekly to trade for flour and corn. On second thought, he was a brilliant choice. We handed him the equipment, and he peered at the box of pieces, looking as happy as a child at Christmas.

"Did you ask if we could have any more medications?" Hamish asked. "We have very little left."

I took this one. Slowly I said, "It was really strange. I asked and asked and kept getting fobbed off but gently. I didn't even realize that I was being fobbed off initially. Responses like, 'Absolutely, happy to help. Let's just finish what we are doing...' But then it wasn't raised again. After three or four times asking and getting nowhere, I stopped asking, as it was becoming embarrassing. Cam and I wondered if perhaps they didn't have enough to share with all the communities and so kept putting me off."

"Well, isn't that fantastic," Sorcha sniped caustically. "We have no pain relief, no anesthetic, and no antibiotics. Even minor procedures like stitching a wound or pulling a tooth need those."

What she didn't mention was that we were also drastically low on salbutamol, the medication she needed to control her asthma. As the only person here with asthma, she alone used it. But it could be life-threatening if we didn't have any. As the questioning morphed into celebrations, I felt people watching Cam and me surreptitiously. "Are they or aren't they?" their faces seemed to ask, looking for a small clue to prove their theory. Cam was oblivious, as usual, and was off chatting to Aidan about the radio equipment.

Maybe he doesn't want to make an announcement so soon? Doesn't want people to know that we are a couple again?

As sad as this made me, I realized I needed to respect his wishes. He had been a part of this community for far more years than I had. He had married one of their most loved residents. I could sense people scrutinizing me. They all knew I had gone after him, but why? What was my motivation? Had he needed help? Were we just friends? My association with Angus wasn't so far in the past that they trusted me entirely, although rescuing Isla, Orla, Mairi, and Lucie the year before had greatly improved my social standing.

Several hours later, as we were about to commence the long ride home, I inquired of Sorcha, "I know it is late, but while we are here, do you think you could check Cam's wound? Maybe see if his stitches can be removed?"

"Wound? What wound?" she asked, surprised.

Hearing the guttural noise of expressed displeasure behind me, I gave a quick overview of the farm and what had happened to us. Sorcha stopped her bike in the middle of the road.

"They did *what*?"

Cam, highly embarrassed, tried to calm her down. "It is fine. It is nothing."

"He has fifty-three stitches," I murmured. "And that is just his chest."

Unable to look directly at his face, I could feel his emotion rise as he pulled up beside me. *Traitor. You will pay.* His posture betrayed his emotions.

Cam and I had disagreed that afternoon while changing into clean clothes before attending the meeting. After a day of heavy gardening, the wound dressing across his chest was filthy. Though he insisted he was fine and refused to let me tend him, I ignored his protestations and gone to take Louis and Katrin off to Di. Now I had the big guns on my side.

"Why on earth....?" Sorcha started lecturing me, and Cam just smiled sweetly.

"Darling sister, I am more than happy for you to doctor me after you have finished with Freyja's wounds. Hers are so much worse. They wanted a plastics consultation for her, and she refused."

All eyes turned to me, and I scowled at him. That was dirty play, and he knew it. His face, just appearing over Sorcha's navy-blue coated shoulder, smirked in the night.

"You refused?" she glowered incredulously. "Why?"

"I had my reasons."

"Right, both of you. Surgery. *Now!*"

Fraser, smirking as he beat a hasty retreat with Isla, recognized that he was in by far the best position today. Cam had once told me, amid hysterical laughter, of a time when Fraser had challenged Sorcha intellectually and had lost in spectacular and very public style.

"Sorcha," I asked, as Cam went to relieve himself upon arrival at the clinic. "I don't mean to be nosey, but is Di okay?"

Sorcha looked at me, surprised. "What do you mean?"

"She... she just seems very unwell. Look, I admit, I have minimal experience in pregnancy in humans, and I understand morning sickness, hormones, and all that, but I can't help but feel that she doesn't seem quite right. I'm a vet, not a doctor. I observe more than I listen. My patients are not the complaining kind. But I have known Di a long time..."

Sorcha wrinkled her nose. "You have noticed that? I keep telling myself that it is her first pregnancy. We don't know what a normal pregnancy looks like for her."

"But you get the same feeling? There is something more going on?"

"Leave it with me. I'll need to manage it carefully."

Cam returned at that point, effectively putting an end to the conversation. But I was pleased I had achieved my goal. Reluctant to have his chest checked, Cam grumbled and moaned, especially when Sorcha wanted to see him first once I explained his stitches were partly intramuscular. But it was healing nicely, even if the dressing was filthy and desperately needed changing. Sorcha removed the external stitches slowly as Cam scowled at me past her for betraying him.

My arms, which I had kept hidden with long sleeves, weren't healing quite so well because of constant movement. Several cuts, mainly those with small loose flaps, hadn't sealed, leaving big, crusted scabs.

"These are nasty," Sorcha said as she inspected each cut, then applied a clean dressing. "I need to redo some of these stitches. You know these will scar badly, don't you? The skin on your inner forearms is quite delicate."

"I do," I responded in my best ice queen manner. Sorcha recognized a resolute tone when she heard one and knew that there was no point in arguing.

Removing some but replacing others, Sorcha demanded, "Tell me the full story of what happened, please."

"On the way home." Cam yawned. "I'm tired, and we have a long way to go. Remind me why we decided to live so far out?"

"So you could live your life in privacy?" Sorcha baited him sarcastically.

"Oh, yeah."

CHAPTER 23

OUR FIRST CHRISTMAS TOGETHER was perfect. Sorcha, Di, and Sam came over early, Sam bleary-eyed and subdued. The children unwrapped their presents, nearly entirely clothes, but some toys and books we had taken from Inverness. Katrin was fascinated with the brown paper wrapping and spent ages shredding it and tossing it in the air. Louis was obsessed with the metal digger we had found in a toy store. Never having seen industrial machinery, he desperately wanted to get it out into the mud and try it out.

"Tomorrow," we told him in unison, his little face falling with disappointment.

Fraser, Isla, and their children came for lunch, and we shared the gifts we had sourced in Inverness. Items the children had never seen: matchbox cars, a spinning top, and music boxes. Books to be shared among all the children and warm winter jackets and boots.

"Here." I shyly handed Isla a rectangular wrapped box. Looking at me perplexed, she opened it, her eyes opening with joy.

"Scalpels! They are beautiful!" Isla hugged me fiercely. Sorcha smiled. I had gifted her a similar set that morning. The men looked at us in astonishment as the three of us gushed over the sharp blades and beautifully balanced handles.

Isla had been close friends with Laetitia, even before she met and married Cam. I was worried about how she would take the news of our reunion. It was important to me that we had not only a good working relationship but that she accepted me as Cam's partner, especially now that we lived in such proximity.

"Knives?" Fraser questioned Cam. "I get her flowers, and she gets excited about knives."

Cam just shrugged.

After a decadent Christmas dinner, Sorcha taunted, "You know, I don't think I have ever seen Cam so happy. Oh, wait. Maybe when mum made him pancakes with maple syrup. That might run a close second."

"Oh, maple syrup!" Cam closed his eyes and licked his lips. "How I miss it!"

Isla chimed in, "Maybe Fraser could grow you a maple tree as a Christmas gift!"

Fraser laughed hysterically. "Cam planted one on his first visit here. We have been waiting for it to mature all this time!"

"How long does it take?" Isla asked curiously.

Cam, blushing furiously, admitted, "About forty years!"

A lightbulb flashed in my mind, and I dashed from the room, everyone staring at me in astonishment. Returning some minutes later, I told Cam to close his eyes, placing the heavy object in his hands.

"I had planned to save this for your birthday, but..."

Cam opened his eyes, and his smile illuminated the room. "Maple syrup? Five *liters* of maple syrup?"

Placing the small wooden barrel on the table, he picked me up and swung me around, his elation evident, making Louis beg, "Me too! Me too!"

Once the hilarity had died down, he asked, "How?"

"From Clava."

"You carried back five liters of maple syrup and never told me?"

"A girl needs to have some secrets." I grinned. "You wondered why I wouldn't let you handle my backpack? I have no doubt you would have noticed that kind of weight increase!"

"This is the best Christmas gift ever!" he pronounced.

As we finished the meal and moved into the living room, stuffed full and unable to move, the adults on chairs and the children playing with toys, it occurred to me that this was the type of celebration I had never experienced with my own family: hilarity, mess, overindulging with delicious food and surrounded by people I cared for, whom it appeared, also cared for me. The children were now playing with their gifts, and wrappings were still strewn across the room. Jam was happily chasing balls made of brown wrapping paper, a small luxury we had also brought back with us. The dishes could wait until tomorrow.

We had celebrated my family Christmases on Christmas Eve, European style, with a formal roast dinner and gift opening afterward. Mum and dad sitting in their chairs, Katrin and I on the floor, carefully opening our thoughtful and nearly always practical gifts. Happy and friendly, yes. But formal, no mess. It didn't have the same sense of camaraderie that I felt now. Glancing around, I felt like I belonged here. Cam and Di had known me for years, and I could always count on them. But Sorcha, Isla, and Fraser too. They seemed to accept me for who I was; I was no longer Cam's first wife. Sorcha knew the truth of Katrin's conception, yet she too no longer seemed to judge me. I smiled to myself as I poured another glass of wine, enjoying the warm feeling of friendship, of family.

CHAPTER 24

"**DO YOU KNOW WHAT** today is?"

"No idea," I mumbled, still half asleep. "Tuesday?" After all these years, I was still not a morning person and couldn't fathom how Cam could be so perky at first light.

"Thursday, actually, but that isn't what I meant."

The kiss that followed, with so much tenderness, pulled me out of my sleepiness.

"Mmmm..." I murmured, liking how this morning had started. After so many years alone, I still couldn't believe that I had him in my bed and in my life. So many nights of longing for the life we had shared before I had been unexpectedly ripped away.

Most mornings, Cam was gone before I woke. *Maybe he isn't in a rush to get going today? Perhaps we can spend some time together...*

With an effort, he pulled himself away. "Today, my darling, is the 20 February."

"Oh." I was fully awake now as that date registered in my brain. August Day. Our anniversary. It would have been five years married and six years together, except for that awful period of separation in the middle. Rolling onto my back, I looked up at him, not sure what to say.

"Do you remember that day in our sanctuary? Do you remember the words you used?"

"Of course." I had spent weeks rehearsing them. It wasn't likely that I would ever forget.

"Would... would you like to use them again?"

My mouth dropped, unable to speak. Never in a million years had I expected that. In the weeks we had been back, we had been blissfully happy but behind closed doors. I had noted that Cam took great care not to be seen with me in public. Sorcha and Di knew. Fraser and Isla, but no one else.

His face was taking on a worried look.

"Are you sure?" I asked. "I thought..."

Cam looked at me directly. "This is absolutely what I want. When we were abducted, and I came to with you rescuing me, getting me off that hook, I knew. At that moment, I had no doubt whatsoever, and nothing that has happened since has given me cause to change my mind. I guess a soul on the verge of death has no time for lies or games. I love you, and I want to be with you. Besides, you asked me last time. I figure now it is my turn. Freyja Jorgensen, will you marry me?"

"Yes!" It came out louder than I expected, and he recoiled slightly, making Jam jump off the end of the bed in fright. "Yes! Yes!"

He looked at me, grinning sheepishly. "Do you think this time, we could say our vows clothed and in front of our family and friends?"

"Katrin, Sam, and Louis, too?"

"Of course. This time, I *do* want people to know how much I love you. We have both lost so much. People, time. I want everyone to know that I love you."

"You aren't a little worried about what people will think?"

"I have thought about that. People will always talk. Better to have them talk about the truth than to gossip about a falsity. I love you, Freyja Jorgensen. I don't care who knows it."

Throwing my arms around him, my heart was filled with joy.

"There is something else."

Fossicking around under the bed, he pulled out a paper-wrapped gift.

Speechless, I looked at it in my hands, unsure what to say. "I don't have a gift for you!" I blurted.

"You just gave me the biggest gift by saying yes. Agreeing to be my wife. Our children will have a mother and a father. Honestly, there is nothing else you can give me."

Carefully opening the paper so we could reuse it, I was astonished to find an emerald-green silk dress and several pieces of black lacy lingerie.

Holding up the black bra, I looked over it at him, my eyebrows raised. Speechless.

Looking much like a naughty toddler, he dropped his eyes, embarrassed.

"How do I wear this when helping birth a foal?"

"Maybe keep it for special occasions?" he suggested, somewhat hopefully.

"How did you even know my size?" I asked.

Cam snorted at that. "Are you kidding? How many times have I held your beautiful breasts in my hands? You don't think I know the size of them?"

It was my turn to flush. "Okay. But when…"

"Inverness."

"Inverness? That was months ago! You mean…"

"I knew. Even then, I knew. Sliced up like a Sunday roast, every movement causing me pain from your stitching, but I knew. I was just waiting for the right time. Our anniversary seems like the perfect time to renew our vows, doesn't it?"

That evening, Fraser, Isla, Sorcha, Di, and all of our children gathered at our home for dinner, Cam greeting them at the door.

"Thank you for coming. It means a lot to have you all here. Before dinner, we have a little surprise," Cam announced.

There were audible gasps as I entered the room in the gorgeous green dress, and Cam removed his jacket to reveal the neat white shirt he had chosen to complement my dress.

With Louis at his side, dressed in a matching outfit to his father, and Katrin in Sorcha's arms, we pledged our lives to each other once more.

As we had the first time, I started. This time, my voice rang out loud and true so that all could hear what was in my heart.

"Campbell Edward William Mackintosh. I love you.
You cannot possess me, for I belong to myself,
But I give you love, which is mine to give.
You cannot command me, for I am a free person,
But I choose to serve you, in order to aid you.

I pledge that yours are the eyes that I will smile into every morning.

I shall be a shield for your back, and you for mine.

I shall not slander you, nor you me.

I will honor you above all others.

When we disagree, we will do so in private,

And tell no others our grievances.

This is my pledge to you,

For this is a marriage of equals."

This time as we kissed, we heard the cheers and clapping from outside our bubble. As we drew apart, unable to stop smiling, Cam looked down at Louis and said, "Are you ready, buddy?"

Louis nodded.

Sensing this was a special moment, I kneeled so I could look into his eyes.

"Will you be my Mumma?" he asked so earnestly that tears welled instantly, and I choked on the lump that formed in my throat, overcome with emotion, unable to speak.

He buried his face in my shoulder as I sobbed, "Yes, my little man, yes! There is nothing I would love more than to be your Mumma. You have always been a part of me, Louis. My heart always knew that you were mine."

Scooping him up in my arms, and with Cam holding Katrin, we turned to face our family and friends. The cheers were likely heard in Garynahine as Fraser whooped and Di cheered. Even Sorcha looked happy.

Sharing our wedding evening with our family and closest friends felt so right this time. We had spent so much time in secret. Now we wanted the world to know.

Hours of laughter, good-natured teasing, eating, and drinking ensued, with music and dancing after Fraser returned home to get his guitar. The children were racing around the house and giggling madly. Finally, we closed the door, our house still echoing with laughter and chatter. Katrin and Louis were having a sleepover with Isla and the girls. For the first time since we had returned home from Clava, our sanctuary was ours at last.

"Will you?" Cam asked and held out a hand.

I took it, and he drew me in, holding me against him, looking into my eyes. With my head resting on his shoulder, I allowed him to lead me in a slow dance around the room. We didn't need music; we followed the beat of our hearts, forever joined, never again to be separated.

"Have I told you how beautiful you look?" he whispered in my ear as I felt the straps of my dress slip down my shoulders and arms, and it slid to the floor in a puddle of silk around my feet. I stepped out of it, and he carefully picked it up, spreading it on the back of the couch.

"Oh, I like that outfit *much* better," he breathed, as he turned back to me, standing at arm's length to admire me in the black lace bra and knickers set he had gifted me. Rather revealing in design, the ensemble left nothing to the imagination. But standing in the middle of the living room, alone, I felt self-conscious. *What is he looking at?* He was taking too long, scrutinizing me, not speaking, and I began to feel the need to cover up the scar across my belly, the scars on my arms—all of my imperfections. Biting my lip, I said nothing and stood there.

"You are a goddess," he said huskily when he finally spoke.

"You don't mind—these?" I held my arms out to him, the web of purplish scars prominent. "Not to mention it is winter, and I am so white I just about glow in the dark."

"Not if you don't mind mine."

He slowly unbuttoned his shirt, displaying the torso length wound from hip to opposite shoulder. Raised, red, and angry looking. I reached out my fingers to touch it, and he pulled me in, kissing my neck.

"God, you are so beautiful. How did I ever get so lucky that I got to marry you twice?"

Unable to stop smiling, I helped him out of his clothing, and we stood there, looking at each other. So little time had passed since our last wedding, but in other ways, it was a lifetime.

"This was how we married last time," he said at last.

"Promise me something," I asked.

"Anything."

"Promise me we will never be separated again."

"That, I promise." His warm, soft lips brushed mine, lingering there for a moment, but moved down my cheek, chin, neck, and chest and to my breasts. Lifting me, I wrapped my legs around his waist, and he carried me to the bedroom.

"I remember the first time you did that to me, in our grotto," he murmured into my ear as he carefully laid me down. "When you wrapped your long, sensual legs around me and made me feel safe. Protected. That was the moment. That was when I fell in love with you."

"Well, you fall easily," I teased, pulling the pillow down beneath my head. "What if I had taken other men to those hot springs?"

He pulled back from me a little, like he had never even considered the prospect.

"I'm teasing," I murmured as I kissed him again, forcing him to respond to me.

"So, when did *you* know?" he asked hesitantly.

"Oh, I can pinpoint the exact moment," I said, a little shyly. "I liked you that first night in the dorm. I knew you were different, but you didn't pursue me, so I just thought you weren't interested. Then on August Day, when you ran me down, I don't know, I took a chance. Some deep-rooted instinct just told me to take you to the hot springs. I didn't doubt the feeling. I just knew that I needed to. But when you took me on that rocky shelf, *that* was the first time I had ever had those feelings. That state of absolute yearning for someone, knowing beyond any doubt that it was *you* I needed. I had relationships before, but that moment was the first time in my life that I had ever felt truly *alive*. Forgot who I was and all of my problems. That was the moment I fell in love with you."

Slowly removing my new underwear, Cam reached over to the bedside table and withdrew a small bottle.

"What's..."

But he cut me off with a kiss.

Unscrewing the lid, the faint waft of almond oil drifted, a sweet scent filling the room. I watched as he poured a small amount in his hands, rubbing them together to warm it.

"Roll over," he whispered, and I obliged, liking where this was going.

Massaging the day from my shoulders, back, and legs, I drifted effortlessly, warm and fuzzy, unable to think. Feeling heavy, too wrapped up in this state of cloud-like oblivion to think, I felt him roll me easily onto my back, paying careful attention to my front. Slowly he massaged the oil into me with long, deliberate strokes, working the sweet scent into my chest, legs, down to my feet.

Slowly I felt him glide into me, solid and dependable, moving within me as I clamped down, and we slid together into rapture.

"Do you have any regrets?" I heard him whisper as I was on the brink of sleep.

"No, I don't believe in regrets," I replied softly. "Regret is time wasted on things you can't change. Why? Do you?"

"Just one."

"What's that?" I asked curiously.

"When you were growing Katrin, I didn't touch you. I didn't get to feel her kick, stroke your belly, talk to her, watch you change, and see her grow. I missed a huge part of her life that I will never get back. I do so regret that."

"Maybe," I whispered, trying hard not to let the emotion choke me. "Maybe we will get a second chance."

"Oh, honey, I hope so." His voice was filled with so much earnestness that I couldn't help but smile in the dark.

CHAPTER 25

"WELL, HELLO THERE, LONG-LEGS!"

The deep, masculine voice boomed across the courtyard, echoing between the houses. Cam and I looked up, startled, as we took our muddy boots off at our doorstep. Evening shadows cast from the nearby greenhouse made it hard to look into the setting sun.

"Luca?" I questioned the shadowy figure.

"Who could forget this ugly mug?" He threw his arms wide and dropping his bag.

My boots untied, I flew at him, throwing my arms around him. Cam stood watching from the front of our house, his eyebrows raised at this unexpected display of affection.

Luca, an enormous well-built man of six feet six inches, lifted me like I was a feather and swung me in the air, one of my boots flying off toward the greenhouse.

"How are you, Princess? I've missed you!"

"Me too!" I exclaimed, kissing him excitedly. "How are you? Are you here for long?" My words tripped over each other in my delight at seeing him again.

Turning, I saw Cam handing out my boot to me. Holding onto Luca for support and hobbling on one leg to put it back on and not fall in the mud, I managed, "Cam, do you remember Luca?"

Cam stepped forward and spoke quietly, subduing my exhilaration. "I do. I never really thanked you for your part in..."

Luca cut him off, but not rudely. "I'm so sorry for what happened. For not getting there sooner."

Before the silence took hold, and not wanting to taint this reunion by dredging up the past, I interrupted. "Guess what?"

"Your man here came to his senses, and you are back together?"

"We are! How did you know?"

"Bliss is tattooed all over your face, Princess. He was always the one for you. *He* just had to work it out."

Cam's eyes popped. "What you are telling me is that the entire world knew that we would end up together, except me?"

Luca shrugged. "Pretty much. Jakob and I talked about it all the time. How the bloke is always the last to work it out."

"Where are Jakob and Nate?" I asked hopefully. "Are they with you?"

While I was fond of Jakob, it was Luca who had been my closest friend and confidante. It had been he who had pulled me out of the downward spiral into which I plummeted over learning that Cam had left August, thinking I betrayed him, and again when hearing Cam was married and had a baby. He had supported me, been there for me, and challenged me to be a better person.

"Ahh, Jake. He met a lovely lass on Newgrange. Nate, well, he chose to stay with Angus."

"Is Angus not with you then?" I asked, surprised. Although after what Cam had told me about Angus and his sister, I wasn't sure I wanted to see him for a while.

"Now, that is quite the story and will need some lubrication. Are you busy?"

Recognizing that this could take some time, I asked Cam to see if the kids could stay at Sorcha and Di's for the night.

"Come on. You will stay with us," I ordered as we turned toward the house, Luca picking up his enormous khaki duffle bag and casting a shadow over me as I walked.

"How did you finally convince your man here? I am assuming you took a hand eventually," he asked cheekily a few hours later over a dinner of mushroom and spinach risotto. Luca had thoughtfully brought several bottles of exceptional French wine. We settled in for a long evening of catching up, a rare child-free night.

Blushing, I looked over at Cam. "I did. I followed him to Edinburgh. We married again, just last week."

"Well, I am ecstatic for you both. You deserve it after everything that happened, all that pain you went through. Some of which could well have been avoided."

"What do you mean?" I asked between mouthfuls.

Luca leaned back in his chair, resting his wine-glass on his chest. "It all started a few months back, in November, not long after Angus ran into your fella here at Kilmartin."

Cam nodded, remembering.

"I wasn't there. Jake and I stayed with the *Selkie*. After Angus and Nate returned to the harbor and told us they had met you, we headed off to Guernsey, and you apparently went to Clava. We have been there once ourselves."

"We did," I agreed. "I caught up with Cam the day after his visit to Kilmartin, when he returned to Edinburgh, and then we went up to Clava together."

"It appears that your visit to Clava set the cat among the pigeons, so to speak."

"Huh?" Cam and I looked at each other, confused.

"How's that?" I asked. "They welcomed us in Clava. They didn't want us to leave."

"Well, you asked about the radio transmissions and some other questions that made them think you knew about Angus's mission."

"Mission?" I asked, perplexed. "What mission?"

"You must have said something about Angus and a mission?"

"I'm sure that I used that word but mainly as you do. I picked it up from you." I grinned at him. I had learned a lot of skills and words from Luca. Much of it was not suitable for the dinner table.

"Ahh, so that is what happened. You don't know then. Well, neither did we. But his colleagues at Clava were furious with him, thinking he had told you something he shouldn't."

Cam looked at me for confirmation, and I gave it. "Okay, mate, we are pretty bamboozled right now. We have no idea what you are talking about," Cam said bluntly.

Luca nodded knowingly. "Well, let me start from the beginning then. Did you ever work out that it was Angus who convinced Heidi to spread the rumor that you were pregnant by him?"

"He *what?*" I just about fell off my chair. "How dare...!"

"You don't think she was that clever, do you?" Luca interrupted before I could completely lose my temper.

Pausing before I really got going in my tirade, I said slowly, "Well, I did, actually. I thought she made it up to hurt Cam and get him to leave."

I blushed at the memory. I had no issue with women. I just didn't appreciate homicidal lying ones who tried to throw me on a bed without consent.

"Getting Cam to leave was just a bonus. She was certainly behind the rumors that Cam killed you. That *was* her. But the pregnancy gossip, that was his idea. He resented having to travel all the way to August only to lose you. Even though he had never met him, he genuinely believed that Cam wasn't worthy of you. The Gardener, he called him."

"He *what!*" I was even more incredulous now. Rage rippled to the surface, and I could feel my skin redden. I barely felt Cam's calming arm around my shoulder as I levitated from the chair.

"Let Luca speak, honey," he spoke soothingly. "Don't shoot the messenger. It isn't his fault."

I made a great effort to simmer down. After all, Cam was the one who had been insulted, and he wasn't enraged. Yet.

"On our first visit, we rushed to get there before Cam could return. Nate, Jakob, and I wanted to stay longer at Kerguelen, learn more about the portals, but he was desperate to get to August sooner. I couldn't work it out. We could have learned a lot more from the scientists there. That was what I signed up for, to explore, learn as much as we could and share that knowledge with other communities. But Angus was desperate to get going and promised we would return that way. At the time, I said nothing. After all, I thought it was for you. By that time that we all would have moved heaven and earth for you."

I flushed as Luca continued.

"Then we got to August, weeks before the solstice, and Cam wasn't there. Which he knew—I should add."

"How did he know I wasn't there?" Cam interrupted. "He was on Lewis when I was on August. When I traveled, you were all mid-way across the Atlantic. He couldn't have known."

"I'll get to that but let me finish the story."

Cam and I nodded in agreement, but I wished Luca would hurry.

Luca took a gulp of wine, swallowing painfully slowly before continuing.

"Angus believed that if Cam were out of the picture permanently, then Freyja would turn to him in her distress. Apparently, deceiving her and getting her any way he could was better than winning her with his glowing personality. Angus deliberately arrived on August well before the solstice, then delayed getting to Melbourne and back, to give Cam time to return and then leave. Heidi did her bit and spread the gossip. Cam, you responded as expected and left before we returned. He genuinely believed that Freyja would hit rock bottom and would rebound into his arms. But people don't always respond in the way you think they will. Freyja was distraught alright, but instead, she retreated into herself. Moped and isolated herself in her cabin. Refused to eat or speak to anyone."

Not wanting this particularly low point of my life analyzed, especially in front of my husband, I asked, "Why would Heidi do that?"

"Like all master manipulators, he fed her obsession. Angus led Heidi to believe that you had come back to August for good and convinced her that you and she would raise the baby together. He had to keep going, and you couldn't raise a baby on a yacht, outside the protection of a dome. All Heidi had to do was eliminate the only threat to that happy family scenario—Campbell. When we first arrived on August, you introduced Angus to the community. He spent a few days working out who was the most gullible, who could be manipulated. He always considered himself intellectually superior to most people. He worked out fairly quickly that she was madly in love with you, hated Cam, was a malicious gossip, and convinced her that the pregnancy was a secret. He thought she would tell everyone, and that would destroy Cam. He had no way of knowing that the person she would tell would be Cam himself. When he heard that piece of news that he was overjoyed. That was the part I overheard a day or so before she attacked you. Heidi telling Angus that Cam knew about the pregnancy and that was likely why Cam left."

"Hang on," Cam interrupted. "When she attacked you, didn't she admit to making it up?"

Screwing up my face in thought as I absently ran my finger along the long original scar, I said, "You know, I can't remember."

"No," Luca interrupted. "Jake and I questioned Heidi while you were off getting stitches. She admitted to telling Cam that Frey was pregnant. She never said she made it up. She was seething, wild, out of control. But she never admitted to lying. All she said was that she had told Cam about the baby, knowing it would upset him, and he would leave. She said that she loved Freyja, and she always knew that they would be together."

"Why didn't *you* say anything?" I asked, my annoyance breaking through. "We spent nearly a year together after that, and you never said a thing."

"I only overheard that small part of the conversation. I thought the pregnancy was genuine and wanted to keep your secret. The way Angus was talking, it was the real deal, and I had no reason to suspect him. You are a friend, and it wasn't my news to tell. When it was fairly clear that you were distressed, I thought maybe you had miscarried or something. You were in a fairly dire state when we left August the second time, but I didn't know why. But over time, it was obvious that you weren't interested in Angus in a romantic sense, although we all got along, so I put it out of mind."

"How did he know to use pregnancy as a reason to upset me?" Cam asked gently.

"I thought we were friends," I said, barely audible, the utter desolation of that time flooding back and threatening to engulf me. "I thought he had my back. Late one night, when I had drunk too much, I told him about how you and I wanted a baby. But couldn't. I think that may have been the only time he ever saw me cry," I admitted.

"Well, he exploited your weakness," said Luca sourly.

Cam tightened his arm around my shoulder. "Okay, so back to my question. He lied to Heidi to get rid of me. How did he even know where I was?"

"He always knew. He has been in radio contact with Clava since the start."

"The start?" Cam looked at him blankly.

"The very start. Angus was a plant. From the day we established the community here, he has been in touch with Clava. Giving them updates about the community, how it was faring, when it would be ready. I was here then. I remember how awful it was in the first year. I was fairly disgusted myself to learn that not only could he have saved the locals, even his own family, and chose not to, but he was reporting on it the entire time."

"If he was their informant, why would he leave with me?" I asked, confused.

"Because his colleagues approved the travel. How do you think he knew the location of the warehouse in Edinburgh? He was a senior official. Warehousing was not under his portfolio."

Speechless, I watched Luca.

"From the start?" Cam repeated slowly. "He knew that there was a settlement on Clava from the start?"

"He did. And he said nothing."

"How did you find all of this out?"

"After the lies about Freyja, I thought he was unethical, at least as far as she was concerned. But unrequited love makes people do things out of character. I could forgive a man for trying to win a woman's heart, even if he went about it in a way I didn't consider entirely honorable. The rest I didn't learn until much later. A few weeks after we left Kilmartin, we had a few drinks with dinner, and I needed to get up during the night to relieve myself. Couldn't get back to sleep, and as it wasn't raining, I went up the deck to get some fresh air. Overheard him on the radio. It took me a few minutes to realize that it even was a radio. I stood in the passage, listening. He was reporting in, receiving instructions from the control room at Clava. When I realized that was what I was hearing, that someone else was setting our mission and instructions, I quietly woke Jake. We listened in and learned that Angus had been tasked with a mission called the Collective. They were cranky with him. Things you had said made them question his allegiance. He was arguing, defending himself, and was likely louder than he intended to be. Probably unreasonably, both Jake and I felt perhaps we should be made aware of any secret missions."

"What did you do?"

"Let's just say that a yacht with four men in the middle of the Atlantic is a very small place indeed when two of them have some skills, and the third is a rather weedy little man."

Cam snorted with the image that provoked. I knew what he thought of Angus. After what I had just heard, the things he had done behind my back, I couldn't disagree.

"We worked out fairly quickly that Nate was in on it, and Jake and I were just the bit of hired muscle. We locked Nate in his cabin and interrogated Angus. Learned what we could, turned the *Selkie* around, and jumped ship in Newgrange. Anyone who could deceive Freyja like that and keep his team in the dark about what he was really up to was no one I wanted to be involved with."

"Thank you." I leaned over to touch his arm. "You have always been an amazing friend."

Then the reality of what he was saying dawned on me. "Hang on, so what you are telling me is that he was in radio contact with Clava since the start?"

Luca nodded in agreement as he shoveled food in his mouth.

"And he kept up that radio contact all the time we were on the *Selkie*?"

"He did."

My voice dropped, barely audible. "He knew Cam had come through the portal to Lewis?" I spoke slowly, unable to comprehend. "He knew where Cam was, and he kept going?"

Luca nodded gravely. "That's about the size of it."

"We could have turned back!" I whispered. "None of this needed to happen. We could have turned back. We would have only been between Africa and Kerguelen. I could have come back here."

We all sat silently, looking down at our bowls as we took that in. Had Angus admitted that he knew Cam had followed me, Luca and I would never have become friends. Cam would not have married Laetitia, nor had Louis. We likely wouldn't have Katrin. But holy hell, how much pain could have been avoided?

Cam caught my eye. "We can't change the past, honey."

"I need some air."

CHAPTER 26

WHEN MY ENTRENCHED LOGIC could finally override emotion once more, I accepted the situation needed to play out this way. Without my travels, Cam wouldn't have been reunited with Di and his sister. They would never have come here. People's lives had changed because of Angus's lies. But all the pain, the heartache Angus had caused Cam and me? I could never forgive him for that.

"What is the Collective?" Cam asked cautiously after a concerned glance to check that I was alright. They had moved to the living room in my absence, and I snuggled up next to Cam on the sofa.

Luca filled his glass again before answering.

"From what Angus told me, under duress, the Collective is what the scientists on Clava and August are calling the amalgamation of communities. Over the past few years, they have been collecting on the ground reports from Angus, their one local source within each community, supplemented with data obtained via their satellites. Imagine my shock to learn that they had been watching us the entire time, including our journeys."

Cam and I nodded. We knew this part. "They told us about the satellites when we were at Clava. But I think it was an accident. The man who told us thought we knew. But a local spy? They told us that there was a broadcast engineer on each site, sent with the original settlement team."

"Well, an informant is likely a better word. Someone sent there with the express purpose of monitoring and passing on information. There is a matrix. An assessment checklist. They were waiting for the point where they knew that a community was desperate in some way. Five years of critical supplies had been provided, but no more. Some places used it faster, others slower, depending upon their circumstances. But roughly the same timeframe. They estimated that was how long it would take for each community to become established, get over any teething issues, form bonds and start having children. The point where each group was settled, I guess you could say. Invested in the success of their community. But five years was also the point where they needed something—stable electricity supply for the colder, darker sites, safe water for the hotter ones, medications, food stocks."

"Well, we are certainly short on medicine here. Pain relief, antibiotics, even asthma medication," I said, thinking of Sorcha. "But it has been seven years now."

"I know, and Angus did too. Sorcha mentioned it to him while she was treating him a year ago. They were just waiting for the best time to make the approach."

"She saved his life!" Cam hissed unexpectedly.

"She did. And he repaid it by secretly collecting information on how desperate the community was, where there were strains, challenges. What they were short of. What could be used as leverage."

"Now I come to think about it, the medical team at Clava were quite willing to give me pain relief for my stitches," I said quietly. "But wouldn't give us any to take back."

"That fits," Luca admitted. "They wanted you to join them. They would give you what you wanted so you would stay, not to take home. What do you mean, stitches?"

Lifting my arms, I rolled up my sleeves to show him my wounds. His mouth dropped.

"Not now," I warned.

"What did Angus do when he visited these places?" Cam asked cynically.

"Form relationships. Be a friend, give them knowledge—not too much but enough. Then, when the time was right, negotiate inclusion into the Collective. In short, signing away sovereignty in exchange for unlimited electricity, medication, radio communication—and here is the kicker—the ability to trade with all other antipodal communities."

"Trade?" I asked, a little perplexed.

"Clava has discovered a way for all communities with a portal to access each other on the solstices and equinoxes. The Nexus, it is called. Every thirteen weeks, any community with an active portal can trade with one other community. As we know, the wormhole doesn't last long, but they worked out a way, using magnetic force, to make them jump to another portal, not just their own antipode. Twenty-four in all. But there was the potential to add more to the nexus, like those communities which had an antipodal point but weren't settled yet like Kilmartin, or those places settled but with no linked community, Orkney and Shetlands, for example. That was why we happened to be at Kilmartin when you arrived, Cam, and why we were planning to visit Guernsey. There is no community at either of those places yet. Only I didn't know it. Angus, however, knew that there was no community there but pretended like there might have been, so we would accompany him. Nate was activating them to connect them to the Nexus."

"Why would they connect them all?" I asked. "I don't see why people moving all over the place is attractive."

It was Cam who replied. "That is a stroke of genius. Imagine you are a tropical country with a surplus of pineapples or coconut but desperately want potatoes. Or have a glut of rice but want wheat. With the radios, all the negotiations can take place beforehand, leaving the actual travel of goods to take place each quarter."

"Come on, Princess," Luca said a little cynically. "You and I have been to enough places. Canada, they were doing well in maple syrup but couldn't grow rice or tropical fruit. New Caledonia was drowning in mangoes and bananas but had no way to make whisky. There is now the capacity to access pretty much anything, for a limited time, and you get to agree on your own terms and who you will trade with. Now tell me why that wouldn't be attractive?"

"That makes sense. Was this a new discovery? Making the portals jump, I mean."

"That was always the plan. They knew people would discover the portals but didn't want to add the complexity of multiple sites until most communities had joined the Collective and they could exercise some degree of control. It was you, Frey, that changed the game by wanting to travel back by sea. They wanted Angus to dissuade you, to travel back via the portal and confirm that one worked in both directions. They never tested it, you know. But you refused, saying that you would go alone. They didn't want that as they couldn't control what you would tell any other communities you found, so they got Angus to spearhead the mission. Cam was the loose cannon and really mucked up their plans. The irony is that you left August the second time and found Bellcamp because of Angus's lies. I'll bet he never told his superiors that!"

"How did I change things?" Cam asked, puzzled.

"When you took a yacht from New Zealand and then gave it to the community at Bellcamp, that changed everything. With people now sailing around, they lost control over who had the capacity to travel and what information was being shared. Information was their most valuable commodity at that point. Angus was then tasked with traveling to all the communities, befriending them, giving them a little information, and essentially preparing them for the time when they would need to fall under the rule of the Collective."

"He pretended like he didn't know about the antipodal portals!" I seethed. "He played me! Now you are telling me he knew all along?"

"Worse, it was he who chose the sites. He seems to have quite a bit of knowledge in ancient history."

"So, Angus accompanied Freyja, ostensibly to take her home, but really to form relationships with the other communities? What a great cover story. Freyja fell through the portal and was trying to get home.

Leaving here was probably a good idea. The people here never trusted him," Cam muttered.

"Which is why you haven't yet been invited to join," Luca finished.

"Who has joined?" I asked, interested, despite the awful news I had learned tonight. I had been to many of these places with Luca and Angus, so I was intrigued about which ones they had deemed ready to join. Desperate enough.

"Clava and Auckland Island are the control centers, north, and south, respectively. Kerguelen and New Amsterdam both signed up straight away. First, they are scientists. Second, they are struggling with the isolation, the constant dark, and lack of food. Their partners in Saskatchewan and Colorado haven't yet signed up. Easter Island and India have agreed, both struggling with a shortage of fresh water. Russia said yes, but their partner in the Falklands said no. Russia is struggling with a lack of fresh food. Cocos-Keeling and Nicaragua both said yes. Both are struggling with the supply of medicines. Africa and New Caledonia said yes. The portal there is unstable, and the African community is facing a lack of water, like India. The Chatham Islands said yes, but Toulouse said no. Gibraltar and Great Barrier Island—both of those communities perished."

"Do you know how?" Cam asked.

"I'm not sure. Angus said that it appears that both communities were sabotaged from within. Frey and I have been to Gibraltar, and that was certainly what it looked like. What they think happened was that one dome was breached, and they attacked the other. But they can't tell for sure which went first."

"Ashton, one of the senior officials on Clava, told us they had satellite surveillance. Could they not check?"

"They tried apparently, but as both portals are inside caves, they couldn't tell who traveled. A lot of the damage occurred at night, so again, they aren't sure. If they had to guess, based on the level of decomposition and damage to the dome, it appears more likely that it was the Gibraltarian community who perished first, and someone from there traveled to New Zealand and damaged their dome."

"And they *watched?*" I asked incredulously. I had seen the devastation firsthand. To think that they sat there and watched...

Luca shrugged. "I asked Angus that exact question. Why didn't they intervene? He said that they didn't know until it was too late. But later, under pressure, he admitted they felt it wasn't their responsibility."

"Sounds almost exactly like what we were told on Clava," Cam muttered to me. "Party line clearly."

"Do they know how the dome was damaged? I mean, we were shown the fabric, and it was fairly robust."

Surprisingly, it was Cam who knew the answer to that. "I forgot you weren't with me when I went to Melbourne to get Sorcha. Tadhg learned that obsidian could cut the fabric. Most likely, that was what was used."

"Obsidian is used in high-end surgical blades," I said thoughtfully. "I used to have some back in Melbourne, but I wasn't allowed to take them with me. They were crazy sharp."

"Well, all obsidian was removed from the domed communities settled from Melbourne, and Fraser said it wasn't naturally found here. But it appears likely that was what happened. Someone cut the dome fabric with obsidian."

I could still picture the haphazard slash marks on the dome fabric, ratty and torn, flapping in the breeze on Gibraltar. The image reminded me of my arms, and I pulled my sleeves down over my forearms.

"Who is still sitting on the fence?" I asked.

"Last I heard, and bear in mind that my intel is at least a few weeks old now, but Machu Picchu and Vietnam are yet even to discover the portal, so they are deemed not yet ready. Newgrange and yourselves are considered ready but not yet approached. August, Bellcamp, Orkney, Shetlands, Canada, and Colorado are considering the offer. Falklands declined, as did Toulouse. But the balance has now tipped in their favor. Eleven have joined, plus Auckland and Clava. Only two declined, four yet to decide, six if you count Orkney and Shetlands, who have no partner. Two not ready. Two no longer settled."

"We need to warn people," said Cam slowly.

"Newgrange knows," Luca said with a smile. "While it was just luck that was the nearest point for us to jump ship, we were fairly persuasive. I can't see them joining any time soon. Orkney and the Shetlands are odd ones. Those portals were charged as test cases, but their antipodal points are tiny atolls in the sub-antarctic region. They deemed the partner sites unin-habitable, but the links are still active, and in the rush to set up the communities and mobilize everyone, they ran out of time to deactivate them. But they can be linked into the Nexus when it is operational, so they went ahead and settled them both, especially as both are fertile lands."

"Is *that* where he went!" Cam exclaimed, briefly telling Luca the story of Ross from Orkney who had fallen into the portal at Maes Howe. "I should radio Will and let him know. They would love to have closure. Poor Ross. They all thought he was mad."

"*No!*" Luca bellowed with such force that Cam jerked.

Luca softened. "Sorry, I didn't mean it like that. I just meant that the radio broadcasts are being monitored."

Cam and I looked at each other. Monitored. Not only were we being watched, but they were listening to us as well.

"Orkney likely won't want to expose themselves to other communities after what happened," Luca said, and Cam nodded in agreement.

"They are still fearful of outsiders," he admitted.

"Is there anything they don't know?" I asked, rather crankily. It seemed that we had no privacy at all. To think Cam and I had seriously considered moving to Clava, taking our children.

"Well, if Angus is to be believed, their monitoring is visual satellite and radio via their local contact only. I would think that anything spoken or inside is probably safe."

"Good to know," Cam said as he poured us all another drink.

CHAPTER 27

FRASER AND ISLA'S NEWLY finished home was the location for dinner the following evening. We had invited Luca to stay with us until we found a more permanent solution for him. After his bust-up with Angus, there were limited places he could go.

Sorcha, Di, and the kids were also there—the entire village, as we liked to call it before we settled on a more permanent name. The adults were seated at one table, and the children were on their own smaller table. It was a special treat, and the six of them loved it.

Isla was awed to host Luca, showing her gratitude for his role in saving her from the raiders the previous year. For Fraser, this meant continually topping up Luca's glass, and I noted, with a smirk at Cam, that he didn't say no.

Judging by the immense array of dishes on the table, Isla had been cooking all day. She had taken the day off as soon as she had learned that Luca was here, and I was famished. But this was her first opportunity to thank him for his considerable role in saving her life, so I was happy to shoulder the burden for a few days. Like all men, the way to Luca's heart was through his stomach. For someone who had spent the best part of the past few years eating packaged and canned foods in a ship's galley, he was in heaven.

"Campbell," Sorcha announced brusquely midway through the main course. *Motherhood may have softened me,* I thought, *but it doesn't appear to have the same effect on Sorcha.*

"What's up?" Cam asked, sensing there was an announcement coming.

"I need to take Di to Clava," she stated bluntly.

That made me look up from my plate. Di just blushed.

"Clava?" Cam asked incredulously. "Why on earth would you want to go there?"

Sorcha paused, her mouth open, as she chose her following words.

"Because we think I have cancer," Di said covertly, trying not to be overheard by the children. A glance confirmed they were still giggling and having a wonderful time.

That took the wind out of Cam's sails quite visibly. All the color had drained from his face, making him look gray and ghostly. Everyone had stopped eating, and all the adults were staring at her, making Di exceedingly uncomfortable.

"Cancer?" Cam croaked.

Sorcha nodded sagely. "We have enough equipment here to do the basic diagnostics, but we don't have any expertise in treating it. I instructed Aidan to ask in a broadcast, and apparently, they have an oncologist on Clava. We leave in two days. They are expecting us."

Aidan had proven to be an exceptional choice for our spokesperson. He thoroughly enjoyed receiving updates from settlements around the world, both antipodean and isolated, and he also enjoyed passing news on. I had never known Aidan to be chatty before, but now he was the font of all knowledge, speaking to everyone on Lewis, and had become the central point for news. The problem was, we hadn't had a chance to share Luca's information from the day before with the others. We had planned to do it tonight, after dinner, but this news...

I looked at Cam. "There is that French oncologist there, remember? Magali. We met her that night at dinner."

Furrowing his brows, Cam's face lightened. "I do. She was there on assignment from Auckland but was heading back in June."

"That is why we need to go quickly," Sorcha finished.

Luca, unsure what to say, sat quietly, looking at his plate.

"Do you want me to come? I have been there, met Magali. I can help," Cam asked, making my heart lurch.

"No, I can manage," Sorcha replied briskly. "But I need you to look after Sam. We don't know how long we will be away. Treatment could take some months."

"And the baby?" I whispered, scared of the response. Di was pregnant, about twenty weeks now. I had suspected she was unwell since Christmas, but *cancer*? That bombshell had knocked even me for six.

"The baby will be fine," Sorcha responded firmly. "We just need to get there."

"I will come with you," Luca said softly but firmly. It wasn't an offer but a statement of fact. Everyone paused and looked at Luca.

I looked at Sorcha expectantly. She nodded. She knew what had happened to Laetitia, and also to Cam and me at the farm.

"Thank you. Can you be ready to leave the day after tomorrow?" she asked gently.

"I can. But first, I need to tell you some things." He looked at me, and I nodded confirmation, sending the children into the living room to play before dessert.

CHAPTER 28

BEFORE DAWN TWO DAYS later, we set off, Cam and I accompanying Luca, Sorcha, and Di to the harbor. Luca and I had spent years together on the *Selkie,* and he was a competent sailor. But the *Eurydice* was slightly different to operate, and I wanted to give him a handover to ensure they could travel to Clava quickly. Squinting, I could just make out a strange vessel, advancing slowly toward the far end of the dock, barely visible in the low light.

Here we go, I thought, and quickly alerted the others who were chatting and hadn't noticed. Luca had, his military training never permitting him to be oblivious to any situation that could pose a danger. I noticed he had already dropped out of sight.

Di, Sorcha, Cam, and I approached cautiously as the small fishing vessel leisurely came into port. A head with long dark hair stuck its head out of the window and waved madly.

"Illy?"

"Cam!"

"What on earth are you doing here?" he called. "Not that I am not happy to see you!"

Watching Cam sweep this tiny, bird-like woman off the dock, I felt my stomach lurch and then tense. Alarmed by the unusual feelings, I watched him embrace her and kiss her on the lips. Trying hard to maintain the smile plastered on my face, I waited quietly until they turned to us. Sorcha and Di were also watching with great interest at this unexpected and overly friendly reunion. Unmistakably, there was something between them.

Cam turned, beaming. "Frey! This is my friend Illyria. Illy was one of the recruitment team in Melbourne, but she now lives on the Orkneys."

"Illy, this is my wife Freyja, my sister Sorcha, and her partner Di."

I blushed slightly at the word "wife." Illy didn't seem to have noticed.

"Lovely to meet you all," she gushed charmingly. *Goodness, so she was lovely as well as pretty and overly friendly with my husband,* I thought uncharitably but maintained the pleasant façade.

"Where are you off to?" she asked, noting the bags we carried.

Cam slumped visibly. "We are fairly sure that Diana here, Sorcha's wife, has cancer. We were taking her to Clava to see Magali."

Di just smiled uncomfortably, not used to being the center of all of this attention or her medical condition discussed with strangers.

"Ahh, I know Maggie," Illy chirped. "She is an exceptional doctor. But you know, I really wouldn't recommend it."

Sorcha bristled. "Why?"

Illy looked at Cam, and he back at her.

"Illy, this is my family. If there is something we should know about Magali, then you need to let us know. I can't lose Di."

Illy's face went through a transformation of emotion, struggling with what to tell us. "Can we go inside the dome?" she asked cautiously and in a very low voice, her face looking down at her feet. "We aren't safe here."

Now it was my turn to look at her with astonishment. "Safe?"

It was Cam who answered quietly. "I trust Illy. If she says to return, we should."

Illy spoke quietly, her face still down. "I will tell you. If you want to travel after what I tell you, I will come with you. But you should know everything first."

Luca reappeared silently, realizing after Cam's embrace that this woman was no threat. One minute he wasn't there; the next, he just was. He introduced himself nonchalantly but said nothing about who he was or why he was with us. Once inside the dome, Illy was delightful and chatted as we started the long walk back to our tiny village. Neutral things, how the community on Orkney was faring: the people, crops, and children. People Cam had met previously. Nothing controversial.

Several hours later, and now full daylight, Illy slowly pulled the blinds shut as she stood beside the window as we settled ourselves in our living room.

"What's with all the cloak and dagger?" Cam asked as he assisted her. Illy pushed him out of the line of sight.

"Well, you know they have satellites?"

Cam and I both nodded. We had heard this from Ashton. Luca had confirmed it.

"Well, they have drones too, with sound. Inside the dome is relatively safe, but inside a stone building is even safer."

"Why would they care about us?" Sorcha asked a little crankily. The look of thunder on her face indicated she was not pleased to have their trip delayed on the whim of some little bit of fluff, even if her brother liked her.

Illy paused. It was Cam who broke the silence. "Illy, this is important, clearly, for you to have come all this way and in the dark. To stop the girls from traveling. If you have something to tell us, please do. I promise we will listen."

Illy looked Cam in the eyes and nodded. Settling in, she started. "The scientific communities of Clava and Auckland have quietly been establishing something called the Collective. Basically, centrally governed communities. The communities of Auckland and Clava jointly controlling all the others. An agreed set of rules, laws if you like."

"We know that already from Luca. He was one of Angus's team. Came to his senses," I interjected to move this along. Maybe if we were quick, the girls could still depart today.

Luca nodded but didn't say anything. But I noted he was alert.

"I still don't understand. What is wrong with that?" Di said.

"Nothing in theory. And communities are agreeing because of what they are promising."

"Which is?" Sorcha asked.

"A return to how we lived before. A consumerist economy, people being paid for their work, and everyone taxed to pay for services such as facilitated trade across the communities. They have learned how to manipulate the portals so that any antipodean point can travel to any other. Plus, they are offering access to technology, medical support. The life we had before."

"Okay, we knew all of that and the way you say it, that all sounds reasonable. Especially the medical part," Di said cautiously. She was quiet, I had noticed, clearly disturbed at her emergency trip being postponed. "What's the catch?"

"They have been waiting, monitoring, observing. Waiting for the right time for the communities to be mature enough."

Luca spoke quietly, "Angus told me they had a matrix to assess that."

"They do. They knew that eventually, people would grow tired of working hard to survive. That people would be jealous when they perceived others to have more. They offered computers that can maintain greenhouses and the capacity to mass-produce chickens, fish, and pigs. This frees up people to have more leisure time and work less. They are offering electric cars and bikes that are safe to use under the dome so that people no longer have to walk. This is why these things were never provided upon settlement. Better electrical systems so we can run more timesaving appliances like clothes dryers and dishwashers."

"It sounds attractive," I admitted, the exhaustion of a long day tending livestock fresh in my mind. But seeing the wild look in Cam's eye, I added hurriedly, "But never worth trading freedom for."

"Exactly. The problem is, they are compelling. Several more communities have just voted and agreed to join the Collective."

"Which ones?" Luca asked curiously. "My intel is a few weeks old."

Illy's mouth quirked at the word intel.

"As of five days ago, August for one. Shetlands and Bellcamp too."

"Really?" we responded in unison. But truthfully, we weren't surprised. Cam and I had spoken at length about the political systems in the different communities we had both visited. August had struggled with factions from the start. Many had resented the lack of recognition and payment. Bellcamp had already been consumerist, so this was just offering an incentive.

"Newgrange?" Cam asked cautiously.

"No. They voted for independence."

"And Orkney?" he prodded gently.

"No matter what I said, I couldn't persuade them," Illyria said sadly. "The Orcadians were almost sold on the idea of external wind turbines linked to better electrical substations. It is a depressing winter on Orkney. But that wasn't the turning point. I could understand the benefits, but it was not worth the sacrifice."

"Freedom?" I asked gently.

"Exactly. Clava watched and waited for the right time. When they felt each community was at its lowest, usually in the middle of a tough winter, he rode in on his gallant steed and came to save the day. How on earth so many people believed that dickwad is beyond me."

"Dickwad?" I questioned.

"Angus MacLeod, of course. Have you not met him?"

Cam quickly filled Illy in on Angus and my history. I noted he didn't tell her about Kat. Possibly his most generous act, although I knew it didn't even come close to balancing out what he had done—to me personally, and to others.

"There is something else," she started cautiously, then stopped. I could feel Sorcha's frustration from across the room.

"Illy, if there is more, just tell us."

Cam was more gracious than the rest of us. We knew everything she had already told us from Luca. We knew, and we still agreed that getting in bed with the devil was preferable to losing Di.

Illy breathed out audibly and said cautiously. "I can't prove this, but I will tell you what I know. The reason the community on Orkney finally agreed to join the Collective was that Will's youngest daughter had lymphoma, and the scientists at Clava cured her."

"Little Thea?" Cam asked, shocked. "Cancer? She was fine when I was there in October!"

"She was. It all happened very quickly. She was very ill, and they asked me to make contact. We took her to Clava. I went too. Magali cured her, and as you can imagine, the community was grateful."

"Okay, so what is the problem?" Sorcha asked, frustration taking hold. "If they cured her, why did you stop us?"

"Because the same thing happened in Toulouse. One of the prominent, well-liked families. The husband was suddenly critically ill. The medical team on Clava cured him. I was there with Thea, Will, and Liesl. I met them."

"I thought Toulouse voted no," Luca added quietly, connecting the dots. "That was what I heard."

"They had previously voted no. Now they are part of the Collective. It happened on the Falklands too."

We all looked at Di.

"Surely not," Cam whispered in stunned amazement. "Even *they* wouldn't infect someone with cancer. For what purpose?"

"I can't prove it. But this is now the fourth time a respected family has had a person suddenly struck with cancer or an illness closely resembling it. Someone the community would do anything for."

We all looked at Di, and she blushed. But it was true. Everyone loved Di—in the year she had been here, she had assisted everyone. No one had a bad word to say about her. She had such a happy, outgoing, and helpful nature. Sorcha, as a doctor, and a very good one, was revered and respected. Cam was loved, especially after Lae's death. If you wanted to convert our community to something, getting Cam and Sorcha onside would be critical.

"I can't believe the scientists on Clava would deliberately infect someone else with cancer," I said crisply and held my hand up to Cam as he began to interrupt. "But I believe you, Illy. As filthy and unconscionable as what you are suggesting may be, the truth is that Cam and I were utterly disgusted by some of the things we learned. Then Luca came a few days ago and told us about Angus and his mission. You have traveled a long way to tell us something you considered important. Illy, I believe you."

Illy and Cam both smiled at me, relief and gratitude clear in their eyes.

"How would they even infect her?" Sorcha asked incredulously, still not convinced. "Does such technology even exist?"

"It does," Illy admitted. "I can tell you that for a fact. They had nanotechnology specialists. It was one of the many reasons I left Clava. There is one other thing I should warn you about. As I left, they were experimenting with psychotropic herbs."

"Psychotropic?" Di asked. "That doesn't sound good."

"It isn't quite as bad as it sounds," Illy hastened to explain. "Psychotropic just means any substance that can alter behavior or mood. Some were readily available in your local health store: valerian, kava, St John's Wort, for example. Lots of people took them."

"I know very well what psychotropic means. Why are you telling us?" Sorcha asked brusquely. She didn't trust Illy. Luca was also sitting back, taking it all in, assessing, but saying nothing.

Illy sighed. "One day, while researching a project, I found evidence that they were experimenting with herbs to make people more compliant. When I asked questions, it was all brushed over. My training and my instincts told me it was all linked."

"Your training?" Sorcha sneered sarcastically.

"Ph.D. in communications and psychology. Major, Intelligence Corps., Australian Army," Illyria snapped, glaring unblinkingly at Sorcha, daring a challenge. Despite coming up to roughly Sorcha's armpit, with that tone, it was abundantly clear that she was no pushover. Trying not to smirk, I recognized that Sorcha might well have met her intellectual match.

"Do you think it is all linked?"

Cam was the one person buying it. But he had the benefit of knowing her. And knowing her well, it appeared. Despite my suspicion of this woman, I had to admit she sounded right. Cam and I had noticed a marked change in our attitudes toward Clava after we had left. I looked over, and he saw me.

"Do you think…?" I asked Cam, meeting his gaze.

Cam nodded gravely. "I do. It all makes sense now. The day we arrived, we were suspicious. But as time wore on, we relaxed. Probably said and did things we ordinarily wouldn't."

Recalling that afternoon out at the cairns, I blushed, realizing that we had been in plain sight. Similarly, on our walks in the woods most mornings. *Did they see us?*

Illy was watching me closely.

"It's true," I admitted. "The first night, we felt like we were in the Stepford Wives. Everything was so perfect, and we were suspicious of everyone. But after that, we relaxed, enjoyed being there. Time passed so quickly, almost like a time leap. We hadn't realized we were there for so long. It felt like six hours, not six weeks. We didn't question our suspicions again until…"

"We were on the boat on our way back here," Cam finished. "Do you remember that we both couldn't sleep, had headaches, and felt nauseous the few days after we left? We thought it was something we ate."

"Withdrawal," Sorcha interjected. "Classic drug withdrawal."

Nodding at Sorcha, Cam said to Illy, "I told you my sister is a doctor?"

At the time, I had fervently hoped that the nausea, which had affected me more, had been a symptom of something else. But after a day or two, it became clear that the situation was temporary.

"Did you warn the people on Orkney?" I asked Illy carefully. I didn't want her to think I blamed her, although she had been one of them.

"I tried," she confessed. "But they were so grateful to the medical team on Clava for saving little Thea's life. And I get that. Will is highly respected. If he said to support them, then they did. The bonus of unlimited electricity in a community that spends months each year with only a few hours of daylight was also very attractive. The community voted just a few days ago. It didn't take much. I went straight home after the meeting, packed my bag, and came here, traveling at night to avoid detection."

"So, how do we deal with this?" Sorcha turned to us all. "I am not prepared to lose Di over politics. Can we play the game? Take her along to Clava to get her treated but refuse to sign over our sovereignty when the time comes?"

"That was what Cam and I did," I said softly. "Just didn't give them an answer and left. I'm not sure they will fall for that a second time. Are there specialists elsewhere?" I asked Illyria.

"Sadly, no. As far as I am aware, there are no other oncologists. Magali was the best of the best from what I heard on Auckland."

"How terribly convenient," Di drawled sarcastically.

We all looked at her, surprised to hear her speak. Here we were, talking about her, but not really asking her.

"What do *you* want?" Cam asked gently.

"Well, I don't want to die," Di said softly. "I want to be here to see my children grow up, watch Sorcha and

I get old. It was a privilege denied to my parents. But," she continued, "I also don't want to be responsible for a political stramash that affects all of us."

"Di, none of us want to lose you," I said. It was true. Everyone loved Di. While I had known her before, she and Sorcha had become good friends over the time we lived together. "But I think a governance decision is one for the entire community. We need Illy to tell them what she knows, and Cam and I can confirm what we learned when we were in Clava. Luca too. I don't think this is our decision to make."

Sorcha started to object, recognizing that this would delay Di's treatment, but relented.

"Agreed. It is a monumental decision. We would be giving up a lot: medical treatment and supplies, access to knowledge, unlimited electricity, and free trade. But can we arrange this meeting quickly?"

It stunned the community to hear the reports from Luca and Illyria. Luca, an original settler in this community, was viewed with suspicion and respect. He had been here at the start, and many had known him. They listened but with a degree of skepticism. Despite being part of the team that had rescued the women from Mousa, Luca had the dubious honor of siding with Angus when Angus was not someone you wanted to be associated with.

Illyria, on the other hand, I was surprised to see they took seriously. She must have been very good at her job, I realized, as she worked the room. She was warm, engaging, and made people feel that each one of them was valued and consulted. She perfected the right mix of listening, understanding, but also getting her point across. She explained about the finite resources, how Angus had spied on the community all along. The satellite surveillance and now the drones. Now, how people were getting sick in communities who refused to join. While they were offering fabulous things, the consequences of not agreeing seemed very high for someone posing as benevolent.

People looked to Cam, sitting quietly next to me, Sorcha on his other side. What did he think?

"Honestly, I could never trust anyone on Clava after I learned they saw our people be taken, and they did nothing. They did nothing when the dome over Gibraltar was breached, and the residents killed. Frequently, it appears, they have had the power to intervene, to save people, but they chose not to. They didn't help us before. I truly don't think we can trust them now."

There were lots of nods of agreement at this. Three men had been killed, and five women kidnapped and mistreated. Laetitia was the only female casualty, but not one member of our community had not been affected by those events.

Hamish looked at me. "And you, Freyja. What do you think?"

I paused. I hadn't expected to be consulted. Finally, I spoke my truth. "When I first came here, it was by accident. All I wanted was to get home to my husband, Cam."

Cam reached for my hand and clasped it in his larger one.

"Traveling through that portal was indescribable. A feeling of being turned inside out, pulled apart, and prolonged, excruciating pain. As some of you know, I suffered a fractured skull when I hit the tomb arriving at this end. I knew I could never do it again, so I told Angus I was traveling back by sea. He chose to come, and Luca did too. I'm so sorry I backed the wrong horse. I had no idea what Angus had done until much later. Many years later, in some cases. I am still learning the things he has done. But at the time, I just wanted to go home and be with the man I love. Now I know what kind of person he is. He played me and was spying on you all this time. He had the power to save those people you saw outside the dome. It is Angus who is being tasked with facilitating this agreement. Ask yourselves: is this someone who has proven himself worthy of your trust?"

Walking home in the dark, Luca spoke quietly from behind me. "You hit the jackpot, Frey."

Cam smiled as his arm slipped around my waist. "You did good, honey."

CHAPTER 29

ILLY, LUCA, DI, AND Sorcha left for Clava the following day, only two days later than planned. Life back on Lewis was suddenly calm after the months of trauma.

"Do you feel like it is the calm before the storm?" I said to Cam one night as we were preparing to go to bed after a long, tiring day.

"I do," he admitted. "Whenever I feel settled like this, a whole shit storm blows up. Is it too much to ask for a little peace?"

We were getting updates on Di every few days. Illy radioed Aidan, who passed the messages on. We knew she was careful with what she said, so we didn't ask for too much. But Di was well, responding to treatment, and they had done their best to minimize the impact on the baby. Given the potential for complications, the baby would be induced prematurely. Sorcha had demanded to be on the medical team, and they had agreed.

"Relented after they worked out what they were up against?" I giggled.

Cam, who had over twenty years of experience with Sorcha and her demanding stubbornness, just said, "Oh how I wish you could have met my mother."

"I would have liked that. Do you think she would have liked me?"

"Mum would *adore* you. Strong-willed, intelligent, determined, opinionated. You, my mother, and Sorcha. You are all very much alike."

"Hey!" I playfully slapped at him. "You don't flatter me much, do you?"

"I forgot generous, caring, and the most amazing lover," he crooned as he kissed me with so much tenderness that I almost forgot what he was saying.

"I'm not sure your mother would appreciate that last trait," I purred as his mouth dropped lower.

"She wouldn't want me to be unhappy." Cam's voice came from somewhere near my navel, as I stretched back, enjoying the attention despite my bone-deep exhaustion.

"And are you … unhappy?"

The kissing stopped, and I felt his voice resonate through me as his chin rested on my stomach.

"Is it wrong to say that despite everything that is going on, with Di and the Collective, that on a personal note, I don't think I have ever been happier?"

"There is one thing that would make me happier," I whispered, barely able to get the words out.

"I know, honey. Working on it."

The impact of missing two key members of our tiny village meant a significantly increased workload for the rest, but no one minded. After all, they had accommodated Cam and me being away for weeks, and we all recognized that this was just part of living in a close community. Setting a schedule, we each took turns to mind the children while others worked. Adjusting the tasks to accommodate Isla's new pregnancy and morning sickness, I tried to take the veterinary jobs that kept me away from home while she saw the clients who could come to our clinic. It was an excellent arrangement, but it kept me away for much of the day.

Fraser and Cam took turns to work in both our greenhouse and the community one in Garynahine. Once a week, they traveled there together, spending an entire day weeding, planting, and generally ensuring that any resident could come and pick what they needed. While there had been community gardens back in Australia, here people respected the work and never left a mess, damaged anything, or took more than they needed.

How much longer?

After seven weeks of punishing work schedule, rising early and falling into bed, exhausted, well after dark, I wasn't sure how much longer I could keep this up. My knowledge of cancer treatment in Australia was that the course of treatment could take months. I sincerely hoped that Di would be well enough to travel back soon. Cam and I barely saw each other for twenty minutes a day, and that was often wolfing down breakfast or scoffing a late meal while the kids got ready for bed.

As I dressed, yawning profusely, Cam entered our room, handing me a cup of coffee.

"I love you," I said with all of my heart as I stared into the dark milky depths. It was going to be a long day. I needed to travel to the northern part of the community, up near Arnol, to geld a stallion. Not my favorite job at the best of times. I had taken an e-bike rather than ride a horse; at least I could charge it before I made the return journey, some 50 kilometers in total. It also meant that all the smaller jobs would need to wait another day, wasting so much time in transit. I still wasn't keen on e-bikes after our experience near Inverness, but I realized that it was by far the best option. *If only we had cars!* I thought for the millionth time that month, remembering what Illy was saying about the Collective offering electric cars. Today I would have accepted the offer gladly.

While at Mann's farm, the stallion was gelded without too much furor, and I was asked to assist with a few other tasks which I felt I couldn't refuse. After all, I hadn't been here in months. There was bound to be a backlog of chores. Castrating bulls, drenching sheep, and worming a whole menagerie of animals took the best part of the day, and the sun was mid-way down the sky by the time I said goodbye, politely refusing their kind offer of dinner.

Knowing it would likely be dark before I got home, I pushed the bike to its limits, a challenge considering the rough terrain. Hitting a deep pothole in the shadowy, dusk light, the bike kept going as I tried to put my foot down. The bike shot out from under me, and I tumbled, my foot dropping into the pothole, twisting my knee painfully and landing on my hip, the bike atop me.

"Owww!" I cried out, but with no one to hear me, I swore instead, profusely, as I kicked the bike with my uninjured leg.

As I lay there in the road, instinctively I knew that this wasn't a minor accident. My foot and ankle were soaked from falling into the hole. My knee throbbed painfully, and I could feel the swelling as the fabric of my jeans grew tighter. Fabulous. And with Sorcha away, too. Well, I had no time to consider it now. Forcing myself up, I picked up the bike, moving it from the pothole, and recommenced my journey. But I slowed, carefully navigating the roads in the dark. They had streetlights in Clava. *Maybe... no.* I snapped my wandering mind back. *No.* They had likely infected Di. There was no way we were negotiating with the devil.

Finally chugging up the final crest toward home, I stopped as I reached the top. An icy wave washed over me. Something was wrong. Usually, there were lights on in both houses. The animals were put away. I could see the chickens fluttering around from here, even in the dim moonlight. The houses loomed dark and quiet.

Flying down the hill as fast as I could with my aching knee screaming at each rotation of the pedals, I called, "Cam! Fraser! Where is everyone?"

My voice echoed back at me, and I tried again. "Hello!"

Dropping the bike, I hobbled into our house. Dark. Empty. *Fuck.*

"Cam? Louis?" I called, trying to project my voice.

Freaking hell, where is everyone? All the kids were gone, too. Six kids made some noise, so the silence was terrifying.

"Meow?" I heard at my feet as Jam rubbed around my legs, looking for dinner.

"Not now, sweetie," I promised. "Later."

Entering Fraser's house, it was apparent that they weren't there as soon as I opened the door. Sorcha and Di's house had been empty for weeks. *What is the logical next step? Garynahine?*

Barely remembering to close the door, I grabbed the blasted bike and began the journey in the dark, desperate to hurry but fearful of falling off again. The more I moved, the more my knee hurt. Shooting pains were now radiating up my leg. Remembering the technique Sorcha had taught me to get through childbirth, I focused on my breathing, exhaling forcefully.

As I reached the outskirts of Garynahine, I stopped, unable to weight bear on my bad leg. *Where could they be with all the kids?* The medical center made the most sense. There wasn't much else that would have kept them away in the dark.

As soon as the white stone building came into view, I saw Fraser and Isla sitting on the benches outside with the kids, Fraser holding Katrin, asleep. Isla with Kari. All the kids ... except Louis.

Fraser saw me approach and, balancing Katrin against his stomach, held his hands up to stop me from panicking. Isla had been crying. Her face was red and blotchy. She looked terrible, and tears started flowing again as I approached. Between Fraser talking, Isla crying, and me trying to ask questions, I finally worked out that Louis was hurt. Unable to understand what Fraser was saying with Isla sobbing, I dropped the bike and pushed past him.

As soon as I entered the main treatment room, I saw Cam. His face was ghostly white and drawn in pain as he sat beside the bed containing Louis. My child was unconscious. Barely noticing how I got there,

I was across the room in an instant and at his side. With my arms on his shoulders, I looked down at him.

"Louis," I sobbed, my head on his chest. "What happened?"

"Mumma?" the little voice asked.

Looking up at his face, I saw him open his eyes, and it was then I noticed the oversized bandage wrapped around his head, blended with the pillow.

"Louis? I'm here!"

A brief smile crossed his face as he closed his eyes again.

"No, Louis, talk to me. Tell me what happened, darling."

Louis' eyelids fluttered once more, and Cam was standing on his other side, holding his hand.

"Hey, buddy! How are you?"

Fighting sleep, he opened his eyes and struggled to focus on us. "Mumma, Dadda?" Then he reached his hands up to his head, grimaced in pain, and cried, "My head hurts, Mumma!"

"Sweetheart, what happened?"

"He fell," Cam whispered as Louis lapsed into unconsciousness again. "Isla was held up with a client. She had Katrin and Kari with her, but Niamh, Iona, Sam, and Louis were playing outside. They built an obstacle course from large rocks, jumping from one to another. Sam made the jump. Louis didn't. He fell and hit his forehead on the low rock wall near the greenhouse."

"Oww!" I winced, envisioning exactly how that had happened. Desperate to be a big kid, Louis would have done anything his hero Sam did. With two significant head wounds myself in recent years, I was in a better position than most to know just how much that hurt.

"Then?"

"It knocked him out cold, so they thought they had killed him. They screamed for Isla, who came running. It was Josh with her, so they left the calf behind, and Josh and Isla carried Louis and Katrin, Sam helped Kari, and the older girls walked all the way here. Sam came and got Fraser and me from the greenhouse here, crying so hard that I couldn't make out what he was saying at first. But I soon realized Louis was injured and raced here."

"Oh darling," I crooned as I held his limp form in my arms, stroking the blood-soaked chestnut hair from his face. "You will be okay. We are here now."

"Where is Hamish?" I asked without taking my eyes from Louis.

"Off delivering a baby."

"Morwenna? Mel?"

"Here. It was Mel who cleaned up the wound, stitched up his head, and bandaged it. He is drifting in and out of consciousness with the pain, but we have nothing to give him. She is hunting through all the cupboards and kits to find something. Anything."

"She stitched him with no pain relief?" I asked incredulously.

"She did. I had to hold him down."

"Oh, God." I thought I was going to vomit. The thought of holding a two-year-old down while a doctor inserted sutures was horrifying. It was bad enough for me with pain relief the first time and drunk the second.

"Can we call Jacinda? She was always so good at knowing what we could use."

"Done that. I sent Josh off to Aidan's house to radio August and see what we can give him that is safe and likely to have. What happened to the bottle of codeine that they gave you at Clava?"

"I gave it to Sorcha for Di," I replied wistfully. "Sorcha was scared that if labor came early, she wouldn't have anything for the pain."

At that moment, I realized exactly how Clava got communities to sign over their independence. *What was it that Luca had said? Wait until they are desperate enough?*

I would have done anything at this moment to ease my child's pain. I said so to Cam, and he nodded grimly.

"I have been sitting here thinking precisely the same thing for the past two hours."

Mel entered the room at that point, a look of anguish on her usually cheerful countenance. She didn't need to tell us. There was nothing.

"I'm going to send Fraser and Isla home with the kids. There is no point in them being here all night."

"Go with them. Take Katrin home."

"No. Louis is my son too," I said firmly. "I will not leave until he does."

Limping around the bed to the door, Cam noticed my unsteady gait. "What happened?"

"Not now. Not important."

Josh came bursting into the room, panting. "Willow bark," he gasped. "White willow bark."

Unable to focus on what he was saying, I felt like he was speaking a language foreign to me.

But Cam was nodding as he stood.

Grabbing a scalpel from the cleaned instruments laid out glistening on a white cloth, Cam was out the door in a shot, heading out the back entrance into the night.

Catching his breath, Josh managed, "Jacinda said the bark of the white willow tree contains the natural ingredient in aspirin: salicylic acid. He can chew the bark, or we can grind it up and make a tea."

"Both," I responded instantly, looking around for a way to boil water.

Not willing to leave Louis, but recognizing that I couldn't leave Fraser and his family outside all night in the cold, I braced myself against the pain and hobbled outside. In the gentlest voice I could muster, I told Fraser, "Louis will be okay, but we need to stay with him. Could you please take Katrin and Sam home? Your girls too. You are all exhausted."

"But..." Fraser started at the same time Sam spoke. "I'm so sorry..." he cried.

Looking directly at Sam, I shut him down. "No. It was an accident. Accidents happen Sam. He will be okay. But I need your help. I need you to look after your little cousin. Could you please take care of Kat for me? I need to stay with Louis a little longer. It would mean a lot to me."

Sam sniffed, stuck out his chin, and said, "I can."

Looking up at Fraser and Isla, I said softly, "He will be okay. We will keep you posted."

With that, I turned and limped back into the surgery. Pain shot up my leg as I moved, but I didn't care. There was nothing that could be done anyway. Mel saw me grimace and started to speak, but I cut her off.

"Not now. You can look at it before we go, but while my child is still in pain, I can't. This isn't about me."

Mel, the mother of three children, nodded, understanding.

It felt like an eternity sitting beside little Louis's bed, stroking his hair, holding his hand. Talking to him. Singing. Louis loved to sing to Katrin. Row, row your boat. Hey, diddle diddle. Incy wincy spider. I couldn't bring myself to sing five monkeys jumping on the bed or Jack and Jill. That seemed wrong in the present circumstances. He cried intermittently in pain and occasionally woke, but mostly, he slept. I was grateful for that.

Please hurry, Cam, I pleaded silently. *I need you.*

Finally, my thoughts turned to Laetitia. His birth mother. I had seen enough photos to know what she had looked like, had seen her a few times from a distance, although I had never spoken with her. He looked like her. I conjured her image and prayed to her.

"Laetitia, I know you probably hate me, and you have every right to. But this isn't about Cam or me. Louis is hurt, and I need your help. We need him here. We love him so very much, Cam, Kat, and I." As I spoke the words, I stumbled a little on Kat's name but pushed on. "Please don't take him from us. I promise you: I will always love him like my own. Care for him. Nurture him. Please. Help him."

Hearing the front door open, I snapped out of my trance and stood without thinking, collapsing, my knee unable to hold my weight. Cam dropped the bark he was holding and was on his knees beside me in an instant.

"I'm alright," I snapped, more frustrated at myself than him.

"You're hurt." It was a statement, not a question. He knew me well enough. Deceiving him was pointless.

"Here, chew this." He shoved a piece of bark at me. I snorted but took it nonetheless. It couldn't do any harm. He helped me to my feet, and I dropped some of the bark in the simmering water and wondered how long to brew it for.

"I never thought to ask Josh," I said regretfully. "Assuming he even asked Jacinda."

"Where is he?"

"I sent him home to his family. Fraser and Isla too. There was nothing they could do here."

"I didn't spare a thought for them, focused on Louis as I was."

Mel returned to check on Louis, his temperature, and his blood pressure. She rolled her eyes when she saw the bark steeping. It wasn't like she had any better alternatives.

Sitting beside Louis's bed, chewing bark, the pain from my throbbing knee eased somewhat. Not to the degree of morphine, but it was undoubtedly alleviated.

When Louis finally woke, he looked over at me and said, "Mumma, why you eat sticks?"

Laughing, I said, "It is medicine, my little man. Do you want some too?"

Between sips of tea, he chewed the bark. Throughout the night, we repeated this. Tea, bark, sleep.

Somewhere toward dawn, he woke. I had fallen asleep, my head resting on my arms at the side of his bed.

"Mumma? Dadda?" his little voice barely reached us, through our haze of exhaustion.

I bolted awake. Cam did too.

"Louis?"

"I love you, Mumma."

Tears flowed. I was unable to stem the tide. "Oh darling, I love you too."

"Love you too, Dadda."

When Hamish arrived in the morning, Louis was sitting up in bed, gingerly feeling his wound. He was still in pain, but it was tolerable now. Fraser arrived soon after, and Cam sent him off to find more willow bark. In the dark, he hadn't been able to see what he was doing, and there was the genuine risk of falling down an embankment or slicing his hand. Without question, Fraser did as he was asked.

Hamish unwrapped Louis's head and inhaled as he saw the wound. So did I. There was a large hematoma, enormous swelling, and prominent bruising under the skin as well as a laceration roughly ten centimeters long, now with neat black stitches holding it together. Hamish swabbed it with the raw alcohol we now used in place of commercial antiseptic. Louis cringed but didn't cry.

As he finished, Cam said forcefully, "Hamish, I need you to look at Freyja's knee."

Protesting, I knew the futility. Scowling at Cam, I needed help to remove my boots, unable to bend my right knee. As I was slipping off my jeans, I remembered I had worn my very revealing black lace wedding knickers, as I did occasionally to stir up Cam. Hamish, with the experience of a well-seasoned doctor, didn't seem to notice. Cam, flushing furiously, most certainly did but looked away until he could get his face under control. Hamish palpated the wound, watching my face as it went through a series of screwed-up expressions. I would not let Louis hear my pain. My back was to him, so he couldn't see my face.

"Can you stand?" Hamish asked.

"Yes," I said, as Cam replied, "No."

Hamish looked at us, confused.

"She tried to stand in the night and fell over," Cam explained. "She can't weight bear."

Glowering at him, I tried to stand to prove him wrong but fairly quickly had to admit the truth.

"What happened?"

As briefly as I could, I explained what had happened.

"Let's just hope it isn't a torn ligament," Hamish muttered. "It's not like we can operate."

Hamish sourced a wheelchair and announced that he was taking me to the radiography room. Cam was torn.

"Stay here with Louis," I ordered. "We won't be long. I'm in excellent hands."

Nodding, he smiled, appreciating that I hadn't given him a choice.

"What are you thinking?" I asked Hamish as soon as we were out of earshot, Hamish pushing me up the hallway in the wheelchair.

"Sprain at best, ACL at worst," he told me. "I'm fairly sure your PCL is intact."

I appreciated the honesty, one medical professional to another. Hamish had always treated me with respect, even when I first arrived here, wet and raving. It was he who had x-rayed my head wound and not betrayed my confidence. Half an hour later, the MRI showed it was a torn anterior meniscus but that both ligaments were intact.

"Thank goodness," I breathed. A torn ACL would need surgical repair, and that was something we had no capacity for. While likely never healing, a meniscus could be mostly symptom free with ice, rest, and exercise.

Returning to the room where Louis lay sleeping, Hamish left us alone as Cam hurriedly helped me put my jeans and boots back on, blushing as he did so.

"So?" Cam looked at me expectantly. As a skier, Cam knew about knee injuries. There was no point in lying.

"Torn meniscus, but the ACL and PCL are intact."

Cam looked at me, recognizing the mixed blessing in this news. There was no way I could walk distances for a while, but it would, in time, heal. Hearing voices in the foyer, I greeted Morwenna, the doctor who had treated me initially upon my arrival here, Hamish, and... Fraser. He was back. Beaming, he thrust a bag of bark at Cam. Seeing me in a wheelchair, a look of puzzlement crossed his face.

"Torn meniscus," I droned.

"How?"

"Fell off the bike."

He looked puzzled, so I elaborated. I explained, despite not wanting to. I felt foolish enough. "How are Isla and the kids?"

"Isla is devastated. She blames herself."

Cam spoke, but Fraser raised his voice. "Really, she is gutted. She keeps saying how you saved her life, and she nearly took Louis away from you. She wants to know what she can do to make it up to you. Please, give her something. She won't stop beating herself up until you do."

"Can she look after Katrin and Sam for a few days?" I asked. "We don't want to leave Louis."

Fraser beamed, knowing that this was both genuinely helpful but would also make Isla feel valued. By allowing her to look after our baby, she would know we didn't blame her for Louis.

"Done."

"Is Sam okay?" I asked. "He was pretty upset last night."

"Poor kid. He berated himself all the way home. Nothing I said made a difference. He is as bad as Isla with the guilt. He won't let Katrin leave his side, which is driving her mad."

At eleven months old, Katrin was mobile and determined, into everything and as fast as lightning. You only needed to lose focus for a split second, and she was off, climbing and jumping off everything with a knack for knowing precisely what you did *not* want her to do. "Our little daredevil," Cam called her, but I knew he adored her. Louis, by contrast, was such a placid child. A healthy, active three-year-old certainly but without the fiery streak of Katrin.

Morwenna returned and assisted Cam in moving the bedside tables and pushing the three single beds together. With the wheels locked, they didn't move, but they were most uncomfortable. As shattered as we were, Cam and I took one each and slept, exhausted after the night's events.

As I woke sometime later, I felt Cam stir beside me. Rolling onto my back, I saw he was lying half on his bed and half on mine, his arm thrown across my waist but lying across the metal edges. It must have been very uncomfortable, but I was grateful for his presence.

"Cam?" I whispered, careful not to wake Louis.

"Mmmmm?"

"Do you remember that house in Edinburgh where we spent the night? During the storm?"

Cam rolled onto his back and cleared his throat before speaking. "Of course."

Before I could speak again, I heard the soft rumbling of his voice beside me as I gazed up at the ceiling. Turning over was difficult and jarred my knee. "I remember watching you sleep and pinching myself, unable to believe what had happened. Feeling like it was the first time. Wanting you so desperately, needing to be with you, touch you, but not wanting to scare you off. I remember a few things we did in that house."

Feeling a little self-conscious, I smiled. That day had been the turning point and had led us to where we are now.

"Did I ever thank you—for coming after me?"

"Not in words, no," I admitted. "But I know what you mean. I am so very thankful I did too. On the journey to Edinburgh, I second-guessed myself a thousand times, wondering where I would go if you rejected me. What I meant was, do you remember those boxes stacked in the house? Didn't they have medicines in them?"

Cam sat bolt upright and almost fell down the gap between our beds.

"They did. I can't believe we didn't think of that before! There must have been five hundred boxes there, and each had a packet of aspirin, I am certain of it."

"That is my recollection too. The hospital in Inverness had no pain medication, but some chemists must. Now I am not suggesting we go back to Inverness, but there are other hospitals. Clinics. Could we not collect..."

"That is an amazing idea. Why didn't we think of that sooner?"

"Because you never think of it when you aren't in pain," I pointed out logically. "It is like never remembering to buy toothpaste unless you are brushing your teeth!"

Hamish and two others led the expedition to Edinburgh the following day, taking Illy's small fishing boat and planning to return with something larger. Attending university there, he knew the city well, and it wasn't hard to describe the location of the house we had broken into.

"Just look for the broken window." Cam laughed. While we didn't want to be another doctor short, everyone realized that having a medical specialist on the retrieval team made sense. They could assess what was available and ensure we got everything we needed. At some point, one of the vets would make a trip seeking veterinary supplies too.

After Hamish departed and more detailed instructions had been sought from Jacinda about the uses of comfrey, arnica, and boneset, Louis made the slow trek home. Borrowing one of the bike carriers, Cam rode with Louis in the trailer. Unable to bend my knee, Mike brought me a horse and a step ladder, although Cam had mostly lifted me onto the quiet brown mare.

"Daisy, is it?" he asked Mike questioningly.

"It is," replied Mike approvingly. "Don't tell me you like horses now? Thought that was your sister?"

"Nope," Cam replied bluntly. "But you may recall that I rode Daisy here a few times, and she seemed calm enough. We just can't deal with any more drama today."

"Aye, she's a gentle soul."

The trip was arduous, but worth it to be home. Louis and I set up in our bed with a warm doona, reading and keeping each other company. Cam went to fetch Sam and Katrin, the latter of whom came flying in the door like a mini hurricane and threw herself at the side of the bed, chanting, "Mumma! Mumma!" until Cam lifted her.

"We need a bigger bed," I said to Cam as he lay back on his side, Kat and Louis between us, Sam sitting on the end.

"Or a bigger house!" he grinned back at me.

CHAPTER 30

A COMMOTION OUTSIDE THE SHED made me look up from the newborn calf I had just finished examining. He was only a few hours old but doing well and feeding. Giving him a quick pat, I hobbled outside slowly with Cam's old walking stick to see what all the shouting was about.

Cam was running up the hill toward four people, one carrying a large package. I squinted into the sun. No, it was Sorcha, I realized in the next instant, her long red hair ablaze as the afternoon sun struck it, making it gleam in the light. It was a baby in a sling in front of her she was cradling protectively. Di's long black hair with a thick fringe radiated beside her, barely up to Sorcha's shoulder.

"Di! You look so well!" I heard him exclaim as Cam swept her off her feet, and she squealed with joy, throwing her arms around her neck. Kissing her. I could hear the interrupting, throat-clearing noise, even from a distance.

"Oh alright," he feigned jokingly, putting Di down and kissing Sorcha's cheek too, over the baby in her arms.

Pushing through the pain, I made it up the hill. Reaching the crest, I followed suit, hugging Di fiercely before pulling back and looking at her.

"Look at you! There is color in your cheeks, and you have put on weight. You looked like a skeleton when you left, despite the bump. Now, you are positively glowing!"

"It is all thanks to Illy," she beamed.

Carefully, I hugged Sorcha, who looked surprised at first, but relaxed, hugging me back over the baby in the sling.

"Congratulations!" I said enthusiastically. "Who is this little person?"

"I would like to introduce you both to Miss Kendra Cairstine Mackintosh," Sorcha announced, as proud as I have ever seen her.

"Oh, Sorcs, I am so happy for you!" Cam beamed at her. She looked ecstatic, although travel-weary and dirty. "Come on. Let's introduce her to the kids."

Isla and Fraser, hearing the noise, had come to investigate and were headed up the path as we carefully wound our way down, followed by Sam, Katrin, Louis, and their three girls. Isla's now prominent bump was on display.

"Look at you!" squealed Di! "Another one!"

"Another one." Isla rolled her eyes. "You'd think I would have learned by now."

Excitedly, I said, "Louis, Sam, Kat—look who came home!"

"Mum!" Sam cried and fell onto his mother's leg. She squatted, slightly unbalanced with the baby, trying to hug him, and I held out my arms to take the baby from her.

Carefully, she unstrapped the baby and handed her to me. As I peeked inside the swaddle, I could see a tiny delicate face with a fuzz of black hair and a miniature fist clenched against her chin. I couldn't quite see the tiny fingernails. She was exquisite, and my heart twinged just a little. How long would *we* need to wait? I sensed Cam watching me, but I had years of experience in feigning indifference. He had two children, three if you counted little Kendra. I was blessed to have Katrin; I knew that. But part of me desperately wanted a child that wasn't born under dubious circumstances. Just one more was all I wanted.

Holding Katrin's hand with one arm and baby Kendra with the other, we walked back to our house, constantly chattering as we tried to catch up on the past weeks. Illy and Luca quietly brought up the rear, carrying bags and paraphernalia.

"Let's get you some guest rooms organized," I said as they arrived in the clearing between our homes. "We can move the kids into one room, so one of you can have Louis's room, and I am sure..."

"We will only need one room," interjected Illy, her eyes glittering.

Cam's eyebrows lifted for a moment before he burst out in a grin. "Well, congratulations!"

"I travel around the world, in and out of communities, meeting hundreds of people, and I end up with the only other brass in existence," Luca said, unable to wipe the beaming smile from his face. At roughly half his size, Illy slipped a tiny arm around his waist and tipped her head up to look into his rugged face.

"I gave him an order," she teased, "and as his superior officer, I expected him to follow it. Captain Cadman," she taunted as he effortlessly lifted her with one arm to kiss her.

"You work fast," Cam teased Luca. "You've only been gone nine weeks!"

We all stopped and looked at Cam in amazement.

"Did you not think that Di and I hooked up quickly?" Sorcha asked acerbically.

"Or you and I?" I asked, equally flabbergasted.

"Fraser came for dinner one night and never went home," Isla said cheerfully. "I still haven't worked out how to make him leave."

"Funny isn't it," said Illy, gazing up at Luca. "Back home, before all of this, relationships were such hard work. Finding someone looking for Mr. Perfect. Or Ms. Perfect," she amended. "Then it was years before it was acceptable to get engaged, get married. All the games we played, people we tried to impress. Don't you think life is just much simpler here? You meet someone you like, and you make it work. You consciously form a partnership, accept that there will be good days and bad, and roll with the punches."

"I think that sums it up perfectly," said Di, her armed interlinked with Sorcha's. "Now, let's go home and clean up. Who is cooking us dinner?"

Dinner was a raucous affair with jokes, stories, and many toasts to the new parents, the expecting parents, and the new couple. Everyone had a turn cuddling baby Kendra and asked Cam and I what had happened in their absence. We told them about Louis's accident and mine, eliciting sympathetic looks.

"Are you planning to stay?" Cam asked Illy. "Now that you are happily partnered."

"Well, if you don't mind," she said cautiously, with a glance at Luca, "we would both like to stay. Here. If that is okay."

"Well, of course, we don't mind!" Cam was exultant.

"What will you do here?" I asked, trying to be diplomatic. Two former military officers had little to offer in the way of practical skill in a self-sufficient isolated community that relied heavily on agriculture. Besides, Illy and Cam had history, and Luca was my best friend which made me uncomfortable.

"Well, I was thinking, if you believe it could work, of establishing a barter business. Like I had on Orkney."

"That is awesome! I definitely think there is a need for something like that here." Cam briefly explained Illy's business on Orkney, and we all nodded agreement. It was a good idea, especially for Sorcha, Isla, and I, who regularly traveled to other crofts, with limited time to grow or make anything ourselves.

"What about you, Luca?"

"Still tossing up options," he said, through the mouthful of potato he was chewing. "Not a lot here for a career soldier. I don't want to join the building team again. Eighteen months of that was enough."

"Do you like whisky?" Sorcha asked unexpectedly.

"Drinking it? Sure."

Sorcha laughed. "That wasn't quite what I was thinking, but it will certainly help. Hamish, as you know, is in charge of the whisky still. But with all the new births, we are run off our feet. We need Hamish back on the med team permanently. He is an exceptional doctor and especially good with complicated births. Now that I can't put in so many hours for a bit, it would be great if someone could take over the whisky-making."

"God, it is exhausting work," Cam chipped in. "I helped a few times on my first visit here. Best exercise I ever had."

Luca laughed but looked interested.

"Sure, I'll track him down tomorrow and see if he trusts me enough."

When we finally finished dinner, we spent ages settling the children in the lounge with blankets, pillows, and snacks for a slumber party. But like all kids, as soon as we tried to leave, someone needed the toilet, a blanket, something.

"Bloody hell," Sorcha muttered. "It is like they have a frigging radar for when adults need to talk about something important. It would have been so much easier for our parents with television. No wonder mum called it video-sedation."

Nearly forty-five minutes later, the little ones were asleep, the older ones talking, and Kendra cradled in Di's arms.

"What happened on Clava?" Cam asked.

It was Illy who responded. "There is so much to tell you. But importantly, we played the game and got Di the treatment she needed. They were very welcoming and willing to share their homes, food, and treatment. It was a little difficult to explain how Luca and I came to be with them, but when we reminded them of your experiences in Inverness, no further questions were asked."

"That's good. I was wondering how you were going to overcome that hurdle," Cam interjected.

"Di was induced at 30 weeks, and Kendra was born prematurely, so a lot of my time was taken up caring for her," Sorcha said quietly. "But it gave me time to watch."

"Illy and I were welcomed," said Luca, "but not trusted. Especially as it wasn't Illy's first time visiting with a cancer patient. Someone was with us wherever we went. Nothing overt, of course, just someone always happened to be there when we were. A technician was fixing a machine. A cleaner. It was all very convenient," he drawled in a tone that made it plain that it was anything but.

"With Sorcha and Di in the hospital, Illy and I started to spend some quality time together," he said, a slight blush rising into his rugged cheeks. Illy just smiled across the table. "It was her idea!" he protested.

Fraser, Isla, Cam, and I all looked over at Illy, confused.

"After a couple of weeks of not even being able to go to the loo alone, I got a bit fed up with the constant company," Illy confessed, her eyes twinkling. "So, I figured, we may as well enjoy ourselves, and it may minimize the surveillance."

"She was right," Luca admitted. "But we both benefitted from the deal."

Responding to the increasing looks of confusion, Illy elaborated. "One day, I was overcome with lust while we were visiting Di, and the medical technician, a man, blushing terribly, decided to give us some privacy. We took the opportunity to disable the surveillance system and get to work."

"What did you do?" Cam asked, intrigued.

"Hacked the computer system. And we learned some very interesting things. First, Di was never the intended target. The infected mosquito was released into your greenhouse. *You* were the intended target. Angus intended for it to be you, Campbell."

"Me?" Cam asked incredulously.

"You." Luca said bluntly. "The problem was, he released the mosquito, not realizing that you weren't even here at the time. They hadn't seen you leave."

"But ... why me?"

Fighting the urge to roll my eyes at him, I answered, "Really? You need to ask that?"

"I don't need intel to answer that," Luca said grimly. "Pure, unadulterated jealousy. For thousands of years, it has been one of the best motivators. For all those years, he was in proximity to the woman he was obsessed with. After the return to August, he thought he stood a chance then. When Cam married Laetitia. Again when Frey was pregnant. The thing was, blind Freddie could see that she only ever wanted you. But he still thought that with you out of the way, she would finally settle down with him."

"Never," I seethed. "How could I possibly love someone who deliberately infected a person I love with cancer?"

"Not just one person," Illy added quietly. "We found the evidence. Five in total."

"Di was pregnant! One of those he infected was a child!" Cam choked. We had talked about it a great deal over the past nine weeks, hoping it was an unhappy coincidence.

"Again, an accident. The intended target was Will's wife, Liesl. The problem of using a mosquito as a carrier—while they are discreet, they bite indiscriminately. He was aiming for someone who the community loved and would be devastated to lose.

Someone they would do anything to save and whose family would be so grateful for the treatment that they would convince the others to sign up. Despite hating Cam, he won either way. Either the community agreed to the proposal and saved Cam, or Cam died. Win-Win."

"It could have been any of the children," I raged. "They all play in that greenhouse."

"They do. But logic doesn't matter when you are trying to get revenge. He convinced his colleagues that Cam was an excellent choice because of Lae's death, Sorcha's value, and your expert contribution here. But truthfully, it was simply payback for Freyja choosing you."

"Who on Clava knew?" asked Cam quietly. He was taking this news far better than I was. If Angus was here now, I doubt he would be able to breathe again after the damage I would inflict. First, being responsible for Cam and me missing each other all those years ago, and now for Di's illness?

"We will never know that for certain, but it was likely upper echelons only," Illy spoke confidently.

"But Ashton knew?"

"I can say that definitively. Ashton knew. It was his name on the reports."

"Magali? Jorja?" I asked, almost scared of the response.

"Magali, I genuinely don't think so. They brought her in from Auckland to save these people, but she made a comment to me that suggested that she didn't know that it was deliberate."

Illy knew this was hard to hear and was doing her best to be gentle.

"Like what?"

"It was when Di first arrived. She seemed genuinely concerned that there had been so many cases presenting similarly. She said something odd, like she was concerned about a cancer cluster. You know, like the dome fabric might be involved, or another commonly used item like the biogas units. It was a strange thing to say if she knew. She just would have said nothing at all."

"Maybe. Or she is just a talented actress," Sorcha interrupted.

"Magali was my neighbor on Auckland Island. I have known her and Nasir for over four years. She is completely committed to her patients. She is an amazing doctor and very caring. She has always struck me as ethical and honest. I really can't see it."

Sorcha reluctantly nodded in agreement. "She was wonderful to both Di and me. Surely this would have been top secret. Only a few people would know."

"More than that if you think about it. The scientists who invented the disease and infected the mosquitoes. Angus. Ashton. There must be half a dozen or more," Luca added.

"That is true," Illy admitted. That made us all pause for thought.

"What I can't fathom," Cam said, a note of steel in his voice, "is that Ashton knew Angus tried to kill me, yet he spent so much time telling me how valuable I was."

"It wasn't about killing you, Campbell," Illy said pointedly. "They had the skills to save you if you asked. It was only ever about making you sign over sovereignty to the Collective. Angus knew everyone hated him, so he could never convince the people here of the benefits. People wouldn't listen. But they would listen to you and Sorcha. Fraser and Isla, by association. You are respected—all of you. The other perspective is that if you, Freyja, Di, and Sorcha all moved there, then the remaining people of Lewis would also likely pledge allegiance as they would assume that you agreed with their governance model. Clava, additionally, gained all of your valuable skills, which they wanted. I saw the reports. It was fairly strategic."

"Except that we said no," I said acerbically.

"Tell them what else you learned," Illy said quietly, placing a tiny hand on Luca's thigh and looking up into his weather-beaten face. "Sorcha, Diana, you too. We couldn't tell you this while we were there. We felt it better to be all of you together."

Luca steeled himself. We all watched his face. What he was about to tell us wasn't pleasant.

"There are two things. The first, and most difficult to swallow, is the *why* of all of this. Why go to all that trouble to select people, keep them safe, but for five years only? Why a community of three hundred, give or take, when the area under the dome would accommodate more? Why not save the relatively few locals who remained? Why allow communities access to one other site via an antipodean portal? But then, when the time is right, provide enough incentive to join the Collective, the Nexus? Illy was right when she didn't trust them on Orkney. It isn't about providing better resources, medicines, or even trade. It is quite simple. What is the most critical resource in the resettlement of the world?"

We all pondered that.

"Water?" said Fraser.

"Food, trees for oxygen?" said Di.

It was Sorcha who sat silently, as we guessed. "Humans," she said bluntly. "We cannot resettle the world without humans."

"Bingo," said Luca. "So, if you want to resettle the world, and you want to control the genes that are released back into the world, what do you do?"

"You choose people selectively?" Cam suggested tentatively.

"You *breed* people selectively," Illy sliced through, the iron in her voice unmistakable.

"Breed selectively?" Isla said. "Do you mean we were all chosen for our genes, and now they are happy that we are reproducing?"

"No," Illy responded curtly. "That was just the warm-up, the practice run. Once all the communities sign up to the Collective, they will initiate a program of selective reproduction. Each woman will be impregnated by a carefully selected male, producing the ideal race."

"A master race?" I gasped. "Surely not. Have we learned nothing from history?"

"It appears not," said Luca. "This isn't about appearance, culture, or religion. It is pure science. Our friend, Professor Ashton, is a world-renowned geneticist. During the screening process, they selected people with ideal genes, those they wanted to be reproduced. They filtered allergies and illnesses out. That was why they put us through all of those tests. Those who were chosen represented the best of the best, genetics-wise."

"That makes little sense," Sorcha butted in. "I have asthma, and they chose me."

"No, you were selected to go to Kiewa. The inland communities were established in part to hide the true purpose of the offshore communities. But the secondary motivation of those sites was to replicate the key genomes they wanted to save. So if something happened to Cam, they would call you up. Same with Di and Kendra. Many people sent to offshore communities were a close genetic match sent to one of the isolated ones. It was Cam who mucked that up by going to find you and bringing you here."

"I was the *spare*?" Sorcha's outrage was barely contained.

"This is one situation where I would happily offer you my spot," Cam said to her, grinning, before turning to Luca and me.

"If Angus always knew about the master plan, then why did he take you to Melbourne? I mean, it was because of that discovery that I found out about Sorcha, Kiewa, and the other communities. If he always knew, why wouldn't he just avoid Melbourne altogether?"

"Because he didn't want to go!" I chuckled. "It was me that pushed it, and then Luca and Jakob agreed it made sense. After we discovered Kerguelen, and I no longer think that was a coincidence, Luca and I talked all the time about where we could learn more about the science behind the geodesic domes. Angus tried to convince us to find more communities, likely to start his mission of building relationships. He had no desire to go to Melbourne. He kept telling us that there was nothing to be found there. It would all be computer-based, and with no power, it would be a waste of time. But he relented as he realized that three out of five wanted to go. Didn't want to draw attention to his actual plan."

"Okay, that makes sense. But what about the list of the ISO communities you found?" Di asked.

"That was a complete accident!" I laughed softly, making Cam look over at me, his eyebrows raised.

"Angus was right. We found nothing. With no electricity and limited paper files, we found nothing much of interest. As we were leaving, Jakob picked up a wad of discarded paper from a recycling bin without telling us. Sometimes we stopped when the weather was fine and built a bonfire on the beach. Just because we could. We used to sit around a fire, talk, drink, sometimes sing. We only took the paper as we used it to help us build fires. It was me that noticed the names but not until weeks later. We had stopped to build a fire, and I was about to feed the pages in when I saw the names. Angus acted surprised. But now I know he knew all along. I always thought that I had a good bullshit meter, but he played me," Luca said dryly.

"He played all of us," Cam replied gruffly. "Why did he present it like it was his discovery?"

"He was the one who wanted to speak." I shrugged. "I wasn't in a good place emotionally; you and I had met the night before. Luca, Jake, and Nate aren't the oratory type. Angus loved holding court, as we used to call it. But I guess he knew that I would have told you, even if he hadn't announced it. He also didn't think you would try to get back and find her. I had read the list and found Sorcha's name. He made some comment like, 'Well, it will be nice for him to know.'"

"Let's face it: he didn't save his own family nor help his sister and niece when he had the chance, so he probably didn't think I would travel all that way to find my own sister."

"Likely not," I admitted.

Isla spoke quietly, visibly shaken. "I need to ask. When you say impregnated by a chosen male, I assume you mean not a male we chose ourselves?"

"Exactly," Illy admitted. "In the reports, it was termed ideal reproductive pairs. Essentially, they would pair up the best genome sequence and force that couple to reproduce. Not to be a couple, mind you. That was one of the brilliant parts of the plan. They hoped that after more than five years together, the community would want to share the raising of children. Let's say, Freyja, that you were chosen to reproduce with Fraser. They assumed that you and Cam would raise the child that selective breeding pair would produce. They don't care about co-habiting or raising of the children, just the end product. If you and he already had one or more children, they assumed you would accept your genetically selected child, even if you didn't care for the father. They knew they could never stop people from having children with a love partner, so they didn't try. But it was all about ensuring those selected pairs would reproduce, and likely not just once."

"We are an experiment?" Di gasped.

"Absolutely. A very well-planned and researched experiment. All of us. Even the team on Clava and Auckland were expected to partake. All of those who survived were scientifically chosen to reproduce with their perfect match. The science behind it was genius. All cultures, appearances, chromosomes were chosen. They were deliberately inclusive. Combine that with each chosen person having a desired skill and intelligence to ensure the community would survive the first five years, and yes, they really did choose the best candidates to ensure the future of the planet."

"How did they know we could or would have children?" Sorcha asked.

"They took reproductive material from each person as part of the selection process. Tested the genetic material. Ensured that each of us was fertile."

We all sat with our mouths open, astonished at what we were hearing. Cam and I had spoken once about waking from the scan in Melbourne dressed in a hospital robe. They had tested me invasively then. I had often wondered what happened while I was unconscious. Now I knew and felt violated. Illy sensed my discomfort and smiled at me across the table.

"What did you learn about the Nexus?" Fraser asked.

"The Nexus is how they described the interconnected communities. Each society would join the Collective, the association. The Nexus was how they were interconnected, the web of portals, if you like. Therefore, Orkney and the Shetlands were linked in, despite no livable antipode at their opposite point. There are a few others like that. They just needed enough space, over the first five years, for all the people with mapped genomes," Illy explained.

"Now we know why five years—so we would run out of resources. But why cap the communities at 300 people?" Fraser asked, his arm around a traumatized Isla.

Luca responded to this. "Each community has slightly more or less, but roughly 300. They scientifically predicted that to be the ideal number—enough diversity to choose a mate, roughly 150 of the opposite sex. But not so many people that it was overwhelming. The community forming a tight bond was also critical. That bond would be essential later to ensure the communal raising of children in the new world order. It would allow people to choose a life partner but raise children that were not biologically of that partnership. They knew other children would be born too, through the chosen partnerships. But the ideal reproductive pairing children would be granted special privilege."

"Let me get this straight." My brain was whirring. "They impregnate us with a child designed to create a superspecies: illness resistant, superior genome and all that. But we can go home and raise this child with our choice of partner?" I said, unable to keep the absolute disgust from my voice.

"That's pretty much it," Luca admitted.

"What happens to this child when it comes of age? What is the special privilege?" I asked, fearful of the answer.

"I don't know. But I can't imagine it is: 'Here is the key to your new car and all the best.' Why would you go to that much trouble and not have plans for their future?" Illy seethed.

"How did you not know?" I asked Illy, recalling she was part of the selection team.

"I didn't. Truly, I had no knowledge of this until a few weeks ago." Illy looked exhausted. Knowing this for weeks hadn't made it any easier to stomach. "All we found was a reference to those two words: special privilege. We don't know if that means that the selected breeding children would be a ruling class, and the children born from relationships would be working class or just that they would get better opportunities like schooling and medical care. That part, we found no information on."

"There is still the second thing," Luca continued as we all sat at the table, speechless. No one was eating anymore. Likely everyone was feeling as sick as I did. "But in context, it makes more sense. In the early days, most communities settled in quite well. Working together, forming partnerships, establishing the foundations for a civil society. But a small number, unfortunately, did not. The community was disjointed, and the people selected simply didn't get along. Some disagreements fragmented the communities. This was the one factor they couldn't control in their assessments of who would be chosen—personalities. To assist, they experimented on the communities by using a substance aimed to promote compliance and dispel resistance."

"They poisoned us?" Fraser was enraged.

"Not you. The community on Gibraltar was fighting, and the village was splitting in two. Disagreeing over resources. It wasn't what they wanted, and to have a failed community, they felt, risked the entire project as people would seek a way out, or they would lose three hundred carefully chosen specimens. One night, using a drone, they released a fine mist into the water supply, a substance designed to quell the anger. Mood control, I guess you could call it."

"But it didn't work," I stated bluntly. "Luca, you and I both saw what happened to Gibraltar. It was a mess. Bodies in the street, some in pieces. The dome slashed. It was deliberately sabotaged. We just didn't know *how*."

Luca nodded. "That is my recollection, too. We only ever went there the once, on the first leg." We smiled over the table at each other. Despite my desperation to get back to Cam, Luca and I had fun on that trip, grown very close.

"The problem was, the substance mostly *did* work," Illy admitted. "Of the population of 300, only two people had an adverse reaction, in percentage terms that is roughly half of one percent. Most clinical trials go ahead with those results. The majority became compliant, mellowed. They stopped arguing and started working together. Started pairing up and falling pregnant. Exactly what they wanted. The two who had the adverse reaction, unfortunately, went completely the other way. Violent, uncontrollable rage, with one of them eventually going on a murderous rampage, slashing the dome. Unfortunately, somehow, he found the portal."

"He did the same thing in New Zealand?"

"He did. But as he had slashed the dome, the insurgent died along with the entire population, and so Clava thought that was the end of it. They didn't try that again."

"Except they did," I said. "They drugged Cam and me to make us more compliant."

"You were, and we found the records on that too. Based on the majority reaction, they thought they should try again. Being in the water supply, they couldn't tell how much each person had been exposed to. You ingested it in low, controlled doses, and they monitored you closely to ensure that neither of you had an adverse reaction," Luca explained.

"We were guinea pigs?" Cam looked shocked, even though Illy had warned us months ago that she suspected the use of psychotropic drugs.

"You were. It was the substance that they intended to use, in higher doses, when they impregnated each pair. Ensure people were compliant. Illy and I were also exposed until we worked it out. You weren't the only ones. They fed most people on Clava the substance."

"The children too?" Cam asked cautiously and looked over at me. "Do you remember how compliant they were in the school that day?"

Nodding, I couldn't verbalize my response. *Using mood-altering drugs on children?*

"What do you mean by closely monitored?" I finally asked. "Were we watched *all* the time?" I was trying not to show how mortified I was.

It was Illy who answered. "Yes. There was a detailed file."

I didn't know whether to be angry, embarrassed, or amused. I was speechless.

"How? How did they feed it to us?" Cam asked Illy.

"It was a naturally growing herb. In its natural and purified forms, it is mildly sweet, so likely in baked goods. That was how Luca and I were being fed it. Under constant surveillance, they could monitor how much we ate, they knew our size, and they could calculate the effects. Luca, being larger, wouldn't be as strongly affected, but he also ate more."

Cam and I looked at each other. After the first night, we had barely gone three waking hours without being plied with cakes, biscuits, pastries, or other pies. We had just thought they were hospitable, trying to make us welcome. But now...

"When we read your file, Ils and I realized that was how they were slipping it to us. We started finding ways not to eat the desserts or secretly vomiting after meals. Like you, we had terrible withdrawals for a day or two. But then, we found we could think with far more clarity. Question what we were being told."

"What about Sorcha and Di?"

Sorcha smiled. "Di was on hospital food, anyway. She was no threat. Me, well, your friend Illy here made sure I knew." She slipped Illy a wry smile, making me suspect there was a story there. I had no time to pursue this, though, as Cam started speaking.

"What about August?" Cam asked. "There were disagreements and divisions on August too."

"As there were here," Fraser mumbled. "The first few months were awful."

"That is true. Only they didn't know about August. There was no spy on August, so they didn't get that intel until much later. By that time, they had lost over six hundred prized specimens across Gibraltar and New Zealand, so they weren't willing to lose any more. Here, Angus advised them that the unrest was temporary. After the locals had perished, then the community would settle down. Start pairing up and having children. He was correct. They did."

"How lucky were we?" said Di. "That could easily have been us. Remember when the first split happened? Kai trying to take the aquaponics ponds? That could easily have led to violence if you weren't there, Cam."

"Oh, I'm not sure I..."

"I wasn't there," I said, speaking over his protests. "But the way I heard it, you were the perfect diplomat. Listened, understood, and negotiated a fair deal for all parties. Everyone was raving about how well you handled it."

Sorcha snorted but tactfully covered it with a cough.

Cam looked at me, surprised. "You never told me that."

"We didn't know each other at that point. I mean, we had spoken that one time, so I knew who this person was that everyone was talking about, but I didn't know you well enough to say something to you."

"People were talking about *me*?"

Di looked at him in amazement. "How could you be so oblivious to that?"

Cam shrugged. "I never really listened to gossip."

"What do we do now?" I asked to move this along. I was shattered and wanted to go to bed.

"I would suggest that the first thing to do would be to deactivate the portals," Illy suggested. "If there is no capacity to move us between sites, we minimize the risk of being forced to reproduce. To do that, they would have to kidnap people and move them forcibly to other sites, and we didn't see any sign that they would do that. We have no real shortage of electricity here, thanks to Sorcha, now that algal bioreactors are supplementing the biogas. It is only medical supplies that we are short of."

"Ahh, about that..." Cam spent the next few minutes filling Sorcha in on the new crops he was growing, plants they were sourcing to provide natural alternatives to many of the medicines we used here. Jacinda had been most helpful and happy to share her vast knowledge. But, most importantly, until we could harvest opium poppies and the natural medications Jacinda had suggested, Hamish had brought back the boxes we had found at the house in Edinburgh. Our recollection had been correct. Each box had contained one packet of paracetamol and one of ibuprofen. He had also sourced an enormous array of medications, taken from every hospital and clinic that hadn't been raided between Edinburgh and Glasgow. Enough to last us for many years with careful monitoring.

"I can't believe we didn't think of that before!" Sorcha gasped, slapping her hand against her forehead.

"Well, necessity is the mother of invention. When we realized how insular we have been, especially under the circumstances, we sent Agneta out to get veterinary supplies. To be fair, there was no capacity in the early years, not knowing how to get out of the dome and knowing it was unsafe. But now that we know we can travel carefully, we thought it was a good idea to stockpile as many resources as possible before we potentially have issues with Clava. So as silly as it sounds, we never really thought about it until it became an issue."

"I have a gift for you," Cam blurted, disappearing into our room, returning with a large, square mirror, and handing it to Sorcha. "Do you remember that night when I told you how much you looked like mum?"

Sorcha accepted the gift graciously, responding, "You know I had access to a mirror the entire time I was on Clava? All it made me want to do was cut my hair! But thank you. I appreciate it. What else did you get?"

"Oh, all sorts of amazing things!" I gushed, making everyone look at me, knowing it was out of character for me to be so effusive.

"She means chocolate," Cam said dryly.

"Chocolate?" All the women chorused in unison, making us all laugh.

"Are we really going to deactivate the portal?" Isla asked when the hilarity died down, making us all turn to look at her. She had been sitting quietly with Fraser during this conversation. Taking it all in. Pregnant with her fourth child, the idea of being forced to have more children was a repugnant concept. "Not that I want to travel myself mind, but it seems so... final. After all, you all traveled here."

"The problem is," Illy pointed out, "August has voted to join the Collective. That places a lot of pressure on Lewis to be part of the Nexus."

"Is that even possible? To deactivate it, I mean?" Di asked.

"It is. But we are going to need help to do it," Luca said.

"I know who to ask," Cam announced.

CHAPTER 31

HEARING CLATTERING IN THE kitchen, I rolled over to hug Cam, only to find his side of the bed empty. This was nothing new. He rose with the dawn and was often gone before I woke. But it had been a late night, and I hoped he would stay so we could talk about everything Illy and Luca had told us. We were so exhausted the previous night; we had barely undressed before falling headfirst into bed.

Rolling out of bed, barely awake, I slipped on a robe and staggered barefoot into the kitchen, bleary-eyed, not registering anything.

"Morning," chirped Illyria.

Fuck. So she is a morning person, just to top off being ridiculously close with my husband, I thought crankily. *Just what I need.*

"Mrrnngg," I slurred, plonking myself in a chair and hoping coffee would find its way to me by osmosis. Remarkably, it did, via Illy. I eyed it suspiciously. Did she want me dead so she could have my husband as well as my best friend?

By the time she delivered a plate of hot buttered toast to me, I had reassessed my opinion. Maybe she was alright, after all. Besides, Luca seemed to like her. He had a particularly good bullshit-meter, although both of us had been taken in by Angus.

"Lu-ca?" I managed.

"Ahh, he went with Cam to the whisky cave."

She chattered away merrily as I plowed through my toast, starting to feel remotely human.

"He was looking forward to meeting up with Hamish and learning the..."

Illy froze mid-sentence, staring behind me.

"Is that..."

Slumping in my chair, I checked over my shoulder, not really in the mood for mice. But it was only Jam, lurking for breakfast.

"That is a Scottish Wildcat. This is Jam. She has been with us for years. I guess you could say she is the closest thing we have to a pet."

Holding my hand down, Jam rubbed around it affectionately.

Illy blinked at the word "wildcat" but squatted and held her hand out. Jam, a very social creature with no sense of fear, happily switched people and rubbed against Illy's fingers, demanding that she scratch under her chin. Within minutes, Jam was on Illy's lap, head-butting her and demanding attention. I handed Jam my toast crust, which she devoured in a few bites.

"The things I miss the most about Australia," Illy breathed as she held the mug of steaming coffee in one of her tiny hands, heaping affection on Jam with the other, "aside from family and friends, of course, are my two cats, Max and Lily. Ragdolls, they were. They were my children. They came on all my postings with me. But when we reached the end, they refused to let me take them to Auckland. I had them euthanized. I couldn't bear to let them suffer."

Not wanting to take her to a dark place, I mocked gently, "Crazy cat lady."

She smiled at me, sad memories filling her eyes.

"Despite being a vet, Jam is the first cat I have ever lived with. As a child, I was never allowed a pet," I admitted softly. "I desperately wanted one. But my parents refused. There was always a reason. They were too busy, or we traveled too much. When we were on August Island, Cam and I had a pet goat named Fred. He even lived with us for a while." Thinking of Fred conjured memories, both good and bad. Fred had shown me the hot springs. But equally, it had been searching for him that had led me into the cave on that fateful night. I never saw him again.

"You know," I said, trying to dispel the image the cave had provoked. "Miss Jam here has already had two litters of kittens. If she has any more..."

"Really?" Illy's eyes lit up with such joy that I felt an instant bond with her.

"Oh, yes. She had eight the first time and six the second. I'm sure we can earmark one for you."

"What happened to them?"

"Most were desexed, and crofters took them, ostensibly to keep down mice, but truthfully, most are spoiled pets. There was a lottery, everyone wanted one, but I'm sure we can make an exception. Aidan has one, you know. Gussie. She is gorgeous, friendly, much like our Jam."

Hearing Katrin cry out, I was off my seat in a shot. I paused as I passed her chair. "We will take care of you, Illy." I wasn't sure why I had said it. It just … slipped out.

A look of stunned amazement crossed her face as she reached for my hand and looked me directly in the eyes.

"No one other than Luca has said that to me in a very long time," she whispered. "I think that is why I fell in love with him."

"It is hard, isn't it? Being strong all the time. Needing to have broad shoulders. People expecting that you are always in control but knowing that sometimes, you just need to be held. Nurtured."

Searching my soul, she responded, "I think we will be very good friends, Freyja."

That afternoon, Cam and Luca, on their way home from their distilling lesson, met me leaving the stables where I had delivered a foal. Mike had been thrilled, and I was filthy and exhausted, smelling distinctly of horse. We walked together companionably. Luca and I had been very close when we were traveling together, much of it at sea, having long discussions well into the night. It was strange to think of us both partnered and settled. If we had been at home and at a bar, he would have been my wingman. I knew I could rely on him for anything, and he would always have my back. But now, I had married again, and he, madly in love with someone I was surprised to realize that I didn't entirely dislike.

"Is Illy okay?" I asked Luca out of the silence. "I mean, about living here."

Surprisingly, Luca didn't respond.

"What is it?" Cam asked cautiously.

"Well, it is just that while we were reading those files on Clava, she read her own, and learned why they chose her."

"And why is that?" I asked suspiciously.

"Well, for her genome, like the rest of us, and her intelligence. But mostly for her skills. Her skills with people, I mean. She is an expert in both human intelligence and signals intelligence."

"I understand human intel, but what is signals intelligence?"

"The monitoring, interception, and interpretation of broadcast transmissions," Luca responded.

"Well, that makes sense. I watched her at work on Orkney. She is phenomenal at reading people, getting them to feel heard and understood, but then getting people to do what she wants. She could interpret something in an inflection or a single word," Cam admitted. "But the role they had lined up for her. I am assuming it was somewhat … unpalatable?"

"She was devastated," Luca confessed, "when she read they had earmarked a primary role for her overseeing the breeding program. Using her skills to encourage reluctant people that it was the right thing to do, for the future of the planet. She was inconsolable. That was why we didn't tell Sorcha and Di beforehand. I needed to get her away first."

"I can see why they would think she would be great in that role," Cam admitted. "They didn't count on her having ethics, did they?"

"Not at all." Luca smiled. "They assumed, being military, that she would follow orders. But my Illy has a mind of her own."

"Well, she has amazing interpersonal skills," I added, trying to steer this back to a more positive conversation. "I'm sure she will fit right in here. I'm looking forward to her setting up a business here. We could certainly use it."

"Poor Illy," Cam said, genuine concern in his voice. "Melbourne to Auckland, then Clava, Orkney, and now here. I hope she can settle here."

"She will. Now," Luca said convincingly, and we continued to walk in silence, our minds dwelling on the breeding program they had selected us for.

"You know," Cam said to Luca out of the companionable relaxed atmosphere borne from a long day's labor, "Illy was on the selection team for me back in Melbourne."

"She told me. She was seconded to help choose the best candidates. Only it appears that she wasn't given *all* of the criteria."

"The control she had was amazing. She had the most thunderous voice I had ever heard. She boomed instructions in an auditorium filled with hundreds of scared, chattering people, and she spoke without a microphone. Everyone just obeyed her. We all shat ourselves and shut up."

"That's my Illy." Luca smiled.

"I called her the military budgie," Cam mused.

Luca stopped walking abruptly and turned, looking at Cam in astonishment. Cam's eyes opened, and his mouth dropped, looking shocked that the words he had been thinking had slipped out—to the partner of the woman he had just insulted no less, who was potentially the only man on Lewis significantly bigger than Cam himself. Luca drew himself up to his full height, and thinking Luca was about to punch Cam in the nose, I began to insert myself between them. My husband and my best friend. Instead, Luca placed his hands on his thighs, dropped his head, and started wheezing with laughter. Gasping for air between guffaws, he finally managed, "Ha! Military budgie. Oh, God. That is *perfect*. Sums her up beautifully. Oh god. I can't wait to call her that!"

"No! You can't! Please! You can't tell her I told you!" Cam looked mortified.

"Oh, I so am. I can't wait to see her face."

Cam's face and neck had turned the color of beetroot. "No, please, please don't. What will she think of me?"

Luca, still unable to breathe properly from hysteria, flapped his hands in dismissal. Finally able to speak unobstructed, he said, "Do you not realize how fond of you she is? You could call her just about anything with the possible exception of little lady. I wouldn't try that if you value your testicles. I tried it, once."

Cam and I both laughed at that, Cam less so, still humiliated at his slip, his private nickname becoming public.

When we had sufficiently recovered enough to walk, I asked Luca calmly, "What exactly did the report say? About us." I hadn't wanted to ask him over dinner with the others there, just in case. It was time for revenge. Luca's eyes glittered wickedly.

"Oh, there were lots of juicy details in there. They were thrilled with the effects on you. But my favorite part was... oh, what were the words again? Oh yes, that the substance had induced, 'Random, frequent, and public acts of lustfulness with reduced inhibition.'" Luca laughed heartily, displaying his gleaming white teeth in his tanned face. "I never thought that of you, Princess. Always thought of you as a behind closed doors kind of girl."

I playfully punched him in the arm. "We were being drugged!" I protested.

"A likely tale," Luca teased mercilessly, but relented, seeing my horrified face. "Truth is, Frey, I need to thank both of you."

"Thank us?" Cam asked warily, evidently still scared of Illy's reaction.

"Well, when we read that line in your file as an effect of the drug they fed you, once we had finished laughing, that is, Illy and I realized it was also being slipped to us. So we stopped ingesting, but thanks to you, other 'random, frequent, and public acts of lust-fulness' may have taken place so that they weren't suspicious. My heartfelt gratitude to you both."

"Happy to oblige," Cam muttered from beneath his flushed countenance as we descended the hill toward home.

CHAPTER 32

ARRIVING ON LEWIS SOMEWHAT unexpectedly, Luca and Illy stayed with Cam and me, at least until we could organize their own place. It was uncomfortable co-habiting with another couple. Aside from the early months of living with Sorcha and Di, and the time on Clava with Bridget and Jorja, we hadn't lived with other adults, and we both, for different reasons, found the transition difficult.

Illy and Luca were fabulous guests and regularly rose early and left for a walk so we could have a family breakfast, or we woke to them cooking for us. Illy was lovely with the children and regularly helped with their schooling. Not being a morning person, I very much appreciated this. But we recognized it as temporary as we made plans for an additional home in our tiny village. After much discussion, we had named our settlement Roseglen. Rose in part for Laetitia, who never got to live here, but to whom I was eternally grateful for giving me the most wonderful son. Cam and Sorcha's mother had loved roses and had a garden full of them. Cam had planned a rose garden in memory of those we had lost, where he would place our beehives. Glen was the name of Isla's father but was equally such a wonderful Scots word that evoked images of the long, lush narrow valley where we lived. Ringed on three sides by silver and purple heather-covered hills, we had a spectacular view out to Loch Acha Mor and beyond. Cam frequently expressed the desire to build a deck so we could sit outside and watch the world pass by, the loch glistening, the trees growing, and our children playing.

"Do you know," he murmured one night as we sat, enjoying the view, "I used to dream of you and I living in a place like this when we lived on August? I just never envisioned other people being here with us. But most of the time, I think I like it."

One Sunday, after many weeks of hard work, we helped Illy and Luca to move into their new home, now partially furnished, thanks to our wonderful community. Illy's market business was taking off, and I saw what Cam had. She had the most amazing innate ability to read people. She sensed a shift in emotion a second before anyone else and could adapt quickly to her audience, knowing when to push and when to back off.

She must have been quite a loss for Clava, I realized, making me wonder how they would sell the selected breeding pairs program now. Illy could sell ice to Eskimos and then make them think it was their idea.

Watching Luca scoop her up effortlessly and carry her laughing over the threshold, I felt a pang that Cam had never done that for me. But then, I reminded myself, I was heavily pregnant with an unplanned child when I had arrived here. He had lived in our tiny cottage first on August, and I had just moved in, leaving behind the dorm with its lack of privacy.

Returning home, as our door closed, I leaned with my back against it and breathed. "Don't get me wrong, I love Luca and Illy, but..."

"You are glad to have our home back?" Cam finished for me. "I know what you mean. It is lovely to have guests, but a little awkward, if I want to take you, over the kitchen table, before breakfast..."

"You will need to ensure the kids are asleep!" I rebuked him. "Louis is far too young to ask questions like that. I can't believe we need to leave them again, so soon."

"I keep telling you, Frey. I can go. You need not leave Kat again. Not when she is finally sleeping through the night and in her own room."

I didn't want to leave Kat or Louis but knew that they would be safe here. I was more fearful of something happening to Cam.

"Let's be honest. Our track record is not great. I fall through a portal, transporting me across the world, and you follow. We have raiders attack our community. You and I are nearly eaten by cannibals, and only a few days later, overzealous controlling scientists drug us, who want to choose who we have children with to create a master race. Forgive me if I don't want to be separated."

"Well, when you put it like that." He pulled me close and held me against him, searching my face.

"When do you want to go?" I sighed. Waiting wasn't making this any easier.

"Next week makes the most sense. I need to finish the planting, and then all Fraser needs to do is water and weed. Luca is no gardener but can help. Isla isn't so pregnant that she can't travel around to the closer farms, and now Agneta is back, she can visit those farther out. If we leave soon, we can minimize the impact on the community of you being away too."

"Now, who is the overly practical one?" I teased.

"Stop talking and kiss me. The kids will be home soon."

CHAPTER 33

THE JOURNEY TO NEWGRANGE took five days on the *Eurydice*. Getting there and learning what Kevin knew about deactivating our portal was paramount if the plan was going to succeed. Arriving at Drogheda, tired and dirty, Cam pointed out the fishing boat that Eoghan had used to take him to Lewis. If Eoghan was here, that was good. Likely it meant most of the community were here so we could speak to them all, giving an update on what was happening at Clava. I hadn't been to Newgrange, but I had arrived unannounced at several communities when I had been traveling. I knew to be cautious. A calm entrance could mean the difference between being welcomed or being shot.

Riding our bikes into the village, Cam was greeted by people who recognized him from his two prior visits, shaking his hand warmly, although something wasn't quite right. People were distracted, removed. Pleasant enough, but there was a faraway look in their eye. Something was going on.

"Jakob!" I called, spotting a familiar figure in the distance.

He turned and ran toward me. We collided, laughing. "So good to see you, Frey! What on earth are you doing here?"

Aware of the audience we had attracted, I said cryptically, "Long story. Luca tells me you left him? That you have a lovely lady here?"

Jakob blushed. "I can't wait for you to meet her. Mikalya is her name."

"Look at you!" I teased. "All in love!" Then, more kindly, I added, "She must be special."

"She really is," he beamed.

Searching the group for Cam, I spotted him, his dark head towering over most people. He saw me looking for him and beckoned me over.

"Kevin, this is my wife, Freyja."

"Ahh, it is lovely to meet you, Freyja. Jakob has told me a lot of wonderful things about you. Now, I'd like to introduce you to *my* wife."

"Wife?" The look of surprised delight on Cam's face was priceless.

"Yes, I said wife," Kevin finished irreverently. "I realized I couldn't mope around after Lynda forever. I mean, she will always hold a special place in my heart, but then I met this lovely lady."

"Darling!" he called. Turning to face us was a petite and very striking blonde lady.

"Katya?" Cam gasped, leaning forward to kiss her. "How are you?"

"I'm well." She smiled. "It is so wonderful to see you, Cam. How are your sister and Di?"

"Both are doing well. They just had a baby. What a surprise seeing you here!"

Standing back, I was trying to recall who this woman was. I was reasonably confident I had never met her.

Cam turned to me. "Frey—this is Katya. She was on Bellcamp and came with us to Australia when I went looking for Sorcha."

"Ahh," I said, vaguely remembering the stories Cam and Di had told. "It is lovely to meet you, Katya."

Cam turned back to Katya. "How did you end up here?"

"Well, I was completely lost after the news that Nadja died," she admitted.

"I could see that," Cam said tenderly. "I know how that feels when everyone around you is blissfully happy, and you are struggling with your own loss."

"I never thanked you for your kindness," she said, turning the most exquisite pair of light brown eyes on him, and my stomach lurched. *Bloody hell, does my husband know every stunning woman left in the world?*

"I went back to Bellcamp, as you know, but I couldn't focus. Couldn't find my groove. I was just going through the motions, but I felt like I had nothing left to give. No purpose. Fast forward a few weeks, and Blake was ready to head off again, and Ian let slip that not only was I a doctor, but I knew how to sail. He invited me to join his crew, so I did. We spent nearly two years traveling before heading back to Bellcamp, just in time for the vote. The place had changed, and sadly, not for the better. It didn't have the friendly sense of community it once had. Everyone was out for themselves, or maybe I had just visited too many other places by then and wasn't prepared to settle. So, on the next solstice, I came here with a few others. We knew Newgrange was going to remain independent, and we knew they would take the few of us who didn't want to stay at Bellcamp."

"And...?"

"Well, and then I met Kevin." She blushed. "What can I say? He helped me out of the portal. I was lying there, feeling like I had been sucked into a concrete mixer, churned and spat out, thinking I had made a mistake. He unzipped my suit, and the first thing I saw amid the world spinning were those stunning blue eyes. He says that I was just disoriented. But for me, it was love at first sight."

"Oh, it was for me too." He beamed at her. "When I looked into her face, my heart skipped a beat. I just didn't dare to think she might like *me*. I also had the minor complicating factor of introducing her to my kids. Fortunately, they adore her." He stroked Katya's slightly swollen stomach. "We are adding to the brood in a few months."

"Wonderful news!" Cam shook his hand firmly and hugged Katya.

I stood back smiling, happy for these people, but they were strangers to me. Plastering a neutral expression on my face, I stood back and observed. The ice queen, I had been called at school, both to my face and behind my back. Better to let people think you were emotionless than to let them see how much something affected you.

"Please come with us," Kevin enthused. "We have a few people coming over for dinner you might like to meet. We have a guest room you can stay in."

"We'd love to. We have a lot to ask you."

"Anything in particular?"

Cam sighed. "We need to de-activate the portal. I can't tell you the conflicting emotions that raises. If it weren't for the antipodes, I wouldn't have lost Freyja, but then I would never have met all of you, been to so many wonderful places."

"Ahh, we are working on deactivating ours. It is heartbreaking that we need to do this, especially before I get the chance to travel myself. It is the end of an era, but it is time. Things are … not pleasant, let's say."

"When?" I asked.

"Soon. At the summer equinox. It is best to do it then, as the wormholes are aligned, and it shuts them off properly, or so we believe. We have done a bit of research on this, and we think either the solstice or the equinox is the best time."

I looked over at Cam. "Maybe we should do the same?"

"Can you explain how you do it?" Cam asked. "I mean, I was there when Tadhg explained to the team on Bellcamp, but I must admit, much of the technical stuff went over my head."

"Because you were stressing about facing that journey again?" Kevin teased gently.

"I was. I didn't capture the finer points. Do you use magnets?"

"Yes, but it is a little more complicated than that. Do you have an engineer on Lewis who can help?"

"We do—several. Most of them civil but one or two electrical. They might enjoy a break from bioreactors and such, although one became a baker a few years ago. We didn't think to bring one of them with us." Cam looked over at me. "I don't think we have enough time to get back to Lewis, then back here again with them. And from what we now know, it probably isn't safe to transmit that information over the radio. Can you teach us? How to deactivate it, that is?"

"Of course, but you will need the equipment. Unless..." Kevin scratched his chin thoughtfully. "Let me have a chat with the team. We will come up with something."

We were ushered upstairs and shown to the bathroom for showers. Although we had cleaned and filled the *Eurydice's* water tanks, as we had previously done on the *Selkie*, it was blissful to stand in a full-sized shower. Like August and Lewis, these were tepid gravity-fed systems using a valuable resource.

As we changed before dinner in Kevin's guest room, Cam asked, "Do you think we can wait? Until the equinox? It is nearly four months away. The speed at which Clava is moving, I am a little apprehensive that they will try more dirty tricks to get us to sign up."

"Sorcha said they had made the formal offer to join, and she said she would take it back to Lewis for discussion. How long do you think we can reasonably string it out?"

"A month or two maybe, but *four*? That is a long time. Remember the pressure they put on you and me?"

"They did, but that was more about our family joining them, not for Lewis to join the Collective. We didn't know about that until Luca came. So officially, the offer is only a few weeks old."

"That is true," Cam mused, lapsing into silence.

An idea was forming in my mind. What I needed was to talk to Luca. Perhaps Illy.

Hearing voices in the living room, Cam hurriedly finished dressing, and I brushed my hair before heading into the main living area. Cam entered first, and a curvaceous, dark-haired woman flew into his arms. He barely had time to get his arms up and catch her.

"Caaaam!" The high-pitched squeal made me want to plug my ears for a moment.

How many women are this keen to see him? I smiled politely, awaiting the introduction of yet another female who seemed on kissing terms with my husband. She was chattering away madly, a tall, quiet man standing behind her. He looked over at me and smiled. Stepping out from behind Cam and the woman, he reached his hand out to me.

"I'm Tadhg. That's Callie. They go way back."

I could see that from the animated manner in which they were speaking. I was most grateful for the introduction. Both Cam and Di had raved about the infamous Callie, the woman Cam had met during his assessment in Melbourne, who had helped him several times.

Finally, Callie turned to me, still babbling away happily.

"And you must be Laetitia! Goodness, Cam raved about you. It is lovely to meet you!"

The name struck me like a bullet, and I let my guard down, just for a moment, before restoring my pleasant, neutral expression.

"Ah no, I am Freyja," I replied, as impartially as I could.

"Oh." The look of shocked bewilderment froze her. It must have only been a second or two, but for the two of us, staring into each other's faces, it felt like an awkward eternity.

Cam had witnessed my momentary lapse before I was able to restore myself and stepped in hurriedly.

"Laetitia died nearly two years ago, Cal. About six months after I last saw you."

"Oh my god. Cam, I am so sorry."

"After Lae died, I was reunited with my first wife, Freyja. You know the one who traveled to Lewis? The one I thought I had lost? Well, we married again and have a daughter."

"That's... that's.... tragic, and... wonderful, and, oh... I don't know what that is!" Callie looked utterly baffled. She had one of those faces that showed her expression clearly. It was a lot to take in. I just stood there as she processed the news, smiling coolly.

It was Katya who broke the uncomfortable silence. "Dinner is ready," she announced pleasantly. With the elephant now squarely in the room, Cam gave an edited version of what had happened over the past two years. The raiders, Laetitia's death, finding me again, and Katrin. Then, in recent events, Luca and Illy, Di's illness, and baby Kendra.

"Di has a baby?" Callie's face lit up. "That is amazing news."

"It is, especially after what is now happening."

Everyone paused mid-meal, expectantly.

"Luca and Jakob gave us some news," Kevin said solemnly. "When they first visited. What else do you know?"

Food went cold as Cam and I explained about Luca and Illy's original intel, then how it had more recently been corroborated by their visit to Clava. Then, we shared the reasons behind our individual selection, the selective breeding program, and what had happened to those communities that hadn't been so lucky. After the disbelief had turned to disgust and finally anger, we got to the point of our visit.

"Now we are looking for ways that we can cut ourselves off from the Nexus, permanently."

Tadhg and Callie looked at each other in the way of married couples.

"First things first," Callie said. "We have just about finished building the capacitors and rig to deactivate our portal. How about we bring it over to you in September and do yours too?"

"Does that mean that you..."

"We live here now," Callie beamed. "Things started getting difficult on Bellcamp about a year ago. So, we returned here permanently. As engineers, we want our skills to be for everyone, not just those prepared to pay for it. We want our children to grow up in a society that cares for each other."

"Oh, I never asked. Number three?"

"Is a boy," Callie beamed proudly. "Ronan is his name. He is nearly two now. Aoife and Aislinn are besotted with him. Think he is a doll. Lug him around everywhere."

"Has it really been that long?" Cam said wistfully.

After our initial awkward greeting, Callie was everything Cam and Di had said. Warm, funny, and excellent company. She spoke constantly, and it was hard to get a word in. Tadhg just sat quietly beside her, smiling. Finally, in a rare pause when Callie stopped to sip wine, I hurriedly asked Tadhg, "Cam tells me it was you who hacked the systems in Melbourne?"

"It was indeed," he responded, a broad grin spreading across his face.

"Cam says you found some interesting information?"

"Well, if you count learning the words to every Kylie and Mariah song interesting, you need to get a life," Tadhg said dryly, his eyes sparkling with mischief. The looks on Callie's and Cam's faces showed they had heard this particular story but were egging him on.

Several hours and many bottles of wine later, we were still laughing hysterically at Tadhg's stories of life with Callie.

"You should have seen my face when she first asked for a dunny," he said, rolling his eyes. "What's a bloody dunny?"

"Oh, Callie!" Cam teased. "No one says that anymore."

"And I don't know why I did! It just slipped out. Six years and he has never let me forget it either."

As the evening wore on, the hilarity died down, and the conversation turned to more serious matters. Callie looked over the table at us and asked, "You said that Di was sick, but well again?"

"She is. My sister, Luca, and a friend took her to Clava. They have an oncologist there who treated her."

"Magali?"

"How did you know?" Cam asked, surprised. "Was someone here sick, too?"

Kevin, Katya, Tadhg, and Callie all turned to look at each other.

"Mikayla," Kevin said mournfully, "Jake's wife."

Cam and I both exhaled heavily. It was happening again.

"Mikayla started getting sick a couple of months ago, but, well, they are newlyweds, so we thought she was pregnant, so it went unnoticed. She fobbed it off. Then they realized she wasn't pregnant, and finally, the med team did some blood tests. Like you, our laboratory is rudimentary, but we had enough equipment and skill to see that her blood cell count was way off. A biopsy and it was confirmed. The problem was, we have no skill in treating it. We radioed for help. Clava noted the request and said that they would get back to us. Several weeks went by, and no response. The next thing we know, Magali and a pediatrician, Nasir, arrive, and ask for asylum in exchange for treatment."

"Asylum?" I gasped.

"That's what they said. Magali hasn't said much, only that she no longer agreed with the governing principles on Clava, so they were looking for somewhere to go."

I caught the word and questioned Kevin, "*Hasn't* said much?"

"They arrived about two hours before you did. We haven't had the time to question them yet. We also felt it was prudent not to rush into trusting them. Making them wait a wee bit isn't a bad thing."

A smile spread across my face. I could see Jake saying that. With several international postings under his belt, primarily to warzones, he and Luca had extensive experience in interrogating prisoners. Not that Magali and Nasir were prisoners, exactly.

Cam was still trying to catch up. "They are here? Both of them?" He turned to look at me.

"You know what this means?"

"Angus is off infecting people, but now they have lost their key oncologist to treat. Wonder how that will go down on Clava."

"Angus?" Kevin spoke a trifle louder than necessary, and we all jolted. "Angus MacLeod?"

"That's him." Cam nodded. "He works for them. How do you know him?"

"Jakob and Luca told us about Angus, to be sure, when they left his company. But it wasn't until later that I realized I knew him from my university days.

Not friends, we were never that. But we have met a few times at conferences and such."

"I thought you were a historian?" Cam asked.

"I am. Well, I was. I'm not sure what I am now, to be honest."

"Why would a historian be in touch with a..." Cam turned to me. "What was Angus's background? I never thought to ask."

"Angus had multiple degrees," I admitted. "A few times he bragged about them after he had a few drinks. He has two doctorates too. Science and history."

As those words left my mouth, I realized what I had said. *Science and history.*

"What field of science?" Cam asked Kevin and me, the caution marked on his face.

"Geomorphology was the field he was lecturing in when I knew him. But I first met him at a conference on Ogham, you know, the medieval Irish written language."

"What is geomorphology?" Katya asked.

"Study of landforms. The origin and evolution of the physical features and surface of the earth," Callie chipped in.

"He had a degree in biology, too," I breathed. "He knew a lot about animals, plants, humans, their impact on the environment. We had a lot of conversations about how life under the domes would likely adapt and differ from that before."

"What about Ashton? Do we know what he did?" Kevin asked.

"Luca told us," I said, straining to remember. "Something scientific?"

"We could ask Magali," Cam suggested.

"You don't need to," Tadhg interjected through a mouthful of food. "I know. Carl Ashton. I've been in his office. His degrees were still on the wall."

We all looked at Tadhg expectantly.

"Bachelor of Science in Biology, Master of Science in Genetics, and a Ph.D. in Genetic Engineering. Lots of other bits and pieces, but they were the ones in the big frames."

"Genetics. Ancient history. Landforms. Biology. You don't think..." I whispered.

"That MacLeod and Ashton were behind it all? They masterminded it together?" Kevin finished for me. "I am wondering exactly that."

CHAPTER 34

THE FOLLOWING DAY CAM and I joined Kevin and Jakob, who the community had tasked to meet with Magali. Nasir would be interviewed later. Sitting in an adjoining room, Cam and I listened in to the conversation. As they had arrived before us, Magali and Nasir had no way of knowing that Cam and I were here, and the Newgrange residents did not know them. We could listen and see if what they said aligned with what we learned from Luca and Illy, or whether this was yet another trick to force the Newgrangians to relinquish self-governance.

Even from the adjoining room, we could tell from Magali's tone that they scared her, but she was quite willing to talk.

"Tell us everything," Kevin suggested kindly as Jakob watched, looming over her.

"Where would you like me to start?" she asked in her educated, French-accented voice.

"The beginning," he said simply.

"I went to medical school on a scholarship," she admitted. "Not being from a wealthy family. The government subsidizes all degrees in France, but the scholarship paid for my living expenses, you know. Then I completed my postgraduate study in Australia. I had met Nasir and had reason to move. After finishing my study, I accepted a position at a cancer hospital in Sydney. I divided my time between research and treating patients. I worked very long hours, and it was very tiring. But I enjoy the work. I do this for several years. Then one day, a man came."

Cam and I sat up a little straighter after hearing this.

"Was he Australian?" Kevin asked.

"*Oui*, he was. He said his name was Professor Ashton, and he had a special project for me. He made it sound wonderful, and I could help lots of people, but I told him I needed to think about it."

"What did he say?"

"He said that they wanted me. They needed my skills. They would offer me just about anything."

"Did you take it?"

"It was around that time that the pandemic first came to Australia. I knew from speaking with my mother in Carcassonne that life in Europe was already quite bad. Food shortages, people fighting in the streets, hundreds of people dying, mostly the elderly. My grandmother was one of them," she said sadly. "I had some understanding of what was to come. I told him I would accept on one condition."

"What was that?"

"That my partner, Nasir, also comes. Initially, they told me that there was no place for a pediatrician; there would be no children where we were going. I declined the offer. I had moved across the world for this man. I would not leave him behind. Ashton tried to convince me. He told me I was critical. But I did not change my mind. Then he insisted Nasir go through the same testing process as me, and after that, they agreed. After all, he had a medical degree and six years of postgraduate study. Just as things were getting bad in Australia, they took us to Auckland Island with the rest of the team."

"What did you do there?"

"For several years, we did not do much at all, and Nasir and I could not work out why we had been asked to be on this project. It made no sense. Please do not misunderstand. We enjoyed our life there. It was relaxed and very easy. We got to spend time together and with lots of other lovely people, especially when we learned that the protozoa had wiped out everything. I even learned to knit and grow things. But we could not work out why we had been chosen."

Cam and I smiled at the lovely way in which she pronounced protozoa in her lilting French accent.

"Then last year, I am told that it is my turn to travel to Clava for one year. Nasir and I were excited. We had heard about this amazing place, and we were thrilled to go. We had met many people from Clava, and there were people we knew from Auckland already there. But especially, I wanted to see the stones. They are much like the stones at Carnac, in France."

Magali paused. "But as soon as I arrive, the patients, they start coming. Cancer, to be sure. Lymphoma, all of them. But it was quite strange. The symptoms they had were almost identical. The disease, it tracked in the same way, and they all had the same response to the treatment. I have never seen anything like it."

"What did you do?"

"I asked Ashton, of course. He is a genetic specialist, you see, and he was in Clava by then. I told him I was concerned that there was a cancer cluster. You know, where a single location or perhaps a product causes a group of very similar cancer cases. There had been a few high-profile ones in Australia while I was there. I helped researchers with one or two. Looking for a common cause."

"What did Ashton say?"

"He dismissed it and told me that each of them had come from different communities. As a percentage of each population, it was minimal. That was true, so I spoke no more of it. I wondered if there was something that all the communities had in common that was causing these people to become sick."

"Then what happened?"

"My friend came. Illyria is her name. She was my neighbor in Auckland, and we got along very well. She used to tease me about my accent, but we were friends. She arrived with a sick child and then, a few months later, with a sick lady. This was the fifth case I had seen, and by this time, I knew that this was not right. I had been on Auckland and Clava for six years, seen nothing, but now five cases in six months? This could not be. I could see that Illy wanted to tell me something, but she was scared. There was a wall between us; we both felt it. It made me sad. Then, many weeks after she left, I found a note. It was in one of my pockets, so it was lucky that I even found it. It was a little, how do you say ... *cryptique*. It said that if I ever wanted to talk, that I should find her, but not to trust the radio. I did not have time to think about it before they called me to listen to the radio message you sent. You asked if we would help, and I agree. But that night Nasir and I made the decision to come," she finished.

We heard a gentle knock on the wall, the signal for Cam and me to enter.

As we opened the door, Magali's eyes filled with surprise at seeing us.

"Freyja? Campbell? *Mon Dieu!* Why are you here?"

"Hi, Magali." I nodded at Jakob. Everything she had said was the truth, as far as we knew.

Sitting down, we joined the conversation, much more open and honest this time. Jakob went to collect Nasir, and he was also stunned to see us.

There was shocked silence as I told them what Luca and Illy had discovered, the mosquitoes, the selective breeding program. Magali looked horrified and kept saying, "*Non!* No! That cannot be! All of us?"

Finally, Cam spoke. "Diana, the woman you treated, is my best friend. Sorcha, her partner, is my sister. We will always be grateful to you for saving her. But Magali, you need to know that these cases were not random."

"*Moustique?* Is that even possible?"

"Apparently, yes."

Magali turned to Nasir. "The nanotechnology *laboratoire*. You ask me once why it is there?"

Nasir nodded, paused considering what he had heard, then finally spoke. Kevin looked surprised that Nasir also had a strong French accent, despite his middle eastern appearance.

"I believe what you say. This all makes complete sense. This is..." he paused, searching for the correct word, "diabolical, but I think it is true."

"We know it is true," I confessed. "Ashton is a geneticist, and he was in charge of who was selected in Melbourne. He chose Cam and me. We know he was testing drugs on us. Linking up the communities and ensuring that there was a spare genome. It all leads to the same outcome."

"Did you know Jorja is a fertility specialist? She worked for an exclusive IVF clinic in Sydney," Magali said sadly.

"IVF?" I gasped. "Really? She told us she was a doctor!"

"Like most of us, she was medically trained. When we lived on Auckland Island, I thought it was strange that they recruited a doctor with a specialty in reproductive endocrinology and infertility. Yet, they did not want a pediatrician." Nasir shrugged dismissively. "Though, perhaps it was just me they did not want."

"Now that you know all of it," Jakob added softly, the first time he had spoken, "what do you want to do?"

"I will treat your wife, of course," Magali responded, not missing a beat. "After all, she is why we came. But perhaps," she looked at us, "we could rest a little first? We did not sleep so well last night."

Cam, Kevin, and I left as Jake showed Magali and Nasir out.

"What do you think?" Kevin asked quietly.

I looked at Cam.

"I genuinely believe that Ashton and Angus are behind it all," Cam admitted. "This was their plan all along, their way of getting people to submit. Why else would you ensure that only one oncologist survived and that single person happened to be precisely where you needed her when the cases started coming in? The matrix, setting up a spy on each community, the limited resources. It all leads to the same end game. Their plan to repopulate the earth with genetically planned babies."

"I have to agree," admitted Kevin. "While I always thought Angus was the type who would sell you his grandmother, I never picked him as a tyrant."

"Nor did I," I admitted. "And I thought I knew him well. But the more I learn, the more I believe it to be true."

"It makes sense why Sorcha, Di's cousin Kendra, and so many others were sent to isolated communities too," Cam said. "Spares in case something happened to the chosen candidate."

"Thank goodness I don't share a genome," I said, a little sadly.

We returned home in silence, unable to digest what we now knew to be true. We were all pawns in a game of science.

"Do you wonder who your chosen partner was?" I asked Cam as we lay in bed that night, unable to sleep. My head was spinning with everything we knew. To learn that Jorja was a reproductive specialist was effectively the last nail in the proverbial coffin. If we had any doubts before about the existence of the selective breeding program, we didn't now.

"I would always have chosen you," Cam breathed in my ear.

CHAPTER 35

ON OUR WAY TO the Newgrange antipodal point several days later, Callie was quiet, unusually so for her. She was always so gregarious and full of life. She was one of those people that everyone just *liked*. She was warm, engaging, self-deprecating, and when she spoke to you, you felt like you were the only person in the room. To top it off, she was naturally funny. An hour spent with Callie was an hour spent with your sides splitting. Cam had once described Tadhg as a natural comedian. Tadhg had regaled his companions with jokes and stories on the journeys between Bellcamp and Australia. But beside Callie, he paled in comparison. I could see why Cam liked her so much.

But today, something was wrong. Cam, not usually attuned to people's emotions, glanced at me for confirmation. I nodded, just slightly. Yes, he was right. Something was off.

He slipped an arm around her shoulders and asked gently, "What's up, Cal?"

She looked up at him and smiled wanly. "I was just thinking."

"About...?"

"What we are about to do. Cut ourselves off from Bellcamp. It was my home for years. Many of those people are my friends. Now..."

"Are you having second thoughts?" I asked cautiously.

"No, not really. It's not like going home from a holiday and knowing that you could always jump on a plane and go back at some point. We are about to cut ourselves off from the entire world. This is a big deal."

"You aren't being cut off from us," Cam replied quickly. "Lewis will always be there to support you."

"True, and we can reactivate, I guess. Didn't you say that the radio signals are being monitored?"

"I did. That makes things a little difficult."

"Unless..." I started but stopped.

"Unless what?" They both looked at me, and I relented.

"Deactivating the portal is the primary goal. I mean, that is time critical. You need to do it at the solstice, and we are keen to do ours at the equinox. But... could we not find a way that we can communicate, just between us? I'm no engineer, and you are about to tell me I have watched far too many movies, but there must be a way. Encrypted messages or something?"

"Something a little more high-tech than tin cans on a string?" Cam grinned.

"It isn't impossible..." Callie thought aloud. "It is certainly right up Tadhg's alley. Shame Blake stayed on Bellcamp. He would have some ideas too."

"Oh, I meant to ask you about him. Why did he stay?"

"Angus convinced Blake that joining the Collective was a good move. Once Blake joined, everyone else fell in line behind him. That left Katya, Tadhg, and me rather out in the cold."

"Oh. Do you know how Angus convinced him?"

"I don't. All I know is that Blake was blatantly against the idea and then overnight changed his mind."

"Very sudden," Cam noted.

"Very suspicious," I said acerbically. "Bribed?"

"I wouldn't have thought," Cam said thoughtfully. "Blake had ethics."

"He did," Callie agreed. "That wasn't it. But Angus said something to convince him. One minute he was all, 'over my dead body'... then next, he was... 'this is in the best interests of everyone.' It was almost overnight."

"Blake was a very logical man," Cam said thoughtfully. "Do you think they told him the truth? About needing all the genetic sequences to repopulate the earth?"

"Tadhg and I have talked about it quite a lot since you told us about that project. It is the only thing that makes any sense," Callie admitted.

Arriving at the ancient complex of Newgrange, its size and sheer presence awed me. Looming up out of the hillside, it was several times larger than the stone cairns at Clava. The large circular-shaped dome had enormous gray boulders marking the outside, a vast wall of rock, a grassy roof forming the top of the mound. As we approached, I could see the curbstones Cam had described, intricate patterns carved on them.

I gasped as I approached. "They *are* the same patterns as the stones on August!"

Cam smiled. "I told you."

"I had no basis of comparison," I admitted. "I have never been here, and to be honest, I had never heard of this place until I went through to Lewis. Is it the only one like it in Ireland?"

"Oh no," said Callie. "There are several, and some more in this region. Knowth and Dowth are in line with this one, although not as well preserved. There is another quite famous one at Loughcrew. Plus, many other ancient sites. Now that we won't be traveling to Bellcamp, we plan to spend some more time exploring the other sites within Ireland."

"Be careful," Cam warned. "There is a site in the Orkneys: Maes Howe. It wasn't supposed to be activated, but it was."

"Where did it go?"

"A rocky, icy atoll near Antarctica, not under a dome. Ross, the poor man who fell through, spent six months nearly dying before he returned."

"Point taken," she said with mock seriousness. "No visits during solstices."

Pulling an electronic device out of her pocket, Callie started pointing it, looking down at the tiny screen.

"What is that?" I asked her curiously.

"I'm just taking some measurements of the site, you know, data required to generate the magnetic charge. We need it to be strong enough to knock the poles from their axis, but not so strong that we blow up the site. We have come a long way from tape measures!"

There was already a lot of metal here, I noted, stepping over at the long pieces of copper pipe lying just outside the ring of curbstones.

"Cal," I called, "why copper?"

She shrugged. "It conducts electricity well, and it is easily moldable. Technically silver is better, but we don't exactly have hundreds of meters of silver lying around. Copper is fairly common hereabouts. Did you know that some of the earliest copper mines in the world were in County Kerry? We revisited the mines with our modern tech and smelted enough to construct this monstrosity."

"How did you smelt it without generating smoke?" Cam asked, concerned.

"We did it outside, of course. Do you think we are complete dafties?"

Cam just grinned at her.

"Do you think the dome over Callanish is about the same height as this one? I'm just wondering if we need to bring more pieces. Or is there plenty of copper on Lewis?"

Cam and I stood looking at the dome overhead.

"Hard to tell, isn't it?" I said, staring upward. The sun was hitting the dome directly overhead, dispersing the light and making it hard to focus.

"Well, Callanish isn't really on a hilltop. I mean, it is elevated but not like this. I would think the dome over Lewis is higher at this point. As for, do we have copper ore, well no. I don't think so."

"Fair enough." Callie disappeared around the back of the enormous structure, leaving us to explore.

Crouching before the enormous curbstones, I ran my hands over the spirals and double spirals, feeling the tingling of familiarity. I called him over.

"Cam, you told me once that these were called something. What was that?"

Crouching next to me, he placed his hand beside mine on the enormous rock.

"Triskeles," Cam responded. "Those. That set of three spirals."

"Why three?" I wondered aloud. "The double ones, I understand. The portal runs both ways, and there is that point in the middle where you change direction. But three?"

"Do you think they thought the portal went to different places?"

"Possibly. It is a little odd, isn't it?"

Tracing my hand over the chevron, I remembered the same pattern on the menhir in the cave on August. I hadn't thought about it for so long, that place where we had become one. Where we had pledged our lives to each other. Smiling to myself, I replayed some of the blissful memories of our time there. The only place we had felt genuinely alone and safe. For so long, I had dreamed that we would conceive our child there. Then it had been ripped away in an instant—a roaring force extracting the life from me. Glancing up surreptitiously, I checked Cam wasn't watching. I didn't want him to worry about me. He did, I knew. Especially since I had started getting blistering headaches again. The pain was emanating from where I had fractured my skull, first on Lewis, but also when the slingshot had hit me near Inverness. It had only been a few weeks, but the frequency of the headaches was increasing, and they were exhausting me. It wouldn't be long before I needed to consult Hamish or perhaps Sorcha.

Moving around the enormous structure, I noted the ring of intricately carved curbstones at the base. Thousands of years old, yet they had withstood the test of time. Beautiful pieces of art that someone, or a group of people, had deliberately wanted to carve here, leaving their mark. There was nothing random about them. I wondered if there were the cup marks here, like Clava, marking a constellation visible above Campbell Island.

I was absently tracing a circle with a knot in it as Cam silently stepped behind me.

"That is an Ouroboros," he whispered.

I didn't know the word. "Ouroboros?" I questioned as I removed my hand, studying the image once again.

"It is an ancient symbol of a serpent, sometimes a dragon, eating its own tail. Ancient Egyptian culture, Greek, Roman, Norse—they all have it, or a version of it."

"But not Celtic?"

"I have no idea. Some cultures say it symbolizes infinity or the cyclic nature of life: birth, death, rebirth. Others suggest it reflects the unity of life, the relationship between men and women. But no matter how you look at it, the Ouroboros is a circle, never-ending."

"Like us?" I asked softly.

"I haven't thought about it," he admitted slowly. "But yes. We found each other when we were both lonely and came together, lived our lives apart for a bit, but we have returned to each other. Come full circle. Now, we are eternally connected through Katrin. The children she may have one day."

"Bloody hell," I snorted. "She isn't out of nappies, and you are talking about grandchildren!"

"I can't wait to see you, gray-haired, with our grandchildren asleep in your lap, singing to them," he whispered tenderly in my ear.

"And you? What will you do?"

"Likely still gardening and complaining each night about how much my back aches." He chuckled. "But I will still be able to take you to bed."

"I'll hold you to that."

We stood there, motionless, staring into each other's eyes, visible sparks flying, oblivious to the world around us. A war could have been going on, but those beautiful azure blue eyes mesmerized me. Eyes that held my future in their depths.

Callie returned at that point, effectively putting an end to the conversation. "Good to go?" she chirped.

"Random, public acts of lustfulness, was it?" Cam whispered in my ear.

Elbowing him in the ribs, I followed them both back down the hill.

CHAPTER 36

I SENSED CAM WANTED TO spend some time with Callie, catching up on the past few years. She was lovely, but I could tell she was busting to ask him questions too. Questions that I probably shouldn't be present for.

"It is so beautiful here," I gushed as we left Newgrange. "If you don't mind, I'm going to go for a walk, explore a little."

"Oh, I am a terrible host!" she exclaimed. "I forgot you had never been here. Do you want me to show you around?"

"That is very kind, but I know you have things to do. I'll be fine. Can't get lost in a domed community, can I?"

Cam, knowing that I was trying to give him alone time, flashed me a look of gratitude.

Leaving me at the foot of the hill, Cam and Callie headed back into the village as I walked along the River Boyne. Following a meandering tree-lined path, it was much like parts of Lewis. I noted the similar trees, bushes, and the general landscape was familiar.

It was hillier here and less rocky than parts of Lewis. Large, ancient trees towered high above, trees that had seen the passing of many generations of people, that had once overlooked the wilderness, then roads and farms, and were now resting for the winter. Discarded stalks of corn and wheat lay on the ground next to the cultivated fields, not blowing anywhere because of the lack of natural wind. There were turbines here, as there were in all communities, airflow being essential to survival, but nothing strong enough to pick them up and scatter them randomly. Dead leaves lay at the foot of the tree from which they had fallen. Choosing a path, I started walking inland, not going anywhere, just following my heart.

In the distance, I could see the ruins of an ancient stone church. One end was still intact with what was once a bell tower, a belfry. The stone frames of the two small windows were still intact, but the bell and roof were long gone. The crumbling side walls were barely a meter high, and sheep grazed nearly, blissfully oblivious of the history in their vicinity. I wandered through the ancient cemetery, absently reading the headstones of people long dead, many of them hundreds of years ago—people who likely wouldn't believe what had happened to the earth wiped out in the space of a year. Or perhaps they would, believing in the apocalypse, being God-fearing folk.

Bizarrely, this place had survived, unlike millions of other revered sites across the globe. Lush green grass lay within the churchyard walls, stone graves scattered in-between with no real semblance of order. Some were ancient, well-weathered, the engraving hard to read. Others were far newer, although nothing that could be called modern.

Walking the outside perimeter walls, I noticed a stile, a set of uneven, rocky ancient steps that led up and over the stone wall. Reaching the top, I sat for a moment to take in the spectacular landscape. From here, I could see the layers of green hills in the distance, the varying shades of green blending into a tapestry. The mound at Newgrange was visible in the distance as well as a nearer one—Dowth, I think Callie had said it was called.

I don't know how long I sat there, a sense of calm filling me, a sense of peace. Meditation had never been a practice I engaged in, but right now, I understood why people actively sought this feeling of serenity. I felt connected, and a sense of utter tranquility descended over me like a curtain. Closing my eyes, I knew without question that I was finally on the right path. I was where I should be and with the man with whom I would spend eternity.

Hearing crunching, I searched the landscape and saw a man walking up the path; I recognized Nasir. He saw me and waved. Not really wanting to move, I waved back but moved slightly, gesturing that he could join me on my perch. He did and sighed as he took in the landscape's magnificence. We sat in silence for a while, and I started back down the stile, intending to take my leave. To my surprise, Nasir followed me.

"Do you want to look around the Abbey?" I asked.

He shrugged. "I am hopeful that Maggie and I may live in this place. If this is so, I will have plenty of time. Do you mind if I walk with you?"

Nasir was quiet, relaxed, and had a gentleness that masked his intelligence. I could see how people would overlook him, not consider him a threat. He spoke little, but when he did, it was with sincerity and wisdom, proving that he had listened deeply and had made astute observations.

"Nasir, can I ask you something?"

"*Oui.*"

"I keep getting headaches—bad ones. I fractured my skull a few years ago when I came through the portal and smacked my head on a rock. Then another decent head wound seven months ago when I was hit with the slingshot near Clava, just before we met. Both knocked me unconscious, and I had a nasty concussion for days, dizziness, unable to focus. But in the past few weeks, I have been experiencing headaches again, and I am so exhausted."

"The headaches, they are new? It sounds like you have been busy, perhaps stressed. Could you be fatigued? The body is a precision instrument. If you do not look after it, it starts to break down," Nasir replied, sounding very French.

"That is possible, of course. But, well, life has always been busy for me. That is nothing new. But the headaches *are*. I was wondering, could you perhaps run some tests?"

"You do not want to wait until you are back on Lewis? Your sister-in-law, a doctor, is she not?"

"She is, but ... well, I want a little privacy. If it is something bad, I don't want Cam to worry about it. Not now. There is so much going on."

Nasir began to object but closed his mouth again.

"*Oui.* I understand. I will need to ask if they will let me use the medical center, but I do not see why not. I was a doctor too, you know, before I chose to work with the children."

I paused, wanting to ask, but was afraid to. We were strangers even though we had met before, on Clava. But we weren't close.

He sensed my question. "Is there something you want to know? Ask it, *s'il vous plaît.*"

"Please tell me if this is rude or invasive. But clearly, you like children. Is there a reason you and Magali do not have children of your own?"

He smiled wanly. "In the early days, in Sydney, we worked very long hours. We both wanted to focus on establishing our careers. We wanted a family, but only when we could both take some time. We wanted to be with our children, you see. Not be always rushing off to leave them. Then the pandemic came. They offered Magali a place, and by association, so was I. We thought maybe then, we could follow our dreams and have children. Auckland was clean and safe and a wonderful place to have a family. But they warned us. We would need to travel to Clava, to work our term. That was the condition of our tenure, you know. They provided a house and food and jobs. But at some point, everyone needed to travel to Clava. When we went through, we understood. No child should go through that. It was, how do you say ... intense."

"Not the word I would use," I smiled at Nasir, "but please continue."

"We worked at Clava, and time is getting near for us to return to Auckland. Maybe then, we think. We are not so young anymore."

"And now you are here?" I probed gently. "Does that change things?"

"If we can stay here, yes, it does. Maybe, now. Maybe we can, especially now that we know more about why they chose us. Maybe that is why they did not want us to have children together? We believe you, you know. Magali and I talked last night. It is disgusting, but from what we know, we believe it is all true."

"How did you meet Magali?"

His face lit like the sun had struck it. "I am from Iran. A refugee. My father, my two older brothers, they disappeared, taken off the street one day. We were Baha'i, you see."

"Baha'i"? I questioned. It wasn't a cultural group I had heard of.

"Baha'i believe in the unity of men and women, equality in all things. World peace. That all religions are equal, and that religion and science can operate in harmony."

"That's very progressive," I admitted.

"It is, but most people in Iran are Muslim, so they do not agree with our teachings."

"So, you left?"

"My mother, she smuggled me out of Iran and into Turkey. I was eight. We spent two years in a refugee camp. Then we were lucky. Canada accepted us as refugees. We settled in Quebec."

"Ahh, so that is how you speak French."

"Yes, I was schooled in French but also English and Farsi. My mother was a learned woman."

"Where did you meet Magali?"

"I was at a conference in Paris. It was about cancer in children. After my own time in the refugee camp and watching all the children get sick, many dying, I always knew it was my calling. I was running late, and I arrive as the speaker is starting. There is one seat left, next to a beautiful woman. I stand there, frozen. I am too scared to sit next to her, but she sees me, and she smiles the most beautiful smile. It lights up the room.

She pats the chair and beckons for me to sit beside her. From that day, I never left her side."

"That is beautiful. But why Australia?"

"My mother, she moved to Australia. Maggie and I visited her several times. We decided it was a good place to raise children. But sadly, that did not happen."

I wanted to ask what had happened to his mother but couldn't. Likely she had perished, the same as all the other parents when the pandemic had struck.

Nasir snapped out of his melancholy and resumed his doctorly manner.

"Tomorrow morning, come and find me at the clinic. I will ask if I can use the laboratory, and we can see about this headache of yours."

CHAPTER 37

THE FOLLOWING MORNING, I awoke feeling terrible. My head ached, and I felt like a truck had hit me.

"Are you sick? Too much wine?" Cam asked worriedly.

"I don't think so." I grimaced through the throbbing pain in my head and nausea rising. The truth was, I had barely drunk one glass at dinner the previous night, feeling unwell. But fortunately, everyone else having such a wonderful time hadn't noticed.

"I am just so exhausted," I admitted.

"You haven't been bitten by a mosquito?" Cam asked, turning his concerned eyes to look at me closely. "Come into contact with water?"

"I don't think so," I admitted. "Not that I can recall, anyway. I just feel like I could sleep for a week."

"I had glandular fever as a teenager. That was much how I felt," he admitted. "Do you want to rest today? I was going to see Callie and Tadhg do a practice run on setting up the capacitors."

"If you can do without me, I think more sleep will do me a world of good," I said with as much enthusiasm as I could muster.

"It isn't long until the solstice. Do you want to wait here, watch how they deactivate it, and then all return to Lewis together?" Cam asked.

"I don't mind," I said dismissively, but in truth, I did. I didn't want to spend more time away from our children. Di and Sorcha were shouldering the burden again, and they had a baby of their own now.

"Why don't you ask Callie and Tadhg?" I suggested as I snuggled under the blankets. "They may have some ideas. They are the experts."

As I tried to sleep, the voices laughing in the dining room weren't loud but just intrusive enough to stop me from dropping off. Taking some aspirin from the stash Hamish had taken from the house in Edinburgh, I drifted off, finally waking mid-morning. I staggered out into the kitchen to find only Katya at home.

"Feeling better?" she asked sympathetically.

"Not really," I admitted. I did not need to lie to her. "Just feeling a bit under the weather. I'll be fine tomorrow. I'm sure."

"Coffee?" she asked with her hand already on the percolator.

"Oh, that would be *wonderful!*" I replied with so much enthusiasm that it made her smile.

"Like *that,* is it?" she teased gently.

"You know, it is funny. When I was growing up, my father drank coffee, and my mother tea. I didn't drink either until I moved to August. All those days in vet clinics on student placements and people would ask, 'tea or coffee?' and I would reply, 'water is fine.' I feel like I am a bit late to the party. It wasn't until I moved in with Cam, and he drank coffee, that I developed a taste for it. Now, I can't function without it. Not a lot. Just one, maybe two cups a day. But it is part of my routine."

"Cam told me what happened to you," Katya said. "That must have been awful, taken away so unexpectedly."

"The journey was awful," I admitted. "But it was the distance that was worse, and the incapacity to contact him. I couldn't just pick up a phone and go, 'Guess what? Went for a walk, and now I am in Scotland. Be home in six months!' I knew he would worry about me, but I had no way to alleviate that fear."

Katya nodded. "Well, it all worked out in the end," she said, striving for the silver lining.

"It did," I agreed. *But not without a hell of a lot of pain and heartache, for both of us,* I thought grimly. *And pain that could well have been avoided.*

Finishing my coffee, I asked, "Can you tell me where the medical clinic is?"

Raising her eyebrows, she asked discretely, "I'm a doctor. Can I help?"

Not really wanting my medical history relayed to Kevin or Callie and potentially back to Cam, I smiled with as much enthusiasm as I could. "Oh, I just want to visit Mikayla."

I found it quickly enough, a small white building, very similar to the one on Lewis. Nasir was there, as was Magali. A young red-haired woman lay in a bed, looking very pale and sickly. Even from where I stood across the room, I could see that she was unwell. Jakob was sitting beside her, holding her hand as Magali was writing on a chart.

"So *this* must be the woman who stole my friend's heart," I said breezily, entering the room. "I'm Freyja. It is so lovely to meet you."

She smiled weakly at me, but it was plain that she was exhausted. I knew how she felt.

"Jakob and I have been friends a very long time, so when you are ready to hear embarrassing stories, let me know," I said, making her look slightly more alert, and Jake look worried. "You are in excellent hands with Magali," I went on, trying to be reassuring. "She helped my friend Diana only recently."

"How is Diana?" Magali asked, her voice filled with concern. "I never get to hear how patients are once they return home."

"She is doing well," I admitted. "It is like she was never sick! Sorcha has taken some time off to help look after baby Kendra. Di has put on weight, and she has color in her cheeks. She just looks *well* again. Thank you, Magali, truly. I can't thank you enough for saving her. She means so much to all of us."

"I'm so glad," Magali responded in such a heartfelt way that I knew it was genuine. "I was most worried about her being pregnant, you know. But baby Kendra, she is alright too? She was born a little early. But it was necessary. Nasir said she was doing well when they left."

"She seems fine. A normal healthy baby."

I saw the look pass between Jakob and Mikayla. So did Magali.

Magali returned her attention to Mikayla, taking her blood pressure. "You know, once we have you treated, nothing is stopping you from starting a family."

"I won't have to ... wait?" Mikayla asked nervously, in a charming Irish lilt.

"There is no reason why. You have a presentation called non-Hodgkin lymphoma. The treatment is radiation in most cases, not chemotherapy. It is chemotherapy that affects your fertility. It is also not a type of cancer affected by hormones, so if you want to…"

Remembering my conversation with Nasir the previous day, I wondered how much of this conversation was relevant to all of us. Nasir caught my eye from the doorway and gestured that we leave, so giving them my best wishes, I left, following Nasir into a small office.

"Roll up your sleeve," he instructed as he prepared a syringe. Nasir sucked in his breath when he saw my inner arms.

"No, I didn't do that to myself," I blurted, not wanting him to think I was suicidal as well as sick.

As he placed the cuff on my arm and flexed the muscle to draw the vein, he asked calmly, "May I ask what happened?"

"When we had dinner that night on Clava, do you remember Cam and I talking about the farm? You know, the men who tortured people and took the scientists from Clava?"

"Ze cannibals, you mean?"

I tried not to smile at the lovely French inflection on the word cannibals. He almost made it sound exotic.

"Yes. Well, they tied me up, you see. My hands were behind my back, and I was trying to cut the rope, to escape."

Nasir nodded, understanding, glancing a fresh eye over my inner forearms as he extracted the blood into the vial.

"Some of them are deep," he noted as he finished, capping the vial and withdrawing the needle, placing some cotton wool on the tiny hole for me to hold in place. "But they appear to be healing well. Let me run some tests, see what we can find. It won't take long, just a few hours. I will come and find you later."

Nodding my thanks, I left. Jakob was lurking in the hallway.

"You okay?" he asked, concerned.

"I'm fine. Just tired, that's all."

Panic crossed his face. "That was Mikayla's first symptom!"

"I'm good. We have already had someone on Lewis infected, and it wasn't me. Mine is likely just a bug I picked up, or nothing at all." I didn't tell him about the headaches, the real reason I was worried.

"How is Mikayla, really?" I asked.

"She isn't good," he admitted. "When we didn't hear back from Clava, I got concerned. Then, out of the blue, Magali shows up, we hear about all the other cases, and well ... what if she is the one who doesn't make it?" he whispered, half-choked. "I waited so long to meet someone, Frey. I can't lose her now."

"You won't," I assured him. "Magali is an exceptional doctor. They chose her as she is the best of the best. My friend Di, and her baby, are doing fine now."

"Was your friend really pregnant? And they did this deliberately? On that note, why Mikayla? She never hurt anyone."

"They did do this deliberately," I said caustically. "And yes, Di was pregnant, so again, we missed it at first. Luca learned that Di wasn't the target though— Cam was. But when you use a mosquito as the carrier, you can't control who it bites, can you? As for Mikayla, short of Angus wanting to get back at *you*, well, I have no idea."

"If I ever see his sniveling little face..."

"Get in line, buddy," I said determinedly. "You'll need to wait. After what he has done to me and my family..."

My eyes must have been flashing warning signs as Jake grinned.

"There's the Freyja I know and love."

"I've missed you, Jake," I said with sincerity.

"You too, Frey." He reached out to hug me.

"She will be fine," I promised. "Now, there is something I want to talk to you about."

Returning to Kevin's house, I found Cam waiting for me.

"You okay?" He looked worried, seeing my worn face.

"I went to visit Mikayla," I explained, mentally making a note to remove the taped-on cotton-ball from my arm before Cam saw. "I just wanted to offer Jake some moral support."

"Is she okay?"

"No, but she will be. Magali has it all in hand. What did Callie say?"

"She said we should get back to our family. They will decommission their portal here on the winter solstice, then travel to us with the equipment, and be ready for the equinox. She asked if they could bring the kids."

"I don't see why not. She knows that the water outside is still not safe?"

"She knows, but figures if they can source a yacht similar to ours, then she can keep them off the decks. She wants them to see some of the world and doesn't want to be away from them for the several weeks it would take to travel to Lewis and back."

"I understand that completely." I sighed, making Cam grin.

"Should we leave tomorrow?"

"That would be *wonderful*."

CHAPTER 38

BACK AT SEA THE following day, I felt exhilarated, enjoying the blasts of wind in my face. The gusts were providing me with some much-needed energy. I heard the voice behind me, "Careful. You don't want to get water in your face. I'm not losing you now."

Turning, I threw my arms around his neck.

"I am so excited to be going home! Every time we return, we say, 'This is the last time,' but then we keep finding reasons to go back out!"

"You look better," he said, holding me at arm's length and studying me. "Maybe you were just homesick."

"Definitely. How fast can we get there, do you think?"

"Four days? Maybe five?" Cam looked at the sky. It was blue with white fluffy clouds, not a storm in sight. "Why the rush, though? Missing the kids that much?"

"So much that it hurts," I told him truthfully. "Also, I need to send Illy and Luca on a retrieval mission before they settle down too much."

"I thought your mission days were done!" he teased. "Retrieving what? And why them? They have barely arrived."

"Jake and I agree Clava isn't likely to give up lightly. Now that we know why they wanted us all, our genes, I mean, they will do pretty much anything to stick to their plan. I mean, infecting people with lymphoma and then having on hand the only specialist who can treat it screams premeditated. If the situation gets nasty, we need to be able to defend ourselves. There are very few military personnel left, and certainly, no one on Clava has any defense training. They told us that when we were there. I thought it might be sensible if Jake, Luca, and Illy collect some *resources*."

"Guns?" Cam flinched.

"Oh, more than that. Between Jake and Luca, they have been posted to several bases on the mainland. They can source some equipment and ensure that we can deploy adequate resources to protect the community. Illyria also likely has knowledge of security systems."

Cam looked startled at that.

"Think about it before you judge," I said, knowing that he was anti weapons of any kind. "This isn't an attack. This is defense. The other benefit, if we are clever, is that Clava will probably see that we are stockpiling weapons..."

"... and are less likely to try anything? It isn't a bad idea," he admitted, a little begrudgingly. "But you said Jake. Surely he won't want to leave Mikayla?"

"He doesn't. But he also acknowledges that Newgrange is as much at risk as Lewis. If the three of them get enough for both communities, then we stand a chance. Especially if Tadhg can find a way for us to communicate that isn't traceable."

"You are my warrior goddess."

His arms came around me, enveloping me in his warmth. I stopped thinking about weapons.

On our return to Roseglen, everyone was excited to see us. While devastated to hear of Mikalya, Di looked so well it was surprising to think that only a few months ago she had been desperately ill. Sorcha was furious to learn that they had infected yet another young woman. There was rapidly becoming quite a mob seeking a private audience with Mr. Angus MacLeod.

I noticed that work had begun on a new home farther down the valley. The frame was in place with some walls and a roof. But it was far from finished.

"If we work hard, do you think that could be ready by the time Callie and Tadhg arrive?" Cam asked hopefully. I knew what he was saying. He loved being home and didn't want to share it with another family for a few weeks as close as he and Callie were.

"Let's see what we can do."

A week later, after a late breakfast and checking the kids, I said to Cam, "Isla is coming to stay for a bit. Come with me. We will need to ride, though."

Raising his eyebrows suspiciously, Cam said nothing, knowing that I detested e-bikes, my knee having not yet recovered.

Chugging through the darkness, the fields alive with color, Cam asked, "Where are we going, honey?"

"Callanish."

Jolting the bike to a stop, he nearly came off. "Are you *mad*? It is the bloody solstice!"

"I know. It is okay. I promise we will keep our distance."

Looking sideways at me, he asked suspiciously, "Are you trying to do away with me already?"

Laughing at his reaction, I said, "No. But it is important."

As we approached, we could see the complex of stones in the distance, the sun glowing warmly behind them, the orange tint making the stones glow with a liveliness I had rarely seen. Cam's reluctance to move toward the stones was blatant. After all, he had made that passage several times. Myself, I had endured it once, and once only. After the fractured skull I had suffered the first time, and the months of headaches, blurred vision, and woollyheadedness, add the nightmares and... ugh. No, I couldn't face that again. Besides, everything I ever wanted was here.

"We don't need to go near them," I reassured him. "I just wanted to spend some time with you."

"You couldn't have picked somewhere safer? And why *today*?"

As we settled on the rocky outcrop overlooking the circle, I spoke softly, "The winter solstice would have been your anniversary. But we likely won't have a portal by then."

"Yes."

"What was she like?"

Cam turned to me, pausing. "Laetitia? Are you sure you want to know?"

"I do. She was a significant part of your life, and I feel like I need to know her better, so I can help teach Louis about her. He knows he is lucky he has two mothers. One who grew him, and one who chose him. But he asks questions, and I don't know how to answer them."

Smiling to himself in the morning light, Cam said, "She was sweet, gentle, and kind. Tiny, like a kitten. Long chestnut brown hair and beautiful almond-shaped brown eyes. Slightly exotic, but now that I know her grandmother was Thai, that all makes sense. She had a kind word for everyone, always stopped to help. Bloody hell, it took ages to get anywhere, as she always took the time to help someone peg out washing or carry something. She always put other people's needs before her own, cleaned their houses, or cared for their children. That night, when I arrived here, she took me in without question. Just took me into her home and cared for me. I was a stranger, and I was in a bad way. But that was the type of person she was. I have told you a little about her life before she came here."

I nodded, encouraging him to continue.

"What I could never work out was how someone so neglected could focus on others so much. I think she made me a better person." Cam trailed off, staring into the distance.

"I'm so sorry for your loss," I said and meant it.

"It wasn't your fault. It never was. And as long as it has taken me to acknowledge it, it wasn't mine either. It was Illy that finally made me realize that. I couldn't have stopped what happened that day. Those men would have found our community. It is so blisteringly obvious from the coast. She would have gone out to Carloway whether we had fought or not. She had planned to go, to help Steph school her kids. Chances were, she was always going to be taken. The part that broke my heart for so long was that she and I fought on that last day. We so rarely fought, not like you and me. I should have gone after her, but I didn't. Now I can never take it back."

We sat in silence for a very long time. Finally, I said in a low voice, "Do you notice how we don't argue as much as we used to? The first time around, I mean."

He looked up from his place on the rock beside me, and I sensed him smiling.

"We are more mature, you mean?"

"Maybe."

"I... I don't know if I should raise this..."

"You can tell me anything," I said, and I meant it.

Cam exhaled softly. "The fight Lae and I had that day. It took me a long time to realize that it was over *you*."

I blushed but said nothing.

"I blamed you for a time. And I am sorry for that. I've told you before that Lae was raised by a single mother, and she had no siblings. Her experience of disagreements was listening to the violent altercations in the adjacent flats, often leading to family violence or the police being called. When we fought the first time, it shattered her, thinking it was all over. It wasn't, but she had never seen the full cycle play out—disagreement, negotiation, reconciliation. I was thinking... are *we* role-modeling the right behaviors for our children?"

"Goodness, you sound like my mother!" I said without thinking. Then hurriedly added, "She was always talking about behavior cycles and role modeling."

"Did they fight? Your parents?"

I considered that. "You know, I rarely even saw them be affectionate to each other. They were a team, a partnership. I don't think I ever saw them argue, although, at times, things were frosty between them. There was no anger but no affection either. And never in public."

"How did you know?" he asked cautiously. "When we used to argue. How did you know it wasn't all over?"

"Because you told me a million times a day how much you loved me, and I believed you. I felt secure in the relationship. I could be myself. Besides, I had my sister. We didn't always get along, but like you and Sorcha, we always worked it out."

"If there was an Olympic category for slamming doors, you would have been a worthy contender," he teased, ever so gently.

Feeling the waves of red rushing to my face, I looked away, mortified as I recalled those times. "I'm so sorry," I said in a low voice. "I was childish and didn't realize how much you meant to me ... until you weren't there."

"Darling, I am teasing you. I was young and foolish myself. I poked the bear, asking questions I knew I shouldn't. Neither of us were perfect. But we were in love. I loved you so very much. I was half a man when I lost you, thought you were dead."

"And now?"

"Now I am whole because of you. Louis and little Kat are my world. Everything I do, I do for the three of you."

As the sky grew brighter, Cam told me stories of Laetitia. He laughed and cried as he remembered each memory of her. Shared them with me. I didn't feel jealous or threatened. I knew now that life had needed to happen this way, to bring us back to each other.

The sun reached its zenith and illuminated the chambered tomb, glowing orange, nestled between the largest upright stone and the edge of the circle. The magnetism was visible, thickening the air with a charge. Clutching my hand, Cam watched, apprehension and fear etched into his face. A crackling sound like static electricity made us focus on the chambered tomb as a large silver ball came tumbling out, rolling a few meters from the entrance. Cam gasped, and I smiled secretly. We waited a few minutes until the static eased, and the sun moved, casting the chamber into semi-shadow once more. Racing to the ball, I unzipped the outer case.

The look of stunned amazement on Cam's face when Jamie's face popped out was priceless. Then Jacinda, Aroha, Kara, and a screaming baby strapped to Jacinda's chest. Jamie looked green and sat on the ground, the two youngest on his lap, looking bewildered and shaken. Jacinda was trying her best to comfort the baby, who was screaming so loudly that the sound was reverberating painfully off the nearby rocks.

Cam stood there, agape, unable to process what he had just seen. Manners got the better of him as he helped Jamie with Kara, Aroha letting me pick her up and comfort her. Jamie staggered to his feet. Jacinda had placed a finger in the baby's mouth, and it was sucking madly. Quiet, for now.

"Now, I know what you meant," Jamie breathed. "Words aren't quite adequate to describe … *that*."

"Try it without a heat suit!" Cam laughed.

"Yeah, no thanks. One-way trip, mate."

"What did you say? Not that I thought you would do this for a Sunday picnic!"

Jamie shrugged. "The community on August is fragmenting. Erica and Kai have split the Green Island community with their bickering. Phil has alienated just about everyone. Things are getting nasty, and people are looking out for themselves and themselves only. Then, they voted to join the Collective. This isn't what Jac and I wanted for our kids, so…"

"So, you came *here*?"

Worry crossed Jamie's usually cheerful face. "You didn't know?"

I rushed in, "I wanted to make it a surprise."

"A wonderful surprise!" Cam gushed. "Welcome to Scotland! I cannot imagine anyone I would rather share my home with!"

Turning to me, he asked, "That is who the new house is for?"

"It is," I beamed. "I have been planning this for a little while. Now that Illy and Luca are here, we will need to finish the other, but it doesn't matter. We have time."

Checking that each of the travelers were okay and able to walk, we started the slow trek back to Roseglen, hooking the bags they had brought on the handlebars. Jamie and Jacinda carried a child each, Aroha holding Cam's hand.

"I cannot tell you how happy this makes me," Cam enthused. "Having all my friends together. This is the best news I could imagine!"

"I have one other tiny piece of solstice news," I said in a low voice from beside him.

Cam's face broke into the broadest grin as he dropped Aroha's hand and turned to look at me. His beaming smile brightened under the midday sun.

"Really?"

"Really."

Dropping the pack and swinging me off my feet, he kissed me, the excitement barely contained.

CHAPTER 39

WE LEFT JAMIE, JACINDA, and the children to settle into Illy and Luca's house while the permanent residents were away on their mission.

"Goodness, ten children!" Cam breathed as we hid in our room. "Thirteen when Callie arrives. Plus Isla's, plus this little one."

He rubbed my bare belly as I lay back on the bed, the protrusion barely noticeable.

"Hello, little one!" he called softly. "I'm your dad. How long have you known?" he asked excitedly.

"Only a few weeks. Since Newgrange. Nasir did some tests to see why I was getting so many headaches and why I was so exhausted all the time. When Nasir told me, I nearly fell off the chair. It was the last thing I was expecting." What I didn't say was that after so many months, I had almost given up hope. "But even then, it was very early. I was scared it wouldn't stick. But I keep growing. And I know how much you wanted to share this journey."

"How many weeks?"

"About nine."

"I wish I had a camera," Cam said wistfully. "I could take a photo of you each week and keep track."

"It's not important," I said, enjoying the attention as he stroked my tummy. I meant it. "We are both here. We won't forget. Not this time."

"How are you feeling?"

"Tired," I admitted, "but now that I know why I am so tired, it is okay."

"What did Nasir say about the headaches?"

"He said that headaches are not uncommon in the first trimester. Rapidly increased hormones likely being the cause."

"So not impending insanity then?" he teased.

"Only if being desperately happy at being pregnant to *you* is an indicator," I retorted, but unable to keep the joy from my voice. "But really, this is what I dreamed of for so long. Us, together, creating a new life. Not that I don't love Katrin," I rushed, "but this time..."

"This time, we will do it together," Cam finished as he ran his hands across my belly and kissed it lightly.

Building another home took much of our time, but being summer, the daylight hours were long. We could all find some time to help in some way. It was difficult to arrive in a new place with children but not settle into your own home. Despite not being particularly handy, I learned to make mud bricks for the foundations and nail shingles on a rooftop. Cam had blown a gasket when he saw me on the roof one afternoon but was stymied by not wanting to let people know I was pregnant. It wasn't until I had finally climbed down that he told me off resoundingly, and I ignored him.

Three weeks after the solstice, there was an enormous ruckus. Pausing in the delicate operation we were performing, Isla looked up, annoyed.

"What's all this clishmaclaver about?" she called, her Scots accent broadening and making me smile. Despite spending her early years at Stonehaven, near Aberdeen, she had spent most of her high school and university years boarding in England, softening her accent. But when Isla was frustrated, there was no doubt of her heritage. Waddling, her protruding belly making her move more slowly, she made it to the door and peered out.

"What is it?" I asked, placing the last stitches in the wound.

"It's... it's a golf cart!" Isla said, the incredulousness in her voice unmistakable.

"It's what?"

"Nae, it's two golf carts," she corrected.

Checking that Gussie was still soundly asleep after removing an abscess, I moved to the door and stood behind Isla. It *was* two golf carts. Slowly winding their way down the steep track to Roseglen.

"It's Callie," I exclaimed, seeing the long, black hair flying behind the slowly moving vehicle.

Wiping my hands, I rushed out to greet them.

"Callie!" I waved from the front of the shed. They pulled up, the carts laden with children, bags, metal rods, and other paraphernalia.

"You travel light!" Isla said jokingly.

"Callie!" Di squealed as she ran across the yard, Kendra in her arms.

"Di! You look wonderful! Is this..."

"This is Kendra. My daughter," Di said proudly.

Callie looked quizzically at Isla, Di, and me. "What is this, a maternity ward?" she exclaimed, looking at Isla's belly ready to pop, Di holding Kendra, and my tiny bump just showing in my t-shirt.

Di and Isla turned to look at me, astonished, and I flushed red.

"Eleven weeks," I admitted.

"Ahhh!!" Di squealed, hugging me with one arm as she balanced Kendra on her hip.

Callie looked embarrassed. "I'm so sorry. Didn't know."

"It's alright," I said dismissively. "We were just hoping to go a little longer, but everyone would have known soon enough."

Tadhg was helping the children down from the carts, the children looking around in bewilderment.

"Come on," said Di. "You can stay at mine. We have guests all over the place at the moment! Besides, Cam got to spend time with you recently. Now it is my turn!"

That night, Di and Sorcha hosted a rambunctious party attended by ten adults and thirteen children. Congratulations abounded, and I couldn't stop smiling, finally feeling like I was part of the fabric of this place.

"Goodness, when Illy and Luca return, and these two are born, we will need a town hall!" Fraser joked.

"You know," said Sorcha thoughtfully. "That's not a bad idea. We are going to need a school soon enough, especially if we keep multiplying at this rate."

"Oh, don't look at me," said Isla, squirming and unable to get comfortable in the last weeks of her fourth pregnancy. "I'm done after this one. If Hamish doesn't fix the problem, then I'll take matters into my own hands. Limits Clava's chances of the selected breeding program, doesn't it?"

Fraser squirmed uncomfortably, knowing that he was the one likely to face the surgeon's knife.

"Oh, me too," said Di quickly. "One pregnancy is enough for me."

"Yours wasn't a fair assessment," said Isla reasonably. "After all you went through. You don't want another?"

"No," said Sorcha and Di in unison.

We had never explicitly stated that Kendra was Cam's biological child but suspected that most people had guessed. When I had asked him, after they had returned from Clava, how he felt about Kendra, he admitted she was like a very close niece, but not a daughter. I was eminently grateful for that, but unsure why. He would always play a significant role in her life, whether or not he was biologically related. But that he saw her as Sorcha and Di's daughter, not his own, made me feel that there was potentially room for just one more.

Everyone looked at Jacinda and me.

"You have three, Jamie. Is that enough?" Cam asked coyly.

"Well, we were thinking an even four..." Jamie said with a glance at Jacinda, who smiled but said nothing.

"I'm just thrilled to be having this one. I have no plans beyond that," I responded truthfully.

"Three is enough for me," said Callie cheerfully. "But we aren't staying. We need to return to Newgrange after we deactivate your portal."

"You are much earlier than we expected," I said. "Not that we aren't pleased to see you. Do you think it will take that long?"

"Ahh, no!" Callie laughed. "But it isn't like we get family holidays all that often, is it? We thought we would come and stay, help a bit. Cam has helped us several times, so we just thought we would return the favor."

A whirlwind of children flew through the kitchen, laughing merrily, leaving muddy footprints in their wake.

"Well, if Clava wants us to have more children, then they can raise them," Sorcha grumbled.

CHAPTER 40

TWO WEEKS LATER, ILLY and Luca returned, looking rather pleased with themselves.

"How are you both?" I greeted them warmly before reminding them that there was a family temporarily camped in their home.

"Oh, that's alright." Illy grinned. "Where do you want us to stay?"

"With us?" I offered tentatively, "Jamie and Jacinda have three children, the youngest only a baby. It is probably quieter with us."

"Although..." Cam added, "that situation won't last."

"I'm pregnant," I explained to the confused looks, realizing that as I did so, that I had rarely used those words during my first pregnancy. They sounded strange to my own ears. In fact, after telling Cam I was pregnant, I don't think I told anyone else other than Angus.

Luca's face lit with joy as he swung me off the ground. "Wonderful news, Frey!" he gushed. "Really. I am so happy for you."

I caught the slightest flicker in Illy's eyes as she smiled and offered her congratulations. Disappointment. Not for me but for herself. I knew that feeling all too well.

As Cam and Luca bounded off ahead carrying the bags, I murmured, without looking at her, "I know how it feels. Being happy for someone else but sad for yourself. It took us a very long time. It felt like people blessed with children constantly surrounded me. But it will happen."

Illy paused and said, "Thank you for understanding. I am happy for you, truly."

I put my arm around her tiny waist and helped carry the bags into our house. "I know."

Catching up with the men, I asked Luca, "What did you source?" with a quick look at Cam. But he seemed interested.

"All sorts of amazing toys," Luca twinkled. Illy laughed at Cam's expression.

"Toys?" he asked cautiously, making me laugh too.

"Oh, weapons, surveillance systems, security systems, all kinds of cool stuff," Luca gushed. "I can't wait to try it all out."

"We have someone here at the moment who might be able to assist with rigging some of it," I said, smiling at Cam. "Didn't Callie say that tech stuff was right up Tadhg's alley?"

Not only was it an area of interest, but upon fetching Callie and Tadhg, it turned out that Tadhg had pre-pandemic experience in surveillance and security systems for military installations. We all stood back, listening to Luca and Tadhg finishing each other's sentences and planning what to do with the equipment they had sourced. They had met, briefly, on Luca's visit to Newgrange when Jake had first met Mikayla. But to listen to them converse, it was like they were old friends.

"Did Jake take some equipment back to Newgrange?" I interrupted at one point.

"He did." Luca grinned. "He got the same kit that we did. Jamming equipment, drones, we even got a full COFDM set-up. He was looking forward to showing Tadhg. But now I get to share it first. We had no idea you would be here." Luca beamed at Callie and Tadhg.

"What is a COFDM?" Cam asked curiously.

Tadhg's eyes lit up. "A Coded Orthogonal Frequency Division Multiplexing unit! That is outstanding news."

"Dare I ask what that means?" Cam quizzed.

"It is a digital, multi-carrier modulation scheme which uses many closely spaced orthogonal sub-carriers," Illy explained.

Cam looked at me. "Was that English?"

I shrugged. It was all beyond me.

"High tech broadband equipment, which means we can communicate with each other, and they can't hack us," Callie explained kindly.

"Thank you for translating."

"We have another surprise." Illy beamed. "We went via the Edinburgh offices and found a laptop that used to belong to Angus, which we managed to fire up, including retrieving his saved password. We worked out how to hack their servers, so now we have updated intel."

"Really?" we all chorused in unison.

"That would be handy," Cam acknowledged.

"We haven't finished yet, but we have already learned quite a bit of useful information."

"Like what?"

"Like why was there life on Mousa."

Cam flinched at the name.

Instead, I asked, "Why?"

"After you told them, the scientists used satellites and drones to surveil the area. They could see it, clear as day. They sent a team, and they discovered that a seemingly insignificant species of moss grew there, and one that appears to counteract the effects of the protozoa."

"A species not found anywhere else?" Cam asked, interested.

"Exactly. But what this means is that we are on our way to a cure. If they can work out how to replicate the moss or breed it, then they can use it to start re-greening areas outside of the domes," Illy finished.

"That is amazing," I admitted. "There really is hope. And in our lifetime, too."

I could see that Cam wanted to ask more about this greening program but was torn by his memories of Mousa.

"What else did you learn?" Callie asked with enthusiasm. She glanced at us. "Sorry, I am still a geek," she admitted.

"We were also hoping," Illy added, "that with Tadhg's help, we may be able to access one or more of the satellites still in orbit and re-task it."

"How many satellites are there still up there?" I asked curiously.

"Oh, about 5000!" Tadhg grinned. "I saw an image once. It is like a blanket of space junk. I'm sure with some time, we can access a few. What were you thinking, Illyria? One over Clava and one over each of us?"

"That is exactly what I was thinking," she agreed. "We can watch them, and we can keep our communities safe."

"Well, our primary goal is still to deactivate your portal," Callie admitted. "That is urgent. But we are most happy to help with security. We can just do that one in reverse. Start here and then copy back home."

The next few weeks flew by, everyone helping with setting up the capacitors to deactivate the portal, planning a security system for Lewis, and in what little free time we had, continuing to build a home for Jamie and Jacinda's family.

"I'm shattered!" I exclaimed as I flopped onto the bed. It had been a crazy day, trying to fit in vet work amidst everything else.

"Too shattered?" Cam asked shyly.

"Too shattered for what?" I feigned ignorance as I slipped off my boots.

"I have been near you all week and no private time to do anything about it!" he hissed, well aware that Luca and Illy were in the next room, and the walls were not that thick.

"Feeling a little frustrated?" I teased, stripping off before slipping under the covers.

"You look phenomenal," he whispered lustfully. "People say a pregnant woman has a glow about her, but you! You positively radiate. I should keep you pregnant. I can barely keep my hands from you!"

Wanting to say something about Clava's plans to keep me pregnant, I didn't, not wanting to kill the mood as he slid in beside me.

"Oh God, I want you," he moaned in my ear as he rolled me toward him, caressing my stomach before reaching around and cupping my backside in his hands and pushing me into him.

I gasped aloud as he slid inside me, and he hissed in my ear, "Shh! They'll hear you!"

I didn't care. After a few moments, nor did he.

CHAPTER 41

BEING SUNDAY, WE HAD a rare family breakfast planned. No one was in a rush to race off somewhere. Louis and Katrin both rose early and were up and dressed, seated at the table, when Illy and Luca emerged, looking blissfully in love but still sleepy. I smiled up at them, sipping my coffee, hoping that they hadn't been disturbed the night before.

Cam, being a morning person, and able to function far better than I, was just serving an enormous platter of pancakes onto the table, along with some of his special maple syrup. Louis's eyes lit up with glee. He loved pancake Sundays. Katrin, too young for pancakes, was gnawing on pieces of fruit and toast beside me.

"Morning!" Cam said happily as he placed another two plates at the table. "Perfect timing."

Illy poured a coffee for herself and Luca. I smiled, watching him drink his black. He had teased me every morning for years about needing milk, not something easy to get at sea, regularly resulting in me using out-of-date UHT milk, powdered milk, or even whitener. I couldn't tell him at the time that it was how Cam had drunk his daily coffee, and it was one of the tiny rituals I had maintained, just to feel close to him.

As Cam was serving his plate of pancakes from the dwindling stack, Jam jumped onto Cam's lap. He was always her first choice. She had chosen him, after all.

"Well, hello, there, Missy Moo. I've missed you."

Jam head-butted him under his chin, forcing him to scratch her. He did but placed her on the floor before commencing his meal. As his hands reached around her mid-section, Cam's face went through the most extraordinary sequence of changes.

"Bloody hell! Kittens! Again! Just what we need on top of thirteen children!" Cam's face proved he was not impressed with Jam's inopportune timing.

Illy's face lit up over the table, and I saw her glance at Luca with wonder in her eyes. My hand resting on my own slightly bulging stomach, I knew the joy this news had brought her.

"Well, I promised Illy two," I said quickly. "After all she and Luca have done for Lewis, I think we can see that happens."

She beamed at me over the table, and I knew I had just given her the best gift in the world.

"We will need to desex them," I warned her. "With no predators, they could reproduce out of control. Also, we still need to ensure the gene pool is diverse, and we already have some of Jam's previous kittens still entire."

"Oh, I don't mind!" Illy gushed with pleasure. "I'm just so excited to be having a cat again."

"They are far naughtier than a domestic cat," Cam warned. "The stories we could tell."

"I'll tell Isla after breakfast," I promised.

"Probably not great timing," Luca chipped in, chewing pancake. "Isla had the baby last night."

Cam and I looked at him in astonishment.

"Baby? We heard nothing."

"I'm a light sleeper," Illy piped up. "I heard Fraser banging on Sorcha's door just after midnight, and Sorcha returned home just before dawn. I assume the baby is born."

Cam looked distressed at this news.

"Are you alright?" I asked, worried. "Are you unwell?"

Sending Louis off to play with his digger outside, Cam spoke quietly, "I'm just worried about bringing children into the world when we are potentially about to go to war with Clava."

My eyes popped as I placed my hand on my rapidly expanding mid-section.

"Bit late for regret, isn't it?"

It was Luca who responded. "I get it, I do. But this is protection. We are setting up systems to monitor and observe. We aren't attacking anyone, Cam. What we want, what Newgrange wants, is to live our lives in peace. We don't want trouble. We just want them to leave us alone. We talked a lot about what equipment would best serve that purpose. We focused on surveillance and protection. That's not to say we couldn't defend ourselves in an all-out attack, but we know from Sunny's time on Auckland and Clava that she was the only military-trained person there. Her specialty is intelligence, and that is why they chose her, but she has combat training. The rest of those communities were civilians, brilliant scientists, and engineers, but none with battle experience. They know that Jake and I do. We plan to be very visible with our equipment set up, make them aware that we have weapons. We did a test as we left the mainland. I suspect they could see that from their satellites, if not their bare eyes." He grinned widely.

"Test?" I asked curiously.

Illy rolled her eyes. "Jake and Luca remote detonated a navy base."

Luca looked at her derisively. "It was a strategic demonstration of force," he announced formally.

"You enjoyed it."

"Oh, did I ever. You could see it for miles!"

Illy looked at us, bemused. "You should have seen him and Jake hooting and cackling on the deck. Boys."

Cam interjected, "So basically, you blew something up just to prove to Clava that you could?"

"That's about the size of it." Luca grinned widely, forking in another piece of pancake coated in maple syrup.

Fraser arrived at the end of breakfast with a sleeping bundle tightly swaddled in a white blanket in his arms.

Cam jumped out of his seat to make way for Fraser, firing up the cooktop to make him some fresh pancakes while we quizzed him on the new arrival.

Fraser looked exhausted but happy.

"So?" Illy asked excitedly. "Tell us."

"I am very proud to announce that after three beautiful daughters, we have a son." He beamed. "Please meet Lachlan Jakob Luca McKinnon."

Luca's face was a picture. "Jakob Luca?" he asked, the stunned amazement visible all over his face. "Why?"

Fraser couldn't keep the smile from his face. "Without you both, I wouldn't have this child. Wouldn't have my wife. So yes, we needed to acknowledge that gratitude formally. Lachlan was my brother's name. But Jakob Luca is for you. We considered Luca Jakob but felt that LLJ was a bit much for the poor wee babe."

In the years I had known Luca, he had been stalwart and solid, despite the challenges facing us. Never had I seen him be emotional, but now he was visibly choked as he stared down at the tiny person asleep in Fraser's arms.

"Can I...?" he whispered.

Fraser gratefully handed over the precious parcel and accepted the mug of coffee I offered him, telling us about the labor, how Isla was doing, how wonderful Sorcha was. But Luca heard none of it. Sitting rigidly, he stared down into the tiny face of the person he helped create.

"Have you never held a new baby?" I asked softly.

"Never," he whispered, not wanting to disturb the sleeping person in his arms.

"Well, you are about to get some practice," Fraser added cheerfully.

CHAPTER 42

FIVE HOMES NOW HOSTED six families in Roseglen. The sense of community was warm and welcoming. People were always willing to share something, lend a hand. You couldn't walk anywhere without meeting someone. I had never lived with such a sense of belonging, despite the projects Luca, Illy, Callie, and Tadhg worked on.

It was only a few days until the equinox, and the setup was almost complete. It had freed Tadhg up to work with Luca, establishing our surveillance systems. Over the past few weeks, I had learned a lot about security systems, including the difference between a tactical ballistic missile, a short-range ballistic missile, and an intercontinental ballistic missile.

"Intercontinental?" Cam quizzed Luca. "Aren't they really long-range?"

"How far away do you think Auckland Island is?" Luca had responded cheekily.

While my first reaction was one of shock, upon consideration, that made sense. "That is clever," I admitted. "If they know that we have the potential to strike both Auckland and Clava, and I am assuming almost simultaneously, they are less likely to strike us. But ... isn't it a little threatening?"

"Yes and no," Illy admitted. "Yes, it looks threatening. But you also need to remember that many countries had ICBMs in the old world. They were rarely used and never for nuclear deployment. Think of the Cold War. Nearly fifty years of tension but no real conflict, although both sides had the capability. The type that most countries had, and we were lucky that the UK had, were multiple independently targetable re-entry vehicles. This allows a single missile to carry several warheads, and each warhead can strike a different target concurrently. Now we have one too," she added a little proudly. "Remember that I lived in these places. I know these people. They started this. We have made no overt displays of aggression. They targeted us by infecting Di, Thea, and Mikayla, and others. If they know we *can*, then they likely *won't* engage with us. It is easier and far safer for them if they just let us go, and likely, that is what they will do. We, in turn, will make no attempt to use the weapons. The longer we don't use them, the more comfortable they will become. Add to that the deactivation of the portal in a few days, and it will be proof that we aren't acting aggressively."

I nodded, understanding. "They let *you* go, and they had plans for you."

Illy grimaced at this reminder.

"And Newgrange?" Cam asked. "They have the same set-up?"

"They do," Illy agreed. "Exactly the same. Jakob also doesn't want to use any of it. It genuinely is just for protection."

Illy was the closest thing I had ever had to a female friend, other than Di. But Di was now with Sorcha, and while we respected each other, as Cam's sister, it was difficult for Sorcha to be someone I could confide in. Each day Illy and I took a walk together after dinner, talking about our day, but really, just disclosing a little more about ourselves. Aside from my sister, I had never experienced a sense of sisterhood. But I was coming to like it and value the time we spent together. She was an only child, born late in life, so like me was independent. I told her once that other women didn't like me, and she snorted, saying that was *her* story. She told me how much she wanted a child but was fearful, partly because of her age, now thirty-four. But mainly due to what she had learned on Clava.

"I still have nightmares about how they would enact that plan," she told me one night. "Forcing people to have children against their will." I slipped my arm around her. She came up to my shoulder, so it was like comforting a smaller child, despite her being older than I was.

"I have nightmares about what they did to me while I was unconscious in the facility in Melbourne," I admitted. "When I learned that, I wondered if that was why it took me so long to conceive."

"If only I had known then," Illy said in a low voice. "I would never have been part of it."

"But you didn't know what they were really up to. You thought you were saving people's lives, and to an extent, you were. Do you know, Cam and I had a terrible argument once, years ago, about the guilt the team must have felt at choosing? He couldn't deal with it, likened it to choosing people to be sent to a concentration camp. I saw the logic. I know that not everyone could be saved. It was important to be selective."

"I didn't make the decisions, you know," she said softly. "I was there to assess their testing, rate their profiles. But I remember most of them. Cam, you, Callie, and Di. Out of all the candidates, we knew we could only choose such a small number. But my part was easier. I assessed against a benchmark, not making a judgment."

"Why on earth did you choose Heidi?" I said with an edge. "She tried to kill Cam and me."

"We didn't," she pointed out. "If her sister was chosen, then she would have been sent to an ISO community. But she never underwent testing, so we didn't know that she existed."

"Also," I added logically, "if you hadn't been involved in the project, you would never have met Luca and ended up here."

"Funny how something so wonderful can come out of something so negative," she said wistfully. "I remember reading once that mountains don't rise without earthquakes."

I paused, wanting to say something, but stopped. Illy, sensing the reticence, said, "Go on. Say it."

"Can you stop doing that?"

"Doing what?"

"Reading me. Knowing when I am about to say something but chicken out."

Illy laughed, making me feel more relaxed. "Sorry. But really, what is it?"

"I was just going to say that you see things with a different prism when you have children of your own. I described it to Cam once as, it is like, the logic is still there. I am hard-wired that way. I will always see the linear approach. But now, there is a thick blanket of emotion that overlays the logic. Now, there is an element of emotion at play with the logic. It balances out my decisions. Does that make sense?"

I couldn't see her face in the dark, but when she finally spoke, it was tinged with sadness. "One day, I hope to feel that too."

"Well, my advice is to pick the most inconvenient time, and that is when it will happen."

"Really?"

"It will happen, Illy. You will be the most wonderful mother. In the meantime, there will be kittens."

CHAPTER 43

THE MOOD ON THE morning of the autumn equinox was subdued. The portal we were about to close had brought many of us here, Cam and me, Di, Sorcha and Sam, Jamie and Jacinda. Callie, Tadhg, and Illy were travelers, although they hadn't come through this one. Fraser, Isla, and Luca were the only three of our community who had initially settled here.

"Are you sure there isn't another way?" Di asked with tears in her eyes. Sorcha looked at her kindly.

"What is wrong?" she replied with more sympathy than I had ever heard from Sorcha.

"Kendra. My cousin. She will never get to meet our daughter."

"You know," I piped up. "That isn't entirely true. There are portals as close as Orkney or Shetland. But don't forget, I sailed from here to Melbourne and back. We still have the *Eurydice*. We could take a trip if you wanted."

Di's face lit through the tears. "Not that I want to. I just don't want to write off the potential of it ever happening."

Callie smiled at her. "So, you call us up and say, 'Set up the gear,' and we come for another holiday and reactivate it. It is possible, you know. It isn't a one-time-only deal. They have been re-activated before. I struggled myself with the concept of closing off the portal, but we can reactivate it if we want to. We know how."

Just as Jacinda was about to say something, a low yowling sound emanated from under the house. Cam got down on his stomach and sighed. "It is Jam. Looks like she is having her kittens. Seriously, could she pick a more inopportune time?"

"I'll stay," I offered. "I have no desire to be near that thing again. But someone else will need to get her out." At nearly 22 weeks, my belly was now protruding noticeably. There was no way I was lying flat on my stomach to retrieve her.

"Sam can do it," Sorcha offered. "She likes him."

That was true, and Jam was a very well-behaved cat. The problem was she was still a wild cat, and she was in pain. There was no way of telling how she could react. Isla and I looked at each other.

"I'll do it," Isla said firmly. Handing me baby Lachlan, she opened the trap door and slithered in on her stomach. We could hear her crooning to Jam and waiting until the contractions eased, then moved quickly, grabbing her from behind the neck and pulling her out.

"Get a box," she ordered as she held Jam tightly against her chest. "Old blankets or towels too. Set it up inside my house so I can watch Lachlan. Go on. It is important you all do this. Close it off. I'll stay with Jam and the little ones. She will be fine."

"I'll stay, too," Fraser added. "This isn't about me. Go. I'll watch the kids."

I looked at Cam and shrugged. It was under control.

Taking the golf carts that Callie and Tadhg had brought from Newgrange, we slowly made our way to Callanish. Sam came with us. At six years old, he barely remembered traveling here two years previously. But we had agreed that it was important that the younger generation saw what we were doing, not just hear us talk about it.

"Why on earth didn't we think to get some of these?" I asked Cam in amazement. "How much easier would it have been bringing Jamie and Jacinda back last time?"

Jamie just smiled in his soft, gentle manner. When he had arrived, I wondered how he would fit in here. Sorcha, Illy, Luca, all being forceful personalities. But he, Cam, Fraser, and Di all seemed to work beautifully together. Children running under their feet constantly, they all adapted their work around their family lives.

As we approached the standing stones at Callanish, I looked over at Cam. He smiled sadly at me. We had both been through that portal accidentally. Now, no one would again. Melbourne and August were in our past. Lewis was our future.

We stood well back and watched as Callie and Tadhg linked the magnets to the intricate copper piping surrounding the tomb. As the sun lowered in the sky and shone directly onto the gray rocks, we saw the lightning charge fizzle down the wire. Callie and Tadhg ran for the rocks we were resting behind and barely made it before a massive tremor shook the earth. I watched the ancient stone circle fearfully, wondering if the enormous monoliths would fall.

"Goodness!" Callie giggled as it slowed. "That was even bigger than the last one!"

"Is it ... over?" Cam asked Callie.

"My friend, nothing is ever really over."

Callie was right. Like the Ouroboros carved at Newgrange, Cam and I had found each other, experienced joy and loss, but now we had come full circle. The trauma of the past seven years hadn't been for nothing. As the new life in my stomach shifted, a mixture of sadness and excitement filled me as I looked forward to the years ahead, surrounded by friends and family.

BOOK CLUB QUESTIONS

1. An ouroboros is an ancient symbol of infinity depicted by a snake or a dragon eating its own tail. What themes of life going full circle are present in the Antipodes series?

2. Infinity documents the best and worst of human behavior. Who do you think are the most evil characters in this book?

The first section of Infinity sees Cam on a quest ＼ discover Laetitia's heritage. How does this ＼nge his view of Lae?

＼ Cam and Freyja reunite, he tells her that f his heart always belonged to her. Is it ⸲ to love two people concurrently?

⸲pter 7, the Antipodes series shifts to ⸲he narrator. How does hearing her ⸲log and self-doubt change your f her?

⸲ed when she learns that Angus ⸲ginal residents of Lewis die, ⸲ved them, but understands

"Goodness!" Callie giggled as it slowed. "That was even bigger than the last one!"

"Is it ... over?" Cam asked Callie.

"My friend, nothing is ever really over."

Callie was right. Like the Ouroboros carved at Newgrange, Cam and I had found each other, experienced joy and loss, but now we had come full circle. The trauma of the past seven years hadn't been for nothing. As the new life in my stomach shifted, a mixture of sadness and excitement filled me as I looked forward to the years ahead, surrounded by friends and family.

BOOK CLUB QUESTIONS

1. An ouroboros is an ancient symbol of infinity depicted by a snake or a dragon eating its own tail. What themes of life going full circle are present in the Antipodes series?

2. Infinity documents the best and worst of human behavior. Who do you think are the most evil characters in this book?

3. The first section of Infinity sees Cam on a quest to discover Laetitia's heritage. How does this change his view of Lae?

4. When Cam and Freyja reunite, he tells her that part of his heart always belonged to her. Is it possible to love two people concurrently?

5. From Chapter 7, the Antipodes series shifts to Freyja as the narrator. How does hearing her internal dialog and self-doubt change your perspective of her?

6. Freyja is horrified when she learns that Angus watched the original residents of Lewis die, and could have saved them, but understands

this would have placed the community at risk. Was he right to do what he did?

7. What benefits would there have been for Cam and Freyja to move to Clava?

8. "Regret is time wasted on things you can't change." Do you agree?

9. Deception by a friend is the worst kind of betrayal. Freyja is furious when she learns that Angus actively prevented her from reuniting with Cam. But the Lewis community also learn that each community had a planted spy, waiting for the community to need resources. Is deceit more painful when it is by someone you know and trust?

10. The scientists from Clava and Auckland Island watched the communities in Gibraltar and Great Barrier Island perish, yet took no action. Are you guilty by association if you watch a tragedy unfold and do nothing? Or is it not your place to interfere?

11. The scientific team actively withhold resources like medications until a community needs it, but then they seek allegiance to the Collective as payment. Discuss how is this different from our society where we are provided with schools, hospitals, and infrastructure in return for adhering to the law?

AUTHOR BIO

T.S. SIMONS IS AN Australian author of Scottish heritage. Living in the alpine region of Australia, she believes in the values of sustainability and community in a world where we place greater value on possessions than people. The Antipodes series addresses the question—if we gave young people the opportunity to start over, would we replicate the mistakes of the past?

She holds Bachelor and Master's degrees from Monash University, and enjoys strong coffee, travelling, mythology and snow skiing, while attempting to live as sustainably as possible. She is owned by two rather bossy standard schnauzers and two rescue cats who co-manage her household.

The Antipodes series includes Project Hemisphere, The Space Between, Infinity, Circle of Protection, and Sessrúmnir. She is now working on a related series, The Latitude Series.

More books from 4 Horsemen Publications

Fantasy, SciFi, & Paranormal Romance

Beau Lake
The Beast Beside Me
The Beast Within Me
Taming the Beast: Novella
The Beast After Me
Charming the Beast: Novella
The Beast Like Me
An Eye for Emeralds
Swimming in Sapphires
Pining for Pearls

D. Lambert
To Walk into the Sands
Rydan
Celebrant
Northlander
Esparan
King
Traitor
His Last Name

Danielle Orsino
Locked Out of Heaven
Thine Eyes of Mercy
From the Ashes
Kingdom Come

J.M. Paquette
Klauden's Ring
Solyn's Body
The Inbetween
Hannah's Heart
Call Me Forth

Invite Me In
Keep Me Close

Lyra R. Saenz
Prelude
Falsetto in the Woods: Novella
Ragtime Swing
Sonata
Song of the Sea
The Devil's Trill
Bercuese
To Heal a Songbird
Ghost March
Nocturne

T.S. Simons
Project Hemisphere
The Space Between
Infinity
Circle of Protection
Sessrúmnir

Ty Carlson
The Bench
The Favorite

Valerie Willis
Cedric: The Demonic Knight
Romasanta: Father of Werewolves
The Oracle: Keeper of the
Gaea's Gate
Artemis: Eye of Gaea
King Incubus: A New Reign

Discover more at
4HorsemenPublications.com